Sylvia +
Otis
from Joan

The West Window

John S. Hall

The West Window

a novel by John S. Hall

iUniverse, Inc.
New York Lincoln Shanghai

The West Window

iUniverse books may be ordered through booksellers or by contacting:

iUniverse
2021 Pine Lake Road, Suite 100
Lincoln, NE 68512
www.iuniverse.com
1-800-Authors (1-800-288-4677)

ISBN-13: 978-0-595-38502-7 (pbk)
ISBN-13: 978-0-595-82883-8 (ebk)
ISBN-10: 0-595-38502-8 (pbk)
ISBN-10: 0-595-82883-3 (ebk)

Printed in the United States of America

To Donna, my wife,
for her undying encouragement.

CHAPTER ONE

Harold Tully drives down Pine Mountain, letting the front wheels of his '39 Chevy follow the frozen road ruts. Snowdrifts linger under the sugar maples that line the roadside. A light snow has come in the night. Harold calls the early spring dusting *sugar snow*. It is melting to slush on the gray gravel where the morning sun strikes the narrow road. The truck tires sink into slushy pools as he travels, spraying an icy fan that lands on the white powder leaving large black holes on the clean cover of snow. His big weathered hands grip tightly to the wheel when he realizes the truck is about to bounce over a hummock. He knows the road well—he's been traveling it for nearly sixty years.

Four forty-quart milk cans drum together in the back of the truck as he's descending the steep hills from his mountain farm. Tire chains keep the truck from sliding out of control where the road is slippery and frozen hard as stone.

Harold's mind is a blank most of the time; life for him is pretty much a long string of monotonous days and uneventful nights. He runs his farm by a mind-numbing routine such as milking his cows twice a day, something he's been doing for as long as he can remember. Of course the seasons change and the work changes with the seasons, but Harold's way of doing things never changes. However, the letter he carries in the vest pocket of his bib-overalls regards a decision he has made that may set his life in a new direction. The thought of hiring help, especially a woman, scares him.

As he's driving down the mountain he mumbles to himself, "I'm goin' to kill myself. Someday I'll fall dead in my tracks if I try the three seasons again; spring's work of forkin' and spreadin' a heap of last winter's cow shit; and swingin' and drivin' posts with that mall, fixin' fence; and summer's hayin'—makes me sick just thinkin' about it; then, sawin' up enough wood in the fall for winter. I near blew my lungs out, usin' that one-man crosscut and bucksaw last fall, only the fear of freezin' to death kept me goin', until I knew I'd cut enough for winter." Harold emphasizes his situation by desperately clutching the wheel. *I need help!*

The truck is approaching a hairpin turn at the bottom of the mountain. Off the edge of the road stands an ancient, odd appearing tree known as Mary Maple. Some believe it to have spiritual significance, but he knows such a belief is all hogwash. Just the same, he lifts his foot from the gas in passing this unusual phenomenon while pondering his situation. He chuckles at himself for even considering talking to a tree. *Hell, I'm desperate.*

Last month, a newspaper ad inquiring for farm work in the Huntersville area caught his attention. He wrote the applicant and offered a job to a woman by the name of Shirley Mason. He was surprised to learn she was the mother of an infant, but she claimed to have had farm experience. He vaguely remembers hearing of a Shirley Mason working for the Iversons across town. Old Jim used to brag in Butson's Feed Store, "I have a good worker that can do double of what my nephews can. A girl, too—still in high school. She's a real looker to boot."

Harold wonders why she would want to work for him. The Iversons are some of the best farmers in town, and she's coming back with a baby. *What am I takin' on anyway?*

He's hired plenty of housekeepers over the years, but he always made sure they didn't have kids, and he made sure they stayed away from the barn. He's a little worried about bein' teamed up with a woman. After all, with most of the teams he's had, the mares can get a might nippy at times.

The truck brakes squeal as he comes to a stop at the milk stand on his way to town to get his newly hired hand. The dull black dented truck chatters in reverse, backing up to a milk can platform that he shares with his neighbors, the Coleses. He hears Zack Coles coming with his milk and inwardly grumbles that a day as big as this is in his life, and he has to face a fuzzy-headed scatterbrain. On the other hand, Zack might know this Shirley Mason. Maybe he'll be willin' to talk to him today.

After backing his truck up to the stand, Zack Coles, a tall slender fellow, walks from his truck to the platform. He's concentrating on the snowy slush that he scuffs with his boots, seemingly unaware of Harold. He climbs the four steps of the 10'x10' milk stand, turns his back on Harold, and drops the tailgate of his polished, nearly new truck. Zack and Harold almost never speak—a practice that suits them just fine. They grasp their can covers, turning them hand over hand, rolling the forty-quart cans upright on their steel rims. Zack's cans slam with a full sound when they slide to a stop on the smooth elm planking. Harold's four cans land in place, making a sloshing sound. He hates being reminded daily that his cows aren't milking as much as the Coleses', and at the same time, he knows Zack is the kind to brag about the fact. But there are good reasons for the differences, and Harold often runs through those reasons as he unloads his milk. The Coleses' fancy Jersey herd isn't because of Zack, and neither is the good hay they feed. His father, Percy, was the farmer. *Zack's just suckin' off the family tit.*

The sun is filtering through the trees, beginning to reach the stand located next to the valley road. The morning air is brisk as puffs of warm breath float from the working men. While standing next to his cans, Harold fumbles in the vest pocket of his bib-overalls for Shirley Mason's letter. He clears his throat. Zack, with a disgusted expression, stops and stares at Harold.

Harold waves the envelope in front of Zack. "I have a letter here I thought I'd show you; but, hell, I don't want to bother the busiest man in town, havin' to tend to your cows."

Not giving Harold the satisfaction of his attention, Zack grabs the letter.

Dear Mr. Tully: March 23, 1948

I'll be arriving in Huntersville on Monday April 5th, on the twelve o'clock bus. I'll plan to meet you at The Market parking lot by one o'clock. I'm looking forward to my new job and a new home for my baby, Steven, and myself.

Sincerely, Shirley Mason

Zack nervously runs his fingers through his curly hair, flushes, and bends weak-kneed, backing up to sit on a can. He holds the letter in both hands and stares at the words saying, "Shirley Mason has a baby? She's coming to work for you?"

"Yup. You know her?" Harold is trying to figure the kid. Why has such a change come over him? He's never seen him act so upset—like his best cow has just dropped dead.

"Well—well, yes. We went to school together and graduated last June in the class of '47. After Dad died, I wanted her to work for us. I think she liked being asked, but she said she couldn't."

Harold absorbs himself in Zack's every word and reaction, trying to learn all he can. Why wouldn't this young woman want to work for the Iversons; and if not them, why not the Coleses? And then there's the baby. "What about her kid?"

Zack's face turns deeper red and, in a dreamy voice, he continues, "She is pretty, all right, and smart; but I don't remember that anyone ever went with her. She's an orphan, a state kid, you know. She and I got acquainted on our senior picnic out at the lake. Even though we were in the same school and the same class, I never knew her well before that day. That's when I asked if she'd come to work."

Harold studies Zack, wondering if this jerk could be the father of her kid. Harold pulls his pipe from his bib-overalls pocket, still not taking his eyes off Zack, hoping for all the information he can get. "This baby of hers…Is it—Is it—by any chance your doing?"

Zack slams his foot on the platform, jumps to his feet stiffly, and yells, "You filthy old hermit! Of course not!"

Harold laughs. "Take it easy. I guess I stumbled onto a hornets' nest."

Zack grabs a can from his truck, rolls it onto the platform, and loses control. It tips on its side with the cover popping off. A gush of milk washes over the stand. Harold catches the can handle and flips it upright. "Golly, Zack, we're only talkin' about you makin' a baby. Don't spill your milk 'cause of what I said. Baby makin' happens all the time."

Zack yells, "You have a sick mind!" He slams the empty cans left from the previous day's pickup into his truck. He jumps from the stand and runs to his truck. The spinning rear tires spit ice and slush at the stand as he heads home.

Harold laughs and drives away, scratching his head. In the process, he moves his cap backward, and then pulls on the visor, yanking it in place while his truck picks up speed. Broken cross chains slap on his fenders, a sound he has come to accept as normal.

A cloud blocks the sun and dimness covers the road. A light spring rain begins to glaze his windshield. Harold turns on the wipers. The worn rubber blades barely clear the droplets of water. Harold drives on, continuing to be puzzled by both Zack's reaction and this woman Shirley Mason.

Having some time before the bus comes, he stops to buy the *Huntersville Weekly* paper. The headline immediately angers him:

TRUMAN'S MARSHALL PLAN TO SPEND BILLIONS

The Truman administration has won the approval from Congress to spend billions in foreign aid for the reconstruction of war-torn Europe. Money will be spent on food, machinery, and other forms of aid.

Harold shakes the paper, angry that Truman may be the ruination of us all. He wonders if this country will be bankrupt before the Republicans can save us. He turns to his favorite column. "Now, this is good readin'. Honeydew writes about stuff that's happenin' right here in Huntersville. 'Course I get the inside scoop on the nights we romp for a spell. Thinkin' of teamin' with a woman, she can get nippy at times all right."

HUNTERSVILLE WEEKLY

April 5, 1948

Driblets of Honeydew
By Honeydew Mullen

The Ladies of the Congregational Church Home Circle have elected Alice Coles as their president and Mildred Perkins as secretary.

The church world service, aid to Europe has been selected as their '48 mission project.

Toby Perkins has been released from prison. He has served time for fathering a child by a thirteen-year-old Huntersville girl. He'll be spending his probationary period working on the home farm.

Joseph Iverson, son of Attorney David and Trudy, we all call him Joe, has been hired as Huntersville County's Agricultural Extension Agent. This is quite the plum for one of our hometown boys. He'll have an answer for all your problems on subjects from dairy cows to laying hens. Oh, by the way, for technical information he said he relies on specialists from the University.

Speaking of Joe Iverson, word has it that he's soon to become engaged to a Vassar graduate, a big-city banker's daughter. Maybe she can bring a little style to us country women. Watch out all you men in bib-overalls—change is on its way. You may be seeing some high fashion prancing around the kitchen table.

CHAPTER TWO

The bus driver drones, "Huntersville, Huntersville." Immediately, anxiety throbs through the girl. The bus pulls to a stop and Shirley Mason steps off wearing a faded gray jacket with threadbare sleeves. She's holding her two-month-old son, Steven, in one arm; a bag strap hangs over her shoulder, and she's carrying a bulging cardboard suitcase. She walks on the sidewalk in front of a brick building by a sign: DAVID IVERSON, ATTORNEY-AT-LAW.

A shiver shoots up Shirley's back and her palms begin to sweat. Warm misty rain collects on her face. She hurries for cover from the rain, entering a dimly lit alley that separates The Market from the seldom-used side entrance to the law firm. She shakily holds the doorknob to the law office entrance. The loosely attached brass knob rattles, echoing down the damp alley.

Unnerved by her lack of self-control, she places her belongings against the brick wall and sits on her suitcase. Her instincts tell her to calm herself before seeing Iverson. The attorney is the linchpin of her plan to return to Huntersville.

She rests Steven on her lap and bends forward, focusing on her child's face. "Yes, you and your mama have got to find a home. What perfect skin you have, like fresh cream, with cheeks the color of a beautiful pink lady slipper. Yes, you like to open those bright blue eyes and put that little fist, with tiny long fingers, right to your mouth. To think you came from me, turning a disaster into beauty. You grew in me stitch by stitch, coming to me as a part of me, but more—like a miracle. Those perfect little ears; your lobes are connected, but mine aren't. So you're a part of him too, because his ears are like yours. But this mama is going to raise you, and that will make all the difference." She kisses her son. "We're going to have a good home—no chasing and screaming." *I remember my foot caught on the chair leg. If only that hadn't happened and I hadn't gotten him mad. Dr. Plumbly was so upset seeing the blood running down my face, and the long gash, oozing, making my hair wet with red.*

She feels for her silver barrette. Its smooth warmth is a comfort during anxious moments. It reminds her of her first home and Mrs. Perkins, who gave her the barrette as a small kid. She really loved Shirley, and cried while holding and telling the girl, "Honey, you've got to leave." Later, that's what others said, but they didn't cry, and they never held her, and they never called her honey.

She turns her attention back to her baby. "Being chased by that bull made me cry and cry but no one cared." Suddenly Steven opens his eyes wide. Shirley smiles at him. "We're going to find a good home, no mean people in your life—ever!" She feels for her barrette again and pushes it into place. "Our home is going to be full of caring. I'm your mama. I'll always protect you."

Pulling a small mirror from her bag, she runs a comb through her hair and resets her barrette. She looks different since cutting her long black hair. Taking a blue denim cap from her bag, she tries it on, holds up her mirror, and smiles. *What a goof!*

She pulls the letter from her bag. The writing is in lead pencil, on dull gray cardboard, cut to fit the envelope. She's already read it many times.

Shirley Mason

I'll hire you. Never hired a young woman with a kid before. Meet me at The Market parking lot at 1 on Monday, April 5th. I drive a '39 Chevy truck with four milk cans in back.

Signed: Harold Tully

Shirley sits, recalling the reaction of the Leland Home director upon reading the note. He protested, "You have so much ability—straight-A student in school, trained as a legal secretary, and yet you're taking a job like this! Why would you want to go back to Huntersville and work for a farmer? From the looks of his grubby note, he's a slob to boot!"

A group picture of the Leland Home trustees hung on the wall in back of the director. Attorney Iverson was in the picture. She wondered at the time: is the director protesting for Iverson or for me?

Unzipping her jacket, she pulls up her sweater and feels the rush of milk. Steven's lunch is ready. While she softly holds his head, guiding him to her breast, she relaxes against the wall and wonders about Attorney Iverson's reaction when she enters the side entrance of his office. *I should have told him I was coming. But if I'd done that, he might have refused to see me.*

She was the only one among the young mothers at the Leland Home who chose to breast-feed, and for good reason: most of them gave their babies up for adoption. With her uncertain future, Shirley would be assured that at least there would always be a ready supply of food for her son.

She lays Steven on her suitcase and changes his diaper. Then she picks him up and looks at him closely. "Okay, Steven. Let's go and see what happens when we meet Attorney Iverson."

She stands and again walks to the door. She enters, places the bag and suitcase on the floor, and pushes the switch button. One bulb hangs from a long cord wired to the high ceiling. The walls are unpainted, dark, and dusty. She starts up the stairs—her legs feel like stumps and her knees are weak. She stops on the landing to regain her composure.

A spider dangles in the hallway, suspended by a minutely thin silver thread. The dim light reflects off the tiny web strand as the insect hangs at eye level, curled in a ball. She squints toward the dirty gray ceiling into a blur of darkness. *My plan hanging by a thread.*

She walks up a few more steps and looks down at Steven. "Your bright blue eyes are so precious; I think he'll understand why I want to keep you."

Despite her trepidation, the overwhelming need for a permanent home reminds her to press forward. Her heart is pounding in her ears. She listens for a moment at the office's back door, since Iverson may have a client. Hearing no voices, she takes a deep breath, turns the brass knob of the heavy oak door, and walks into the attorney's office.

Attorney Iverson is seated in a plush leather chair. Startled, he jumps to his feet. A man in his early fifties with graying hair at the temples, he's impeccably groomed with a maroon tie perfectly squared tightly to his stiff white collar. His three-piece suit is spotless and the crease in his pants is as sharp as the edges of his legal documents. She sees nothing common about this man as shown by his dress and his cultivated demeanor.

Seeing Shirley carrying a baby, his face turns typing-paper white and then darkens to an angry rose red. "You returned with the baby, taking no one's advice as to what would be best for you!"

Ignoring him for a moment, she sits to gain composure. The office is elaborately finished in mahogany and is immaculate. Two walls are lined with law books. The entire floor is covered with a deep red Persian carpet. A television is placed on a stand in a corner near his desk. At the far end of the long rectangular office is a fireplace mantel decorated with ornate wood carvings, on which sits an eight-day Empire Clock. The *click-clock* sound can be heard throughout the room. Iverson is nervously pacing on a slightly faded path from his desk to the fireplace. She's well aware, having worked for him, that the clock acts as an integral part of his thought process. His pacing on the thick pile is quiet, while his steps are in perfect time with the resonating *click-clock.*

Thinking of her pressing need, Shirley refocuses on her mission. She steps into Iverson's path and stops him. "Meet Steven Alan Mason." He glances at Steven. Firmly, she says, "Hold him," and hands him the baby.

Iverson takes Steven as if he is a bundle of firewood. He allows himself to look into the child's face. He quickly lifts his head with his neck muscles tightening, causing his face to reveal a heightened tension as if he's just been charged with a serious crime.

Shirley takes Steven back and speaks forcefully, "He's beautiful and worthy of special care, and should have the benefit of what most children enjoy—don't you think?"

Flustered, Iverson continues his pacing. "You intend for me to be a part of this—this child's life?"

"I certainly do!"

The sound of her voice fuels Shirley's confidence. She waits for his reaction like a wild animal ready to pounce for the kill. His face contorts into a deep concentrated frown. He stops at the mantel. Taking a white handkerchief from his vest pocket, he lightly polishes the face of the clock, peering closely for dust to clean. "So what do you expect from me? I've done all I can."

Iverson's fussing over the clock irks her. She flushes and speaks with determination. "Steven Mason is always going to walk in the front door of life with pride and dignity. I'm raising him and I'm staying in Huntersville."

Iverson nervously straightens his tie, clears his throat, and walks to his chair. "This is unusual, having a woman as young as you leave the Leland Home without having given your baby up for adoption, or at least relocating to begin a new life. Have you told anyone who the father is?"

"No I haven't. No one has to know—ever." Shirley continues to speak assuredly, "I need support for Steven. Working at Harold Tully's farm isn't going to give me enough."

"Harold Tully! Everyone calls him Hermit Harold. You amaze me. I get you a good job away from town, and yet here you are, planning to work for the likes of this despicable old man."

"I want most of all to be a good mother and for Steven to live and grow up on a farm where I can be with him, yet still work for my room and board. In order to carry out my plan, I'll need support for Steven."

The attorney shakes his head. "I tried hard to right this whole mess. But here you are back in Huntersville!"

"As we've discussed before, I don't think of this as my mess."

"Yes, yes." Iverson's voice rises to a lofty tone. "The whole mission of the Leland Home is to make a better life for wayward girls."

"Hey, get this straight: I was never wayward," Shirley says, her eyes flashing.

"Well, yes—yes. I only use the term as a manner of speaking. As I was about to say, I'm not sure your going up on Pine Mountain with Harold Tully will be accomplishing the purpose of the Leland Home."

"Maybe it isn't what you or the Leland Home had in mind, but this is my plan. I didn't take a secretarial job because I want to be for Steven what I never had: a mother. I'm an orphan, remember. I never knew my mother. Any child of mine is not going to experience what I had to."

Iverson again starts pacing. "I do have some limited funds. We'll work out a plan. But I'll be surprised if you can tolerate Harold Tully."

The old Empire strikes one *gong*. "I need to leave now. Thanks for your help."

"I would prefer that you make an appointment before you come next time."

"I hope to come to town every Wednesday. Could I see you then?"

He sits with a sour expression, but with resignation in his voice. "Yes, I guess so."

She opens the side door and hurries down the stairs, breaking into a smile of satisfaction. She nimbly slips the strap of Steven's bag over her shoulder and grabs the handle of her suitcase, and in a near run, heads for The Market parking lot.

She locates Harold Tully's truck and taps on the passenger-side window. Through the mud and the smear, her eyes capture a profile that could be on Mount Rushmore, ridged and stony; but otherwise, it looks far from presidential.

Shirley puts her face up to the glass and shouts, "You Harold Tully?"

"Yup."

"I'm Shirley Mason. You know, the girl you hired."

"Get in."

After putting her suitcase in the back with the four milk cans, she opens the truck door. She's nearly overcome with barn smell, but climbs in just the same and slams the door. Neither speaks as Harold takes his pipe from his bib-overalls pocket, fills it from a can of Prince Albert, and strikes a match on the dash, and drags deeply, filling the cab with smoke. Even though he knows her age, he is surprised to see such a young woman. *Smart-lookin' eyes. Just as I expected: nothin' dull about this one.*

Steven begins to cry. She rolls down her window. She doesn't know if the cry is from the smoke, the smell, or hunger. She unbuttons her coat, pulls up her sweater, and nurses him, covering herself with Steven's blanket. "I don't know why he's crying, I just nursed him a while ago. Maybe he doesn't like the smoke." *Great. I have to feed him right next to a total stranger.*

Harold rests his pipe on the dashboard. "So you're the modern kind, lettin' him feed whenever and wherever."

"I don't think of breast-feeding as modern. Mothers have been doing this since the beginning of time."

"Guess I ain't used to seein' it. The babies I've seen drink from a bottle."

"Call me modern if you like. It's fun to try new ideas, and try new ways of doing things."

"I—I ain't modern. Hell no, I ain't modern."

"That's fine with me. Maybe we can learn from each other." Her stomach tightens. *I don't like how this conversation is going.*

"I can see you've got a lot to learn. I ain't changin' nothin', whether it's in the house or out in the barn."

Shirley's stomach knots tighter. The cool breeze from the open window chills the perspiration on her neckline. *Uh-oh, maybe I've made a mistake taking this job. After all, a nice apartment and a good-paying position is nothing to sneer at.*

She looks closer at her new boss. White stubble covers his face. He's wearing dirty bib-overalls and a red flannel shirt. The cuffs are glazed with oily grease and dirt. His knee-length boots are caked with cow manure.

The truck bounces over the rough gravel parking lot to the clattering sound of empty milk cans. He glances her way. *Damn. What am I thinkin' of, hirin' such a young woman? Yet she ain't a woman—just a girl doin' a woman thing.* "You know, I'll be footin' the bill for the keep of both of you." Harold feels his power and hold over her. "You can have the egg money to run the house, buy provisions, and that'll be all."

"How much is that?"

"I reckon I don't know. The hens ain't layin' much right now, and it depends what it takes to feed you both. Oh, and I ain't got a telephone. You ain't havin' to be wastin' your time talkin'."

She gets the message: She'll work herself to the bone and it will still probably be hard to make ends meet. But she has been successful with Attorney Iverson, and at least there will be a place to live with Steven.

After a long silence Shirley asks, "Why no phone?"

"It costs too much to string the wires up the mountain."

After a moment, she raises her voice, speaking directly at Harold to confirm an understanding. "I'll work my best for you. I know I can make a good home for the three of us. But I want you to know that my room will be my own private place."

Harold's eyes open wide, and his bottom jaw clamps shut. He again reaches for his pipe. He mumbles, "Yup, that's what all my housekeepers have said."

Shirley forcefully counters, her sharp brown eyes catching his attention, "We can live in the same house, but the minute you set foot into my room, you're going to be sorry. You understand?"

"Okay." *Damn, she's a sassy one. She's good-lookin' all right, but she scares me—seems more strong-headed than any woman I've known.*

Satisfied she's made her point, Shirley takes a deep breath and relaxes. They pass the milk can stand next to the road, and the truck begins to climb the steep hills to Harold's farm. As they round the hairpin turn at the bottom of the first hill, there's a long, almost vertical slope with no guardrails. She gulps. At the bottom of the bank a huge maple stands, but it has no central leader. It has two large limbs that grow skyward in a sweeping bend below the point of an apparent break of the tree trunk.

Turning her head over her shoulder as the truck starts up the hill she says, "That's a strange looking tree."

"Yup. Some call her Mary Maple."

"You make the tree sound like a person."

"My ma thought so. She was sort of religious and claimed the odd bend in the branches was like the outstretched arms of the Virgin Mary. My old man said she was nuts. He said the tree was one left from about a two hundred year-old stand of timber. Ma and my old man argued to beat hell over that tree. She hated to say 'virgin'. It must've reminded her too much of an untried woman. So she always called the tree Mary Maple."

"I like that—Mary Maple. I guess if you can name animals, you can name trees."

Harold snorts, "Yup, well, namin' stuff sounds sissy to me."

Steven has finished nursing. Shirley rests him on her shoulder and lightly pats his back to burp him. The truck engine roars and the transmission whines as they creep up a seemingly unending hill. Finally they reach the top and the road levels somewhat. Out her side window, she sees pussy willows with their brown fuzzy buds, one of the first signs of spring. Mrs. Perkins used to say they wore fur coats to keep warm during the cold spring nights. As the truck starts to climb yet another hill, Shirley feels uneasy, and she finds herself on the verge of crying, remembering Mrs. Perkins. *I'd like to be holding her hand. When are we going to get there?*

Her heart sinks as the farmstead comes into view. The cow barn, on the left-hand side of the drive, is a two-story unpainted wooden stable. Many of its windows have been broken and old burlap bags have been used to replace the glass. The hay storage is above the cow barn with a plank ramp, or high-drive entrance facing toward the house. *That's the saddest looking barn I've ever seen.*

As they come closer, she sees that the winter's supply of manure is overflowing the first level and oozing out into the barnyard. They pass the milk house, which is next to the high drive, followed by a henhouse and a small tool shed. Shirley looks at the house. It's barren, bleak, and in need of paint. The clapboards are the color of dark slate with only flecks of paint here and there, showing that once it had been painted white. The front door seems as though it is never used. It's decorated with a Christmas wreath with evergreen needles that have turned rusty brown. *The house is as bad as the barn. This whole place looks like it needs a friend.*

But as she turns her attention away from the buildings, she's struck by the beauty of her surroundings. The sky has cleared, allowing her to view distant mountain peaks. For Shirley, the scenery is breathtaking. As she scans the grays and greens of trees set against the mottled sky, mist is rising from the melting mountain snow. Rolling meadows and pastures lie in the foreground. She's surprised at how much snow remains in the fields. Stony ledges only occasionally appear above the tapestry of white.

Most impressive is a grove of centuries-old white pines towering above the house. With the ebb and flow of a warm southerly breeze, they sound like a huge musical instrument. The whooshing tones rise and fall from the wind like a vocalist singing a musical scale. *I understand why this place is called Pine Mountain.*

Harold turns off the truck and watches Shirley. *Just look at her takin' in everythin'. I wonder what she's thinkin'. I know my place ain't much. What in hell does she expect, that I own a palace? She's like an Indian scout travelin' in new territory.* He draws a deep breath and forces himself to open his door. *Damn it. Lettin' her see my house is like gettin' undressed in front of a doctor.*

The afternoon sun filters through the trees bordering the edges of the little fields. A number of crows are perched in the very tops of the branches catching the afternoon's sun. They seem to peer down as if checking on the new arrival. She can hear a crow's lonesome call as it soars effortlessly along the thermals.

The two make their way toward the one-and-a-half-story farmhouse. Shirley, clutching Steven in one arm, has the bag strap over her shoulder and the suitcase in her other hand. Harold trudges slowly, with his head down, kicking bits of icy snow. *If this isn't the biggest mistake I ever made—just to get a little help. In the past I only hired old broken-down women that never helped outside and never stayed.*

Shirley remarks, "I'll bet you don't have visitors very often."

"Nope. Not ones that stay."

Inside the kitchen a once-white plastic clock shows it's two o'clock. Shirley can barely make out the time because wood smoke and flyspecks blacken the face. A Glenwood kitchen woodstove is the only apparent source of heat and hot water. The kitchen table is covered with dirty dishes, dried-on bits of food, and yellowed reading material. A Windsor chair is pulled up to the only cleared spot on the table. It was once green, but most of the paint has been chipped and the arms have been worn to the wood. There are four more chairs of the ladder-back variety, placed around the table. The chair seats are piled with magazines. A Morris chair is in the corner of the room next to a window facing west. Shirley takes a deep breath, filling her lungs with stale wood smoke.

Harold leads her to the bedroom that used to be his but will now be hers. It's next to the kitchen. The room has a rocker and a bureau. The bed is just a thin mattress placed on wire springs. The side rails are slightly bent so both the headboard and footboard tip toward each other. No sheets are on the bed.

Harold nervously laughs. "My last housekeeper was a heavy bitch—the bed was a might small for the two of us."

Shirley sharply remarks, "This bed will be fine for just me!"

Harold notes her frosty expression while they find an old bureau that is empty and carry it to Shirley's room and carry Harold's to an unused room. She closes her door. Steven wakens acting hungry. She sits in the rocker, relaxes, and feeds him.

Harold yells through the door, "Come to the barn by four. I'll see how good you are at doin' chores." Before leaving the house, he looks toward his new room. *After all these years, I've got to sleep in a different room, one that's cold and damp as a bastard. Hirin' class cuts me out of a warm bed. Damn it, I can see I ain't thought about this hirin' business much.* He smiles as he walks the narrow snow-packed path to the barn. *It would be great slippin' in beside the likes of a Shirley—but what am I thinkin'? She's just a kid. But just the same, this evenin' will be interestin'. Lookin' at her makes me feel young again even though I'm sneakin' up on sixty. She must have let some fella around her; Zack, maybe? Her little one is livin' proof.*

Shirley removes her silver barrette, wraps it in a kerchief, and places it on her bureau for safekeeping. After organizing her room and washing a pile of dishes, she puts on barn clothes, boots, and her blue denim cap, looks in a mirror, and laughs. Anxious to see all her new surroundings, she leaves the house and walks the path to the barn. She carries Steven in a clothes basket she found.

The milking machine pump belts a high-pitched *whir,* spewing sound and oil out a pipe placed through the milk house wall. The outside boarding is oil soaked, and Shirley sees the oil droplets running off the end of the pipe as her thumb presses the latch of the barn door. The strong smell of manure almost chokes her. She watches Steven grimace as he coughs. Moisture is dripping from the ceiling. The walls are wet from the foggy air exhaled from twenty-some-odd cows, eight or so heifers, and a few calves tied wherever there's space. The cows stand in one long row on a wood floor. She wants to open the door to let some fresh air in the barn but thinks better of it. She carries Steven and opens a large door leading to the horse barn. The horses whinny at the sound, apparently hungry. The two dapple-gray work horses are thin, with ribs showing. She yells, "What are the horses' names?"

"Jeanie and Lassie."

She instantly likes them and feels sorry for their condition. "Can I feed them?"

"No! Come here and milk. I'll feed my own horses."

Placing Steven's basket beside the wall behind the cows, she decides that next week Attorney Iverson should give her money to buy a carriage for Steven.

Shirley knows the milking routine, and continues after Harold gives her some brief instructions. The cows are a mixed herd with most being the result of crossbreeding between Jersey, Guernsey, and Ayrshire. They stand listlessly with their hide covering only bones. *These are by far the poorest cattle I've ever seen. The hay is poor, too, and I'll bet he doesn't grain them very much.* She can see that he cares for his cows the way he does his horses. *Probably hunting, fishing, and women take up most of his time.* She finishes milking and carries the machines to the milk house for washing and rinsing. She returns to the barn for the wash bucket and a half pail of milk. Looking into the can after straining the remaining milk, she is amazed at how little the herd is producing. *This is pathetic!*

CHAPTER THREE

While Harold feeds out the hay, Shirley returns to the house and finds a casserole, and a basket of rolls on the kitchen table. Propped up against the casserole dish sits a note:

Welcome to Pine Mountain. I hope to meet you soon.

Sincerely, Alice Coles

Shirley sighs in relief for the prepared meal. *Alice Coles is the kind of person I'd like to get to know.* She feels the warm dish and is comforted to know there's someone close by she can turn to for help if need be.

She clears the table, washes the worn oilcloth, and finds a radio that works. She moves an accumulation of newspapers and junk into a back room: boxes, beer bottles, a pile of *Lost Love* magazines, a big pile of *Hunter's Gazette*, an old radio that doesn't work, and a pile of monthly newsletters from The Lovelorn Club. There are no farm magazines, not even the *American Agriculturalist.* She remembers that all the farmers she knew received that magazine. *Maybe he isn't even considered a farmer*. Shaking her head, she sweeps the floor.

By the time Harold sits down for his meal, the kitchen already looks more livable. He eats three helpings of the casserole. After the third, Shirley nervously laughs. "You must have been hungry, or maybe you just eat a lot."

"Nope, it was a mighty good-tastin' meal. Alice is a good cook."

"I'd say it's a nice neighborly thing to do—bring the dish all the way up here."

"Yup, maybe—she thinks the whole world is her friend. She's all for sendin' aid to Europe. We just got through bombin' the place; now we got to spend money to fix what we just busted."

"I don't understand what you're talking about."

"It don't matter, all I'm sayin' is that she's a goody-goody. You know, the church type, they tell you to love your neighbor. 'Course, Alice does it because someone told her to."

"I don't care what you think or why she did it, but I know I appreciate her sending up a nice meal. It was a friendly thing to do."

"You and she prob'ly think the same—just like peas in a pod."

"Not exactly, but being friendly and giving is a good way to live. It's a lot more fun. At least that's what my counselor, Dr. Meyer, said. He should know, he's a psychologist."

"Alice gets her ideas from the church and you get yours from some fool couch doctor. Well, I'll tell you, the church and this Dr. Meyer ain't had to milk cows for the last forty years, and fight the cold winters. Life's a bastard. You learn fast up here that you look out for yourself and to hell with the rest of the world."

"This sounds like the Gospel According to Harold." Shirley dips a pan into the hot water chamber of the woodstove and pauses for his reaction.

He gets up from the table and sits in his Morris chair, pulling his pipe from his bib-overalls pocket. "I'll tell you, Harold knows. I'll bet that Dr. Meyer never froze his ass off when it's twenty below with the wind blowin', huggin' a woodstove. There's been many a winter's night up here when I'd push that stove just as tight as she'd go, just to keep from freezin'." Harold rubs the bowl of his pipe and turns to face Shirley. "Talkin' about Alice Coles, Zack tells me he knows you."

"Zack. Is he Alice's son?"

"Yup. Poor woman, only a mother could love that kid."

"He didn't have many friends in school." With her hand, she sweeps her hair away from the side of her face. "I guess he might be okay in his way."

"Huh, in his way, but I can't stand his way. You must be seein' somethin' I never did. I showed him your letter—he's kinda sweet on you."

Shirley blushes and Steven begins to fuss. "I've got to feed and change my boy and put him to bed." She quickens her steps to her room and firmly closes the door.

Harold lights up his pipe. *She's coy, that one is. I'll bet Zack made a move on her, but on the other hand Zack ain't normal.* Harold builds up the fire for the night, waiting for Shirley. *He might've tried. I know I would've at his age.* Harold walks toward her room and yells, "I need some help movin' a bed."

"Just a minute."

Shirley enters the kitchen ten minutes later and they find an old studio couch and carry it to Harold's new room. She makes his bed with yellowed sheets, ragged blankets, and a flat pillow. "It looks to me as though you're going to be sleeping in as good a room as I am."

"Yup, but it's cold as hell in here."

They return to the kitchen and Shirley goes to her room, leaving the bedroom door ajar so the stove can heat the room.

Harold stands over the stove with outstretched hands, more out of habit than need, and later sits for a smoke before leaving the warm kitchen. It's been more than forty long years since he's been near a woman as young as Shirley. Not since Maria. *Now, if Shirley was Maria—well, but she's got more class, and seems like a good worker, too.*

Wonder how long she'll stay? His pipe smoke curls up toward the ceiling in the stillness of the warm room. Soon he heads for his new bedroom. The old spruce flooring creaks and snaps, bearing the weight of each step.

Harold tries to adjust to his new surroundings. The damp cold bed makes him irritated, and he keeps waking. The night seems endless. He isn't by nature a poor sleeper, but the dampness is working its way to his bones. However, due to his own foolhardiness, he has given Shirley the room that has always been his. He lies awake sizing up the situation and his relationship with his new hired woman. *She's a strong one, with a body the likes of which has never passed the doors of this house—well, maybe except for Maria. What the hell is she doin' up here with an old worn-out codger like me? Ah, I can't stand this damn cold anymore.*

He gets out of bed, goes to the dark kitchen, and stands by the stove. The moon is full and it casts light through the gray smoky windows. He pulls a chair up to the stove and sits soaking up the warmth, rubbing his cold weathered hands. *I sure as hell would like to be sleeping in my own room.*

Although Steven is an easy baby, Shirley still has to wake in the night to feed him. She has just finished, and goes back to bed. Harold gingerly moves over the noisy spruce flooring, with each step breaking the stillness of the night. *She made it damn plain she didn't want me near her room. But who in hell is she? Tellin' me what I can or can't do in my own house. Maybe I should show her who's boss around here and check in on her.*

Through the partially opened door, a moon shadow of Harold strikes the wall in Shirley's room becoming larger with each forward step. Her bed springs clatter, signaling that she's gotten up, but he keeps slowly moving.

When he reaches her doorway, he balances himself near the threshold by grabbing the doorjamb, while peering into her room. Suddenly the door slams on his index finger, sending a blinding jolt of pain up his arm.

"YAOW!"

Harold yanks his hand free, throwing his arm up as Shirley opens the door. He stumbles backward, howling and crashing on the kitchen floor. "Damn it all! All I was doin' was checkin' on you. Bastard, look what you did!"

Shirley stands over him with her hands on her hips. "I warned you, Harold Tully; my room is my private place!"

Steven wakes and cries out. She runs to comfort her son, while yelling at Harold, "Stay out of my room! Get that through your dumb head!"

Steven continues to cry as she holds him, rubbing his back, trying to calm him. After a few minutes he settles down. She lays him down and returns to the kitchen, turns on the light, and kneels beside Harold. He's flat on the floor groaning in pain. The weight and force of the door closing has crushed his index finger. Blood is spraying in several directions. He howls, "You're fired! Get out of my house! You're a no-good bitch—too smart for your own good!"

Steven starts to wail again, so she runs back to her room to comfort him. He takes several deep breaths and stops crying. She lays him back in his basket.

Harold, still moaning, remains on the floor. "Bastard, my right leg is numb." He's rubbing it with his left hand. "You're leavin' right now!"

She helps him to his feet as he tries to put weight on his leg. "Harold, sit at the table," she orders, while helping him walk toward the Windsor chair. The bright redness of his blood has sprayed onto his ashen face and settled into his white stubble.

"What are you goin' to do?"

She looks in the bathroom for some disinfectant to clean the wound and finds a bottle of pine oil. The bleeding is slowing, but he continues to curse and threaten. She runs to his bedroom and, with determination, lifts one end of his bed off the floor, but the other two legs squawk and dig as she pulls the heavy bed into the warm kitchen.

She again orders as she helps him from his chair, "I want you on your bed!"

"Damn, my leg! I ain't able to bear any weight on it." He flops to lie down.

She dips some water from the stove's hot water reservoir into a shallow bowl, tempers it from the tap at the sink, and adds the disinfectant. She rests the dish on his stomach and puts Harold's hand in the solution. All the color has drained from his face and sweat runs down from his brow. She finds some aspirin, holds his head up, and has him swallow two while drinking some milk.

Wow, it's three o'clock. I hope I can calm him by chore time. Maybe I can find something better for his pain. She quickly scans old bottles among the medicines and notices a small vial among them. She blows the dust from the bottle, which reads For Pain. "This will help."

"Woman, you're givin' me enough med'cine to kill me, and the way I feel right now, I hope it does." She wraps the wound with a strip of white sheeting. He asks, "What makes you think you know what you're doin'?"

"I took first aid in school and used it caring for old Jim Iverson when he was dying."

"Oh." Harold's pale eyelids close.

By morning chores, he is continuing to rest quietly.

At five, Shirley dresses and bundles Steven for the barn. She unplugs the radio and places it in the clothes basket at Steven's feet. *Maybe this will brighten my spirits.*

She walks toward the barn, using the light of the open sky to guide her way. She's enjoying the crisp spring air and the peacefulness of the early morning. Reaching the barn, she opens the door and turns the black knob on the light switch. All of the cows turn their heads and bellow. *Gosh, they look thin and act hungry. Their hay looks terrible: gray, coarse, mostly goldenrod and break fern—as poor as any hay I've seen.*

Early morning radio is enjoyable listening: the weather report, the maple sugaring report, the milk prices, the local news, and, most interesting, the Agricultural Extension Service program. Joe Iverson, the agricultural agent, visits over the airwaves, his friendly voice reverberating throughout the barn. *Joe sure has done more with himself than his brother Jimmy.*

She pulls open the scuttle boards located behind the cows' rear feet and hoes stiff manure into the pit below. The daily manure removal and urine accumulation since the previous fall has caused what's stored below to flow out into the barnyard.

After freshening up the old hay beneath the cows, she starts milking. None of the cows' udders are very full like the ones she remembers. Joe is talking about the problem of cattle lice. He lists signs and symptoms. As she listens, Shirley looks more closely at the cows and she's dismayed to see what he's referring to: incrustations on the cows' bodies, rough hair coats, hair falling out—all indications of lice. Some cows are wiggling their tails, irritated by the crawling, blood-sucking insects.

Dried dung balls hang from long tail hairs. While the cows' tails swing, the dung balls hit, like balls of wood knocking out a tune on some medieval instrument. Joe's closing statement on the subject stirs Shirley the most: "Lice can suck up to a quart of blood a day from a heavily louse-infested cow. Cows can't give milk and blood too."

She shudders and goose bumps scamper up her back. *Gosh, I need to get rid of these lice. Harold may want me to go, but he definitely needs me.*

She finishes milking, washes up the utensils, and feeds Jeanie and Lassie. They are friendly, not a bit nervous; but she's appalled to see only hide and bones. Out of pity, she feeds them some cow grain, realizing that Harold never does, since the cast-iron mangers are dusty. They ravenously dive for the grain, as dry particles of ground corn and bran blow from their flapping mouths. Shirley stands and watches. "Poor things."

Steven has been sleeping the whole hour and a half it's taken her to do the chores, but now he stirs. She smiles as he opens his bright blue eyes and waves his tiny fists. She picks him up and then settles on a milk stool. "Good morning, Mama's little joy. You're so good. Sorry about last night, but we're going to make out just fine." She kisses him on the forehead and feeds him. While relaxing against the wall, she spots a brown rat running down the manger, searching and nibbling at flecks of grain. She remembers hearing someone say, "See them in the day and there are a hundred or more. They breed like flies." She shudders. *The henhouse must be crawling with them.*

She places Steven back in the clothes basket and steps outside the barn. The early-morning sun is shining through the pines. Shards of orange and yellow light illuminate the trees. The bright light reflects and glitters off the waxy dark green needles. *Nature's gift, more beautiful than any decorated Christmas tree.*

The bright spring morning outweighs her problems: injured Harold, a dirty house, lice, rats, skinny cows, and hungry horses. *Problems and more problems—always. But the gifts of nature: the rising sun, the trees, the birds, the pussy willows, the meadows, plus a precious son to raise make this the perfect place.* She only enjoys the sight for a moment because a fast-moving cloud floats over Pine Mountain, hiding the sun.

Concerned for Harold, she passes by the hens. *I'll feed them and collect the eggs later.* She walks through the entry. With its handles crackling, she balances the basket on one knee to free a hand to open the kitchen door. Harold's ugly mood covers the living space like the dark cloud that just passed.

"Ain't you smart, runnin' your little behind down to the barn. I suppose you have all the chores done: cows milked, hayed, and cleaned out, and the horses fed, and everythin'. Bastard, I'm in pain."

"I'll fix you up." She gives him three of the remaining pain tablets.

He continues to rant, "If you think you're takin' over here, forget it. I've never seen the likes of it. You ain't been here for a day, and I feel like a man ninety years old."

"I guess you know where we stand now, don't you? I'm not having you snooping in my room! I only work here!" She zings him with her piercing brown eyes, and points. "You're never to set foot in that room."

"Well, holy shit, look who's marched in and taken over in MY house!"

Shirley calms herself. "You know, we could have a real good life here together; you, me, and Steven. You could sort of retire. Take up with someone in town, hunt, fish, and I'll work the farm, cook your meals, and make a nice place for you to come home to. We both could benefit. You need me now, Harold. You're in no shape to go to the barn."

"Yup—you snared me but good. I'm a-layin' here helpless while you're just a-bossin' my life." He looks at her in anger. "How lucky can I be?"

"Now, as soon as your pain lets up some, we're getting in the truck and taking you to see Dr. Plumbly. I'll load the cans and leave them on the stand, and then we'll go and get you fixed up."

"You sure like to run things!"

Shirley snaps, "By the looks of your place, you need someone to run things." She immediately tempers her tone, not wanting to overstep her position. "You've worked all your life—you need me. I'm young and can help you."

"Some help! I was a whole man just a day ago and now look at me."

Shirley ignores him. She picks up Steven in his basket and heads outside, gets into the truck, and backs up to the loading platform at the milk house door. She views the eight-can McCormick Deering cooler with a different perspective than at milking time. In the morning as milk was poured into a fourteen-quart strainer, the forty-quart cans settled into the cooler water. Now she prepares herself to lift the cans from the cooler.

The buoyancy of the water allows her to lift the first can to the top edge of the cooler with more ease than she first thought. She holds each handle, lowering the can to the milk house floor. The first one is the lightest because the level of the water in the cooler is at the highest point. Each succeeding can is heavier. *Wow, I did it! I wasn't sure I could. I've lost a lot of strength, sitting around the Leland Home for the last few months.*

She hitches the chain in front of the truck body that holds the cans. Steven is crying. Shirley jumps off the loading ramp and opens the truck door. "How's my boy doing? You're just the perfect baby, yes you are. Your big blue eyes are wide open, and your little fists are flying. Well, your mama is going to feed you right now and change your wet diaper."

After feeding him, she finds a wooden box that is the right size for the front seat of the truck, and folds a baby's quilt to place in the bottom; then she gently rests him in it. She drives the truck up to the house. *Now I have to deal with a much larger problem.*

Leaving Steven in the truck, she goes into the house. She loads the stove with wood and wakes Harold. "Come on, big man; let's see if we can make it to the doctor."

"Bastard, I'm a wreck. I tell you if I had a choice, you'd be out of here, that's for sure." He sits up weakly, carefully holding his injured finger away from his body.

"What a pity for both of us that we don't have much of a choice. Put your arm over my shoulder and let me help you to the truck."

"Hell, if we even touch, you'd probably bust me up more."

"Don't worry, in your condition, you're no threat to me."

"Bring my pipe and tobacco."

She helps him into his seat where he slumps over, holding his hand. Shirley fills his pipe, sticks it in his mouth, and strikes a match. Loaded with pain medicine, Harold can barely draw on the pipe; a fact for which she is thankful, since Steven is bothered by his smoking. He slumps further down in his seat, opens his mouth to talk, and the pipe drops on the floor. "The stand, ba—the truc—up, I—number 21 'n' Coleses' number 25."

"I don't understand a word you're saying. I guess you share the milk stand with the Coleses?" Harold grunts in answer.

The engine races in second gear, slowing the truck as it descends the steep hills. The tire chains crunch and slap on the fenders. She intently watches the road, spinning the wheel to avoid the deepest ruts, rocks, and muddy pools. "All I know is that I've got to back up to the stand and unload these cans."

She carefully maneuvers around the sharp turn at the bottom of the last hill. Shirley's and the Coleses' trucks simultaneously arrive at the stand, and they back up side by side. She walks up the rickety steps and smells sour milk. The elm planks are as slick as black ice from the milk spilled the day before. Fat in the curdled milk has bubbled through the cracks in the floor. She takes note of the number of cans in the Coleses' truck. While stepping toward the back of Harold's truck, she adjusts her barrette.

Zack opens his door and stares at Harold and Steven. He slowly walks toward the stand, continuing with his head turned in their direction, yet moving forward toward the steps. He mutters to himself, "Harold and her—her baby!"

He reaches the stand, but he's still distracted, and stumbles on the steps and slips with feet and legs in the air and hands clutching space. Throwing himself forward, he lands facedown on the putrid elm planks. In alarm, Shirley holds her hands to her face, but then quickly kneels by his side. She firmly grasps his shoulder. "Are you okay, Zack?"

For just a moment, he lays quietly, his nose and face in sour milk. She continues holding his shoulder. "Are you okay? Zack? Answer me!"

He finally lifts his head. Strings of curdled milk drip from his face. "Hi, Shirley. I love the touch of your gentle hand."

She quickly stands and backs away saying sharply, "I was afraid you were hurt." *What a fool he is!*

She returns to the truck to get an extra diaper and hands it to Zack, who stands with sour milk dripping from his face to his front. He stares at her with his mouth gaping open. "Wow, you're good look—well, I—I haven't seen you since the picnic."

Shirley realizes he's right. As Zack cleans himself up with the diaper, the details of the picnic come back to her. How all the girls were lined up at the shore by the lake, waiting to stand on the guys' shoulders, held there by firm boy hands pressed into soft girl flesh. How they giggled as their toes gripped into unsteady footing. Then they dove, like Olympic swimmers with outstretched arms and hands splitting the water. She remembers that tall and handsome Jimmy Iverson had enjoyed the longest line of waiting girls. They had screamed with delight, as he hoisted them with his strong iron grip to stand on his brawny shoulders.

Shirley had sat by herself, not wanting to take part even though she could swim. A loner, Zack had stood close by, acting miserable. He mumbled something like, "Iverson thinks he's hot stuff."

Shirley remembers that she laughed, thinking that Jimmy didn't look too hot at five in the morning when he had to go to the barn. Zack had asked, "Want to go for a walk?"

After hesitating for a moment she had said, "Sure, why not?" As she thinks about it now she feels a deep regret. *What a mistake it was to have taken that walk*!

Zack finishes cleaning up and hands the diaper back to Shirley. "Thanks. That came in handy."

"This sour milk is nasty stuff."

He stands staring at Shirley, seemingly incapable of making the next move to unload his truck.

I wish he'd quit that. She says, "I want to meet your mother and thank her for the casserole and rolls. What a nice thing to do!"

"That's my mother, always doing for others." Zack gestures toward the truck. "What happened to Harold?"

"He jammed his finger. I'm taking him to see Dr. Plumbly."

"I see you have a baby."

"Yeah. His name is Steven."

"Oh, Steven." After a pause, Zack blurts out, "I wish you'd come to work for us. We need the help. Anyway, it's a lot nicer at our place than living up there with Hermit Harold. He can't keep help. I'll bet he's had more housekeepers over the years than Mary Maple has leaves."

"Thanks for the offer, but I want to give this a try."

"Maybe you'd come to supper some night. How about tomorrow night?" Zack brightens. "We could go to the barn and I'd show you our cows."

"How about next week? I want to make sure Harold is all right."

Zack slumps his shoulders, and he bites his bottom lip while nervously running his fingers through his curly hair.

She speaks assuredly, "Just be patient. We'll come to supper soon."

"We'll? I—I mean just you!"

"I'll see." She feels a knot in her stomach thinking of the picnic, as she counts ten cans in Zack's truck. While driving away from the stand, she questions if that much milk could ever come from Harold's cows, and what are the Coleses doing differently? *They must have quite the herd.*

With Steven in one arm and the drugged Harold on the other, she climbs the stairs to the waiting room. Dr. Plumbly, a kindly, rotund, balding man comes to greet them. His face brightens and breaks into a big smile upon seeing Shirley. "Hi, Shirley. Glad to see you're back in town. You work up on Pine Mountain?"

"Yeah, for Harold."

Shirley feels a rush of anxiety as she enters the doctor's office. The last visit was the worst day of her life. The words "You're pregnant" lodged in her head like a bullet. She hardly knew what the word meant. But then Dr. Plumbly said, "You're going to have a baby." She saw her whole life's plan unraveling at that very moment. She was numb watching the doctor pick up the phone. In her dazed state of mind she remembers hearing "Attorney Iverson," and something about how she must use the side entrance.

Harold, holding his hand, scuffs into the doctor's office. Dr. Plumbly looks at his finger. "So you're a little bunged up this morning. My word, what a nasty wound!"

Harold winces. "It pains like hell, my leg too."

The doctor answers, "We'll fix you up in short order."

After attending to Harold, Dr. Plumbly calls Shirley into his inner office. "How's the baby doing? Let me look him over." He examines Steven very thoroughly, checking for reflexes and alertness. "He appears to be a bright boy." He holds Steven for Shirley to take him. "I hope you're all right way up on that mountain with this man. Over the years, he's sent plenty of women in here crying from all sorts of ailments."

Shirley is sitting in view of the stirrups each side of the examining table. The words "You're pregnant" continue to echo in her mind. In a flash she runs her hand over her hair and nervously smiles. "I think Harold and I can come to an understanding."

"Appears so, since he's the one in pain this morning. You're one gritty gal to handle Harold."

"Thanks, Dr. Plumbly. I hope we don't have to see you for any further such visits."

Riding back home in the truck, Harold moans and groans for a while, but quickly falls asleep. Once they reach the farm, Shirley brings blankets from the house to cover him. She takes care of Steven and starts the washing, and then rearranges the kitchen for Harold's bed, and takes the opportunity to sweep the kitchen floor. Finding a colorful pink porcelain vase, she picks some white pine bows for a centerpiece on the table.

She fries some bacon, cuts it into bits, and mixes it with a can of corn chowder, stirring and warming the soup on the stove. She hears the truck horn and smiles. *A good sign we'll be staying on Pine Mountain; he needs my help. It sure would be nice if we could settle in one place. I don't need an Esther Erickson hysterically calling a social worker and yelling, "Come quick and take this girl. I don't want her in my home!" And all because I had flattened her bratty kid.*

With Shirley's help, Harold makes his way into the house and sits at the table. He tastes the soup and slurps down two full bowls. "I hate to give you any credit, but this soup tastes good."

She laughs. "You don't have to give me any credit. I have to eat, too."

He looks at her and says nothing. *Golly, she's quick.*

She writes a note to the Agricultural Extension Agent, Joe Iverson. *I haven't seen Joe since the summer old Jim died. Joe was always nice to me, and I liked working at the Iversons, especially when he came home from college. He had enough edge under that smile to control Jimmy, like no one else could.*

Dear Joe:

It will be great to see you again. I need some help. Please come soon to Harold Tully's place. Oh, and congratulations on being hired for your new position. I read it in Harold's paper.

Sincerely, Shirley Mason, Pine Mountain

After lunch Harold sits in his chair and groans, "I'm feelin' powerful pain."

She doles out more pills. "Let's move you to your bed—you'll feel better. I'll get you a magazine to read."

"Forget it. How can I read, layin' here achin' like a bastard? You're tryin' to mother me more than your own kid."

"Well, the squeaky wheel gets the grease." Shirley brushes strands of hair from her face.

"You're a snappy one all right. Always have an answer. Everything I got to say, you roar back at me like a tiger."

"Remember this, whatever pain you're in is your own doing."

"You're just too smart for your own good," he says, as he settles in his bed and closes his eyes.

Carrying a wire egg basket in one hand and Steven in the other arm, she follows the path to the henhouse. Outside, she hears the hens. *These poor chickens are hungry. Oh, there's that high-pitched singing call.*

Pressing the door latch with her thumb, she enters the small building and shivers, seeing several rats scurry for their burrows. She's dismayed to find gnawed holes in the grain bags piled in the granary. She knows rats cost a lot of money in feed consumed and damage done, such as eating eggs and the live flesh of hens while they roost at night. She remembers seeing hens in the morning still alive with great caverns eaten into the interiors of their bodies.

Fearing for Steven, she holds him while gathering eggs, placing them carefully in the wire basket. She counts forty. *Well, the rats are certainly doing their damage. With a hundred hens, I should be collecting at least eighty eggs.*

Going to the truck, she places the eggs on the seat, feeds Steven, and sits thinking about the rat problem. She decides to take action. Leaving Steven sleeping, she returns to the poultry house. After a little hunting, she finds barrels that have been used for storing feed. She empties all the remaining grain into the rat-proof containers and covers them. After some more poking around, she finds some plaster of Paris that's on a shelf. She mixes it with feed, and places the baited feeder in the granary where the bags were piled.

She knows that seeing dead rats as a result of the poison will take a while as their rock-hard intestines would not immediately cause death. Jim Iverson's wife, Janice—Jimmy and Joe's aunt—taught her that rats are very intelligent. If the poison works too quickly, they won't continue to eat the bait.

Returning to the henhouse from the granary, she catches three dying hens that have been attacked by rats. She holds them by their pale scaly legs. They hang lifeless. Taking them to the woodshed, she places each bird's head and neck on the chopping block. With her free hand, she swings the ax, and the blade severs the head from the neck and bites into the wood. The head and gasping beak lie on one side of the shiny blade, and the headless body lies on the other. She repeats the process for each hen. For a moment, the necks spray streams of blood and the wings flap in a dying reflex. *Death is a friend to these poor things.*

After doing evening chores, she checks on the rat bait. Shining a light through the granary window, she points it at the baited feeder. It is completely brown with rats, devouring the bait. *What a problem! They're so many I can't count them.* Jarring the door, she enters. The rats scramble out of sight into their burrows. She refills the feeder with the deadly mix.

CHAPTER FOUR

Agricultural Agent Joe Iverson drives into the Tully farmyard in his new '48 Ford coupe. Shirley notices the car through the west window and quickly bundles up Steven and runs across the kitchen floor toward the entry. Harold is half-awake. "Where are you headed in such a rush?"

"I'll be right back."

He lifts himself from his bed and sees the car and grumbles, "I'm bein' taken over, losin' my grip on this place. OH—damn this pain. Plumbly said, 'Just a little bruise.' What a bunch of hogwash. I'm crippled for life all because I was stupid enough to hire a young thing with springs on her feet and a fire-cracker in her pants. We make one hell of a team: a young spirited filly and an old horse, fallen in his traces! When and if I get feelin' better, she's got to leave. I'd rather drop dead than to try and tame her."

Having left the house, Shirley waves at Joe as she walks toward his car.

"Hi, Shirley." Joe Iverson is in his early twenties, tall and slender. He has a ready smile. "I must admit this is the first time I've been here. Harold isn't the kind of farmer to call for help."

"You're right. Harold would never ask for advice."

"Gee, you have a baby!"

Shirley lifts Steven off her shoulder and rests him in her arms. "Isn't he about the sweetest kid? Are you going to open those big blue eyes for Joe?"

"He's beautiful, Shirley! The last time I saw you, you were headed for Burlington to take a secretarial job." While talking, he stares at Steven.

"I know—then Steven came. We've moved back to make a new home for ourselves."

"Your husband got left behind?"

Shirley pauses and takes a deep breath. "There wasn't one to bring."

"Sorry for asking. Personal lives aren't my job, but I think of you as being almost a part of our family."

"Yes—almost." *But I'm still the state kid, right?* "Those were some good times living with your Uncle Jim and Aunt Janice, especially when you visited from college." *But then again, there was always Jimmy.*

"You should have written Aunt Janice. She would have given you a job."

With Jimmy! "Probably, but I saw Harold's ad and answered it. I guess there wasn't much competition." Joe and Shirley both laugh. She continues, "Don't you think a farm is the best place to raise children?"

"I sure do. Jimmy and I had a great time living and working for Uncle Jim and Aunt Janice. We always dreaded having to go home for short visits. Where's Harold? I expected he'd probably meet me with a shotgun. Not many folks in town have ever been up here except for all the down-and-out women he took in that were headed for the poor farm."

Shirley laughs. "You aren't serious! Harold wouldn't greet you with a gun. He isn't that sort."

"Maybe not, but you know how stories get started."

"He's been hurt, so I've got to take care of things for a while." She turns toward the barn. "Let's go. I want you to see the cows."

Steven, wrapped in his blue blanket, again catches Joe's eye. "You're waking up for Joe? He sure is a contented baby."

"Thanks. He seems to be." Shirley opens the barn door.

Joe takes a step backward as he enters. "Wow, do you ever need better ventilation. Cows need good fresh air to do their best and remain healthy."

"What can I do?"

"You need a barn fan. I'll tell you what: you buy the fan, and I'll help you install it."

"You will? I thought you'd be busy with your Vassar friend. Aren't you about to be married?"

"'Don't believe all that you read' is certainly true with that news. Honeydew got that tidbit from my mother. I only dated the girl a couple of times. In regards to installing a fan, I can't do it during the day, but I could help you at night." He carefully looks at the barn. "On warmer spring days, keep this door open. Also, open the haymow door; then you'll get some good cross-ventilation. But you should really have a fan."

Shirley wonders out loud, "How can I ever get money from Harold to buy a fan? I'm still new in his life. I need to wait at least a few weeks before I discuss needed improvements. I don't even know if I'll be staying here." She pauses. "But Joe, one thing I did do was cover these cows with louse powder, once I heard your talk on the radio."

"I see that. They sure are in poor condition. Getting rid of the lice should help a lot. They can probably give more than twice their present production if you make a few simple changes. I'll be back tonight to give you a hand." Joe smiles at her.

"You will? Thanks! Don't think you have to, but I won't turn you away." Shirley returns his smile, feeling flushed.

As Joe leaves the yard she's satisfied that she's found an old friend who knows farming and is willing to help her. She finds herself thinking eagerly about tonight when he returns.

During the next few days, she continues to feed the rat bait and dust the cows with louse powder, figuring these are two things she can do without interference from Harold. Joe stops by every evening for short visits to help feed the cows and horses. He also feeds the calves and the hens and collects the eggs. She appreciates him as she has found that her days are full: doing chores, caring for Steven, washing diapers and clothes, preparing meals, and cleaning the house. She likes working with the animals, but most of all she likes being in charge of her own life. *I'm free of the Esther Ericksons of the world! No one can tell me where to live and what I should do—for the moment, anyway.*

Tuesday night Shirley sits at the kitchen table grading eggs. The following day she has to drive to The Market, deliver the eggs, buy Steven a carriage and a crib, stop at Attorney Iverson's office, and get grain at Butson's.

Harold lifts himself off his bed and walks to the Morris chair. "Damn, my leg and back pain me whenever I walk or stand."

"Why don't you ride into town with me tomorrow? Getting out would be good."

"Yup, and let everybody see how Shirley Mason has to drive me around. I'm goin' to feel better one of these days and you can go along and tend to someone else's business." He waves his hand in emphasis and hits his injured finger on the arm of the chair. "Ouch! It'll be a few days before I can milk a cow. I never in my life have known pain like this and you're the cause of it!"

"Harold, don't talk like that. I'm trying my best to help and make life better for you. I hope we can come to some understanding. I'd like to stay here with Steven."

"You would? You're the first woman that's ever told me that—we'll have to see." Harold turns toward the west window. Shirley notes he has a slight smile.

The next day after shopping for groceries and delivering the eggs, Shirley stops at the furniture store that's next to The Market. She selects a carriage and crib for Steven. After loading the items, and with the receipt in her pocket, she carries Steven and walks to the side entrance of Attorney Iverson's office. She stops for a moment and straightens Steven's jersey top and takes the edge of a clean diaper and wipes drool from his chin. "You're a lucky boy to have a crib to sleep in and a nice new carriage to ride in."

She opens the side door to the office and starts climbing the stairs. She checks her barrette and looks for the spider, but it's gone. *Maybe this is a good omen and he won't give me a hard time, having to pay for the crib and carriage, plus an allowance for Steven.*

She enters his office. He is seated at his desk reading from a Vermont law book, and looks up. "So—you haven't forgotten!" He clears his throat, and straightens his tie.

"No, I didn't forget. Here's a receipt for two items I had to have for Steven." She hands him the paid invoice and then sits holding her son in her lap.

He checks the receipt. "These are reasonable, but…" He begins to scowl and shakes his head in exasperation. "I'm trapped in this whole matter. I have no choice but to pay for your child." He gets up from his chair and starts pacing while the old Empire Clock sounds the beat—*click-clock, click-clock, click-clock.*

"Pardon me, Attorney Iverson, but you have no idea how I felt the day Dr. Plumbly told me I was pregnant. Talk about being trapped—that was me. This child has altered the whole course of my life. I could be bitter, but I'm not. All I'm asking for is some support, with no grousing over the situation." She pauses and then blurts, "Please!"

His face is red with anger. "Okay, I get your point!" He takes his seat, pulls out a checkbook and begins writing. "This will do for now, but I'm going to make some inquiries to be sure this is my responsibility."

Now Shirley is the one to get angry. "What do you want? For me to press charges, review the whole ugly mess, and go to Honeydew Mullen? She'll be pleased to tell the whole town what *really* happened."

The attorney stiffens in alarm. "Oh heavens, don't do that!" He then sighs deeply. "Come, as we've agreed. I'll continue to support your baby."

Relief washes over Shirley, but she tries hard not to show it. Standing, she takes the check. "Thanks. I'll see you next week."

The attorney drops in his seat, seeming to be in a sour mood.

While she's driving to Butson's Feed and Farm Supply, tears start trickling down her face. *Trapped—If only he knew. But, as Dr. Meyer said, "Feeling sorry for myself won't help." So pull yourself together, Shirley.*

The truck enters Butson's yard. She backs up to the loading platform and climbs the stairs to the mill with Steven. The machinery is in full operation. The hammer mill whines, making a loud blowing hum. The sound of whole grain rattles, hitting the metal pipe leading to the grinder. Very fine particles of dust blow and swirl from tiny cracks in the machinery. It seems as though she's walking into a driving snowstorm. The workers are covered with a yellow-gray powder.

Covering Steven's face, she hurries to the mixing and bagging room. The next door leads to the salesroom. Through the dusty glass window, several farmers can be seen standing around a large potbelly stove talking and laughing.

She opens the door and enters. The salesroom immediately becomes silent. All that can be heard is the crackling sound of wood burning in the stove. All that can be seen are men dressed in bib-overalls, denim farm coats, and boots, standing and watching. She is dressed in a brown sweater and skirt, wearing loafers. *I know women don't come to this place very often, especially young women carrying their babies.*

The proprietor, Elmer Butson, pleasantly greets her. "Can I help you?"

"Yes, I'd like eight bags of twenty percent cow grain, one bag of horse grain, and six bags of layer mash." She whispers, "It's for Harold Tully." She senses the piercing eyes of the men.

While waiting for Elmer to write the sales slip, she turns her head to the left. *It's been a long time since I've been here.* Suddenly a hundred-pound burlap bag zips down from upstairs on a wooden chute. Shirley smiles to herself. *That could have been me as a kid, flying down the chute, squealing in laughter, and then running up the stairs for another turn. Coming here used to be a big deal, just to get a chance to take a slide. But that was a long time ago. Now I want out!*

Elmer gives her the sales slip and she pays him.

"Thanks. We'll have you loaded right away. Oh, by the way, I got a carload of citrus pulp yesterday from Florida. Some farmers are short of hay and need a substitute until spring. If Harold is short of hay, this might be something he'd like to try."

"It sounds like a good idea, but I'll have to ask."

A voice from behind blurts, "Elmer got more than a load of citrus from Florida." All the farmers laugh.

Shirley nervously looks at Steven. *What's so funny?*

A farmer steps forward. "Hi. Remember me, Harry Durkee?" He greets her with a big smile. "You're Shirley Mason. I heard you were working for Harold Tully."

"Yes, it's good to see you. I'm here doing some errands for him. He got hurt and is unable to come to town."

"Glad to see you back in Huntersville. How badly is Harold hurt?"

"He jammed his finger and fell. I think he'll be up and around in a few days."

Shirley hurries toward the salesroom door and Harry follows. Outside, she relaxes, knowing she's in the company of a friend. "What was so funny in there?"

Harry chuckles and adjusts his cap. "When Elmer opened the freight car door this morning he found a Negro man lying near the door, appearing to be almost dead. There was an empty wine jug beside him, and I guess the wine was what kept him alive."

"Oh, the poor fellow, I wondered if they were laughing at me." Suddenly, Steven kicks. Shirley smiles and quickly holds him at arm's length. "Meet my baby, Steven."

Harry moves closer. "He's a bright boy." He pauses and continues in a sympathetic tone. "I was sorry you were asked to leave our place. Louise and I don't always agree. It was a shame that bull got loose and especially scary that he chased you. That cussed bull had to go. The whole incident gave me a good excuse to shoot him. Louise continually harped that it was your fault. Of course it wasn't. I'm sorry she blamed you."

"Thanks for telling me. That bull sure gave me nightmares. And even though it was long ago, I still shudder when I think about it. I realized at the time that Louise wanted a good excuse to get rid of me."

"Probably so, but I never felt that way." Harry speaks with concern in his voice. "You know, Toby Perkins is out of prison. I hope you can stay clear of him. His brother, Elbridge, says since prison he's grown into a monster and he's obsessed with the desire to get even with you. It's good that you're working for Harold, if you can stand him, because few of us folks have ever been to his place and I'm sure Toby could never find the road to Pine Mountain."

"Thanks for your concern, Harry." She leaves feeling a deep chill thinking of Toby and what sort of revenge he might dole out. *Yeah, I'm sure Harry's right. Toby will never be able to find me on Pine Mountain.* She forces herself to think of something else.

The drive home proves to be a distraction. The truck has a heavy load for the road conditions and the hills it has to climb. The tires sink in the soft gravel where the sun has had a chance to warm the road and thaw the frost. In these places, the truck almost comes to a complete stop as the wheels spin and the mud flies. She is tense, wondering if the truck will make it, and she feels relieved when the farm comes into view.

I bet Joe will come again for night chores and will unload the truck for me.

She enters the house, goes to the bedroom to nurse and change Steven, and then rests him on her bed while she works at assembling his new crib.

Harold grumbles. "What did you do, spend my money on new baby stuff?"

Shirley looks up and sees Harold watching her from the doorway. "No. I hope you trust me enough to know I wouldn't do that. Can you help me with this crib?"

"Yup, I guess so. This broken-down old body can at least use one hand. Did you have any money left after I set you free with my big check?"

"I'll get it, since you're so worried." Having cashed Iverson's check, she gives Harold the money due him and the receipt from the grain. "Elmer told me he has citrus pulp now and wonders if you wanted to buy some. I guess some farmers are short of feed."

"No, I ain't buying any such thing as citrus pulp. We'll make it to spring turnout with what I have in the mow."

"I thought that's what you'd say." Remembering the conversation she laughs and adds, "Inside the rail car, he found a Negro man with the citrus, nearly dead."

"A black man? Golly, wonder the ride didn't kill him."

"Yeah, all the way from Florida. I guess it nearly did."

Harold looks at the Butson's receipt. "What are you doin' buyin' so much cow grain and horse grain? Twenty percent protein for cow grain! I always buy sixteen percent. It's cheaper."

Color rises in Shirley's cheeks and she says firmly, "The cows will give more milk and will more than pay for the grain."

Harold grudgingly consents, "Maybe the cows' hay is gettin' sorta poor. But hell, I've never fed those horses a bit of grain, especially since they ain't workin'!"

Shirley restrains herself from making a comment.

By the second week, Harold's wounds are well on their way to being healed. He's still limping, and occasionally walks with a cane. Shirley is pleased that the cows are milking better, as evidenced by the almost full cans. *It's the twenty percent grain and no lice. "Cows can't give blood and milk too."*

Harold is sitting in his Morris chair looking out the west window. He watches Shirley walking toward the house. *Damn, she's a worker and I'm a lazy bastard.* He stands and winces from stiffness as he limps on his way to get an armload of wood. She is startled as the two meet in the entry. "Harold, you must be feeling better!"

"I ain't got any choice. You runnin' around puts me to shame."

Shirley laughs. "You poor man. How about helping me load the milk and you taking it to the stand after breakfast?"

He fills the stove to the clatter of steel griddles and throws the remaining sticks in the wood box. He scratches his white stubble. "I guess I can help—steer with my bum finger off the wheel and sit slant-like on the seat. I suppose I can make it down and back without wrecking the truck or myself." He moans as he sits back down in his Morris chair. "I've been thinkin' that maybe you're just too much for me. Maybe a young high school kid would have been better, one that ain't as smart as I am. Someone I can boss around, that don't think, but just works while I watch. Then everything can stay the same and change ain't havin' to nudge me all the time." Harold nods and continues with confidence, "Take no offense but soon's I feel better, you can make plans to leave. You don't have to hurry—no, don't hurry about it, but you just be thinkin' that way."

Shirley's early-morning hours and work have led to weariness, and tired anger erupts. "What? Is the house too clean, clothes too clean, and the food too good, or is the fact that I'm doing all the chores just killing you? Oh, and the cows are no longer loaded with lice and I've killed most of the rats."

Harold jumps to his feet, forgetting about his leg. "I—I'm just thinkin'. You always doin' and makin' work look like it ain't work is goin' to kill me tryin' to keep up, and this business of always wantin' change—well it—it scares me a might. I ain't used to it."

"I can't believe you want to go through life living like you did before I came. You can start helping around here a little more, that might make you stop thinking so much."

Harold sits down at the table, seeming deflated now. "When people ain't feelin' right about each other it's time they split. That's all I'm sayin'."

Shirley feels a lump in her throat the size of a butternut. "Speak for yourself. I'm not complaining." She holds back tears. *Getting along with him is impossible.*

They sit in silence. She clears the table, checks to see if Steven is sleeping, and walks to the entry, puts on her barn coat, and heads for the milk house. Harold limps along behind, using his cane, watching Shirley's determined stride.

She pulls the milk house door handle hard and fast. It swings beyond the strength of the spring and bangs against the outside wall. Harold gulps. She yanks the cooler handle and flips the cover open. The metal lid flies against the wall with a bang. Harold jumps. They pull the first can from the icy water and lower it to the floor. He looks at her frosty expression. "Damn, these cows are milkin'. Must be the twenty percent."

She glares at him. *Cows can't give blood and milk too, you old fool.*

She goes to the house, not bothering to take off her barn coat. She sits down at the kitchen table, flops her head down on her folded hands, and sobs. *I don't want to leave, but that's been my life, the "state kid" who bounces from place to place.*

Harold tries his best to drive slowly down the mountain to avoid irritating his bruises, thinking of what he said to Shirley. *She's doing one hell of a job with the cows and bringin' almost twice the eggs to the house. She's even taken care of the rats that had damn near taken over the place and I ain't givin' her credit. Damn, Harold Tully, wake up and look what you've got!*

The truck tires hit a rut. The steering wheel spins, snapping his sore finger. "Ohooo ouch! Of all the luck!" He passes Mary Maple on the turn. *I suppose some would say you did that. Payin' me back for bein' such a miserable bastard.*

From the turn, and through small saplings of maple, birch, and beech, the Coleses can be seen parked at the stand with the morning sun reflecting off their clean truck.

"Damn, my first day out and who do I have to meet up with—Zack."

Harold's mud-coated truck bucks and chatters, shaking chunks free from the fenders as he backs up to the stand. He slowly pulls his corn-cob pipe from his clean bib-overalls and starts to fill it with Prince Albert. Shreds fall onto the curled index finger of his left hand. He sweeps the tobacco with his right thumb and carefully gathers each stray shred and then presses the moist tobacco into the bowl. He's startled when something moves, noticed from the corner of his eye. A welcome smile strikes him like a sunbeam on this crisp spring morning. *The prom queen.* He rolls down his window.

"Well, look who's here—Alice Coles. I ain't seen you in an age."

"Well, same here. How have you been? Zack tells me you got hurt." She steps closer so she can hear over the sound of banging milk cans.

"I'm better now, thanks." *Still the prom queen and not a gray hair out of place.* Her delicate hand and milky white nails grasp the edge of the partially rolled-down window. She bends nearer. "Doesn't seem to me like you're all better. Fresh blood is showing on your bandage."

"Oh, I just dinged it on the wheel as I was rounding the turn by Mary Maple." He chuckles. "She's paying me back for being such a bastard."

Her face blooms in laughter. "You don't believe that—you've always told me the tree was only good for firewood." Alice raises her voice toward her son. "Zack, please unload Harold's milk. He's in bad shape." Zack tightens his lips and scowls.

Harold quickly opens his door. Alice steps back as he unfolds his body and stands, letting out an uncontrolled low groan—and limps toward the back of his truck, slightly dragging his right leg. He hears the chain that holds the cans in place drop in a dull thud onto the floor of the truck. "Hey, Zack, stay away from my truck. I can do it myself."

Zack laughs. "Relax, you old geezer, handling the tea-cup amount you produce is a snap compared to my cans." He grabs the can handles as he's talking. "Oh, my gosh, this can is almost full. Amazing!" He rolls it hand-over-hand from the cover and then holds a handle, landing it in place. A deep *bong* resonates. "Harold, you've never made this much milk! It looks like Shirley Mason knows her cows."

Alice frowns at her son. Harold, still standing on the ground, turns to limp back to his truck. "How can a real decent woman like you lay claim to such a wiseass of a son?"

He groans while getting himself back in the truck.

Alice says, "Now, don't pay any attention to Zack."

But Zack yells in a high-pitched tone, "Right about now, I'll bet she'd be willing to come to work for us. Two weeks up on that mountain is the limit for most of the women you've hired."

Harold yells back, "She's ain't the same as most women. How do you know, but what she might *like* livin' on Pine Mountain."

"We'll see. I'm inviting her to supper."

Alice gently puts her hand on Harold's arm and asks in a low coaxing voice, "Why don't you come, too—Friday night?"

"I ain't never been to your place before to eat. I—I don't know."

"Goodness' sake, it isn't that you haven't had a chance. When Percy was living, he asked you a number of times."

Zack jumps from the stand and crowds by his mother. "Yup, right about now Shirley would like working for us; all I've got to do is ask."

Harold yells at Zack, "I'm coming Friday night to your place for supper and I'm bringin' Shirley. We'll see what she says."

Alice stands erect, seeming surprised. "About seven?"

Zack whips his head around toward his mother. "WHAT?"

Harold jams the pipe back in his mouth and nods while pressing the starter of his truck. For a moment the engine groans, but soon the valve lifters click in rhythm and the truck spins with the slapping chains, spitting gravel at the stand. Exhaust pours from behind as it lurches toward Pine Mountain.

Damn, my life has sprung out of a can and it's runnin' away on me. I hate the thought of goin' to the Coleses' for supper: handlin' fancy silverware, eatin' food from fancy dishes, plates restin' on fancy linen, and only seeing from the flickerin' light of candles. Just like you see in pictures at a Thanksgivin' dinner—all because of that Zack. Shirley and I ain't teamin' up just right but—but him wantin' her makes me think I'm a fool for lettin' her go. Make up your mind, you old bastard. Ah, she sure has me in a twist!

The empty cans bounce and drum in the back of the truck. The bright spring sun has dried the earthen road in most places, but the deep tire tracks remain as hard as if fired by a potter's kiln. Holding his blood-soaked bandaged finger straight out, he rests the palm of his hand on the black knob of the shifting lever. The truck ascends the hills slower than usual, as he sits in mental anguish. The thought of socializing with the Coleses is more torturous to him than his physical pain. He squints ahead at an unfamiliar object. *What in all hell?* The truck approaches closer to what's in front of him. "Oh bastard! How do I handle this one?"

Shirley lets the baby carriage travel down the hills on its own inertia. In places she holds it to keep it from rolling too fast. Her strides are long to keep up. The sun and slight breeze have dried the stream of tears on her face to a white film. Her cardboard suitcase is stuck upright in front of the carriage, resting on the thin mattress at Steven's feet. His diaper bag is draped over the chrome handles. *I feel just like the homeless in Europe during the war—displaced persons, searching for a new home, traveling the endless road ahead, carrying all their belongings. Well, I've learned that in dealing with difficult people, as in matters of war, the surprise attack works best.*

A flustered Harold, with a fast-moving Shirley coming right at him, momentarily forgets his driving, and lifts his foot from the gas. The truck sputters and stalls on the steep hill and immediately starts rolling backward faster than it was going forward. He jams the brake with his sore leg, but a lightning-fast leg pain overcomes him. In reflex, he holds his leg with both hands as the hardened ruts turn the front wheels. The truck veers toward the ditch, coming to rest with a crash against a big boulder. The empty cans bust their hitch, rolling in a thunderous sound of chaos, and most pop their covers.

She hurries down the hill toward Harold with the bouncing carriage in the lead. He's sitting dazed in his truck. When he sees Shirley he manages to sputter, "How—what—what are you doin' and where do you think you're goin'?"

Without answering, she looks in the truck's open window at a feeble curl of tobacco smoke coming from between his feet where his pipe rests on the floorboard. Blood is dripping from his bandaged finger while he holds it upright near his chest and rubs his right leg with his left hand. She asks in alarm, "Are you okay?"

"Hell yes, I travel this mountain every day goin' backward! You runnin' off leavin' a half cripple behind to fend for himself?"

She shouts back, "Seeing the shape you're in, I guess I'd better stay, but don't think for one minute that I feel sorry for you. I'll help you out, because if I were to leave, I know the kind of care you'd give the animals. Right now I think more of a brooding hen than I do of Harold Tully! You hear?"

"Oh, thanks. I suppose I've got to do one hell of a lot of apologizin' to rise above the likes of a broodin' hen. Well, forget it. Harold Tully ain't that kind!" He continues rubbing his right leg and then before he knows it, he says, "But I will say this. You've been doin' a good job with the house, the meals, the cows and the hens, and I've been dumb not to have said so."

Shirley smiles in surprise and laughs. In spite of his pain, he starts a low rumbling chuckle that opens into a full-blown roar. They laugh together for a moment, and then she opens the door and reaches to the floorboard. "Here's your pipe. Slide over, and I'll drive."

He stops laughing and frowns at her, suddenly feeling his pain again. "Hell, I don't have a choice. I'll just have to let superwoman take over."

She rests Steven on the front seat, goes to straighten the cans, loads the carriage, and looks at the damaged truck. She slides in behind the wheel. "You're lucky—the crash only smashed the taillight and bent the rear fender. I think it best if we turn around and climb the mountain from a running start."

"Do as you mind to, my finger is painin' like it's caught in the jaws of a steel trap."

Heading up the mountain, Shirley stops the truck at the hairpin turn and closely observes Mary Maple. "What a remarkable tree." She says excitedly, "The two largest limbs do have a graceful bend and grow skyward like welcoming arms. The morning sun is hot today. See the mist rising from the melting snow, collecting in a soft swirl between the outstretched limbs?" She leans to look closer. Her face is near Harold's shoulder, transfixed by what's before her. "I think I see a face—there is a face! But it's changing as the mist rises."

Harold grumbles, "Look, don't lose it over that tree. Will you get us home? Now!"

"No, I'm serious! Turn your head! The mist this very moment is circling like silver hair, and there are even open spaces for eyes and a friendly tender mouth."

Harold isn't interested and can't control his impatience. "Let's get home! I need some med'cine—my finger is painin' like fury!"

She doesn't stop observing the tree while the truck creeps slowly backward to the sound of squawking brakes. She knows he's in pain, but she wishes he would at least try to see the beauty in the tree. *Mary Maple—please help me with Harold.*

Beside the road on the steep hills ahead buds are bursting from cover caused by the warm sun. Snow is visibly sinking, and small streams of water trickle down the mountain. Ridges of brown grass, dead goldenrod, and dead purple asters are poking through the crystallized snow.

Shirley steers the laboring truck over the mushy road where the sun has melted the frost. She's deep in thought. The solution of her conflict with Harold comes to her: *Try being Harold's friend. That's it! That's the answer!* She remembers what Dr. Meyer told her: "Work on making friends and your life will be a whole lot easier." She turns Harold's way, his face is straining in pain. *Friends with him—yes, with him!* The truck picks up speed as it travels near the farm. The broken cross-links of the tire chains extend and slap in perfect time against the fenders like the sound of a spoon beating on a tin can. *Yes, with him—yes, with him—yes, with him.*

Arriving at the farm, Harold laboriously opens the truck door. "It's time the chains came off the truck. The racket gives me a headache. I'm takin' some pain med'cine."

Since Steven is sleeping on the front seat, Shirley takes a moment to relax and enjoy the warm sunny day. The fields are losing their snow cover, showing patchy brown here and there. She spots a robin bouncing along like a jumping jack near the front of the house. She chuckles to herself. The robin wasn't on the lawn but on an accumulation of dead grass and matted leaves. The wetting and drying of the surface gives the impression that the bird is suspended on a mat of papier-mâché. *Could a lawn be called a lawn, since Harold has never mowed it?*

The bird continues to search through the mat, sounding very much like its bill is pecking on a paper bag. Occasionally the robin lifts its head and is aware of Shirley. *Mrs. Perkins was always the first to spot a robin in springtime. She used to say, 'Listen for its song: cheer-up, cheerily, cheer-up, cheerily.'* To Shirley, the bird brings hope and happiness, because with spring comes longer days and a warmer sun.

The westerly breeze, fluttering the needles of the white pines, makes for soft background music. She lays a grain sack on the ground next to the truck's rear wheel. She drops to her knees on the sack, and rolls onto her back to unhook the tire chains, pulling the links for slack and unhooking the connectors. When standing, she rubs and slaps her hands to rid them of dried mud. She notices that her hands are no longer soft, but callused and rough. Dragging the chains to the shed, she realizes that she also feels more strength in her arms than when first coming to Pine Mountain. She hangs the chains on some rusty nails. She pushes the carriage to the house and goes to the sink to wash up. She holds Steven. "My heavens, you're getting to be a big boy, and do I see a smile? Are you trying to smile at your mama?"

Harold's pain has now subsided. While sitting in his Morris chair, he watches her talking to Steven. "He's some handsome kid. Who's his pa?"

"I don't know as that's any concern of yours," Shirley says indignantly, sweeping hair from her face.

Harold smiles slyly, "Oh yeah, it was prob'ly some sorta happenin' that he started to grow in your belly. You know, I guess the religious folks would call it a miracle."

Shirley stiffens. "Steven *is* a miracle. I'm lucky to be his mother."

"Oh, so you consider yourself like the Virgin Mary, the real saintly type? Probably the same as the angel face you claimed to have seen in Mary Maple."

Shirley turns her back on Harold while wiping Steven's face. "This conversation is leading nowhere. I've just taken off the chains. I think I'll visit the Coleses this afternoon."

"To hell you will. I mean, I mean you don't have to. We're goin' there—Friday night for supper."

"We are? And—you are?"

"Yup, that's what I said. Alice feels she has to do her social work and invite us to supper. Zack probably wants you all to himself; but I said I'd go, thinkin' I could sorta control the whole scene. Hell, that's a joke!"

"What do you mean—control?"

Not wanting to reveal his new fear of losing her to Zack, he sputters, "Well—well, he—oh, forget it. But we *are* goin' to the Coleses' Friday night for supper—seven o'clock."

"Well, that will be fun—something to look forward to."

"Oh right. I can't wait. I'll have to act like somebody I ain't used to actin' like. Damn, this place is beginnin' to stink! See what's causin' it, will you?"

"Why don't you? I'm starting to do the washing."

"Because I told you to, that's why. All you've caused me is trouble!"

She retorts in a sarcastic tone, "You poor man, probably sitting around this house has taken its toll. If you're feeling well enough to go to the Coleses', you can find out what's causing this stink."

"You think you can tell me what to do?" he growls. His finger and leg start throbbing again.

"Yes! You're going to get fat on my cooking if you don't start doing more."

He explodes, "You've been a-turnin' my life upside down since you've come. Get out! Leave! You hear?" He lifts himself from his chair and shakes his fists at her. She quickly takes Steven to his crib and returns to the kitchen. Harold has grabbed his cane and begins whipping it over his head in a circular motion. She walks toward him. He pauses, holding the cane at eye level, poised in a threat to hit her. She reaches for the end and twists it from his hand. His mood changes from piercing anger to cowering fright.

"Harold Tully, don't you ever threaten me!"

He can't believe his lack of strength and his inability to wield his power over her. She is now wild-eyed, staring at his gray unshaven face. His eyes are wide open as he steps back to his chair, awestruck with feelings of hate, fear, and respect—all churning in his mind. To punctuate her hold over him, she points the end of the cane at his midsection and pushes. He lets out a loud grunt as he lands in his Morris chair grimacing in pain. He sits, seething with anger and slumping in humiliation.

After a moment of silence, Shirley pulls a chair up close to him and sits. "I'm sorry this just happened." She firmly grips his uninjured hand. He tries to pull away, but her strength holds it in place. "Harold,

I want you to be my friend, and because I do, I haven't acted as friends should. I'm sorry I upset you."

He looks at her, a young face earnestly reaching out to him. He feels the warmth of her touch. *Maybe she does care for me like nobody ever has, except for Ma.*

Shirley looks at him with sincerity in her deeply set brown eyes. "Harold, let's try and help each other more. You know—that's being friends. We're going to like it here a lot better if we can come to that."

Harold clears his throat. "You're askin' a hell of a lot. I—I ain't never been around a woman and just called her a—a friend." *Damn, that sounds sissy-like.*

"We can do it, I know we can." She stands. "I'm going to start the washing."

Harold pulls himself out of his Morris chair. "I guess I better figure out what's causin' this stink. Prob'ly it's a dead rat."

HUNTERSVILLE WEEKLY

April 29, 1948

Driblets of Honeydew
By Honeydew Mullen

Elmer Butson, owner of Butson's Feed and Farm Supply, got the surprise of his life this week when he opened the door of a freight car loaded with Florida citrus pulp. He found a Negro man near death lying by the door with an empty jug of wine at his side. The folks at the loading point claim that the door was locked and sealed in the night. They didn't know the rail car had an occupant.

Dr. Plumbly reports that the patient is doing fine and will be released in a few days. His name is Pensacola Sam. He would like to go back home by bus. He has no money. Elmer has put a jar on his store counter for anyone wanting to contribute to the stranded man's bus ticket.

Parmenter Silver, chairman of Huntersville selectmen's board, is worried that the town will have to pay for his hospital bill. Rev. Comstock has admonished his congregation for making disparaging comments in regards to the stranded man. He proclaimed, "We are all children of God." Ester Erickson said, "I think charity begins at home and not in some far-off place like Florida."

Gabby Pilford, our town policeman, has been put on probation by the Board of Selectmen for sleeping too much in the town's police car.

CHAPTER FIVE

It's Friday evening. The Ford coupe is parked at the milk house. Harold paces the floor, the kitchen clock reads six. He's already made three trips to the shed to fill the wood box, poked up the fire, and filled the stove. He stands at the west window examining his wounded finger. *Damn, this thing ain't lettin' up—thumpin' with every beat of my heart, and my big mouth has got me cornered into goin' to the Coleses'. Now that just ain't the normal Harold Tully, lettin' myself fall into such a quandary.*

The Ford coupe is leaving. *There goes that car and here comes Shirley practically on a dead run—'course, her normal way, but she looks to be a little faster tonight.*

She barges through the entry door holding Steven, breathing hard, with pink cheeks from the brisk run and the crisp evening air. "Harold, we don't have much time to get ready!"

"I just decided. I ain't goin'. It's my finger." He takes off the bandage.

Shirley grimaces. "Oh, your whole hand looks swollen and red. Take two aspirin and bandage it. We'll have Dr. Plumbly look at it in the morning." She turns toward her room. "Here, I've got something for you." She goes and returns with a large bag and a shoe box and places them proudly on the kitchen table. "Try them on while I give Steven a bath and get him ready."

"You ain't hearin' me, I said I ain't goin'!"

"Sure you are! Look in the bag and see what I bought for you with egg money."

He stands motionless in the middle of the kitchen floor.

"I'll show you." She opens the bag to the crackling sound of soft paper, and holds up a navy blue wool shirt. "You like it? And here's a pair of gray gabardine pants, a new belt, a pair of new work shoes, and new socks." She holds up each item for Harold to see. "I was going to get you dress shoes, but I thought that might be a bit much for Harold Tully."

He continues to stand motionless. She waits for some response. He moves toward the table and feels the new shirt and pants. "Huh, I suppose 'tis spring—time for the old buck to shed his cover he's worn for damn near sixty wintry years."

Shirley smiles at him. "The sign on the showroom window at Brimblecomb's Men's Shop says, 'Clothes make the man.'"

Harold scoffs, "Maybe that's what the sign says, but I'm thinkin' Harold Tully's already been made, and set in cement. These clothes ain't goin' to make a scat of difference. But it will be sorta interestin' to see what Alice thinks of these new duds."

Satisfied, Shirley checks the clock, takes a wash pan from a nail behind the stove, and ladles hot water into it. Walking toward the bathroom with the full pan she says, "Bring your new clothes and shoes, and shave those white whiskers off. In a few minutes we'll see the new Harold Tully."

Shirley rests Steven in his crib after having bathed and dressed him. He squirms and begins the familiar chugging sound before opening out into a full-blown cry. She hurriedly washes in a basin at the white agate kitchen sink, and then goes to her room to change into her brown and beige outfit. She feeds Steven, having just noticed that the large hand on the clock is edging toward twenty of seven.

She slips on her jacket and bundles Steven; but, as yet, Harold has not emerged from the bathroom. The big hand on the clock is at five of seven.

In the bathroom, Harold has put a new double-edged blade in his safety razor. He dips his brush into the mug of warm water and soap powder, whipping the powder to a lather. His whiskers soak up the white shaving foam. *Holdin' this razor feels awkward as hell, like signin' my name with my left hand. If my face wasn't such a shriveled-up prune this would be smooth sailin'.*

He strokes his face with the razor, showing clear paths of weathered skin beneath the thick white cover, but Harold knows small nicks are inevitable. *Bastard, I'm beginnin' to look like I just sniffed the tail end of a porcupine. Maybe clothes make the man, but I've got a bloody face that will scare the hell out of Alice. 'Course, I don't care what Zack thinks—the mealy-mouthed jerk, he's the cause of me goin' in the first place.* He tears small pieces of toilet paper from the roll to soak and dry the bleeding of each nick. *I might's well plaster the whole damn roll on my face, and go as I am, speckled as a newborn fawn.* He opens the bathroom door, clopping into the kitchen in his new shoes.

Shirley beams. "Harold, you look just great! The clothes fit fine. I guess the measurements were right. Oh, your poor face!"

"And my gut. This belt is holdin' me so tight, there ain't goin' to be room for any of Alice's good cookin'."

"Let me cut a new hole with your jackknife."

Harold shakes his head in wonder. "What a woman—you have all the answers." He scuffles over to the drawer and gets the jackknife for Shirley, who hurriedly twists the knife into the leather and pierces a new hole.

"There, see how that feels."

"Better, now I can blow air out of my lungs. I'll bring a cloth to clean up my face."

"We'll be late, which is too bad for our first visit to the Coleses'."

"Oh, don't worry—Alice will understand. Besides, she never thought I'd come."

"I'd better drive. I don't want you to hurt your finger again."

"Yup, I'll let you drive, so you can race off this mountain faster than a scared rabbit just so we can rush to eat somebody else's food."

As they rumble down the mountain, she takes her eyes off the road for a moment and emphasizes, "Being on time is the polite thing to do, and accepting an invitation to eat out is called socializing, something neither of us has ever done."

"Yup, somethin' that ain't me, dressin' up in fancy clothes and all. You know, I ain't worn anythin' but bib-overalls, even when I went to school. Now that I think about it, that's why most of the kids called me 'the hick from Pine Mountain'. But all them town kids sayin' that didn't make me want to change. Prob'ly 'cause I knew my old man wouldn't buy school clothes—the cheap bastard."

"At least you had a father."

"Yup, and what a miserable prize he was."

A stiff warm southerly breeze whips the tree branches and brush that hang near the road, promising a weather change. Most of the snow has melted and the roadside color has taken on a dull gray-brown, as seen through the fading evening light. She slows at the hairpin turn, and both look at Mary Maple in passing, but the outline of her limbs can barely be seen in the dim light.

Turning right at the bottom of Pine Mountain, she drives a short distance through a narrow valley leading to the Coleses' farm. The road is lined with maple trees with hanging sap buckets. The farmyard has a circular drive. A well-kept lawn is in the center and a large farm sign pictures a Jersey cow and reads in black lettering: COLESES' REGISTERED JERSEYS. The white story-and-a-half farmhouse has the front porch light on. The house appears even whiter with the glow of light reflecting off the clapboards. A shed is near the drive, as are the cow barn, horse barn, and henhouse. The farm buildings seem freshly painted barn red with white trim. The dimness of the night covers any suggestion of imperfection in the neatly kept farmstead. Shirley can see a new Ford tractor parked in the shed.

Harold is wiping the specks of dried blood off his face, using the truck's side mirror, since the porch light reflects enough light for him to see. Shirley is standing by the truck inspecting Steven. She quickly checks her silver barrette, while at the same time watching Harold examine his face. "You're fine. I'm sure by now Alice's dinner is getting cold."

He throws the cloth through the open window of the truck, draws a deep breath, and follows Shirley onto the porch. *Hell, this is just like jumpin' into a barrel of snakes.*

Alice opens the front door wearing a blue dress, a gold necklace, and a welcoming smile. Her white hair is pulled neatly into a bun, strikingly contrasted by a fair complexion with just a hint of natural pink in her cheeks. "Come in. You're Shirley Mason—I'm so glad to meet you! Let me hold your baby while you take off your coat. Isn't he just about the most adorable boy? Yes, you are, and you have a wonderful smile for me, too!"

Alice stares at Harold as if he were a stranger. "Oh, my goodness! Where have you been keeping your handsome self?" Both women laugh. "Harold Tully, you look great!"

He stands with his right hand held tight to his chest and puts on a wry smile. "Yup, I pulled all the dry skin off the old onion, and now I'm ready to make all the women wail and cry waitin' to get their hands on me."

Alice winks at Shirley while she passes Steven back to her. "Have you come here to see if you have a prospect?"

"Hell, no! I've come for some of your good cookin'!"

Shirley notices the worn sleeves and cuffs on Alice's blue dress, and immediately relaxes, especially since they haven't met Zack yet. Harold looks around the house. *Hell, this ain't as fancy a place as I always figured it was.*

He's in deep thought as Alice asks him to take a seat in the living room. "I'll bring a drink while we're waiting for Zack. And Shirley, I'd like to hold Steven while you go to the sugarhouse and see how much longer Zack will be."

Harold hears the word "drink" and takes a seat in an overstuffed chair that has a faded flower print with threadbare arms. Alice comes to the living room carrying a tray. "I have an old bottle of scotch that was Percy's. I thought we'd share a drink from it."

Harold glows. "Alice, this will hit the spot and maybe dull my thumpin' pain."

"That finger of yours should have been healed by now."

"I know, I know. I try not to think about it. Doc Plumbly is takin' a look at it in the mornin'." He lifts the glass and takes a sip. "Speakin' of Percy, I really miss him. It was just a few years ago that we worked together buildin' the milk stand. Hell, he didn't have to invite me to share the thing; you people make all the milk. I remember he come to me sayin', 'We'd get more money for our milk if we shipped to the Huntersville Coop, but we'd have to build a stand because the big truck that carries the cans couldn't travel the bad roads to our farms.'" In one swallow he finishes his drink.

Alice adds, "I vaguely remember that. It's just recently that I've been involved in the farm. Let me refill your glass. Here, you hold Steven."

Harold watches Alice leave the room. *She's damn good-lookin', the prom queen.* He glances at Steven. "Now, see here, you little devil, don't start givin' me a hard time 'cause I ain't your ma. What do you know? You even smile for me, too."

Alice returns from the kitchen. "Here's your drink and I'll take Steven. What a good baby! Just as happy as can be. He's certainly not the way Zack was. I declare, my boy was a sick baby from the day he was born—colic, what a horrible condition. It didn't matter what I did, he continually fussed and cried."

"Yup, I can imagine that must have been bad." *And he never got over it.*

Alice puts on a thoughtful expression. "We haven't had a visit like this since our long rides to school. Well, until Maria, and then I kind of missed your company." With a smirk she adds, "And in recent years you've had other interests in town."

She's hintin', wantin' me to talk about Honeydew. Well, I ain't bitin'. "So, you missed our talks on the way to school. I didn't s'pose anybody would ever miss me." Harold feels a glow from the drink, and relaxes even more into the overstuffed chair. "Golly, you were a looker all right. Remember when you were elected prom queen?"

"Sure do. I couldn't imagine that my classmates thought that much of me."

"Yup, especially with Trudy, Trudy—whatever her name was before she was married. You know, Iverson's wife, prancin' around like she was some showgirl. The town boys clung to her as thick as black flies in a cedar swamp. That was funny at assembly, Principal Gifford telling us all in his namby-pamby way—always talkin' like he was tip-toein' through a pasture speckled with cow shit. The high-and-mighty bastard was standin' above us all on the stage, saying something like, 'Only those planning to attend the prom can vote for queen.' Junior Campbell and I practically laughed out loud."

"What was so funny?"

"Junior always figured any rule Gifford made was a rule to be broken. Junior and I and a bunch of other farm boys voted for you. That idiot Gifford. How did he know we weren't going to the prom? We figured that the only girl in the whole damn school that would bother to speak to us deserved our vote, and besides that, had to win, too."

Alice scowls. "Principal Gifford's idea of voting for the queen of the prom was a silly one, but at the time it meant the world to me. Now you're telling me the election was a fraud."

"Fraud, well—well, let's just say you had friends. Junior and I and a few of his country buddies just wanted to help you out a little."

"Oh, I guess after all these years, I should say thank you. But as I said earlier, voting for a prom queen seems so unimportant now considering the day-to-day problems and issues we have to face, such as a war-torn Europe and trying to make ends meet...."

As Alice and Harold continue their conversation in the living room, Shirley walks out the back door onto planks that she can barely see. The dim house lights reflect off shallow pools of water that are on either side of the planks, the aftermath of melting snow. The temporary planking sags and squishes as it presses into the soaked ground from the weight of her steps. *Why hasn't Zack come? Maybe this is his plan for us to be alone.*

Her throat tightens and builds to a lump. The damp air is just beginning to spit rain. She locates the sugarhouse, which is on a high knoll a few hundred feet away. Fire from the sugaring arch casts a glow. Yellow window shadows dance outside the building with the ebb and flow of the embers in the fiery arch. She reluctantly walks toward the building. Looking through a window into a steam-filled room, she sees the outline of a figure standing stooped over the boiling pan—motionless.

She draws a deep breath and enters to the hot, pleasing smell of maple. The huge arch and sugaring pans almost fill the room. The thick steamy air fogs even more densely from the rush of outside cool air. Zack is shutting down the process. Red coals are already fading into gray ash and black charcoal. The spout on the boiling pan is open, running syrup into a pail on the floor. He stands by the pail watching the golden liquid race through the opening with his hand on the shut-off. Waves of steam swell from the pail, making him barely visible and then totally obscuring him.

Her mind flashes with bad memories. How he held her to the ground with a lock-tight grip on each wrist. She pleaded with him over and over to stop.

She's now surrounded by steam and her face feels damp, but her throat is dry as she nearly chokes, saying, "Is that you, Zack?"

"Yes, of course. No one else will do my work."

"Your mother sent me. It's time for supper."

"Start without me. I'll be late. I've got to hay and bed the cows."

"Really? I'm sure she'll be disappointed." In the dim light and through the foggy steam she can see an unshaven face, red nose, and sad-dog eyes. *Too many hours collecting and boiling sap, while at the same time trying to care for a herd of cows.*

She hears his quivering voice as he talks into the sugaring pan. "And *you* won't be disappointed?" Without warning, strong hands of steel reach from the wall of steam and firmly hold her by the upper arms. The points of her shoulders nearly touch her ears. Almost in a cry, he pleads, "I need you!"

She's too frightened to think or to move—both her mind and body are paralyzed, while standing in the midst of maple sugar vapors.

He continues, "What has changed since the picnic?" The pail beside them wafts steam in their faces, and although his hands are sweaty and warm, they jab cold chills through her. The pressure of desperate clutching feels familiar and frightening.

Her voice strains to answer, "A lot has changed. The picnic—the picnic was last year. You may remember it fondly, but for me it was more like a nightmare."

"Oh, but nothing has changed in the way I feel about you." He releases his grip and yanks the spout shut.

Shirley is too fearful to answer his comment. She backs out of his reach toward the open door. "Come to the house and let's enjoy your mother's meal and good company."

"Huh, you call Harold good company? I can't believe Mother invited him."

"You can't do much about that now. He's here. We'll start without you."

"I can't take the time to just sit and talk."

Opening the door, she walks into the rainy night. Shivers consume her and she feels cold to the core, even having just been in a hot room. Rain hits her face. Her head throbs, dizzy from the heat and heavy from fear, while she locates the buildings to acclimate herself. The house and barn lights cast their oblique window shapes across the yard. From the view on the knoll all the backsides of the buildings, partly hidden in the shadows, are shabby gray and unpainted. She hurries for cover from the rain, which pelts like marbles, ruffling the shallow pool beside the planks. In the entry she takes off her gray jacket, shakes it, and then quietly enters the kitchen to the pleasant smell of food. She overhears Alice say, "Toby—I can't imagine having him in my home!"

Harold blurts, "The no-good bum!"

They hear her footsteps and both abruptly stop talking, but Alice resumes quickly as Shirley enters the room. "Is Zack coming? If he doesn't, Harold and I will get downright silly, drinking Percy's scotch."

Shirley checks on Steven in Alice's arms and is relieved he's sleeping. "Zack won't be coming for a while. He has to hay and bed the cows."

Alice first scowls, but then she smiles down at Steven. "What a good-natured baby; I've never held a child like this."

Harold, glowing and with pink cheeks, is relaxed in the sofa chair, acting very much at home. He laughs. "His good nature must have dropped from the sky, because it sure as hell ain't in his mother."

Shirley sits, her eyes darting between Harold and Alice. "No wonder, look what I have to put up with." Both Harold and Alice laugh, while Alice stands and passes Steven to Shirley. "Let's start supper."

They sit at a table covered with a blue-checkered oilcloth. Alice serves a meal of roast beef and baked potato on very used blue willowware. Hairline cracks on Harold's plate remind him of streaks of white lightning, except they are rust colored set against the blue pattern. He examines them while awkwardly using his left hand, pushing food around his plate with a fork. The scotch has fired up his good humor and he laughs. "By golly, Alice, you're a good cook. This sets just right with me."

Shirley joins in. "It's a good-tasting roast!"

Alice smiles. "Just Jersey beef, a well-fattened cull cow. I wish Zack was here enjoying this with us."

Harold looks up. "Zack don't enjoy much, does he? Must have been the colic."

Alice scowls. "He works too much. I wish he could get away from the farm, or at least come in for meals on time instead of staying in the barn until all hours. I know he misses his father, and now he's trying to do all the work by himself."

Shirley has a somber expression. *I wish we didn't have to talk about Zack.*

Harold observes, *damn she's quiet tonight.* "I ain't never had that problem—staying in the barn too long. 'Course, I don't have cows the likes of yours."

Alice continues, "I'm not sure in the final analysis what it all amounts to. I watched my father die a young man, then Percy, and now Zack seems to be headed in the same direction. He thinks mechanization is the answer: tractors, balers, and motor-driven barn cleaners. All this costly equipment is going to put a lot of us out of business. Frankly, I can't afford to buy all the things Zack thinks we need."

Harold firmly adds, "I ain't buyin' any new farm equipment. My horses can do all the work I need done—if I hire extra help."

Shirley can't contain herself. "Make that *hard* work! The Iversons have a tractor and mower, plus a gutter cleaner in their barn. It sure makes farming a lot easier."

Alice looks distracted. The wrinkles on her forehead and around her eyes and mouth have deepened. Her laugh and smile have vanished. "Don't talk to me about the Iversons. My goodness, Janice Iverson looks old and she's barely forty. She's worked herself to the bone, plus they have twice the cows we do. No wonder they can afford equipment."

Harold adds, "Old Jim was pie-eyed most of the time. I don't imagine he helped Janice much, and their nephews ain't much to write home about."

Shirley retorts, "You don't even know the Iverson boys. Joe is a nice guy. You know, he's our county agricultural agent. He's got a lot of good ideas."

Harold adds, "Yeah, that's his Ford coupe that's parked at the barn every night. It ain't takin' him long to find you. I'm sure he's got all kinds of ideas."

Alice chimes in, "Yes, Joe does seem to be a nice fellow, but I wonder how much he really knows about the economics of dairy farming."

Harold is studying Shirley for a reaction. "I noticed you didn't say anythin' about Jimmy." He watches her jaw set. *Whatever's inside that good-lookin' head of hers is clampin' shut, damn tight.*

Shirley blurts, "Why should I talk about Jimmy? As far as I know he's still helping his Aunt Janice." *And drinking, and probably trying every girl that sets foot on the place.*

Alice looks toward the window and deeply frowns. "I wish Zack would come. Let's have some apple pie, and then we can all go to the barn. We'll bring him his supper."

Alice places the pie on the table and serves Shirley and Harold both a piece.

Harold remarks, "My golly, this is good pie."

Shirley asks, "What's in the filling? It's delicious."

Alice smiles. "It's all in my head: canned apples, tapioca, nutmeg, cinnamon, and sugar." Alice cuts a big piece. "This will be for Zack." She gets up from the table.

Harold clears his throat. "I'll set on the couch—watch the baby while…"

Shirley counters, "I'll watch Steven while you two go to the barn. I've already seen Zack once tonight." Shirley adds, "I'll do the dishes, Alice."

"Oh thanks." Alice urges, "Come on, Harold, Zack will enjoy showing you our cows." She places a plate of food covered with wax paper and a mason jar of tea in a wicker basket that is by the sink. Harold watches her nimble hands close the basket cover and slide the wooden catch into the wicker loop. *She does this most every day, I'll bet.*

He follows Alice as they hurry through the rain. *What a miserable damn endin' to a good time out, gettin' my new clothes wet and havin' to face Mr. Sunshine.* Alice opens the barn door, and Harold closes it behind them. Zack is bedding the cows for the night, throwing pine sawdust under them. The light brown bits fly off the shovel, spreading a wide swath for a soft clean bed.

Harold is surprised at how fresh the barn smells. He hears barn fans humming, filling the barn with fresh air. The cows stand contented. *Golly, these are a fancy bunch of cows. Silky hides, good tight bags, big cows, and milky-lookin' too. No wonder he brings ten cans to the stand every day. Look at the hay he feeds, green and tender as tea leaves.*

Zack sits down on a milking stool with the plate in his lap and the jar of tea beside him on the sawdust-covered floor.

Hell, he eats his food like a dog. His nose ain't six inches from his plate.

Harold says, "By golly, Alice, Percy bred a good bunch of cows. You can see he knew what he was doing when it come to choosin' the right bulls."

Suddenly, Zack throws his plate onto the barn floor. Harold watches it skid several feet. *No wonder Alice has jagged cracks in her willowware. That comment sure brought him to life. He's standin' tall like he just sat on an old dried-out bull thistle.*

Zack runs his fingers through his curly hair. Each curl acts like a spring, sending bits of hayseed and sawdust flying. He is within a few feet of Harold, yelling, "I'll have you know I was the one that selected the bulls for this herd, and have been ever since I was a small kid. My dad let me do that."

Alice nods. "The cows are Zack's life. They always have been."

Harold steps back. "No offense, but you had some good stock to start with. I know your grandfather bred registered Jerseys on this farm." *The idiot, he'll find some way to take credit for that, too.*

Zack fires back, "It's only been in recent years that this herd has been given national recognition for both production and type by the American Jersey Cattle Club."

Alice disgustedly glances at Harold, nodding again. Harold clears his throat. *I'd better back out of this place while I'm still in one piece.* "Well then, Zack, you've done one hell of a job. If you've gone national with these cows maybe you can hire President Truman to help you with chores. It'd be a good place for him."

Alice forces a laugh, but Zack stomps away, and almost trips over the jar of tea while heading for the sawdust cart.

The rain hasn't stopped. Harold follows Alice as they hurry back to the house. Once inside the kitchen, he asks, "Have you got some aspirin? My finger is botherin' me." Alice reaches for a bottle on a shelf and passes it over without looking at him or offering a glass of water. He helps himself, noting that she's been quiet since leaving the barn.

Once they have their coats on, Alice turns to Shirley. "Bring down some mending soon. I'd enjoy your company."

Shirley sleepily smiles. "I'll be sure to do that. Thanks a lot for the meal."

Harold adds, "Much obliged for the tasty meal, Alice. I had a good time"—*exceptin' for the trip to the barn.*

Alice continues to look at Shirley, ignoring Harold. "Good night."

The rain pours off the roof and spatters on the steps as they run toward the truck.

"The old stand that Percy and I built is gettin' a good washin' tonight—clean up some of the dried stinkin' milk his clumsy son spilled. 'Course the stand ain't never goin' national like their cows, but it will always remind me of my good neighbor Percy."

Shirley shifts into second gear. "You miss Percy."

"I sure do!"

The mud and steep hill slow the truck. Water is rushing down each side of the road. The truck engine labors and slows and she shifts into first gear. Harold grumbles, "This night's been fallin' apart ever since drinkin' Percy's scotch and eatin' Alice's good food." He pauses. "You're goin' to have to put the chains on the truck to make it. The next hill is shaded too much. The frost ain't out of the ground yet. Unless I'm wrong, about halfway up this truck is goin' to sink like a bastard. You might's well stop right now."

Shirley has a tense tone in her voice. "What chains? I hung them in the shed."

"YOU WHAT?" Harold whips around to face Shirley, his eyes wide in disbelief.

"You told me to take them off. So, I hung them in the shed."

"Damn, woman, you know a lot, but you sure as hell don't know it all! The chains are always kept on the headboard of this truck! That's the first commandment in what you call the Gospel According to Harold." He shakes his head vigorously. "Bastard, we're up a creek without a paddle, or worse yet, in the middle of Pine Mountain without chains, and son of a bitch look at it rain."

"Well, we aren't stuck yet," Shirley says quietly, trying to remain calm.

"Will you give me a little credit for knowin' somethin' after livin' here for almost sixty damn miserable years?"

"Let's at least try and *see* if we can make it!"

"No, we ain't trying it! Even *with* chains we'd need to get a run on this hill, keep it in first and floor the old girl. Maybe then we'd make it by the skin of our teeth. You try it without and we'll land in the middle of that hill stuck clear to the axle."

"Maybe I can back down the hill and we can have Zack pull us home with his new tractor, or maybe they have a set of chains. We can at least stay the night with them."

Harold adjusts his cap. "I ain't in no hurry to go back to the Coleses'. I feel as though I got frosted outta the place."

"Let's not be too proud. I'm willing to ask for help, if you aren't. What went on to change Alice's mood after you went to the barn?"

"Oh, I said all the wrong things, but I'll be damned if I'll bow and scrape to that idiot, Zack. Anyway they've always run smaller truck tires. I know they ain't got chains that fit. I've never seen them use truck chains. They use their tractor in bad goin'. As for stayin' the night, forget it! I'll sleep in the truck. There's only one way to get us outta this mess. You walk to the farm and get us those chains. I would, but with my bum leg I'd never make the mountain."

Shirley is incredulous. "In this rain? I'll get soaked, and we don't have a flashlight, plus I'm only wearing my loafers. I'd lose them first thing in the mud."

"Son of a bitch, it's black out, all right. 'Course, if we wait long enough it will start to get light. About by then my finger will be drivin' me crazy."

Shirley turns to face Harold. The dim lights on the instrument panel allow her to know he's there in outline form only. "I think we ought to back down the hill, go to town, and have Dr. Plumbly take a look at your finger and see if we can locate a set of chains."

"Good idea, only you're talkin' about Harold Tully. I'm smart enough to know I ain't the most popular around town. 'Course, Junior Campbell would help us out, but the creamery trucks all run bigger tires. As for Dr. Plumbly, you tell him who he's got to get up in the middle of the night for, and he'd just roll over in bed."

"That's not true. Dr. Plumbly would see you."

"Anyway, I ain't lettin' you back the truck down this mountain. Hell, you can't see a damn thing. We'd end up over the bank restin' against Mary Maple, and we'd find those so-called tender lovin' arms are son-of-a-bitchin' hard if we hit her, sliding backward at about fifty miles an hour. We're settin' right here till dawn."

Shirley's voice reveals her resignation. "Then what?"

"As I said, you can walk to get the chains, pick your way in daylight."

"Pick my way? You know that's impossible. I'll still be into the mud up to my ankles or higher. Like it or not, I'm trying this next hill before Steven wakes up."

Ahead of them, water is rushing down the ruts and spilling over the whole width of the road. They sit in silence for a moment, each contemplating how to convince the other. Harold asserts, "It's dumb to try it. There ain't no way to put chains on a truck that's stuck in the mud. Go ahead and be a fool, but I know what I'm talkin' about."

"I figured this much out. If I walk up the mountain, I'm coming back on a horse. She can pull the chains down here and pull us out if we get stuck."

"One green horse—hell, she'll be as limp as a rag, havin' stood in her stall all winter. You'll need the team, and they'll be jumpy as a bastard when they first come out of the barn. It will be chancy to bring the team, 'cause if you ride one horse, it will be hard to hold the other."

Shirley sets her jaw in determination and starts the truck going in first gear. She shifts to second with the vehicle barely moving, but then the tires spin toward bedrock, catching on the hard surface, causing the truck to lurch ahead. Torrents of rain pound the windshield. The wipers barely move, making it almost impossible to see the road.

"Remember, woman, I warned you!" Harold is holding on to the dashboard, his whole body tense.

Shirley grits her teeth. She pulls the black knob of the shifting lever back into first and presses the gas pedal almost to the floor as the truck begins to climb the hills. Her hands are clamped tiger-jaw tight to the wheel. She can hardly see the road.

Harold's face is now within inches of the windshield. The wipers are worthless as he strains to see through the glaze of rain. "Here comes the place I was talkin' about. Floor the old girl—look ahead—oh, it's just a sea of mud, the rain is meltin' the frost to beat hell." Harold's voice rises as they near the mud hole that's bigger than the truck. "This will be just like jumpin' off into a big bowl of soup. We're moving fast, but not fast enough!"

The engine makes a deafening roar when the truck dives into the gray muck. They move ahead, but the mud sucks and they feel the truck begin to sink. They inch ahead slower and slower. The speedometer registers fifty; but the truck has stopped. Shirley slams the truck in reverse, but it's no use—they don't move. She slumps against the seat.

Harold takes his hat off and slaps it on his knee. "Now are you satisfied? You're so smart. Hell, I don't know a damn thing! Have you ever handled horses? I hope so, because it'll take two to pull us out of this mess. Bastard, look at it rain!"

Shirley answers, "Yes, I've driven workhorses, but I've never taken them out of a barn after they've stood in one place all winter. Most farmers I've known let their horses out every day to keep them in working condition."

"Ah, I used to, but in late years, I've taken to doin' things the easy way."

"Yeah, *doing things the lazy way.* We've got to sit here and wait for a few hours. As soon as I can see some light, I'll try to get the team down here."

"And I've got to do somethin' to forget about this finger. It's killin' me! You'd better bring some monkey repair links and a hammer so we can fix those broken cross chains." Harold grimaces in pain. "This mountain is too much for a truck anyway. Hell, for most of my life all I've used is horses to lug the milk to the stand. When I was a kid my old man separated milk right at the farm. I can remember gettin' our first cream separator. That's when he cut and sawed the lumber and built the milk house."

Shirley props her arm on the door and rests her head in her hand, and rests her other hand protectively on Steven.

Harold settles himself in his seat as he continues reminiscing. "My old man was mean, but he was a worker. He did almost everythin' himself. When I was no more than seven years old, he'd call me around five in the mornin' to come to the milk house to separate. Ma and he'd milk all the cows by hand, twice a day, and I'd turn the crank on the separator. One spout ran cream into a twenty-quart cream can and the other ran skim milk into a barrel. We fed the skim milk to the hogs and chickens. Golly, that was hard work turnin' that crank. My arms would ache, mister man they'd ache. Ma made sure she carried all the milk and, without my old man knowin' it, she'd take the crank for a few turns. Yeah, as a kid it was Ma and me tryin' to stand up to the meanest man I'm sure was ever created. Anyway, the creamery made sour cream butter so he only had to take it in twice a week. He lugged it on a pung in the winter and a wagon in the summer."

"What's a pung?"

"A horse-drawn sled."

Shirley's eyes are closed as she quietly says, "I'm sleepy, but keep talking if it will help your pain."

"Well, maybe I can make it if I keep my mind off this damn finger. As I was rememberin', Ma almost never went to town with my old man. He'd buy all the provisions. I rode on the back of the wagon or pung to get to school. He didn't care if I was late, and most days I was. Ma didn't like it but she never said anythin'.

"The days I didn't ride on the pung or wagon, I'd walk, sometimes usin' snow-shoes in the winter. Those days, I'd meet Alice and her father takin' her to school. Alice's folks were good to me and she always was too. Thinkin' back on it, she was always dressed to the nines, while I wore bib-overalls, and stunk of wood smoke and cow shit."

Rain continues to pelt the windshield. Harold pauses for a moment. He rests his head against the window. When he starts up again, his voice is softer.

"I was Ma's link to the outside world. Poor Ma, she didn't get away from the farm very often because she'd have to go with my old man and, hell, bein' near him was like walkin' through a patch of burnin' nettles. She'd ask me to bring books home from school, or old newspapers to read on the sly when my old man wasn't in the house. He'd let her read to me some, but most of the time he wanted her workin'. Lots of days, if the weather was good, Alice and I'd walk home from school together. I remember we used to talk about what we'd do when we grew up. She was goin' to go to college, but I knew way back then that I'd prob'ly never leave Pine Mountain."

Steven begins making his chugging sound, startling Shirley. Her head snaps up and she blinks her eyes in confusion. "Oh, I must have fallen asleep. For a moment I didn't know where I was." She looks down toward Steven. "Poor baby, you're having a rough ride home."

"Yup, and we ain't even home yet, far from it. You mean to say I've been talkin' to myself? It does help to talk because I sure as hell ain't sleepin'. This pain—if I had an ax, I'd chop the thing off. But yet, that's my trigger finger."

"Sorry I fell asleep. I guess I'm just tired." She picks up Steven and cradles him in her arm. "You're so precious; all you need to do is eat and sleep."

"Yup, until you grow up, and then life blows your doors off, and you're faced with the fact that it's one uphill pull with no end in sight."

Steven nuzzles for her breast and starts nursing hungrily. "Oh, Harold, stop talking like that. I think life can be a lot of fun."

Harold laughs. "You'll see in a couple of hours how much fun it is. I wish I had your thinkin'. 'Course, you're young yet, and I'm just a worn-out old bastard. Now you take Alice, for example. Hell, in high school you'd think she had the world by the tail. She was into the woman's suffrage thing, travelin' to meetin's all over the place. She and David Iverson were always into politics. Some thought they'd make a good pair, but her folks saw where that was headed and kinda set her straight—so they thought. The spring before we graduated she was all set to go off to college. Her folks had different plans. They up and left the farm for a few days—hired Junior Campbell to do chores. He come up the mountain to have me help him out of a few jams—and he had plenty, I remember.

"Seems that Alice and her folks were up to the Aggie School gettin' to know some of the graduates. They were pickin' one to hire that summer. Really it seems what was goin' on was they were pickin' a husband for their daughter—someone to pass the farm on to. I must admit they did a corkin' good job, 'cause Percy was a prince. Only thing wrong with the man was he had shriveled nuts." He pauses, waiting for a reaction from Shirley. "Golly, have I put you to sleep again?"

"No, I'm just pretending I didn't hear that last bit of gossip."

"It ain't gossip, it's the truth. Junior Campbell told me."

"What a great source!"

"It's the truth, 'cause I'll tell you why. Alice and Percy got on damn well that summer. Come fall, she goes off to school, but by the next spring they got married. That was the year Honeydew started writin' for the paper. She did a smackin' good job writin' up the weddin'.

"A number of years pass, and Alice has no children; but she's still doin' her politics with folks around the state, and of course with Iverson too, while Percy was home workin' the farm with his ailin' father-in-law. Back then Junior Campbell was workin' at The Market. They stayed open until nine on Friday nights. He said Alice would come in the store around seven, do her shoppin', and leave. One Friday night at closin' time he noticed her runnin' outta the side alley to her car, prob'ly from Iverson's office. David's father had the law practice then. I guess young David had the keys to the place.

"Junior took notice the next week that the same thing happened. She comes out from that alley around nine runnin' to beat hell to her car. Junior told me about it and I told him, 'I've known Alice all of my life. She's a religious woman.' All he'd say was, 'We'll see'; and I'll be damned, in a few months she was showin' she was pregnant. That's when Junior told me she was now doin' her shoppin' Friday afternoons. He also said she drove out of the parkin' lot after he helped her with the shoppin' bags, 'cause now she had what she wanted—one in the oven."

Shirley retorts, "This is all pure gossip. I'd hate to think what people say about me."

"Maybe so, but Alice ain't just a nobody; she's been my neighbor for all these years, and that whiny son of hers—there ain't one part of him that's like Percy. I'll tell you, Shirley, I've thought on this for a long time. He resembles the Iverson boys a lot more than he resembles Percy. I know—I've had to take his crap for almost twenty years."

"I still say there's no proof, just because Junior Campbell saw Alice running. It doesn't mean Attorney Iverson is Zack's father. I've heard enough of this gossip." Steven has finished nursing. She holds him over her shoulder and rubs his back waiting for a burp. "How's your finger doing?"

"Painin' like a bastard."

"I'll bring some pills back for you. Look, it's stopped raining."

Harold rolls down his window and holds out his hand. "Yeah, so it has."

Shirley places Steven back on the seat, and rests her head against the window. Her silence gives Harold the signal to continue his walk down memory lane.

"After my old man strung the electric wires up the mountain, my ma and me bought a radio and hid it under my bed. He wanted electricity to pump water to the cows, to hell with the house. Then he found it was easier to own a refrigerator than having to lug ice for an icebox. So he had a plug-in and one light put in the kitchen. I snuck a radio home and Ma and I used to listen to it when my old man wasn't in the house."

Shirley wakes again. "Sorry I wasn't listening. I'm so tired."

"Well, I was sayin'—we just got too slipshod with the radio and he found it. Bastard, was he ever mad. He beat the livin' hell outta both of us, and we, like fools, stood there and just took it. Ma with her skirt up was bent over clutchin' the chair across the table. He was lacin' her ass with his belt. Every thrashing stroke he laid on Ma cut me right in the gut. My turn was next. Ma staggered to her room and shut the door. Somehow, I knew it wasn't because of herself that she left, but me. She just couldn't stand to see her own flesh and blood tortured—just because we were tryin' to enjoy life a little."

Shirley says sympathetically, "Your growing up years were awful—and I thought mine were bad." She strokes Steven's head softly, sighs, and looks out the side window. "It looks like it's cleared, and there's some faint light. I can see by moonlight. I guess I'll leave now—and I hope Steven sleeps."

"It will be a damn miracle if you and the horses get down here in one piece, with all the stuff you've got to bring. Make sure you ride Jeanie. She's used to workin' single."

Shirley slides her hand over Steven's back, checking to see that he's covered, and then she quickly leaves, closing the door quietly so as not to wake her baby.

Due to the lack of light, Harold can only make out her darkened form jumping from ledge to stone, her faded gray jacket flying up in back. She's reaching for roadside limbs to balance herself, trying to avoid stepping in mud, and then she's gone. A grinding pain sets in. Sweat starts running down the side of his face and for a moment he thinks he's going to faint. But soon the dizziness passes. He shivers and waits.

CHAPTER SIX

Shirley alternates between a walk and a run. She is drenched. With every step, her feet squish in gray gritty loafers. Soaked white socks have fallen to her ankles. She is hot but her skin is cold, being next to her wet sweater and sopping wet coat. Her hair is in strings and it sticks to her face.

She's anxiously mulling over the upcoming task of harnessing and controlling a pair of frisky horses. *Maybe the generous amounts of grain I've given them wasn't such a good idea. With all that extra energy they'll be spirited for sure.*

Her face is streaming from rainwater and sweat, and her lungs are aching as she gasps to catch a breath while running up the slope toward the house. She kicks off her loafers in the entry and opens the door to the welcoming warmth of the house. She turns on a light and notices the wet footprints she's leaving on the black pathway of the worn linoleum. She glances at the kitchen clock in passing. *Two—plenty of time to get the truck back here before chores.*

She puts wood in the stove, changes her sopping clothes, and then fills an old mustard jar with water and puts Harold's pills wrapped in wax paper and the jar in her barn coat pocket. She runs to the shed, connects the tire chains together and hooks them with a logging chain to the evener of the whiffletrees, and empties a box of repair links into an empty pocket of her barn jacket, with a nail hammer. When she opens the horse barn door, Jeanie and Lassie blast ear-splitting whinnies. They begin prancing and treading in their stalls. Shirley pauses and swallows hard. Remembering that Harold said to lead Lassie, she decides to harness her first, and tie her to the hitching post.

She pushes on Lassie's collar and buckles it at the top of her neck, slides the harness over her back, and buckles the wooden hames in place. She bends over to catch the bellyband, snaps it in place, and pulls Lassie's tail out over the breeching. Unbuckling Lassie's halter, she starts to slide the bridle over the mare's head, but Lassie rapidly works her mouth trying to reject the rusty bit. She throws her head high and rears, backing in her stall. Sliding past Lassie, Shirley rushes to shut the barn door, but the mare has already turned, and barges free.

The force of the opening door throws Shirley to the ground, but she quickly bounces to her feet and rushes for a bucket of horse grain. Lassie prances, snorts, and whinnies and isn't about to let Shirley near her head. Her heavy hooves sink into the rain-soaked earth. Mud flies while she trots back and forth, not straying too far from the barn and Jeanie. Shirley places the bucket of grain next to the barn, but to Lassie the grain is no substitute for freedom.

Jeanie is acting wild in her stall. She's snorting, throwing her head, pawing the elm planking with her front hoof and prancing with her rear hooves. Shirley shuts the barn doors and cautiously harnesses her.

Back at the truck, Harold is holding his aching finger above his head and supporting his right elbow with his left hand. Steven begins his chugging sound. "Oh, here comes trouble. I'd help you out, boy, but hell, I'm worthless. I can't even feed a little kid."

Steven opens out into a deafening hunger cry. Harold reaches over and rubs his back, but it gives the child only momentary comfort. "Golly, boy, you're small but your lungs must be the size of a bullhorn."

Ahead, there's movement in the dim light. "Good, she's coming. Mighty Woman has done it again. No, she's not coming, only one lathered-up horse with no bridle." He swings open his door and jumps out to stop the horse that's galloping toward the truck. She stops when Harold commands, "Whoa, Lassie! Whoa, girl!"

The horse is blowing steam from her flaring nostrils, with her sides heaving and collapsing at a rapid rate. Harold weaves for a moment and can't focus. He struggles to lift his new shoes from the mud and falls backward, his left hand is grasping for support from the hood of the truck. Pulling himself back, he sits on the edge of the bumper. Steven's wailing can be heard in the background. Harold moans, "Bastard, we're in trouble." Then he hears Shirley's voice. Although near him, in his state, she sounds far off.

He faintly feels the sensation of being shaken. "Harold, take these pills and drink this water." Through a fog, he senses that she has a grip on each arm, helping him to stand. Weakly and slowly, he drags his feet through the mud. She opens the truck door; he falls backward onto his seat. She leaps through the mire in front of the truck, opens the driver's-side door, and holds Steven. Harold is moaning with every breath. She sits, nurses Steven, and mulls some sort of strategy. *I need help! Harold needs to see Dr. Plumbly.*

Her head is pounding from fatigue, while Steven smacks and gulps. After a few minutes he settles, and she leaves the truck. She leads each horse downhill toward the back of the truck. They act worn down enough to be contented to just stand. She hooks one end of the chain to the eye of the evener and the other end to the axle of the truck, which she has found by digging in the mud. The cold mud has numbed her hand, but she's satisfied with the hitch. She starts the truck, puts it in reverse, and lets the rear wheels slowly spin at an idle. She turns to the team and slaps the reins. They start to pull and plunge into their harnesses. Their hooves kick mud back at the truck and Shirley, but the truck moves just a few inches. The horses falter and Lassie throws her head skyward and lurches backward. Shirley tries them again, slapping Lassie's rump with the leather rein. The truck moves some more, and all of a sudden the slow spinning tires catch on ledge. She drops the reins and dashes to the truck seat to slam the brakes. The truck stalls.

Steven begins crying again and no sound is coming from Harold, whose head is now resting against the window. After tying the team to some branches, Shirley begins backing down the mountain, around the hairpin turn, and past the milk stand. She stops the truck to ponder her next move. *I need Joe's help, and I've got to go to the hospital.*

She's somewhat aware of Harold's grave condition, remembering the night Jim Iverson died, and how a body looks once lifeless. The gas pedal is nearly to the floor while the truck bounces through the ruts and mud toward Huntersville.

The dim light from inside the truck allows her to see Harold more clearly. He hasn't moved and she glances only momentarily at his puffy inflamed hand, while she tries to avoid the soft spots in the road.

Arriving in town, she runs up the porch stairs of the doctor's house, leaving mud with every step on the gray flooring. She bangs on the front door and waits. She turns the bronze wing of the mechanical doorbell—waits—waits and bangs again. Finally Dr. Plumbly comes, tying the string of his bathrobe. He hurries across his living room. "Shirley! What's the problem?"

"Come quickly—Harold is terribly sick."

He goes to the truck in his slippers. He lifts Harold's hand and takes his pulse. "Go to the hospital immediately; I'll call ahead with some instructions." From the street light she can see the alarm on the doctor's face.

Speeding through town, she whizzes down an almost empty Main Street, traveling as fast as the Chevy truck will go. She passes Gabby Pilford's Huntersville police car, doing at least fifty in a twenty-mile zone. *Gabby must be patrolling around the clock since being put on probation. I hope he was sleeping—nope, there goes his red light.*

The Huntersville police car follows the truck. Shirley ignores Gabby and races into the hospital for help. Shirley and nurses come running with a stretcher. Harold is lifeless.

Gabby has arrived on the scene and comments, "Harold looks to be in a bad way." Nurses and Shirley pull him onto a stretcher while Gabby holds one of the handles. One of the nurses jokes, "You're a real Johnny-on-the-spot this morning, Gabby. Must be you've turned over a new leaf."

"Just doing my job, just doing my job," answers Gabby in his wheezy voice.

Shirley runs in the hospital to call Joe and makes arrangements to meet him at the milk stand. *Poor Steven, no one even thought of him.* He's crying and Gabby is trying to comfort him while standing by the open door of the truck, supporting himself with his hands pressed into the seat and his head within inches of Steven's face. Gabby's foreign-sounding voice causes Steven to cry louder. Shirley jumps in the truck behind the wheel and holds her son and starts rubbing his back. "You poor baby, you're scared to death." Shirley turns toward Gabby, forcing a weary smile. "Thanks for trying to help."

The Huntersville man in charge of traffic safety seems lost for words. "Uh, uh, what happened to Harold? Uh, uh—you look familiar. Who are you?"

Shirley reaches over, causing Gabby to retreat, slams the passenger door, and drives away with a crying Steven in her lap. Parking the truck away from the hospital, she feeds and settles her son and changes his diaper. As she does so, she recalls the last time she saw Gabby. It was the day he came to the Perkinses' to investigate the near death of Toby. Gabby kept asking, "Why did you do this?" Shirley remembers she was crying so hard she couldn't answer him. Mrs. Perkins told him to leave. *That was the worst day of my life.*

HUNTERSVILLE WEEKLY

Driblets of Honeydew
By Honeydew Mullen
April 19, 1948

Vandalism recently struck the number five one-room school at the branch. A duo of a pet sheep and a donkey owned by the Hiram and Bertha Soule family entered the school and did considerable barnyard damage. The two pets have been attached as partners for years. They've been seen roaming the branch road at night on several occasions. Herman, the donkey, is well known for opening gates, slipping under barbed wire fences, and opening doors. Snoopy, the sheep, having less intelligence, has always followed her partner. It has been known that the two have frequented the schoolyard for several nights this spring to graze on the front lawn. Apparently the two gained access by nudging the woodshed door.

The greatest damage was done to a map of the world that hung in the front of the classroom. Most of Argentina and Chile along with some ocean are completely missing, torn from the map and in all probability consumed by Herman. Snoopy is too short to reach. Apparently the taste of the Latin American countries was to Herman's liking. The large three-by-six atlas was found on the floor. A heap of donkey manure was left covering the Soviet Union and China. It has an oilcloth finish; therefore, it was easily cleaned and put back in its place. Other damage included: sheep droppings strewn the whole length of the two aisles between the rows of desks; water missing from the fish tank containing frogs' eggs; chalk chewed and spit on the floor. The two also urinated at least twice in the night.

Bertha Soule reported, "Golly, did the school ever stink. We're lucky the kids have next week off for mud season. We washed the floor and raised the windows."

CHAPTER SEVEN

Shirley drives as fast as she dares to meet Joe at the stand and arrives before he does. Steven is sleeping. She runs up to where the horses are tied and starts driving them down to the truck. Through the whippets of young trees and brush, she can see Joe's car parked.

Her face, barn jacket, and pants are spattered with fresh mud, flung from the horses' hooves. She greets Joe warmly. "Thanks for coming. Am I ever happy to see you! What a night we've had."

Even with Joe's uncombed hair and sleepy eyes from being called at such an early hour, he manages a sympathetic smile when greeting Shirley. "I'm here to help. What do you want me to do?"

"Would you put the chains on the truck?" She reaches with a mud-speckled hand into her jacket pocket. "Here's some links and a hammer to fix the broken cross-chains."

She unhooks the line of truck chains that follow the evener and begins unhooking the trace chains. Joe understands what to do and helps unhook both horses from the whiffletrees. Shirley unsnaps the reins, to separate the team. She knows if Jeanie is ridden Lassie will follow.

Checking in the truck at a sleeping Steven, she places her foot on Jeanie's neck yoke strap and swings her leg up over the mare's back. "Joe, pass me Steven, would you? I hope you can make it home with chains. If you would please milk, I'm exhausted."

"Sure. If you don't hear the truck, you'll know I'm stuck."

"Harold said the truck can climb the mountain with chains. Let's hope he's right."

She tightly wraps Steven in his blue flannel blanket. Popping the top snaps of her barn jacket, and using the lower snapped part of her jacket as a sling, she rests Steven next to her bosom. He settles into the comfort of her warmth. The team starts up the mountain in a slow pace. Shirley relaxes, knowing that Joe will take care of what has to be done.

She sits with one hand holding Steven in place and the other holding a brass knob of the harness hame. The horses know the way. The heat from the morning sun is evaporating the wetness, causing mist to rise from the drenched earth.

She fights sleep. Her head slumps forward and sleep wins. Her arm that's holding Steven relaxes. The horses avoid another mud hole by dancing to one side while Lassie steps in line to follow Jeanie. Shirley is jarred by the horse's quick movement. She snaps her head awake and tightens her grip on Steven.

She bites her lip and forces her tired voice to hum. *Thank goodness we're about home.* Now relaxed, feeling the trip up the hills has ended, she closes her eyes to again relieve the sting. Her neck and shoulders slump with arms relaxing as Steven slowly slips with each step of Jeanie's forward motion. Shirley's head drops further forward, and Steven rolls onto the brass knobs of the hames. Jeanie's next step rolls him onto the horse's slender neck while his tummy rides nestled onto the black mane.

Steven screams a frightened cry as he tips and slides down Jeanie's neck. Shirley jerks awake, clutches instinctively at the blanket, but it's too late—she only has the corner in her hand. Steven lands by the horse's front hooves, his face sunken in mud, his head and neck struggling to lift from the mire. Shirley yells, "WHOA!" She flies off Jeanie's back, reaches around the mare's chest, and scoops up her son. She falls backward, sitting in mud, but Steven is in her arms. Her boots are stuck in place, while Jeanie and Lassie calmly stand. The baby screams; his face is covered with mud. He only stops crying to gasp for air. She reaches into his mouth with her index finger and pulls the mud from his tongue and gums. She breaks into a cry of relief. After cursing the mud, she reminds herself that it cushioned his fall. Leaving the horses to walk home on their own, she runs with Steven past the barn and toward the house. From a distance, she can hear the whine of the truck. *Thank God we're home at last and Steven is okay. What a terrible night!*

When she enters the house, the dead smell is overwhelming, and she fights the urge to gag. While washing Steven, she looks in the mirror over the sink, and is horrified at her mud-spattered face, but even more that her barrette is hanging from the ends of her hair. She sets it on the drain board. She washes her face and combs her hair. She can hear the horse barn door slam, and soon after, the low muffled sound of the milker pump. She dries Steven, dresses him and rests him in his crib. Taking off her muddy clothes, she slips under the blankets, and falls into a sound sleep.

*I'm running as fast and as hard as I can but they keep gaining—arms and hands as strong as a northern gale swipe at my coat, which flies in the wind. Steven is drowning, and I can't reach him. I'm suffocating, buried in mud. Hooves are pushing me deeper and deeper—*bang-bang*—smoke pours from the gun. Toby is laughing—I'm bleeding from my nose.*

"Uh—Joe!"

Joe says through her partly opened door, "I've been knocking, but you wouldn't answer. We've missed the creamery truck at the stand so you'll have to take the milk to the plant. I think they shut down at noon."

"I'll be right there." She throws the blankets off her bed and notices grit and dried mud on the sheets. Her upper lip is wet from a runny nose. Sitting on the edge of her bed for a moment, she blows her nose and looks in the crib at Steven. *Thank goodness you weren't hurt in the fall. Makes me realize a guardian angel must be watching over us.*

She has no clean street clothes, so she buttons her flannel shirt and pulls on clean bib-overalls and goes to the kitchen. Joe has made coffee and sandwiches. She says to him, "Oh, thanks for the food."

Joe remarks, "I need to go to work. Although I left a note with Dottie that I wouldn't be in the office until noon, I'm sure she's taken some calls for me."

Shirley sips her coffee and asks over the rim of her cup, "Dottie. Is that Dottie Candy the cheerleader?"

"Yes, I guess she used to do that. I don't know. I was in college. What happened in school doesn't seem to matter much once you hit the real world."

"You're right." Shirley nods and asks, "How were the cows?"

"Fine. They gave a lot of milk and were plenty hungry. Oh, I loaded the truck for you and I'll plan to be back tonight to give you a hand."

"You don't have to. You've already done enough today."

"No, I like helping."

She smiles. "Okay, I won't turn you away. Gee, I wonder how Harold is doing. I want to stop and see him. Poor man, he looked near death." Shirley sips her coffee. "Do you think I can get back up the mountain okay? I'll have a load of grain."

"With the chains on I didn't have any trouble." Joe leaves by the entry.

Watching him from the west window, she smiles. Suddenly, she catches herself daydreaming and briskly goes to the bedroom to get Steven. She hurries out of the house so as not to keep Joe waiting, since she has to take him down the mountain to his car.

They travel with Joe holding Steven. "You're a brave little boy to have taken a bad fall and you can still smile. Gosh, Shirley, he's good natured."

"Yeah, I'm lucky. Most babies would demand a lot more attention than he gets."

They've reached Joe's car. He puts Steven in the box on the seat beside Shirley and leaves the truck. "I'll see you tonight."

"Thanks again Joe." She waves.

Shirley drives into the creamery yard. After unloading the cans, she enters the building. Junior Campbell records each producer's milk weight on a receiving slip. The muscular redhead takes a rubber mallet and taps off each can cover. He then places the covers and cans in a rotating washer which rinses, washes and then sanitizes them. The final stage is a blast of hot air directed inside to thoroughly dry the can.

Junior comments while Shirley loads the clean cans, "You're doing quite the job for Harold. He ain't never made this much milk in his whole life. Where is the old duffer, anyway? Probably still in bed after staying too late at Honeydew's."

"Honeydew? He's never mentioned her."

Junior chuckles. "He wouldn't, it's his secret. Some secret! Everyone knows; but maybe since you come to work for him, he ain't had a hankerin' to see her."

Shirley, dressed in her bib-overalls, and barn boots, has the look of a common farm hand, but her response is anything but common. She puts her hands on her hips and snaps at Junior. "You understand this!" She stretches her neck and leans closer to him. "I only work for Harold!" She pauses and watches his naturally ruddy complexion blossom toward red.

"I—I'm sorry. That ain't something I should've said."

"That's right!" Shirley jumps in the truck, leaving the creamery yard with cans rattling and tire chains crunching on the hard pavement, heading toward Huntersville.

CHAPTER EIGHT

At the hospital entrance, Shirley walks behind a very large woman with dyed carrot-red hair that's fixed in a bouffant style. Shirley sits and waits to ask the receptionist to hold Steven while she visits Harold. The woman attempts to catch her breath, as she sits down next to the desk. She's made up with penciled eyebrows, a powered peach-colored face, and scarlet lips. Opening her purse, she pulls out a mirror, and with a comb she touches up her hair. Apparently satisfied, she turns toward the information desk, asking the receptionist for a list of patients. As she scans the list, her naturally cheery expression changes to a serious frown. She takes a hankie from her purse and pats her forehead. The receptionist looks at her. "Is something wrong, Honeydew? You look like you're going to faint."

Shirley draws a deep breath. *So this is Honeydew Mullen.*

Honeydew tries to regain her composure. "Well—well, no—nothing is wrong, for some reason the memory of my poor Archie came before me. Even though he's been gone now for some time, I still mourn his loss."

The receptionist mouths her much-rehearsed phrase, "It's so hard when you lose a loved one." But she adds with a smile, tapping her desk with her pencil and running her tongue over her teeth, "Did you see that Harold Tully's here?"

Honeydew quickly puts on her business face. "Why—why, yes. I wonder why? I mean—I mean, do you think it's anything serious?"

The receptionist answers as trained, "You know better than to ask me." Then as an aside, she speaks in a low voice, but loud enough for Shirley to hear, "He came in on a stretcher, stone cold, looking to be near death."

Seemingly horrified, Honeydew lifts her big body from the chair and walks away, shaking with emotion. From a distance, she can be heard sobbing. Shirley stands and walks to greet the receptionist. Honeydew enters a room down the hall. Shirley redirects her attention to the receptionist and asks, "Would you mind holding my baby while I check and see how Harold Tully is doing?"

The receptionist reaches for Steven. "Sure, since he's sleeping it shouldn't be too difficult. What a cute kid!"

"Thanks, I won't be gone long."

Shirley locates Harold's room; the one she saw Honeydew enter moments earlier. She glances and notices Dr. Plumbly at a distance, coming down the hall. He follows her in the room. The doctor looks her up and down. "Well, Shirley! Quite the transformation from the way you looked this morning."

She's wearing a brown cardigan sweater with a beige kerchief, tan slacks plus white bobby socks, and a pair of shiny new loafers. Her silver barrette is neatly in place. "I needed some new clothes after last night. I sure wasn't coming in here wearing my barn clothes. How is Harold doing?" She turns toward Honeydew while asking the question and reaches her hand out in greeting. "I'm Shirley Mason." She pauses for a response.

The heavy woman slowly stands and straightens her dress. Shirley drops her hand. There's a moment's silence. Dr. Plumbly looks up. "Shirley, this is Honeydew Mullen. Sorry I didn't introduce you. I thought everyone knew you, Honeydew."

Shirley backs away from the speechless woman. *What's wrong with her?* She shifts her gaze to Harold. His face is as white as cold milk. His cheeks are sunken, with his lips caved into his mouth. He's sleeping, and his closed eyes have a bluish tinge. "Do you think he'll be okay?" Shirley asks.

Dr. Plumbly says, "He's gravely ill, a bad infection plus blood poisoning. If we didn't have the new drug, penicillin, I would have to amputate below the elbow. We'll give him twenty-four hours to see if he begins to recover; if not, I might have to anyway."

Honeydew, with a hankie in her hand, is quietly wiping away tears. Shirley says, "I can't stay. I left the receptionist holding Steven."

Dr. Plumbly asks Shirley, "Can you be here by nine tomorrow morning? We'll decide then what needs to be done. Bring your baby along. I can't see any harm in that."

Honeydew stares at Shirley while talking to the doctor. "I want to be here as well."

Dr. Plumbly nods. "That's okay."

CHAPTER NINE

The sun and the warm afternoon breeze have dried the path to the barn. The fields around the barn are now free of snow, and all the outcropping of ledge is visible. Even the snow under the pines in back of the house has almost completely melted. To the west, the sky looks dark and foreboding as black clouds move rapidly. She can feel a warm sprinkle collect on her face and she stands, waiting for the storm to break open. Puffed up to the size of mountains, the clouds move closer and closer, and hard rain begins pounding the ground. She runs, pushing Steven in his carriage. They reach the barn, and Steven is awake, smiling, his little fists flying like crazy. She strokes his cheeks.

Again the stuffy air in the barn confronts her. As Joe has suggested, she leaves the door open and opens the one leading to the hayloft. Immediately, fresh moist air moves throughout the barn. The blast of fresh air is pleasant, but still she worries about Harold's condition and what will happen if he doesn't recover.

For distraction she closely inspects the cows. The lice are now under control. Most of the cows are bred to calve in June, so their production is dropping. Several are due to be dried off for their two months' rest before calving, but there are still a few in a stage of moderate production. Just the same, the cows are scrawny. There isn't a single one that looks as if she has the body condition to produce much. While milking the first cow, she remembers the conversation she had with Harold concerning how he got his cows bred. Harold had said, "I buy a bull from a cattle dealer in mid-September and keep him until just before Christmas." He puffed on his pipe, and bragged that he always made money on the bull when he sold him for beef. The cows that didn't breed during that period, he never wintered, thinking it was good dairy management. Harold had scoffed, "Those farmers that use artificial insemination are crazy—payin' to have someone come to breed their cows. That costs a lot of money."

Frustrated with Harold, she shakes her head as she thinks about his attitude. Joe had told her that artificially sired animals produce considerably more milk than those sired by farm-raised bulls. He explained that the stud bulls were selected for transmitting high milk production to their daughters, whereas dealer-purchased bulls usually had no proven lineage for production and were just raised to breed cows. Shirley thinks indignantly, *Joe should know, he's the county agent!*

A cow is finished milking. She removes the machine, lifts the cover, and pours the milk into a pail that's sitting in the alley. She does the same with the second machine, and puts both on cows she has washed and prepared.

As she is carrying the pail to the milk house, her thoughts jump from the cows to the good hay she helped the Iversons put up. Joe had told her that feeding earlier cut hay was the best thing they could do to improve production. Shirley wonders how they can ever put up good hay with just Harold, even if he does recover. They should hire at least two extra people. Knowing Harold's tightfisted attitude toward money, she doubts he would ever agree to the extra costs.

She recalls that when living with the Iversons, there were at least four workers during haying and sometimes more when Joe was around. She also recalls building loads and loads of loose hay while Jimmy drove the horses. He almost never let her drive. When Joe wasn't helping he loved to boss Shirley, such as telling her to go to the mow and level the hay as it came into the barn on the grapple fork. Janice led the horse that pulled the hay fork rope. Jimmy always ran the fork on the wagon—the easy job. His Uncle Jim used to let Shirley do the light work until he got too sick.

She squats down beside a cow to wash her udder and prepare her for milking.

Shirley continues remembering her hay days with the Iversons. She almost always handled the hay off the loader. She can see it now, hay falling onto the wagon. She would fork as fast as she could to put it in place for easy unloading. She'd yell to Jimmy, "Stop the horses, it's coming too fast." He'd just laugh. On one hot day, late in the afternoon, Janice told Jimmy to give Shirley a break and let her drive for a change.

She takes off the machine, pours the milk, and puts it on the next cow.

Continuing to think about haying, Shirley flashes on an image of big shirtless Jimmy with the broad chest and big muscles trying to show Shirley how to build a load of hay. The snappy team of Belgians moved across the field at a good clip as the hay poured onto the wagon. He was too proud to ask her to slow the horses, so she didn't. He placed a big forkful of hay on the front corner. The hay kept coming and coming, tumbling onto the wagon. She kept the horses moving, straddling the windrow. She turned around to look. Jimmy had fallen backward. Apparently he had caught his feet, but the hay kept tumbling onto the wagon. Yet, no word came from him to stop. The team moved on and Shirley, with a slight smirk, looked again. All she could see was his head.

Shirley stopped the horses and pulled the fork from the front rack, to help straighten the load. He got up and was he ever mad. She could tell by his sullen expression. Neither of them spoke, but tugged on the hay with their forks. They continued loading hay, only now she stopped the horses occasionally to give him a chance to handle the hay.

Afterward, he jumped off the load, unhooked the loader, and ran toward the barn. *I paid that night and in a big way.*

She carries more milk to be cooled and pours it into the strainer. She holds the pail in the pouring position as she stares off into space, remembering that night.

It was hot upstairs. There was hardly a breath as Shirley lay dressed in a thin nightie. Jimmy didn't come to her room as he usually did, to sit on her bed and just talk. Old Jim was dying. Maybe Jimmy was with Janice. Maybe he was tired or maybe he was still mad.

A slight breeze rustled the maple leaves outside her window. That's all she heard. The sweet scent of fresh hay from the barn was wafting through her window. Even as hot as it was, she was tired and slept soundly. When did it happen? At what time? She doesn't know. It was like a horrible dream. She woke screaming, remembering that a pain shot through her like a red-hot poker. When the light came on, she squinted, seeing the horrified look on Janice's face. That knifing pain, shooting through her was relentless.

"What happened?" She saw the fear in Janice's eyes. Shirley lay in a pool of blood—blood looking redder than blood, set against the whiteness of her legs. Janice brought her cold packs to stop the bleeding. Later Shirley heard Janice's angry voice, coming from Jimmy's room.

Dr. Plumbly examined her the next day. Afterward, he was angry, too.

Having dumped the milk, she walks back to the barn feeling limp. She pulls a washrag from the bucket of water and cleans the udders of two more cows.

Shirley's memories linger: A few days later when Janice asked her to load the steel syringe with liquid medication for a sick cow, something seemed out of place. She didn't have to put the syringe together; the parts weren't in the jar of rubbing alcohol, a place they were always stored. The stainless steel shell, glass barrel, and threaded cap of the plunger were already assembled. She looked closely and in surprise she saw dried blood embedded in the few threads showing at the top of the syringe. She dropped it back in the jar and continued looking at it in horror. *So that's what he used!*

She visibly squirms and is prayerful for Harold's recovery. *Even with the problems of haying, I'm relieved to be living on Pine Mountain.*

At that moment Joe Iverson walks through the door, and stands in the shadows. Shirley is bent over. Her back is to the aisle as she removes a milking machine. He says in a soft voice, "Hi." She jumps in fright. He catches her as she throws herself backward.

These aren't like the arms that once held me. But at the same time she yells, "You scared me! And are you ever wet!" She pulls away quickly.

Water is dripping off his rain jacket. "I'm sorry to have frightened you."

"I didn't hear you come in. I guess because of the rain and I was busy milking." She picks up a pail of milk and starts toward the milk house.

Joe walks between two cows and bends down to take off a machine. He raises his voice as Shirley is at some distance. "I didn't make the hills. I had to park the car."

Shirley stops and rests the bucket on the floor and takes a few steps back to talk to Joe. She offers, "How about staying for supper so we can talk more about the farm?"

He smiles. "Sure, that's a deal."

After supper and after Steven has been put to bed, Shirley and Joe go to the sitting room in the north corner of the house. They're on an old broken-down sofa. Joe wraps a blanket around both of them. She feels frozen inside, and thinks the home-cooked meal has relaxed Joe a bit more than usual. *Having him here alone scares me, but I'm really lucky to have a walking agricultural encyclopedia right next to me. A good time to make plans for the coming spring and summer.*

"Now, Joe, I want to talk business."

"Oh, that's too bad. I wanted to talk about you and me."

He laughs but Shirley sits stiffly as he puts his arm around her. His warm body feels okay, but she still holds herself rigid. She wants to tell

Joe about the jerks in her past—Toby, Jimmy, and Zack; how the memories are all jumbled up into one big ball of fear.

"You're beautiful, you know that?" He senses her resistance and pulls his arm away.

"Joe, I like you, but I—I'm sorry. I'm not ready for more." Shirley feels like crying and slumps forward with her head in her hands.

"That's okay, but I won't take back what I said." He momentarily rests his hand on her back and quickly changes the mood. "Sitting next to a pretty gal, making farm plans—now this is a first for me. We need a pencil and paper."

Shirley sits up, blowing her words past the tightness in her throat, sounding like a garble. "I have it right here. Of course any planning for the future of Pine Mountain depends on Harold's recovery." She rests the pad on her knee with a pencil in hand.

"Yes, I realize that. However, with the new drugs we have today, he stands a better chance than if it was just a few years ago. Let's talk as if Harold will recover. I like being positive." Joe rests his elbows on his knees and appears thoughtful.

"I agree. It's easy to slip into a negative mood especially being around Harold."

Joe sits up, nods, and continues with his hand on his chin. "Let's see, haying is coming up soon. Why not work with the Coleses? They have a tractor and mower. You buy a tractor and baler and you're in business. Talk to the Coleses about buying a front-end loader for their tractor. Spread your manure together so that your spring's work can be completed: fences fixed, young cattle put out to pasture, and you'll be ready to hay when good weather comes by the first of June."

Shirley turns toward Joe and remarks, "This all sounds easy but you're forgetting that I have to get Harold to agree to all of this."

Joe nods. "I realize that. Maybe I'm thinking too much of the perfect world. If you put up earlier-cut hay, milk production would increase dramatically."

Shirley laughs. "Joe, let's get back to reality. How could I ever get the money to buy any new equipment?"

"Well—figure up the total cost, and see if you can sell Harold on the idea."

Shirley stares off into space, "That would be a hard sell."

Joe exhales a deep sigh. "I realize that's the case. We'll have to think about it."

She has a puzzled expression. "It sounds as if we're going into business together."

Joe says, "I plan to help. I like coming to Pine Mountain."

"For the whole summer?" She knows that he's sincere and she's relieved, but also strangely chilled at what a relationship with Joe might mean.

"Sure, why not?" He senses her conflict and changes the subject. "By the way, how are the hens doing?"

Shirley thinks past a relationship with Joe and starts to relax. "You won't believe this, but I've found over sixty dead rats. And the walls of this house have a few I haven't found. The grain consumption has gone way down, and now with the longer days, the egg production has risen. I'm getting over eighty eggs a day. They've begun to really make some money. What a turnaround in such a short time, and with very little spent."

Joe takes her hand. "That's enough business talk. Now let's talk about us."

Shirley's anxiety returns and the palms of her hands begin to sweat. "I was hoping we could avoid that subject."

Joe puts his arm around her. "Shirley, you're the most exciting person I've met in a long time. I could really become very fond of you if you'd let me."

Shirley remarks, "Joe, let's just—take this slowly. I'm scared."

Joe answers, "What you're really saying is, you don't want a close relationship."

Shirley nods and again slumps forward with her face in her hands. She replies through her spread fingers, "For right now, let's just be friends."

In an attempt to soothe her, he places his hand on her shoulder. "You seem so frightened. Why?" Unsure of how to act with her, he pulls his hand away.

She sits up. "I really would rather not talk about it."

Joe watches her expression and chances a statement. "Toby Perkins's brother Elbridge told me that his brother was always mean to you."

Shirley can feel tears roll from her eyes and reaches in her pocket for a tissue. "What a creep! It got so bad I ended up having to leave the Perkinses'."

"I think everyone in town knows that." Joe continues to pursue the subject, and continues to watch her expression. "Is there anyone else?"

She stiffens. "Joe, this all makes me sick!"

Joe holds and hugs Shirley. She sits motionless, unable to respond. Joe whispers, "Let's say good night."

After Joe leaves, her mind races anxiously, but she likes how the hug felt. She loads the stove, and gets ready for bed, praying that someday she might feel differently toward Joe. She wonders if she's asking for the impossible. After a quick peek at Steven, she goes to bed. The rain continues drumming on the roof, and it lulls her to sleep.

CHAPTER TEN

Harold moans as he awakes. "Where am I, anyway? Prob'ly in some nuthouse, white walls and all."

A nurse enters. "Well, you're awake. It's time for your next shot and some pills to help your pain. Roll over. This will only sting for a moment."

"And just what do you think you're doin'?"

"I'm giving you a shot of penicillin in your buttocks." The nurse draws the white liquid into a syringe. The nurse rubs the injection spot with cotton soaked in rubbing alcohol. She buries the needle deep into his flesh. "Oh, son of a bitch, that hurts!" He grimaces in pain. "Up where I come from, I call that part somethin' else, a little easier to say than but-tocks. 'Course, I guess this place has to be more civilized. I take it I'm here because of my finger." He holds out his hand to look at it. "Hell, it's all wrapped up so I couldn't tell if I had one or not."

"The doctor lanced it. The bandaging is for your own protection."

"I'll bet he had a good time doin' that—takin' the old knife right to Harold Tully after all the bother I've caused him over the years."

"Dr. Plumbly is a very good doctor and a very nice man as well. I'm sure he did what he thought was best for you."

Harold smiles. "Yup, thinkin' back, I got kicked in the—the but-tocks once in a while by my old man. I guess he figured that was best for me, too, but it sure as hell hurt more than that needle."

The nurse looks up when the door opens. "You have a visitor—we'll have some breakfast for you soon. Take these pills for your pain."

Honeydew enters as the nurse leaves. "You're feeling better!"

"Well, look who's come to see me." Harold lifts his head from the pillow and swallows his medication with a drink of water. "How's my lover?"

Honeydew puts her finger up to her mouth. "Quiet! Don't talk so loudly!"

"Who cares? I think most people know anyway. I suppose you're here to write about me. Hell, tell the whole town Harold Tully's hand is in a bad way. That's big news—me and Truman sharin' the front page."

"No, I've had a terrible night. I just feel awful—guilty about the way I've lived in the past, being unfaithful to a wonderful man yet worried, wondering about you. And what about this Shirley Mason? She looks like she could be on the cover of a teen magazine."

Harold talks, with eyes focused on the white ceiling. "Well, I ain't been away from that farm this long in my whole life and oddly enough, I've come to realize while layin' here helpless that everything is goin' along just fine up on Pine Mountain." He rolls toward Honeydew. "You know it takes a hell of a woman to do that. I realize more and more that she's quite the find. Old Harold did all right for once in his life."

Honeydew whips around with her back to Harold and throws up her arms. "It doesn't hurt that she's built like a fashion model. I suppose Harold Tully never noticed that. Huh, I guess you have!" She sits in the chair near the window, scowling in anger.

"Look, don't even think that there's anything between Shirley and me. Hell, I'm old enough to be her grandfather. And anyway, she's quality through and through. People in town have given her a bad rap like she's the work of the devil."

"Well, she did almost kill Toby Perkins."

"Golly, Honeydew, she was only a kid. You be decent to Shirley, she ain't deservin' to be snubbed." Harold raises himself to lean on his elbow. "You hearin' me?"

"Yeah, I guess I believe you." Her face turns to a worried expression. "I was terrible to her. I wouldn't shake her hand to introduce myself."

His head is back on the pillow. "Ah, that ain't no way to act! What has she ever done to you? Nothin'!"

Honeydew sniffs and quietly cries. She starts wiping tears. "I'm awful."

"Oh hell, I'm just tryin' to clear it up between you and me. I ain't wantin' you to get the wrong idea of how Shirley figures in my life. Come over here and I'll give you a big hug and kiss. Crawl in my bed if you like."

"I knew better than to tell you my troubles. Our relationship is only sex, that's it—nothing else." Honeydew walks toward the door, glancing disgustedly at Harold.

He turns his head as she passes by the bed, and draws a deep breath, taking in the smell of lilac perfume. He smiles, remembering his many visits at her house. "Damn, when you get right down to it, there ain't much else but sex between a man and woman. Well, unless you're into enjoyin' my good company, which ain't always been too good."

She turns around at the door and walks past him toward the window. "You missed the point. I've asked myself a million times why I allow myself to think fondly of you, but I do for some crazy reason."

"Well, I know why. I'm just so damn irresistible, that's why." He laughs.

"I'm not in the mood for your corny humor."

"Look, life's goin' to get better for you. My hand's startin' to feel better. I'll be around to see you. Just don't snub Shirley, she ain't needin' that." He starts to feel groggy from the medication as his head sinks into the pillow.

"That's my problem, I guess. I'm jealous of her. You've been in my life for almost thirty years when I shouldn't have allowed it. You seem to forget that I was married for all that time to a dear man, and look how I treated him as he worked on the night shift to support me." Honeydew breaks into a sob, overcome with guilt and jealousy at the same time.

Harold mumbles, "Hey, just be sure of one thing, I ain't laid a hand on Shirley Mason—hell, no. She's got a baby. Whoever fathered her kid must have been a hell of a man, but I ain't knowin' and I ain't carin' who he is. It really don't matter, and it shouldn't to anyone else, so no need to snub her." He shuts his eyes, and then suddenly jerks his head, opening his eyes again, to make one last comment before going to sleep. He turns in his bed and says, "As far as you and I are concerned, you were married to a nice guy, all ninety-eight pounds of him. He was good in his way, but as the sayin' goes, he didn't weigh much; you know—a little light in the brain department. I always figured he worked the night shift for one reason: not wantin' to take care of matters at home. Then I came along."

"My hero!" Honeydew wipes tears, freshens her makeup, and combs her hair.

An aid announces, walking in the room with a tray, "Time for breakfast."

He half wakes and moans, "Yup, thanks." He closes his eyes, and begins snoring.

Honeydew looks at the food and at him. "Harold, don't go to sleep yet."

"Oh, forget it. Don't worry." He starts snoring again.

"I'm awfully bothered not knowing what to say to Shirley Mason when she visits. Maybe I should come right out and admit that you and I are lovers, and that I was jealous thinking you'd left me for a more attractive woman—no—that's too honest." She lifts a half slice of toast from his tray and downs it in one gulp. "I was worried out of my mind about Harold—no." Another piece of toast slips in her mouth. The fried egg is in the palm of her hand as she lifts it to her wide-open mouth. She sucks it in with the force of a vacuum cleaner. While munching, the orange yolk squeezes out onto her lips before she swallows. After licking her lips, she swallows again.

"You been talkin'? You're keepin' me awake."

She slips two pieces of bacon in her mouth. She crunches and mumbles, "Well yes, I'm trying to think of what to say to this Shirley when she comes."

"Say nothin' and let me sleep."

"How about if I said..."

"Go out in the hall and rehearse your lines, will you?"

"How about, 'You looked so lovely and I look so terrible, I was out of my mind with jealousy'—no, that would make her feel badly." She glances at Harold's tray for more food. Pressing her chubby fingers into breadcrumbs, she licks her fingers, and waits.

Just then Dr. Plumbly and Shirley, carrying Steven, enter the room. She sees Honeydew with a hankie in her hand and a quivering bottom lip. Shirley offers, "How would you like to hold my baby, Steven?"

Honeydew brightens. "Isn't he sweet?" Reaching her arms out, she cries, "Sure, I'd love to! You know, I can't remember the last time I held a baby. It's been years." Her high-pitched voice brings a smile from Steven and Honeydew's puffy wet face also breaks into a smile.

Dr. Plumbly is unwrapping Harold's hand while Shirley watches. Harold groans and opens his eyes. "Well, I'll be damned, what an audience I have. You'd think I was going to die by the looks on your faces."

Examining Harold's hand, Dr. Plumbly says, "It sure has improved in just this short time. I guess we won't have to amputate after all."

"Amputate! My trigger finger? I guess not. Hell, that's all I live for is deer huntin'."

Dr. Plumbly is bandaging his hand. "You can thank penicillin for such a fast improvement. Just two or three years ago I wouldn't have had a choice but to amputate."

Harold turns his attention to his onlookers. "I always figured lady luck was asleep when Harold Tully knocked on her door, but I guess I must've been leaning on the doorbell because she answered this time."

The doctor smiles. "I'd say you were pretty fortunate to have Shirley taking care of the farm for you, and having Honeydew as your good friend."

"Yup, life's a bastard most of the time, I ain't used to countin' my blessin's."

Dr. Plumbly prepares to leave. "You'll be here for a few days so we can be sure to rid you of this infection. I see you ate a good breakfast. Keep up the good appetite, it will help you heal."

Harold looks at Honeydew, seeing a trace of orange at the corner of her mouth, and chuckles. Then he turns toward Shirley. "You up to caring for the farm for a while? Oh hell, why do I bother askin'? You're already doin' better than I ever did."

Shirley grins. "What a relief to see you feeling better! I'm so thankful!"

"Just what do you mean by that?"

Shirley answers matter-of-factly, "Well now I know that unless you kick me out, Pine Mountain can always be my home, mine and Steven's. The way you looked when you came here, I thought you might die. If you did, I would have had to find a new home."

"Ah, don't worry about leavin'. Like it or not, you and I are stuck havin' to put up with each other." He chuckles.

Shirley's voice rises, "You really mean that? I'm grateful I found Pine Mountain and that you were there to take me in."

"Well, it's been a hell of a burden." He winks at Shirley and laughs.

Shirley says in high spirits, "I've got to leave now." She tugs on the zipper of her faded jacket, which won't zip all the way. She bends to pick up Steven. "Thanks, Honeydew, for holding him. You'd be a great babysitter."

Honeydew remarks, "Thanks for letting me hold him. I'm sorry about yesterday when I was introduced to you. I…"

Shirley says, "Think nothing of it. We were both worried about Harold." She leaves the room, tucking a blanket around Steven while walking away, smiling and waving.

Honeydew relaxes into her chair. "This is really strange. I feel drawn to her. How could that be? She's had such a terrible bringing up, but yet she's so friendly."

"I know, that's just her. I think we both owe her, prob'ly me more than you, but I'll let you in on it. We should think of a way we could show her—we are her—friends." Harold turns to his side, holding his hand out over the edge of the bed. "I ain't likin' the word much. It sounds sissy."

Honeydew scowls. "'Friend'! You never used that word in your whole life, and you never acted as if you cared a hoot about anyone else but yourself."

"Maybe it's time I started thinkin' different. She'd appreciate it all right, knowin' she had a couple of people that cared about her. I guess you could call it bein' a friend, if you mind to. Doing that just makes life a lot more fun."

"'Fun' and 'friend.' This hospital stay has already done a world of good for you, because this sure doesn't sound like the Harold Tully I know!"

He rolls to face the ceiling and grimaces and raises his voice. "Well damn it, maybe I've had a change of heart." After a moment of silence, Harold rolls to his side again and glances at Honeydew. "How about me buyin' Shirley a new jacket and you helpin' me pick it out? If Doc Plumbly knows we were buyin' something for Shirley, he might let me outta this place in a couple of days, for just the afternoon."

Honeydew acts surprised. "Well, that's a nice idea. Of course you've never bought me a thing—ever. Now this slim pretty young thing comes into your life, and you're talking about being a friend and having fun; besides, you and I have never been seen together. I'm not sure I'm ready for us to walk the streets of Huntersville."

"If you think we're such a scandal, would you at least pick out the jacket? I'll go down street myself and see if I like it. If I do, I'll buy it."

"Okay, I guess I can do that. But I'm still not sure of your motive." Honeydew ponders for a moment. "Shirley looks good in beige and brown. Maybe a light beige jacket with a red lining would be best for her; it would make her look really sharp, as if she needs it. If I lost about a hundred and fifty pounds, maybe I'd get a jacket, too."

"I like you just the way you are, gives me more to hang onto. Come here for a kiss."

She bends to his side and kisses him. "You're such a joker today. I don't know what to believe. Whatever the case, I've got to leave, people will begin to wonder about us two. On my way home, I'll see if I can find that jacket."

"Much obliged for the help." Harold looks at his breakfast plate. "I'm hungry as hell, even after the good breakfast I ain't had a chance to eat." They laugh.

HUNTERSVILLE WEEKLY

May 10, 1948
Driblets of Honeydew
Honeydew Mullen

Pensacola Sam has recovered from his near-death ride. He will be staying at Mrs. Jones's boardinghouse until enough money can be raised for a bus ticket home. Mrs. Jones is having him do odd jobs to pay for his board and room. She says he is a better worker than her late husband, Charlie, ever was. She claims Charlie spent his declining years in the bathroom reading love stories.

Ethel Pilford is complaining that she never sees her husband, Gabby, since he has been put on probation by the selectmen. He's apparently living in the town's police car. Ethel has to bring his meals to him. Louise Durkee says he needs to cut out eating so many jelly donuts. She says he's getting too fat and couldn't chase a runaway thief if his life depended on it.

Joe Iverson, our newly appointed agricultural agent, warns, "Don't drink raw milk from cows that have not been certified Bang's free. Drinking unpasteurized milk from infected cows can result in getting undulant fever. The disease is not always curable."

Harold Tully was admitted to the Huntersville Hospital and is recovering from blood poisoning. Shirley Mason, nineteen, is running his farm, and from all reports is handling the job without a problem.

CHAPTER ELEVEN

Shirley is pushing Steven in his carriage, heading to the barn for evening chores. She stops and waves when she notices Joe's Ford coupe coming.

She looks at the box he's carrying. "What have you got there?"

He swings away, hiding it from her view. "A surprise for you!"

"Let me see!" She's thrilled to see him and in such a playful mood, too.

He gently stiff-arms her away. "I'll show you in a minute."

She eagerly looks at the box and reaches for it. "What's this surprise all about?"

Smiling, he continues to hold it from her. "I'll tell you when we get to the barn."

She pulls on his forearm. "You're a tease!" They both walk toward the barn. "After lunch I laid down with Steven, and we just woke up. I hope the cows won't mind being milked almost an hour late."

"I'll help so we can make up the time."

Shirley stops and turns to face Joe. "The big news is that Harold's better, but he's got to be in the hospital for a while."

"I'm concerned for you—and for Harold, too, of course. How are you going to do all this work alone? Fences to fix and manure to spread. This would overwhelm me, and I haven't even mentioned Steven, the house, and chores!"

She collects the hair by her face, and tucks it under her cap. "I don't know."

"How about this? I can take some leave time, and with this weekend, it will give me seven full days to work on the farm. I'll make up that cot and sleep in the front room."

"Oh, I can at least do that." She nervously smiles and turns away from him thinking about the consequences of a close relationship, but at the same time she likes his idea. "You shouldn't have to help, but I won't turn your offer down. I hope I'm not coming to depend on you too much. There just isn't much time to do extra jobs. I need to visit Harold at least once a day; but, Joe, I still think that's a lot of time for you to give to the farm."

"I wouldn't offer if I didn't want to."

She timidly puts her arms around him. Bad memories flash before her. *Those strong arms and my desperate screaming.* Quickly pulling away from Joe, she chokes and coughs, trying to regain her composure.

Joe momentarily stares at Shirley's reaction, and then abruptly turns and walks toward the barn. She's beside him, glancing down while pushing the carriage. Joe bends over and checks Steven, whose blue eyes are wide open. "What a good looking boy you are." Steven smiles while his tiny fists fly in delight.

The barn, the cows, the familiar odors have a calming effect on Shirley as Joe and she enter the barn. Joe places the box on a shelf and lifts the cover with Shirley intently watching.

She says, "What are they for?"

"I thought you might like to name these nameless cows."

"What a great idea!" She reaches inside the box to feel the heavy paper cards.

Joe adds, "There are twenty here, a red crayon, some tacks, and a hammer. There's also room to write breeding dates, calving dates, and production information. Tomorrow morning we can weigh each cow's milk and do the same tomorrow night, and write the totals for the day on each cow's card."

Shirley says, "It will be great naming these cows. We can both do that as we milk."

They set to work. While milking, Shirley reports to Joe, who is graining the cows. "You know we are now shipping four cans a day, and they're almost full even though I've stopped milking and dried off a few. No lice, and the twenty percent grain and more of it has really made a big difference, thanks to your good advice."

Naming the cows is fun for Shirley. It's like having twenty newborns in one day. They discuss all sorts of names: Molly, Dolly, Lolly, April, May, June, Sue Sue, So So, Sunshine, Susie, Such & So, Sally, Sumi, Patsy, Pansy, Popi, Posy, and, naturally, Daisy. And on and on, they reel off names starting with almost every letter in the alphabet.

She picks the name she thinks fits each cow the best, and can't remember having so much fun. She saves the name Daisy for a cow that reminds her of a favorite from her past.

Due to their preoccupation with naming cows, milking doesn't seem to take very long. As they finish up, Steven begins his hungry cry. Shirley sits and starts nursing him. She begins planning the next day's work. "In the morning, when I take the milk to the stand, I'll go into town to see Harold and stop at Butson's to buy some fence posts, barbed wire, and staples. Harold's fences are in sad shape, and these cows will probably be let out in about two weeks—don't you think?"

Joe sits down beside Shirley. "I guess that sounds about right."

Shirley looks at Joe, her demonic thoughts return. *Jimmy is bursting with anger, while trying to catch me.* She forces herself to attention. "If you would feed the horses and hay the cows, I'll go to the house and make some supper."

Joe agrees. "I'd like it if you would let me bring Steven."

She looks down at Steven. "You want Joe's company for a change?" Steven kicks his legs and smiles. "You're a sweetie." She glances toward Joe. "Sure, you can bring him along. It would be good if he heard a man's voice for a change." She walks from the barn and grins over her shoulder at Joe, watching him give Steven some attention.

Shirley exclaims when she breathes in the rotten smell while entering in the house, "P-u!" *This stench is really bad tonight. I'll wash the floor with pine oil before Joe comes.*

She livens up the wood fire, starts heating a cooked roast, puts some potatoes in the oven, and then washes the floor.

Joe and Steven enter the house. "Nice clean smell. I like it."

"Do you think it overrides the dead odor?"

"Seems to have." He stands holding Steven.

"Do you know how to give him a bath and get him ready for bed?"

"Sure, I think so." He looks at Steven. "Us guys are going to see if we can manage some child care."

She watches them enter her bedroom. "Thanks, Joe. I'll put supper on."

Before setting the table she places two yellow candles in old brass candlestick holders, and centers them on the table, either side of a just-freshened white pine centerpiece. This week she has purchased a new oilcloth with a yellow and green daisy print. She lights the candles.

They sit down for supper. The glimmer of candlelight reflects off Joe's young and close-shaven face. *Some change from looking at Harold.*

They eat in relative silence. Shirley's mind is jumbled with contrasting thoughts of appreciation and fear of Joe. She keeps reminding herself that she has never been close to anyone in a romantic way, yet Joe isn't like anyone she's ever known. For the moment anyway, she tries to repress her fears. Dr. Meyer told her that she should accept romantic thoughts as normal. Maybe someday she'll be able to forget the past. She nervously feels for her silver barrette.

Joe stops eating and puts on a puzzled expression. "Yoo hoo over there. What are you thinking about?"

"Why, yes—yes I'm sorry; my mind is a mess." She blurts, "I can't help but be afraid of what might happen—you know, between—between us." Her voice strains as she speaks. "You know—the more you come—the more familiar we become—the more that might happen."

Joe lays his fork on the plate and places his arms and hands on the table and remarks firmly, "I won't make any move toward you in any way that might scare you." He pauses for a moment. "Let's turn on the radio."

Shirley begins to relax. The *Hit Parade* is playing as they both help with the dishes. Going to her room, she feeds Steven and puts him to bed for the night.

Joe is reading when she returns to the kitchen. "My Happiness" is floating over the air waves, and sentimentality fills the room. He stands, takes Shirley's hand, and asks, "May I have this dance?"

Shirley immediately stands ramrod straight. "I don't know how to dance!"

He encourages, "Let's learn together." He shows her the basic steps as "A Tree in the Meadow" plays, and they awkwardly move around the kitchen table, feet scuffing over the black worn pathways of the linoleum. Occasionally Shirley or Joe catch a toe on a chair leg, and they both nervously laugh.

She feels the sweat trickling from beneath her arms while moving as stiffly as a scarecrow. "You're Breaking My Heart" begins to play. He draws her close and she rubs against his chest. She immediately pulls back as her foot catches a chair leg. *The chair leg! Red-faced Jimmy was chasing me—that's when I caught my foot.* She draws back further and asks, almost choking, "Can we take a break?"

They sit next to each other at the kitchen table. He remarks, "You're doing great."

Shirley holds Joe's hand. "I hope you can put up with me."

He laughs. "How lucky can I be? You're so easy to take." He pauses, and then says, "It's time for bed. How would it be if I came to your room to say good night after you're in bed?"

"WHAT ARE YOU SAYING?" Her hand flies up to touch her barrette.

Joe reasons, "Look, we'll just be like friends. You can then get used to me being close to you, and it will strengthen your confidence that I won't harm you. I guess they call it positive reinforcement."

"Oh my gosh! Oh my gosh! This sounds like a repeat of what Jimmy used to do."

"Jimmy! You mean he came to your room nights?"

"Yes, he used to. He sat on the edge of my bed and talked, usually about himself."

"You let him do this?"

She takes a candle from the brass holder and watches the flame flicker. "Why not? Every girl in school was after him, but I had his attention at night. I liked it, until he got mad at me for making him look bad, all over loading hay."

"What did he do?" Joe holds her hand and pulls the candle in reach of his breath and lightly blows on the flame.

"I'd rather not talk about it." She holds the other candle in her hand, repeating what Joe has just done and slowly exhales. The flame flickers.

"Well, whatever it was, it must have frightened you."

She places the candle back in the brass holder. "This flame is like bad experiences. They continue to burn in my memory. You can try and blow them away but they still linger. I'll never forget that night with Jimmy. It was horrible. He did apologize. But after that, I didn't want him in my room. He came anyway. He'd ramble on while I lay feeling that Mr. Rigor Mortis had just invaded me. Then the day old Jim died and Janice was gone was the last time and the worst."

Joe reaches for her hand. "What happened?"

She starts lifting the hardened wax that's spilled on the tablecloth with her thumbnail. "The heifers got out in the road after supper, and Jimmy and I ran to head them off. They ran for a while and then stopped to eat leaves from a roadside bush, giving us a chance to gain on them to head them back to the pasture. The big sports hero lost his wind. I passed him and headed the heifers in the right direction. It happened the first of May. We had just let them out to pasture."

"He lost his temper over that?"

"Yeah, in a big way. That's when Dr. Plumbly called your dad and demanded that he find a new home for me. Jimmy apologized to me again and he seemed sincere. I think he really was sorry, but it was too late, I was headed for Mrs. Jones's boardinghouse."

"Oh, I wondered why you left so abruptly. And that's why you worked at Dad's office for a short while last summer." Joe squeezes her hand to get her attention and she turns to him. "But Shirley—remember this: I'm not Jimmy."

"I know you aren't. If you promise that we'll just be friends, I'll go along with your idea of you coming to my room." She removes the remaining wax stuck on the oilcloth and sweeps it into her hand.

"Good. I really think this can help you learn that at least I won't hurt you."

"Oh gosh, my stomach is in knots." She walks to the wastebasket and throws the wax and then heads toward her room. *I didn't tell him about Zack.*

Last June at the picnic, Shirley saw Zack standing off by himself watching the swimmers and felt sorry for him. So when he invited her to go for a walk, she accepted, thinking it sounded okay. When they entered the woods and came to a small opening of moss-covered ledges, he acted like a young child, lying down, and rolling on the natural green carpet. He invited her to do the same. She felt a little foolish, but it was a new experience. It was soft and gave to the pressure points of her body. Under the cover of the cool wooded area, they could see the new summer growth on the sugar maples, the aspens, the firs, and the hemlocks. He seemed so tentative with her, so innocent, so harmless while they tried to see how many trees they knew from that one spot. Lying on their backs, it felt safe as they played their game like two puppies, rolling, looking, and laughing—and lightly touching each other. Tree identification was like a review of the botany class they had taken in high school. The only difference was, they were rolling in moss, far away from anyone and plenty of time before they were due to go home. Then, by accident, their faces met as they rolled, or she thought it was by accident. At the time, it seemed that way, but now she wonders if Zack planned it. The moment their faces met, he acted like an attacking animal. *I yelled stop, please stop!*

Joe walks into her room. She is lying on her bed, curled in the fetal position. He sits on the edge. "Holy mackerel, this bed! It's going to break your back. Shaped the way it is, like a crescent moon."

Shirley uncurls and rolls toward him. "You mean you don't like my bed?"

Joe remarks, "I don't think you know what a decent bed is like." In jest, he continues, "I've got an idea. Why don't you sleep crossways in this thing?"

Shirley laughs. "It isn't that bad."

"Of course you're shorter, but it would feel like a torture chamber to me." They both turn giddy.

Joe reaches for her hand. "I'm going now, and tomorrow I'm buying you a bed."

The next morning she is childlike in her excitement of weighing each cow's milk. Joe gives suggestions for graining cows in relation to their production. She can see that knowing what each cow gives will enable her to feed the expensive grain more wisely.

By mid-morning, she has left the milk at the stand, and is driving into Butson's yard to buy fencing supplies. While at the counter she notices the jar containing a few pennies and some silver change for Pensacola Sam's bus ticket.

Shirley remarks, "Poor fellow, he probably feels like he's in a foreign land. I can't ever remember seeing a Negro in person. It must seem strange, being in the North among all us white folks."

Elmer Butson says, "At the rate we're getting donations, he'll be at Mrs. Jones's boardinghouse for a long time."

Shirley pulls a dollar bill from her pocketbook and drops it in the jar. Jules Erickson is sitting in a chair by the potbelly stove. He angrily says, "That's just like Shirley Mason to side with a nigger."

Shirley feels herself blush, then turns and steps toward Jules. "I know well enough that Jules Erickson would never help the poor guy, so the dollar makes up for cheapskates like you. You're so tight-fisted; I could kill you by aiming for your wallet."

Jules bursts in anger. "What a smart-mouthed bitch! I got a good mind to slap you!"

Shirley puts her hands on her hips. "Oh, yeah, I just spoke the truth! And it isn't nigger, it's Negro, you stupid bigot!"

Elmer comes out from behind the counter and steps between the two. "Now, now, I don't want to hear that in my store."

Harry Durkee and two other farmers walk to the counter and contribute dollar bills.

Elmer tips the jar to estimate the amount it holds. "I think we have nearly enough for a ticket, and if not I'll make up the difference. This whole matter has dragged on long enough."

Jules grumbles, "Harold Tully would never give to a boozing loser."

Shirley takes a dollar from the change Elmer has given her and drops it in the jar.

"Harold Tully just donated. Now the man can buy a sandwich and a cup of coffee on his way to Florida."

Jules sneers. "Someone needs to smack you a good one!"

Shirley retorts, "It's too bad it won't be you!"

While riding home, she's still nerved up over having had words with Jules. *To think I had to live with him and Esther for a year. Thank God the social worker moved me to the Durkees. Harry was always good to me.*

She begins to travel up Pine Mountain. As she passes Mary Maple she wonders about friendly spirits and guardian angels. Do they somehow connect to the many blessings that have come her way? Such as: Dr. Plumbly caring about her like a father, Steven falling and not getting hurt, finding Pine Mountain as a home, and Joe wanting to help. She wonders how this could happen to her, the "state kid," who got pregnant.

After the climb up the hills, she notices at a distance Joe's Ford parked at the barn. She sees him walking from the house, already in his work clothes. *Spring's work is about to begin and I have the best help.*

Shirley stops the truck by the milk house. Joe leans on the door and talks through the rolled-down window. "I checked the pasture fences next to the woods while you were gone. You know, Harold never has had any fence on the woods side of his pastures."

She rests her elbow on the steering wheel and turns to him. "Well, that old bird. How could he ever keep track of his cattle?"

"Probably he expected they would always eventually come home."

Shirley worriedly raises her voice. "What about a fresh cow? Heavens sakes! She could go off and calve and we might not find her for weeks."

"Let's just work on one pasture. We can string a wire from tree to tree next to the woods, and I think that will hold them fairly well. At first we can let out the milk cows, dry cows, and bred heifers all in one pasture. That will get us by the spring's rush."

"Could we work on spreading the manure pile this afternoon so we can cover some of these meadows before the next rain?"

"Sure, it's all got to be done."

Walking to the house to change, she notices the new bed parts by the back step, and instantly feels her stomach tighten. Such an uncontrolled response causes her to be disgusted with herself. *I tripped and flew through the air, cracking my head on the refrigerator. Jimmy landed on top of me. That's all I remember.*

After changing, she leaves the house, pushing Steven in his carriage toward the horse barn. Joe comes from building fence to help Shirley with the hitch-up. She looks at Jeanie and Lassie's feet. "Oh darn! Their hooves have to be trimmed."

She feels edgy, wanting to start work. After hitching the horses to the manure spreader, Joe ties them to the post in front of the horse barn. He steps out from in front of the horses and stands beside Shirley.

She glares at him. "What are you doing?"

Joe holds her arms firmly. "You're all wrought-up over this work. It's time to eat, I'm hungry, and you never mentioned the bed."

"Oh God, the bed! That's the furthest thing from my mind!"

Joe raises his voice. "Hey, I paid for that with my own money. It's for you! Can't you at least say thank you?"

Shirley never heard Joe's flash of anger before, and it startles her. She admits to herself that she's agitated. *All my past that, for some reason, I can't forget when I'm around him. Zack holding me to the ground, laughing. "Come on, Shirley."*

She runs to the house, forcing back tears, to put some sandwiches together.

Joe enters the kitchen, carrying Steven, and doesn't speak. He rests the baby in his basket and sits down. For the moment, Shirley feels as though she is drowning in her memories. In a panic, she rushes to sit down, and rests her head on the table with her face covered by her hands. She sobs.

After a long silence Joe speaks. "You know, Harold has been on this farm for years doing about as little as anyone could, and he still kept it going. He did precious little for anyone else and sometimes he had a housekeeper besides. Now you come along, bound and determined you're going to run an outstanding farm, do the housework, take care of Steven, and deal with this fear thing that you have. It's too much!"

"I'm sorry, Joe. Thanks for the bed. For some reason, I can't stop these thoughts."

Joe finishes making the sandwiches. She gets up from the table and picks up Steven, who's acting hungry, and sits nursing him while she eats.

Joe suggests, "Let's set up the bed. You take a nap, wash the heaping pail of dirty diapers, and then do the chores. In the meantime, I'll deal with the manure pile. Several loads can be drawn, if just the meadows close to the barn are spread."

Shirley says, "But I wanted to help. That's what I was looking forward to."

"You can do that tomorrow. Tomorrow can't possibly be as full as today has been."

Shirley cheers up a bit, thinking Joe has a reasonable plan. She does have a pile of washing to do, and he deserves a good supper.

They put the new bed together. During the process, Shirley is still tense, looking at her barrette on the bureau.

Joe leaves and Shirley starts the laundry, rinsing the diapers, occasionally watching Joe from the west window pitching the manure into the spreader, forkful by forkful. There looks to be a mountain of it. She doesn't think Harold has spread the whole pile in years. She rolls the Maytag into the kitchen next to the sink and fills it with rinsed diapers. Waiting for the washer, she takes a broom and sweeps the floor around the Morris chair by the west window. Outside, the parked spreader hides Joe's body. She watches for his head to appear as a forkful flies into the spreader. *Can I ever get over my fears and have Joe for more than just a friend?*

She dips her hands in the water and feeds the diapers through the wringer, letting them drop into the tub of rinse water. After passing the rinsed diapers through the wringer again, she throws them in a wicker basket. Carrying the basket full of wet diapers out through the entry, she goes to the clothesline. While pressing the wooden clothespins onto the hanging wet diapers, she tentatively waves to Joe as he drives the horses away from the pile toward the meadow. She reminds herself, *if it had been Harold, I wouldn't have bothered to wave.*

After doing her washing, she goes to the front room to make Joe's bed. An opened letter catches her eye that has apparently fallen from his pants pocket. She sits on his bed with it in her hand. *This is none of my business. But maybe it's just a letter from a farmer.*

April 28, 1948

My Dearest Joe:

I missed not seeing you these past weeks. I understand if your work keeps you in Huntersville. Especially if you're helping out an old high school friend on his farm. I'll bet he really appreciates you.

On June 30, the club is having its spring formal, a real dress-up affair with evening gowns and white tuxedos. What fun this will be. A big band has been hired. There will also be an open bar, and banquet, featuring pheasant-under-glass. The club is going all out this year. I hope you can come.

You can stay over in our beach cottage. Afterward we can share a bottle of Dad's vintage wine. I'll let you pick. I hope it will be a moonlit night so we can sit and sip our wine at the water's edge. How romantic! Let me know if you can make it.

Love and Kisses,

Gloria

Shirley can feel the blood throbbing in her head and her arms and hands feel rigid as if every joint is locked in place. She sits staring at the writing. She doesn't know how long she sat on his bed, but moments later she realizes she had no business reading the letter and surely will never tell Joe. She replaces it in the envelope and slips it in the rear pocket of his khaki pants that are hanging over a chair by his bed.

She goes to her room, checks on Steven, and flops on her new bed. *This feels great!* She tries to brush off the memory of the letter, with no luck. *Why is he giving me all this attention? This Gloria acts like she'd die for him. So he's helping an old high school friend on* his *farm. How clever,*

Joe. Shirley smiles, realizing he sees something in her that she never knew existed. She relaxes and falls asleep.

By early evening she is in the barn milking. A cow she has just named Dolly is starting to calve. Shirley throws some fresh hay in back of the cow so the newborn calf will be kept clean. The cow's water bag breaks, and then the feet begin to show, encapsulated in a fluid-filled membrane. In a moment the tissue breaks and silver-colored fluid flows to the gutter. A contraction, a push, and a dainty black muzzle is showing, pressed tightly by two black front hooves. An additional contraction, Dolly pushes, and the calf's brown head is showing followed by the front shoulders. The calf's head hangs lifeless with its muzzle pointing toward the floor. In a moment a quantity of thick silvery fluid runs from the calf's mouth. It shakes its head and blows fluid from its nostrils. It then flops on the hay. Dolly lets out a low, mothering *moo.* Shirley smiles. *It's a heifer!* She puts the calf in front of its mother, so Dolly can lick and dry her newborn.

Several more cows are due in a few weeks. Shirley anticipates the herd will produce considerably more milk, since by the end of May there will be more cows milking.

Joe comes into the barn when milking is almost finished. His face looks drawn and tired. He opens and closes his hands, commenting, "Hands that shuffle papers don't do well handling a pitchfork."

Shirley is weighing milk. "Oh, your hands do look sore!"

He sits on a stool next to the wall. "Whew, I'm not used to all this work." He takes a deep breath and rests his head against the wall. "I think those horses' hooves can be dealt with in the morning. I'll call the blacksmith when I go to my office."

"You've put in a long day."

He slumps forward and holds his face in his hands for a moment, then raises his head. "This seems odd to say, but I enjoyed it."

She steps from between two cows with a machine. She takes off the cover and pours the milk into a pail that rests on the walkway. "I'm almost done milking. Can you feed the calves? Dolly just calved and her calf needs to be fed colostrum. When you finish, could you bring Steven? I'll wash the milk dishes, feed the hens, collect the eggs, and get some supper." She takes off the second milker from the last cow and dumps it. She weighs and records the amount in the pail, and carries it and the wash bucket to the milk house. She returns for the two machines.

That night they eat in silence. Afterward, Joe asks, "How are you, Shirley?"

She's lost in the thoughts of him coming to her room, and so she jumps at the sound of his voice. "I'm fine! I'm fine!" Nearly tearfully, she says, "I can't wait to go to bed and have you come to my room!"

Joe remarks, "If you don't want me to come and say good night, I won't."

She sweeps her hair into place. "I'll be all right. Maybe I just think too much. I should be dwelling on the fact that you're giving the farm all your time."

"I'm terribly tired tonight. Just think of me as a warm body hardly able to talk."

Shirley musters a chuckle through her tears, and they both get ready for bed. She is in bed face up and flat out as Joe enters the room. "You're thoughtful to have bought me this bed. I've never slept on one as comfortable as this."

Joe sits on the edge. "Some different than your old one." He grips her hand, and stands. As he leaves the room he says softly, "Good night."

She gets up at five for chores, leaving Joe to bring Steven when he wakes up. Walking into the barn she spots another cow, Beauty, starting to calve. Her ears are ice cold and she lies in her stall with her head and neck swung around, resting on her body. Shirley recognizes the condition called milk fever. It frequently occurs when a cow calves. She surmises that Harold probably pumps air into their udder to stop the milk flow, but that way almost always causes an infection, and no doubt he doesn't know that most farmers now inject liquid calcium into the bloodstream for a safer cure.

The tire pump is hanging in the barn. *Yeah, that's what Harold uses. The Coleses must have a supply of calcium on hand, plus a sterile tube and needles. As soon as Joe comes to the barn I'll go to the Coleses.*

After Joe takes over milking for her, she drives down the mountain, and enters the Coleses' yard. She leaves Steven sleeping in the truck, and goes to the barn. Zack is pouring milk into a pail that's in the alley. He lifts his head and says nothing.

She puts on a friendly front. "Hi, Zack, how are you this morning?"

He runs his fingers through his curly hair. "Tired and worn out as usual."

Shirley says matter-of-factly, "Why don't you hire some help?"

Zack walks between two cows and bends down to put the machine on. His head is next to the cow's leg while he talks into the gutter. "Mother says we can't afford to. She's trying to take Dad's place. It isn't working. We haven't even started spring's work yet."

"There's still time."

"Mother saw in the paper that Harold's in the hospital. I suppose you're doing just fine up on the mountain all alone."

"The days are long, but Harold will be home by the end of the week. His pain has left and he's just waiting now until Dr. Plumbly thinks it's safe for him to come home. Zack, I have a cow with milk fever. Do you have some calcium, a tube, and a needle? I'll replace it as soon as I can get to town."

Zack, expressionless, walks to the medicine cabinet, opens the doors, and passes her what she needs. "Keep the tube and needle and I'll even give you the calcium, if you think it might be possible for you to come to work for me."

"Thanks, but I'll return everything by late morning on my way back from town."

"I don't get it. You aren't the same as you were on our picnic."

"Yeah, last spring was last spring. Now I've come to understand a lot. Mainly, I've learned it isn't necessary for a girl to put up with a guy forcing himself on her."

Zack turns red. "I thought—I thought that's the way..., you know what I mean."

"I was beginning to think that too, but now I know better. I haven't fully figured it out yet, but I think love enters in there somewhere."

"But, but I could—could easily..."

"No, you couldn't, Zack, I'm sorry, but you couldn't. Some things just aren't meant to be." She hurries out of the barn and shuts the door, leaving Zack standing in the aisle with slumped shoulders and an open mouth.

She heads back up the mountain, waving to Mary Maple in passing. *Don't you think I handled Zack okay, said the right thing and all?*

As soon as she reaches the farm, she rushes to the barn with Steven and the supplies. Beauty looks lifeless. Joe stops milking and goes to her aid. He searches for the vein on her neck and presses his fingers against it. Blood pools in front of his thumb, enlarging the injection site. He pushes the large intravenous needle into the turgid vein and blood flows onto the floor. He connects the tube to the bottle and holds it upside down above the cow. The liquid calcium slowly flows into Beauty's bloodstream. In a few minutes her ears warm and she seems to act normally. Her contractions begin, and soon the calf flops on the clean dry hay that been placed in the gutter behind the cow. Joe lifts the newborn's rear leg, and announces, "Another heifer." He pulls the calf in front of the cow. She stands to dry and mother her calf with her rough, sandpaper-like tongue.

After chores Shirley, carrying Steven, walks with Joe from the barn to the house. He reaches for her hand. She feels secure and vibrant with this gentle grip. "Gosh, it's warm this morning," he observes.

She turns to look toward the meadows that lie in back of the barn. "Sure is. We've gone a few days without rain, but the fields are still wet and after today's heat, the grass will really shoot up."

At the breakfast table, they begin to plan the day. Shirley says, "After I take the milk to the stand, I'll go to the hospital, but I won't stay long."

Joe remarks, "And I plan to get the blacksmith first thing to trim the horses' hooves."

Shirley has cut her hair rather short for easy care. She's washed it and is drying it with a towel. She puts on a white jersey with light brown horizontal stripes, her brown cotton slacks and her new shiny brown loafers with white bobby socks. She looks in the mirror and combs her hair and snaps the silver barrette into place. She wonders why it matters, but she has to admit she looks a lot sharper than normal for Shirley Mason, who usually wears that dumb looking blue barn cap and baggy coveralls. When she comes out of the bathroom, Joe looks up. "Aren't you snappy looking this morning?"

Her face turns slightly pink. "Thanks, Joe. Dressing up makes me feel a little more normal, especially getting out of those barn clothes."

"Well, I think you look more than normal. I would say more like—beautiful."

She smiles at him and leaves by the entry, carrying Steven.

While driving through town on her way to see Harold, she passes Dottie Candy walking to work at Joe's office. Due to the warm morning, she has shed her winter attire, wearing a short tight skirt that hugs her body and a short-sleeved pink V-neck jersey. She's added a few pounds since high school. Just the same, she looks very sexy. Shirley can't imagine wearing something like that. *I wonder what Joe thinks of her.*

Turning the truck into the hospital parking lot, she hears an unusually loud engine knock, but she ignores it and leaves the truck. She sits in the hospital lobby, since it is too early for visiting hours, and sends a message by the receptionist that she is waiting. Harold eventually comes, wearing a hospital bathrobe. Shirley is sitting with Steven in her lap. She asks, "How are you doing this morning? Getting ready to come home?"

Harold sits down beside her. "Yup, whenever Plumbly makes up his mind. He and the nurses are so damn jumpy about this hand. They keep it wrapped and in this sling. It hasn't seen the light of day since I've been here."

Dr. Plumbly, carrying his bag, walks in the door and stops at the lobby. "Hi, Shirley, how are things?" He looks at her as if he's really concerned for her welfare.

"Fine. Harold and I were just talking, wondering when he might be coming home."

"We'll see. I realize you want him home as soon as possible, but I know before I even take a look at his hand that he should be here for at least two more days. A farm is no place to be exposing an open wound."

Dr. Plumbly leaves and Harold looks at Steven. "Let me have that boy right here for a minute." Shirley places the baby on Harold's lap. "Yes, you're a good kid. You and I have got to become buddies, since your old lady will be runnin' us ragged for sure."

Shirley is pleased that for the first time he's taken an interest in Steven. She can see that his hospital stay has mellowed him—she hopes.

He bends forward to talk to Steven. "Look at you smile for old Uncle Harold."

"Uncle Harold. Huh, I like that. It's sounds like we're a family."

"Well we are as far as I'm concerned." Harold face turns to a scowl. "How are you managin' without any help? You look damn nice for a woman havin' to work as you do." He brightens as if answering his own question. "Oh, I remember, the Ford coupe. Maybe you're hoping I ain't coming for a GOOD while longer! Now, now, woman, look at the color come to your face."

Shirley picks up Steven and catches Harold's eye and says firmly, "Don't think but what I want you home soon. You're right, Joe is helping me. I'm thankful he is."

"Well, good. That makes me feel better, settin' here not doin' a whit of work."

Shirley says, "Oh by the way, you gave a dollar to buy Pensacola Sam something to eat on his way back to Florida."

He jerks to attention. "I what?"

"You know, the Negro man that ended up at Elmer Butson's. I donated for you. Jules Erickson and I had some words. He claimed you would never give to any cause like helping a guy lost in the North so I called his bluff and put in a dollar for you."

"Well, probably I wouldn't have, but since it was Jules, I'm happy you did. He's known for bein' a cheap bastard and I'd just as soon not be put in the same class as him." Harold pauses and watches Shirley getting ready to leave. "I'll see you tomorrow." He lifts himself from his chair and walks toward the window as she leaves.

With Steven in her arms she says good-bye. Walking back to the truck, she feels satisfied that she's had a good start on the day. The truck starts, but an enormous amount of smoke comes out from under the hood. It runs for a while and then stalls with a loud *bang*. She tries starting it again but can't. She sits motionless and Steven begins to cry. She feels like crying, too, as a black curtain slowly lowers on Shirley's mood. *Another day of spring's work gone down the drain.*

She walks back into the hospital and meets Harold, who is still watching from the waiting room. "Holy shit! Of all the damnedest luck I'm havin'." He continues to grouse. "My whole world's cavin' in on me. I'll have to call Perry Bent, the Chevy dealer. He's a slippery cuss. He'll be wantin' to sell me a new truck."

Shirley glumly plops in a chair. "I can see no spring's work will be done today."

He paces. "I ain't carin' about spring's work, I'm just worried about my truck."

She snaps, "Stop your pacing and go call Perry Bent. You remind me too much of Attorney Iverson, always having to walk around in order to think."

"I'll call right now. I'm worried about what Bent will say."

"Well let's get him here and find out." Shirley fidgets with her hair and barrette and changes Steven's diaper.

Harold returns. "Perry's comin' right over. Thanks a lot for comparing me to David Iverson. I ain't at his level and just as glad for it."

"Well, I am, too."

In a few minutes, Harold walks to the window to look at his truck. "Here's Bent. He's lookin' over my truck, liftin' the hood; now he's on his knees checkin' under the engine. Damn, I know he's got bad news." He plunks down beside Shirley.

In a few moments Perry Bent enters the waiting room. "Good morning, Harold, and let's see, you must be Shirley Mason."

Bent is a short stocky man wearing a suit coat, tie, and dress pants. He sports a gray fedora and walks with a strut. He comes right to the point. "Your truck has a blown engine. The block is busted and it's leaking oil. It's hardly worth towing away."

Harold jumps to his feet and confronts the Chevy dealer. "Hey, wait a minute. I paid $450 for that truck, new. It's done me good. Now you ain't tellin' me it's worthless, 'cause I know better."

"I'm giving it to you straight, Harold. That truck is just junk; but I'll tell you what though, I have a new '48, a real beauty, ton and a half, that just came in. I need to pay for it today. I'll take your truck and charge you just what I have to pay for this unit, 1,256 bucks. It's got ninety horsepower. That will climb Pine Mountain as slick as grease lightning."

Harold looks like a grump. Shirley can't read the situation. Maybe he doesn't have the money. Time is flying by. Joe will begin to wonder what happened to her.

Perry just stares at Harold, who is looking grim. After a long silence, Harold says, "Okay, you've got me hog-swaddled. I bought that truck new, and the next one ought to be new and I ain't got much choice but to buy from you. You'll have to let Shirley take your car up Pine Mountain though, for a bit. Will you go outside so I can talk to her?"

Perry Bent leaves and Harold starts in. "He's makin' out like a bandit on me, and I know it. 'I'll let you buy it for just what I have to pay for it.' What a line of bullshit!"

"Okay, okay, Harold. Let's get on with it. This waiting around is driving me nuts."

"It's my bankbook. No one's ever looked at it but me and the bank. It was my old man's and I've just kept addin' to it. You know, keepin' it for a rainy day."

"Yeah, well, if you keep stalling, it *will* be a rainy day."

"Golly, I hate to have you know all my affairs."

"Your affairs! What are you thinking? You're bringing your money to the grave?"

"I ain't got no choice. You've got to have that book, take it to the bank, get the money, and pay Bent for the truck. I'll call the bank and let them know you're comin'."

"Well, tell me where it's hidden!"

"Damn, I've got to do that, ain't I?" He sinks into his chair.

"Harold Tully, you're wasting my time! I don't care what's in your bankbook!" Shirley is now driving her impatience through a whisper.

"It's in my roll top desk in the top center drawer. Reach in and you'll find it."

Shirley, holding Steven, rivets her eyes on Harold. "You be in this waiting room at nine o'clock tomorrow morning. If you aren't, you'll be sorry!"

He smiles for the first time since his truck broke down. As she turns to leave, the baby's blanket is hanging askew off Shirley's shoulder. *She reminds me of a high-strung filly leavin' the startin' gate.*

Shirley rides with Perry Bent back to his dealership, discusses the truck transfer, and then, as Harold has instructed, she uses the dealer's car to go back to Pine Mountain.

She approaches the farm, seeing only the team and spreader at a distance. Joe is on his back under the spreader working on repairing its bed chain. She stops the car, picks up a hungry Steven, sits down in some grass by the spreader, and begins nursing him.

Joe comes out from under the machine to sit with Shirley. She tells him what has taken her so long. Joe scratches his head. "No kidding, Harold's going to buy a new truck. Looking at the condition of things here, a truck is the first thing he's bought in years."

"Well, it was painful, waiting for him to make up his mind."

Joe explains the problem he's having with the spreader, but he treats the breakdown as a normal event of the day. "That bed chain is badly worn, but I bought a supply of links this morning to replace the worn ones as they break."

She squeezes Joe's arm. "You're good for me, being relaxed about these obstacles."

"Well, farming is a life filled with hindrances. If we work at it, we'll meet our goal; maybe not today or tomorrow, but in due time we'll have done what we've set out to do."

"Any goal?"

"No, not any goal. It has to be reasonable."

Steven finishes nursing. She stands to burp him and continues rubbing his back while his tummy lies on her right shoulder. Joe is standing by her. She says, "I want people to think of me as a good farmer, even though I'm a woman. I want good cows, good production, a painted house, a neat barn. Are these reasonable goals?"

"Yes, over time, but you can't do it all at once."

"I guess you're right."

He puts his arm around her and gives her a kiss. For a split second they pull away at arm's length, looking at each other as if spellbound by a new discovery. She feels a tingle spring through her body that she has never felt before. Whether it was the kiss or the lack of fear, a feeling of relief comes over her. He sits down and rolls under the spreader. She turns away and walks to the car, joyfully talking to Steven.

Back in the house, she searches for the bankbook in the roll top desk. She gathers it in pieces. Apparently a rat has chewed the glued binding. Looking at it, she sees that Harold hasn't added to it very recently. The last time was April 1946, when he made a fifty-dollar deposit. She notices he has ten thousand six hundred dollars in his account.

She does housework, frequently watching for Joe from the west window.

An hour later she leaves the farm, and returns with a beauty of a new truck. It's black with a shine like nothing else on Harold's farm.

Joe walks toward the truck. "Wow, Harold Tully has something new—amazing!"

Shirley smiles. "What a difference in the way it climbs the hills!"

Joe holds her hand. "Let's get something to eat."

They sit eating their sandwiches and drinking milk. Shirley suggests, "I think we should have a rest before the afternoon's work."

Joe looks surprised, but agrees, and gives her a hug and a kiss. She remarks, "I'm having feelings I've never felt before."

Joe murmurs, "You're not alone." He turns and walks to the front room for a rest.

By one-thirty they are both back loading the spreader, forkful by forkful. Steven is content in his basket, holding a rattle. Shirley is surprised at how much manure has already been spread. "I think the five-and-five field needs manure badly. That's at the top of the hill. You have to follow the field road past the entry of the house to get there. That will slow the spreading because of the distance the horses have to travel."

Joe suggests, "While you're gone with a load, I can be fixing the barnyard fence." He turns toward the horses. "You notice that Myron did a good job of trimming?"

"Gee, their feet do look a lot better."

The team is well matched as they dig their hooves into the soft dirt of the farm road and their rear leg muscles bulge as they start climbing their way to the five-and-five field. She rests them midway up the hill, since they are not yet in top physical condition. After a few moments, she lowers the reins and gives the team a gentle tap. She doesn't have to yell or command for results; they instinctively give of themselves.

Having entered the field, she squeezes and pulls the lever to engage the spreader. The manure moves on the bed chain, riding into the beaters that rotate, breaking the chunks into small particles. It flies five to ten feet in all directions, making a spread pattern. An ammonia-like smell fills the air. Shirley looks to the west and sees clouds, which tells her that rain will come soon to soak the manure into the warm soil.

She heads back to the barn. Joe and Shirley work until late that afternoon. Near the end of the day he sticks his fork into the ground, and looks at the pile, and then looks at Shirley and smiles. "We've made good progress."

That evening over a late supper, Shirley asks if the cows can be let out for the first time Sunday morning, after milking. Joe feels that's doable, barring unforeseen problems. They will have one more day to finish the manure and to fix the necessary fences. They both are tired by early evening. They say their good nights and go to bed.

The next morning Shirley walks to the barn. The light is just emerging. She pulls the switch to the milking machine pump and rinses the two DeLaval milking machines in a chlorine solution. With a hammer, she taps off the cover of a can, puts it in the corner of the cooler, places the strainer on the can, and is ready to start milking.

Joe comes to the barn when Shirley is about half done. He takes over her job while she tends to Steven, grains the cows and feeds the calves.

She remarks, "Hey, don't you think the cows that have calved are doing well?"

"They sure are!"

After breakfast, Joe continues rebuilding the fences. Shirley, with Steven, takes the milk to the stand. She meets Zack, and inwardly sighs in regret. He stares at the new truck. "How'd you ever get that out of Harold?"

She answers in a matter-of-fact tone, "The old one quit at the hospital."

"You don't mean to tell me that Harold has that kind of money for a new truck?"

"He paid for it in cash."

"Cash!"

She nods. He looks at her and quickly counts five cans. "How can you be doing all that work and still look—well, look as you do?" After a long pause, he continues. "I've been thinking that maybe you should—should be with me. You know, about the picnic and all." He looks toward the truck. "Could your baby be—I mean could I be…"

"I've taken care of Steven's support, Zack! Don't even give it a thought!"

CHAPTER TWELVE

Harold walks out of the hospital wearing the pants and shirt that Honeydew has cleaned for him, plus his work shoes which she has polished. He needs a shave and haircut, wanting to look as sharp as he can before going into F.D.'s Women's Boutique to buy the jacket for Shirley. He keeps clearing his throat, feeling very conspicuous; he's wearing no bib-overalls, no boots, and no barn hat. Out of habit, he reaches in his shirt pocket for his pipe, but he reminds himself that he's left it behind. He enters the door next to the turning red-striped pole and sits down.

The barber comes from a back room. "Who in the world—is this Harold Tully? At first I didn't recognize you. If it hadn't been for your beard, I would have thought you were a stranger." The barber motions as if directing traffic. "Take a seat in my chair."

Harold stands and walks to the chair and slides back on the leather seat, lifting his work shoes onto the footrest. "Well, I've been away from the farm for a few days, hangin' out at the hospital with this lamed-up hand."

"No foolin'. That's too bad. Shirley Mason been runnin' the place for you?"

"Yup, she's been doin' a great good job, too. 'Course, everyone in town knows she's up on the mountain workin' for me."

The barber flicks the button on the clippers. "The usual?"

"Clip it close around the ears, it's spring."

"For an orphan kid that had a bad name around town, Shirley Mason sure has turned out better than anyone ever expected. She has a baby, doesn't she?"

"Yup, Steven. He's a cute kid."

The barber's hands work quickly with the comb and clippers. "No husband?"

"No. Hell, you know the answers, anyway. Seems that everyone does."

The barber chuckles. "I'll bet you don't mind hirin' a gal the looks of her."

Harold's anger flares and he raises his voice. "Don't get any ideas; she ain't the kind to carry on with the likes of me. She's a real decent young woman!"

The barber stops his clippers and forces a nervous laugh. "Sorry, I didn't mean anythin' that wasn't proper."

"Proper or not I'm just tellin' you the way it is!" Harold lifts his chin and stretches his neck for emphasis. "Folks ain't needin' to get the wrong idea! I ain't mad or anythin', just gettin' it straight. Golly, we're on good terms, ain't we? I don't want you cuttin' my throat with your straight razor when you're shavin' me."

The barber laughs and flicks the button, continuing to clip great quantities of hair which float to the floor.

Harold leaves the barbershop feeling more exposed than ever with a shaven face and a close haircut. He's made aware of his condition because a cool spring breeze is bracing his face and head. He inhales the scent of talcum powder the barber used, being reminded that he smells the same as Steven after having a bath. And he feels about as able as Steven in buyin' a woman's coat in a fancy store. He, nevertheless, is satisfied with his looks, thinking no one will know who he is.

He hesitates before entering F.D.'s Women's Boutique, a place he has never been, nor has he ever looked at their display window as he's doing this very moment. *Damn, real live lookin' women dressed to kill. A place for fancy women to buy all their fancy duds, from lacy hats to high-heeled shoes, and Harold Tully thinks he has the guts to go in this place?*

Before entering, he reads Honeydew's directions:

The jacket is straight through to the back of the store, the second rack of jackets to the left, the fifth jacket from the end. It has light brown water-repellent cloth with a red lining, three-quarter-length with a zipper and button-down pockets.

Harold mentally repeats the directions while entering the store with his head down, walking directly toward the back of the store. "May I help you, sir?" He keeps going. "Sir, may I help you?"

He hesitates, not really wanting to stop, because it goes against his plan to grab the jacket, pay for it, and leave. He glances up at a woman's face framed behind a counter between a mannequin torso wearing a Playtex Living Girdle with garters and a mannequin bosom displaying a Lovable Bra by the Lovable Brassiere Co.

Harold says in a flustered tone, while quickly glancing down the counter at a pair of long mannequin legs, wearing Kayser Hosiery, "I—I ain't wantin' the body parts department, I've come to buy a jacket."

The clerk retorts, "We don't sell body parts, but only the finest hosiery and lingerie."

Harold chokes, "Well—well, yes—yes, 'course I meant to say somethin' like the stuff that covers the under parts of a woman."

The clerk coolly instructs, "Follow me."

He reads the promotion signs as he goes to the back of the store: Lucien LeLong lip service for smoother lovelier lips, Florshein Shoes, Air Step, the shoe with the youthful feel, and finally Hostess Coats.

"Which size and type would you like?"

Harold looks up and is faced with several women trying on spring jackets and coats and two other clerks helping out. He spots the jacket

Honeydew picked out, as it this very moment is being taken off a hanger and slipped on an older woman. He overhears the clerk: "Honeydew Mullen was in yesterday looking at this jacket. I can't imagine why, Trudy—can you?"

He turns to his clerk. "Go about your business, this jacket buyin' may take a while."

"Well, okay, whatever suits you."

Harold steps back in an aisle of dresses trying to act inconspicuous as the women hunt through the two racks of new spring arrivals. Trudy Iverson is looking at herself in a three-sided mirror wearin' the very jacket Honeydew has picked out. *I have the damnedest luck at anythin' I try to do.*

Trudy tips up the collar around her lacquered hair. "Woo, does this red lining ever look sharp or what! Why would Honeydew be looking at this jacket? She'd need one twice this size."

The clerk smiles. "She said she was looking for a friend."

Trudy puts her finger to her lips. "Now, who would that be? I just can't imagine. I talked with her over the phone just yesterday and she never mentioned coming in here." Trudy pivots, observing her profile in the mirror. "How do you like it on me?"

"It looks gorgeous."

Trudy pulls on the jacket at her midsection. "Plenty of room."

From behind the dresses, Harold blurts out, "Baggy as hell."

Trudy looks quickly in Harold's direction. "Who said that?"

The clerk turns around and sees no one. "I don't know."

Trudy pulls again on the coat. "Plenty of room, maybe too much. I'd like to keep looking. I'll think about this one." She unzips it and lays it over the rack and walks away as the clerk suggests other jackets. Harold steps from behind the dresses, walking as quietly as possible toward the rack, takes the jacket, pays the clerk, and has it boxed. With the box under his arm, he hurries out the door, feeling good about himself. *That's the first time, and probably the last, that I'll ever get one on Trudy Iverson.*

CHAPTER THIRTEEN

Shirley is eager to get up Sunday morning. It's turn out time, and she's due to bring Harold home after she takes the milk to the stand. The grass in the pasture is abundant. The tender green shoots look like a carpet as soft as the silkiest hide on any cow. Here and there she can see a yellow dandelion. They are just beginning to bloom and put on their spring flower show. She smiles as she remembers how Mrs. Perkins had taught her how to make bracelets and necklaces out of dandelion stems. It was fun because there was no end to the supply.

The barn doors are open and the cool morning air flows through the stable. The cows stand in contentment while Shirley milks in rote fashion. The milker pump hums from the exhaust pipe outside the milk house. The pump creates a vacuum in the pipe that runs the length of the barn and is fastened to the stanchion line. The air draws on the vacuum hose connected to the machine, sucking the slide in the machine's pulsator: milk-rest, milk-rest, milk-rest. She waits as the teat cup clings to the cow's teat: open, close, open, close, open, close. Sixty times a minute: *psst slosh, psst slosh, psst slosh.* The constant rhythm and constant beat are soothing—good background sounds as she kneels against a warm flank, waiting for the machine to take what the cow so freely gives. The cow's body heat and oily scent from the smooth hide make for a comfortable moment.

She smiles, feeling thankful for Joe. He was thoughtful to have taken Steven and thoughtful to have done Saturday night chores. Going for a walk was a special treat. The huge pines in back of the house were playing their haunting tune louder and louder as the breeze quickened, hitting a crescendo and then quieting to a low, very low tone, so low she could barely hear it when the wind slowed and the sound faded.

Farther up the hill, white pines also stand at the entrance of what she thinks of as a beautiful cathedral, the five-and-five field. It's all there for anyone to soak in and enjoy. No admission is needed to enter this upland meadow, surrounded by different shades of green. The maples, with their new greenish brown leaves the size of mouse ears; the tamaracks, showing their emerging light green needles; plus a few dark evergreens, all blend to make a fresh spring scene. There are also the light green leaves of the trembling aspens fluttering in the breeze. This new green tapestry comes only in May. At ground level, the field is also surrounded by thick mats of mayflowers, starflowers, wild onions, and even red trillium, which Mrs. Perkins used to call nosebleed. Yesterday Shirley watched three deer, having survived the winter on starvation browse, eagerly feeding. Their coats were ragged since they were in the process of shedding their thick winter hair.

Shirley methodically milks. *Oh—and I saw those very rare lady slippers. Mrs. Perkins told me what they were.*

She sighs. Mrs. Perkins treated her like a daughter. Springtime brings back the memories of the walks they used to take. She taught her a lot about trees and the untamed natural world, but then it all abruptly ended. *Just because of Toby.*

"Good morning, you luscious queen."

Shirley is jarred. "Oh, hi! As you would say, I was in dreamland, recalling my beautiful walk yesterday. I don't feel much like a queen, though, in this barn outfit."

He smiles. "Beauty is in the eye of the beholder."

"I'm going to miss you. These five days have been some of the best I can remember. You've done a lot of work and have helped me with my fear."

He agrees and nods. "I realize that. Maybe visiting by your bed at night isn't such a hot idea. We could get pretty carried away with the good night kissing."

Shirley laughs. "Yeah, that's for sure."

With milking finished, she washes up in the milk house, scrubbing each pail, rinsing them in a chlorine solution, and placing them on a rack to dry.

Joe is haying the cows and feeding the calves and horses. He remarks, "The cows should get some fill before going to the lush grass. It will taste like candy to them."

They walk to the henhouse to feed the chickens and collect the eggs. Shirley mentions, "I've really neglected this place during spring's work. Their nests need to be cleaned. I'll do that tomorrow. Harold won't feel much like working when he first comes home. I'll ask him to sort and box the eggs for Wednesday."

While both of them are walking toward the house, Steven is grabbing Joe's shirt and trying to bring it to his mouth. Shirley walks in back of them, watching her son. "You want everything in your mouth, don't you?" He smiles at the sound of her attentive voice, taking a deep breath, which causes him to hiccup while catching his breath. "Oh, aren't you about the cutest kid!"

She serves oatmeal that she started soaking the night before. Placing a box of raisins on the table for the cereal, she serves toast with butter and jam, and milk. "Joe, I've been thinking. It would be nice if I had the care of a young girl who could help with Steven. Maybe I could be like a mother to her the same way Mrs. Perkins was to me."

"You've never talked much about Mrs. Perkins before. They're good farmers."

Shirley gets up from the table, starting to clear the dishes. "I think of Mrs. Perkins often—how much she meant to me. I'm hoping the girl could be with Steven some, watch him when he begins to creep and crawl and starts walking. I can't expect Harold to watch him. I saw your father the other day and asked if he might know of someone, since he's a member of the Leland Home Board of Directors."

Joe also leaves the table to help her with the dishes. "Yes, he might." He pauses and asks, "How was it living with the Perkinses?"

She pours hot water from the Glenwood chamber into a dishpan. "At first it was great. She had the four boys, and wanted a girl, so they took me as an infant from the Leland Home. I left the Perkinses when I was nine." She loads the pan with dishes.

Joe pulls a dishtowel from the drawer and is wiping the first plate. "Do you know who your folks are?"

Shirley stands by the sink with her hands resting in dishwater. "I'm told my mother had no family. She died suddenly at the home after I was born. There's no record of my father. I tried to locate some of my relatives when I was in Burlington, but all my efforts came to a dead end."

He again glances at her while continuing to dry the plates. "I've heard some gossip, but really, why did you leave the Perkinses?"

Her hands move deftly in the dishpan. "Uh—that gets into my sordid past. I'll tell you sometime after I've chilled some of my feelings toward boys and men. You know, the ones that are pumped up with testosterone."

"Huh, that's a big word. You think I'm not?"

She flicks the water from her hands into the sink and begins wiping them on a towel. "Dr. Meyer used the word a lot to explain why you guys act the way you do. Somehow, you're different, though. You control yourself in a nice way." *Some different than Jimmy or Zack.*

Joe remarks, "Let's lighten up and turn out the cows." He walks toward the door, turns, and comments, "By the way, I like your idea of having the help of a young girl."

Shirley lets Dolly out first. She sniffs cautiously at the doorway, and then walks out of the barn and down a wooden ramp. At the bottom, she twists her neck and lets both her hind feet fly in the air. Immediately all the cows become restless and start to bellow. The baby calves catch the excitement, and they too kick their heels, even though they have never experienced turnout time. One by one each cow acts with trepidation, slowly traversing the ramp; but once on the ground, they change gears and feet and legs fly while they run to their remembered freedom.

The bred heifers have to be pushed some at the door, since they fear walking down the wooden slope. Some jump from the doorsill to the ground, clearing the ramp entirely. None of the cattle grazes at first. They grab mouthfuls of tender grass and kick up their heels while running to the end of the pasture. They follow the fence line, checking the boundaries. Their heads held high, they breathe rapidly, snorting and bellowing in the joy of being free, as if celebrating the new season. *Aren't they great? What if I jumped up and down every time I saw Joe coming to the farm? He'd think I was nuts.*

Even Jeanie and Lassie are excited, as loud whinnies echo throughout the nearly empty barn. Shirley remarks, "Gee, it's too bad they can't be let out, too."

"I'm working on the small pasture at the south end of the house. We can put them in there with the yearling heifers, maybe by tonight."

Shirley fondly looks at Joe. After a moment, she says, "I've got to go now and take the milk to the stand and bring Harold home."

"Oh good. It will be nice to have him home."

At the hospital, Harold is sitting in the waiting room holding the box with Shirley's new jacket. He stands and looks out the window as his new black truck enters the parking lot. He comes out of the hospital carrying the box. *If that ain't about the best lookin' rig in town.*

Shirley gets out and greets him. "Well, don't you feel great being out and having a new truck to drive home?"

He remarks, "Golly, you've got five cans in back. You makin' that much milk? I ain't shipped that much in years; well, I guess since my old man died. The old bastard, now mister man, he was one hell of a good farmer. For me, I had no choice. You might say the place was dumped in my lap. Well—it was passed to him when his father died. He liked it, but for me it was like being given a prison sentence, or, well, until just recently. You might say I've been put on probation."

"Pine Mountain doesn't seem as bad to you now, does it?"

"Yup, you could say that. The heft of all that damn work has been taken from me and that feels mighty good. For that reason and others—I ain't knowin' how to say this, but I have somethin' for you. Payin' you for all that you've done. You know, what you were talkin' about—doin' for each other." He passes her the box. "Here, this is for you."

"Gee, it's for me?"She takes the cover off the box. "Oh, my gosh, look at this beautiful jacket. I've never owned one as nice. I feel like crying. No one has ever given me something this nice! Can I try it on?" She places the box on the hood of the truck and slips into the jacket. "It fits perfectly."

Harold smiles. "By golly, it looks sharp all right. Honeydew picked it out and I paid for it. You might say it's from the both of us. Now you can throw away that gray thing you've been wearin'."

"Thanks so much!" Harold's standing by the front fender. She turns and gives him a hug and he steps back in surprise.

He wipes his hand across his brow. "Whew, I ain't used to a young woman huggin' me." He opens the driver's side door and sits behind the wheel, and breaks into a wide grin. "Ain't this nice, Shirley?"

"It sure is."

They leave the hospital parking lot. He turns right instead of left.

She raises her voice. "Hey, where are you going? You aren't headed home."

"Hell, woman, do you always have to work? I want to go for a little Sunday ride. You know, in my new truck, try it out a little."

"There's people just going to church, and look at all the children. I want Steven to go someday. Mrs. Perkins used to take me. I remember one of the songs we sang.

"*I would be friend of all the foe, the friendless;*
I would be giving and forget the gift;
I would be humble for I know my weakness;
I would look up and laugh and love and live."

"Golly, you have a mighty pretty voice."

"Would you go with me sometime? To church, I mean."

"Who, me?" Harold sounds panicky. "Hell, no, the timbers would bust if I walked into church. Goin' to church is only for the goody-goody. That don't fit me."

Stately maples surround the white church and a marble walkway leads to the front door. Shirley turns to look out the rear window. "The sign in front reads 'Everyone is Welcome'."

He grumbles, "Well, that's bullshit! You've got to learn what's true and what ain't in this world. There's all this fakery ridin' along the surface of life, but down under in everyone's gut is where the truth sits. Yup, down in everyone's gut."

They travel farther up the street and come to a brick building with Greek revival columns, supporting a portico. There's a sidewalk by the street with a large lawn and walkways leading to the front steps. Shirley remarks, "Oh, there's good old Huntersville High. That brings back a lot of fond memories. I was the fastest typist in Miss O'Shea's class. I remember I was so proud."

"Yup, I remember the place. Gifford was our principal. Speaking of a fake, he sure was. Junior Campbell and I had a great time. But that son-of-a-bitchin' Gifford didn't like me because I was a farm kid, and stunk. He couldn't stand that. He was a bastardly fake. Yes sir, he was."

They leave the village and travel through rolling open country. Shirley's voice rises in excitement. "Look, there's the Perkinses' farm. They have a new Ford tractor with plows. Look at the plowing they've done, probably for corn. They always grew a lot of corn. I remember getting lost in it as a little girl. Mrs. Perkins would hear me cry and she'd yell out, 'Don't get scared honey. Just follow the row. Just follow the corn-row, and you'll find your way out.' I'd do that, and it always worked."

Harold takes his eyes off the road for a moment and turns her way. "How do they ever put up with their horny son Toby? Remember when he knocked up Attorney Iverson's daughter? He must have been twenty and she was only twelve. Did he ever get burned over that! 'Course that's the public version. Honeydew has her own story of what happened in that mess."

"What's her story?"

Harold is concentrating, trying to remember. "I ain't really sure. You know, she raised her eyebrows and remarked, 'That's what everyone thinks.' Just the same, Toby got pinned for the rape. I see he's just been let out of prison."

She grimaces. "I know, I read it in the paper. I hope I don't meet up with him. He had some hot blood all right. He sure had testosterone problems."

"Test what? Where'd you come on to that word?"

"Oh, I picked it up in my past."

Harold looks Shirley's way. "Don't try to use big words with me."

"Sorry—it means being horny."

"Oh, he's that, all right. Honeydew told me that Iverson's wife, Trudy, is pickled most of the time. Why hell, she drinks from mornin' 'til night. The last time Honeydew saw her, she was so loaded that if you lit a match next to her, she'd go up in a puff of smoke. That daughter of theirs, now there's a real loser. You know she went off to find herself—that's bullshit—she's out of it. Honeydew says she's on some kinda drug. Iverson just keeps sendin' her money. I guess to keep her out of town. Last Honeydew heard, she's down in Greenwich Village. You told me their son, Joe, turned out to be a nice guy. I guess you should know, since he's been helpin' you. 'Course, his folks are tryin' to get him married off to some Vassar girl, somebody with class."

Shirley feels an instant pain in her stomach and sweeps the hair from her face, searching for the absent barrette. She sits in silence for a while and then changes the subject. "Would you ever buy a tractor like the Coleses and Perkinses?"

"Hell, no. I'm just fine the way things are goin' right now."

She raises her voice. "You make me more than a little upset sometimes."

"Why's that? Because I ain't spendin' money? Blowin' it on new-fangled stuff like tractors and such?"

"No, not only that. You know why the farm is going just fine? It's because of me!" *And Joe.* She calms herself. "Look, how about you letting me run the farm?"

"Hell, that ain't new. You've been runnin' it ever since you set foot on the place."

"No, I mean really run it. Buy all the supplies, buy and sell cows, order the baby chicks when we need them—run the whole thing: start a checking account, deposit the milk check, and pay the bills. Just turn the whole farm over to me."

"Well, if you ain't the biggest livin' wonder. Shirley, that's what I like about you, there ain't no fakery in you. You lay it all right out so everyone can see it. Damn, that's scary sometimes. You little whip, you took a gander at my bankbook, so now you're schemin' on ways to use it, mentionin' a tractor and the like. For all I know, you'd prob'ly fancy havin' a baler."

She looks at him. "Yes, I would."

He nods his head in agreement. "Yup, I knew it, I knew it!"

"Harold Tully, you remember at the hospital, I told you I didn't care how much money you had. Can you believe that?"

"Yup, bein' you, I can."

"How about this? You work for me and I'll pay for everything. What I give you will be your spending money. Let's say fifty dollars a milk check?"

"Oh hell! I've got to mull all this over. I ain't thinkin' I could ever work for a woman. But Shirley, I'll tell you this, though: I've never had any children, but if I did, and you were my daughter, I'd be proud of you."

"Thanks! You mean that? If I was really your daughter, wouldn't you want me to run the farm for you?" Harold avoids her question and reaches for his pipe, rubbing the bowl in one hand with the other on the steering wheel. They've ended their Sunday ride and the truck is now beginning to climb Pine Mountain.

"Golly, this truck does zip up these hills. It sure has plenty of juice in its pants."

Steven is waking up and Shirley talks to him, "Well, look at you, little boy. You've been sleeping all this time."

Harold reaches over to tickle Steven's chin. "You know, your old lady's been a-blowin' me away with all her wild ideas."

"This will always be your farm, Harold." She takes her eyes off Steven and directs her comment his way. "You'd just be letting me run it."

He throws his pipe onto the dash. "Well, let me think on this deal for a while. Look at that! All the cows are out to pasture, the yearlings—Jeanie and Lassie, too."

Shirley smiles in satisfaction. "Well, what did you expect? It's the middle of May—turnout time."

CHAPTER FOURTEEN

"This is too much! Does it ever smell in here!" Shirley yells as she enters the house. "Let's get some air! I think we should start painting the kitchen tomorrow. Maybe the new paint smell can cover this awful odor. Oh, my gosh! Look, Harold, a television, just like the one Attorney Iverson had in his office when I worked for him. But with his, all you could see was a snowy picture."

"Well, I'll be. I've seen them in the store window, but I ain't never thought I'd have one in my house."

"I'll bet Joe brought it here. Maybe it's a coming-home present for you, Harold."

"For me! Hell, I ain't never met the guy before. Let's turn it on and see if it works."

"Look, the pattern—it's clear!"

"I'll sit and watch the pattern while you paint; I ain't never laid a stroke of paint on this place since I owned it."

"We could get done faster, and you could enjoy television sooner, if you helped."

"I think my ma was the last one to paint this kitchen."

"It's supposed to rain for the next couple of days. It will be a good job to have done. Aren't you sick of this everlasting smell? Well, I am!"

Joe walks through the entry and stands in the kitchen. Shirley is jumping with excitement. "What a surprise—a television!" She reaches for Joe's hand and says, "I want you to meet my friend, Harold Tully."

"Glad to meet you, Harold, how are you doing? You all ready to go and start running this farm again?"

"I don't know. If Shirley gets her way, I ain't runnin' it anymore. She wants to manage the place."

Joe pauses. "What do you think of that idea?"

"Maybe she deserves a try at it, I dunno—she's so full of piss and vinegar. I suppose it would give me a chance to ease off some, but hell, workin' for a woman—and you know Shirley. She—well, she has to have everythin' done yesterday. I'd prob'ly feel like I was bein' yanked around like a puppy on a chain." He looks up at Joe. "Much obliged for the television."

"It was one that didn't work in the village. I thought it might here, and from the looks of the pattern, it will."

Shirley comes back in the kitchen from taking care of Steven, wearing her new jacket, with the red collar tipped up, turning around on the kitchen floor with her arms held out. "How do you like it, Joe?"

"Wow, do you ever look great!"

"Harold gave it to me. Isn't it about the sharpest jacket you've ever seen?"

Joe smiles. "Gee, that's great, Harold, but don't you think the gal makes the jacket?"

Harold laughs. "Honeydew picked it out. She knew what she was doin' all right. It sure looks like it was made for her." *A hell of a lot more so than for your mother.*

Shirley, still in high spirits, jumps in front of the television. "And, Joe, what a surprise present to bring to us!" She throws her arms around him and gives him a big kiss.

Harold adds, “I can see a lot’s been happenin’ up on Pine Mountain since I’ve been gone. Spring has really sprung!” Joe and Shirley look at Harold, as she still has her hand cupped around Joe’s neck. “I was meanin’ spring’s work’s all done and the cows out to pasture and all.” Harold laughs.

Shirley adds, “Yeah, thanks, Joe, for letting the horses and yearlings out.”

“Let me tell you, the yearlings came hard, digging their hooves every step of the way or else they’d shift gears and run so fast I could hardly keep up.” Joe is watching them out the west window toward the heifer pasture. “There they are, though, all seven of them. Look at them run. I hope they stop for the fences.”

Harold watches. “Yup, kicking up their heels havin’ a hell of a time. Somethin’ I never did when I was young. Havin’ fun, I mean. My old man worked me like a bastard.”

Joe backs away from the window. “I’m setting up a water tank for the cows. One I found stored in the barn. It looks like it goes in the barnyard. The pipes are all there.”

“Yup, I used to set it up, but I stopped babyin’ the cows a few years ago.”

Shirley glances in disgust at Harold.

Joe adds, “I’ll take care of the hens and then I’ll go. I’ve got a lot of desk work.”

“Well, you’ll eat dinner with us, won’t you?”

“Sure. I can’t pass up a good meal.”

“Harold, I want to cook you a good homecoming dinner. Would you poke up the fire for me?”

“Yup, I guess so. I was just gettin’ interested in watching this test pattern.” He groans to his feet, shuffles to the woodshed and carries in a few sticks, and then collapses back in his chair.

Shirley comes into the kitchen and places Steven in his lap. “Here, maybe your Uncle Harold will hold you for a while.”

“Sure, why not?”

She's at the clothesline, folding Joe's clothes, tucking them in a bag. Harold, looking out the west window, watches her quick hands move, collecting the pins. *She works like an engine at full throttle.*

She walks through the entry door, carrying the clothes with alert brown eyes.

Harold asks, "I suppose a lot of sparkin' took place here while I was gone?"

"What's a lot of sparking?" Shirley glances at him. "Joe and I did a lot of work."

"Hell, what a borin' answer."

She fixes her hair. "You're lucky to get any at all."

He laughs. "You're a plucky one."

Joe enters and sits down. "It must seem great to be home. How's the finger doing?"

He holds it up, checking it while he talks. "Good. It ain't all healed yet, but I got rid of that bastardly pain." He turns toward Joe. "You know, I ain't never had someone of your type ever set foot on this farm. I guess I'd call you educated in farmin'. Now don't get me wrong, you're a good fellow and all, but I think I've done right well on this place just usin' my common sense. I ain't needin' no ad-vice."

Joe smiles and doesn't say anything, allowing Harold to expound at will.

"I call folks like you educated fools." He gestures with his hands attempting to soften his harsh comment. "Don't need to take no offense, but if you had to run this farm on your own, you'd fail. I've seen it time and again. New-fangled ideas can put you under. They cost too much money."

Joe doesn't comment.

"By golly, I ain't got the best cows, or put up hay that would win a prize at the county fair, but I'm makin' money."

Steven begins to cry, and Shirley asks Joe. "Could you please change his diaper? I just folded some clean ones and they're on top of the bureau in my room."

Shirley looks at Harold with fury in her eyes. She talks while setting the table, taking her anger out on the china and tableware, slamming the settings into place. The plates hit with a loud clatter. "Why is it so hard for you to be nice? Joe is our guest. Take it easy on him, will you?"

Harold says nothing. He sets his jaw while his skin pulls taut on his face. In defiance, he takes out his pipe, loads it, and bites so hard on the stem that she expects his teeth will slip out.

She can't help but laugh. "Heaven's sake, don't lose your teeth."

Holding Steven, Joe sits down at the table.

"Thanks, Joe. The chicken pie is ready, and I have some bread here that's Harold's favorite, along with some grape jelly."

Joe has heard some of the earlier conversation and realizes that she is trying to humor the man. He joins in. "I noticed a thirty-ought-six in your gun cabinet. Is that what you go hunting with?"

Harold relaxes. "Sure is. I shot a nice five-pointer with that rifle last deer season."

"Really? Where did you get it?"

"Right up in the back field. I call it the five-and-five field. The land on both sides of the center field road is sorta sidlin' to the woods' edge. I was drivin' my team with a load to spread, had the gun on the seat, put the spreader in gear, and was movin' when I spotted a big buck watchin' me. I think he was curious as much as anythin', because when I drove closer he just stood there. So I took my rifle, aimed, and fired it right from the spreader seat. He dropped in his tracks—scared the hell outta my team. They were clear halfway to home before I could bring them under control."

Harold continues to talk about hunting and fishing as Joe pumps him with questions. Shirley brings on a custard pie. When finished, she stands to take Steven for his nap. Joe offers, "Now, that was a tasty meal. Thanks a lot."

Even Harold has a twinkle in his eye. "Yup, she's a damn good cook. I ain't sure what she's better at, cookin' or bossin' me around." Joe and Harold roar with laughter.

Shirley leaves with Joe to say good-bye. "This will be some adjustment for me to get used to having Harold around instead of you. Thanks for all of your help." They hug and kiss, and Joe leaves.

When she walks back into the kitchen, Harold notices her tense face and watery eyes. *I think they've plowed some new ground while I was away.*

Shirley takes a deep breath, "I guess I'll start washing the ceiling until chore time."

Harold sits in his Morris chair, looking out the west window. "You know, my ma was prob'ly the last one to wash this ceiling. It sure as hell wasn't any of my housekeepers. Most of them couldn't get out of their own way. They just sat around and listened to the soaps and cried. I guess I was into always hirin' women that were worse off than myself. 'Course, Alice always tried to be neighborly, but hell, they were way beyond rescue. Her befriendin' them never seemed to help."

In determination, Shirley is scrubbing over her head with wash water running down her arm. "I need to go and see Alice, since she invited me to come down sometime. Maybe I can do that after we paint this room, but I don't want to have to face Zack."

"Yup, I know what you mean. But I get the idea that he'd do anythin' to get you to work at their place."

She dips her wash rag in the pan. "That's just the problem. He won't take no for an answer." After working for over an hour she asks, "Would you please help me get the milkers back in the barn? Probably after that a television program will be on."

"Okay, I guess it's time I did a little work." He follows her into the barn and looks at the cards over each stall. "Names! If that ain't the most namby-pamby idea."

She ignores him. "You drive the cows in a few at a time. I'll tie them up."

The cows amble slowly toward their stalls. Their slow movement tells Shirley they are tired from all the running they've done. Some cows' muzzles have turned from white to pink from the sun. Their long winter coats have been lapped by rough tongues, showing areas of warm-weather hair. This is the first time since fall that they've had a chance to clean themselves. Shirley doesn't think they look very filled; probably the taste of freedom was more important to them than the new lush grass. She starts milking and finds production to be off considerably, but realizes that by the next day they will be more settled into grazing.

The kitchen comes to mind as she milks. She decides that the ceiling should be white, the walls off-white, and beige for the wainscoting. *That should look snappy.*

That night after chores, Shirley continues washing the ceiling. Her arms and shoulders ache, but she works through the pain. Harold watches her in utter amazement. *She's superwoman at work.*

Forty years of wood smoke and fly specks stick, making it difficult to clean. Steven begins to fuss. Shirley remarks, "That's strange. He's only been in bed for an hour or so."

She checks and his forehead is warm to the touch. She refers to her child-care book.

It reads, "For a mild fever give aspirin, and place a cold cloth on the child's forehead." She crushes half an aspirin into a spoon and dissolves it in warm water. Steven tries to reject the medicine, but she gets him to take most of it. Placing a cold cloth on his forehead, she asks Harold to hold him. Steven continues fussing and crying while Harold tries to comfort him, but with little luck. She, meanwhile, continues scrubbing the ceiling as her hair flies in all directions, with arms twisting back and forth with the washrag.

"Hey, will you lay off that for tonight and take care of your kid?"

She reluctantly stops and tries to comfort Steven, going to her room to nurse him. She can tell he has a cold coming on because he's stuffy and doesn't nurse as usual.

While sitting in her room, holding Steven, she thinks of Joe—how much she misses him. She wonders if he feels the same. Where does this Vassar girl fit into his life? Then there's Dottie, his secretary. Being together so much of the time, he must have some thoughts that she's sexy and available. Would he ever date her? This feeling of jealousy is an emotion she's never known.

Steven wakes several times in the night, but the aspirin seems to have helped his fever. He fusses during the morning's milking. She stops and tries to comfort him but he continues his crying. She takes him to the milk house for water to dissolve another half aspirin. "You poor kid. This is not like you to feel so miserable."

Harold comes to the barn to load the truck and is walking along the line of cows, grumbling, "Look at these dumb names—Lana. I wish it really was Lana in person, and Liz. Here's Maria. Now, that's a good name. I wonder what she'd think to have a cow be given her name. At this point, the way she's prob'ly livin', I can imagine the cow looks a mite better than she does. I guess, considerin' everythin', Shirley's one hell of a woman. Maria just ain't in the same class."

Shirley comes back from the milk house, and sits for a while, holding Steven, waiting for him to fall asleep. "My poor little boy has got a cold; he doesn't feel very good. Now—he's finally going to sleep."

Harold is feeding the calves. "Well, he ain't bein' neglected. Reminds me of my ma; she was good at carin' for me, too. She came from up Burlington way. Her school came to Huntersville to hear a debate, and there was a big town dance that night. My old man met Ma at the dance. She didn't have much of a family. I can't remember her ever sayin' she had close kin. She graduated from normal school that summer and moved down here to Pine Mountain and married my old man.

"Long as I can remember, he took on as if he hated her. Maybe 'cause she was better than he was. She was, too. Maybe, too, he was mad 'cause I was a-comin' and he had to marry her. Just like me, my old man took this place over when he was young. His old man was killed in the woods. My ma told me that much. My old man was fellin' a tree and it swung the wrong way, killin' my grandpa and a skid horse."

Shirley is only half listening, but she did hear his last words. "That's awful!"

"Yup, and it seemed like my old man never got over it. The whole situation sorta repeated itself, since I was the cause of my old man bein' killed. I was sorry at the time, but I never let it eat at me, like I think the killin' ruined my old man. Maybe 'cause I felt he wanted it that way—bein' dead. He was walkin' hell, that's the way he acted, like walkin' hell; but my ma saved my life. I think I was what kept her a-livin'. I knew all my numbers, and could even read some before goin' to school. I was the smartest in my class. 'Course, there was only three of us in my grade until I went to high school.

"Ma read to me a lot—Charles Dickens and other books. I read to her, too. It was fun. My old man was jealous, 'cause me and Ma got on so good. He'd start yellin' around nine o'clock. 'It's time that boy was sleepin. You're makin' a goddamn baby outta him.'

"You could see the fear in her face at the sound of his voice. She'd kiss me good night and lots of nights the fightin' and yellin' would begin, terrible, just terrible. He beat her and beat her bad, the old bastard. She would look so sad in the mornin'. It must've been hell for her. At breakfast and most meals, my ma nor me ever dared make a noise. I guess my old man didn't want to hear any talk. He was the sourest, ugliest man I ever knew, and did he ever beat the shit outta the cows, and for no reason. I might get mad at a cow, but I could never hammer on a cow like he did. He was a mean one, I'll tell you, but the odd thing was his care of the cattle was good. Hell, he was into the cows all right. They milked like fury, but at times he'd throw a whing-ding. No kidding, he'd near kill a cow."

They leave the barn and walk to the house with Harold still wound up telling his story. They eat breakfast and Shirley clears the table and does the dishes while listening. She interrupts, "We'd better go with the milk. I'll take Steven to see Dr. Plumbly for a check up. This is the first time he's been sick so I want to be sure he's okay. Would you buy the paint at the hardware store and some supplies while I'm at the doctor's office? Here's the list and some money to help pay the bill."

"No, you keep the money; I want to get rid of this stink as badly as anybody. How do you know so much about paintin' anyway?"

"When I lived with Jules and Esther Erickson, I did a lot of it."

"So, you lived with the Ericksons?"

"Yeah, for a year, and I hated every minute of it. I was like a slave to them. Willy Smithson worked there, also. He still does. He's mentally slow, but I came to love Willy. It was myself and Willy against Jules and Esther, and their two miserable sons."

"Yup, he thinks he's better than most. I never did like the man. How come you left?"

"Got in a fight with one of the boys. Esther was scared to death I was going to kill the kid, so she called the social worker and demanded that I leave."

"Well, I guess she *would* be scared, since I heard you damn near killed Toby Perkins. 'Course, I'm barely rememberin' when that happened. I guess I forgot most of it."

"Yeah, well, I'm not proud of it. It cost me Mrs. Perkins. She loved me like a mother and she's the closest I ever came to having a mother."

They walk to the truck, drive down the mountain, leave the milk, and head toward the village. Harold parks the truck in front of the doctor's office. Shirley climbs out with Steven. Harold tells her, "I'll go to the hardware store, and then wait for you."

Coming from the office, holding Steven, she reports, "Dr. Plumbly said Steven is fine. He just has a cold. I've got to bring him in next week, though, for some shots." She doesn't tell Harold that Dr. Plumbly promised when he had a moment he would look at her chart and absolutely confirm who Steven's father is. He told her he could compare the date of sewing the gash on her head with the date of the picnic.

The light rain continues. The truck passes lush green fields and wooded areas adorned in their fresh tender growth. "Harold, we're missing a good meal of dandelion greens. If they're dug before the buds open and cooked with salt pork, they're good."

"Yup, my ma always dug them, but hell, were they ever bitter. I always had a hard time gettin' them down. My old man would give me an ugly look, and I'd force myself to eat them. Ma knew I didn't take to them so she didn't dig them very often.

"I was about in fifth grade when my ma really changed. My old man kept yellin' and beatin' on Ma so much she started gettin' real sickly lookin'. The only good thing he ever did for her was to put in a bathroom. Before that, we always went to the outhouse in the shed. It was freezin' in the winter and pure misery to sit on that cold hole. Maybe the bathroom was as much for my old man as it was for anybody. The only joy Ma got outta life at that point was when I read to her. I spent a lot of time in her room. My old man stopped sleepin' with her. It was like she wasn't even in the house, far as he was concerned. During the summer between sixth and seventh grades, I took care of her just about all the time. I helped her to the bathroom and brought her food. Far's I can remember my old man never took her to the doctor, the cheap bastard. Maybe he did, but I don't remember it. It was then that my old man brought Maria to Pine Mountain to live with us. She was only sixteen, but hell, she had all the makin's of a twenty-five-year-old. The old bastard started sleepin' with her the day she set foot in the house, the son of a bitch, right in front of my ma. Maybe she didn't care, but it bothered the hell outta me."

The truck enters the farmyard. He unloads the paint and supplies and she asks, "Would you please take care of the hens? I didn't do that yet."

"Yup, suppose I can do that, I ain't seen the chicken house for more than a month." He walks in to feed the hens and remarks, "She's tidied this place up, too. I guess those rats were costin' me a heap of money—what a lot of eggs!"

While carrying the eggs back to the house through the rain, Harold's reminded of an old saying: "A cold wet May means a barn full of hay." *Damn, that means a lot of hot, hard work ahead. 'Course, she and that Joe friend of hers had to get all the shit spread before this rain. We'll have more hay than ever. I'll watch a little television. It'll take my mind off hayin'.*

"Harold, would you help me move some things out of the kitchen so we can start painting?" As she asks, she unplugs the television.

"Woman, will you give me a minute to myself and plug that television back in?"

"What, to watch the test pattern?" She laughs.

"No! I was waitin' on the programs to begin."

"Well, okay, you watch television while I make us some dinner."

They eat in silence. She looks around the walls and tries to imagine what the painted kitchen will look like. Harold looks at the walls, too. *I wish we didn't have to paint.*

Shirley asks, "Would you help me move the refrigerator? We'll move the television and your chair into the front room for just a short time. Is that all right?"

"Yup, I guess so." They move the refrigerator and are surprised to find two dead rats. "Well, that's where all the stink's been comin' from. Now we don't need to paint."

They've decayed to the extent that they appear to be melted onto the floor with their fur spread and flattened. They have holes in their skull where there were once eyes. Shivers run up Shirley's back. She realizes that there were so many that these had migrated to the house looking for food. They stick slightly to the floor when she lifts them by their ropy tails. She wrinkles her nose from the stench and carries them out of the house and throws them across the road in some grass. She returns and confronts Harold who is sitting in his Morris chair, watching it rain from the west window. She stands at his feet with her hands on her hips. She firmly says, "Harold, I really want to paint this kitchen and I think you'll like it."

He just scowls at her with no response.

Steven begins fussing and Shirley comforts and feeds him in her room. Harold plugs the television back in and places it on the kitchen table. Shirley comes out of her room. "Oh, I thought…"

"Yup, you thought you wanted me to move some more stuff. Can't you relax a little and not work all the time? Damn, why do we have to paint this kitchen, anyway?"

She sits down next to him. "Remember our talk about being friends? We both do for each other, and it makes life easier."

"Oh, all right. I'll get off my ass. I'll help you, but remember I ain't never painted. I guess I'm a lazy bastard, and you run like an electric motor that never stops. What a pair!"

Shirley smiles and he chuckles. They continue the painting project while Steven lies awake in his clothesbasket on the kitchen table.

Harold remarks, "I warned you about me paintin'."

"I'll lay some cloths around so it won't matter if we drip some."

He says, "I was thinkin'. My old man, he'd never do anythin' like this."

"From what you've told me, I'm lucky not to have had a father like yours."

"Well, there was one time of the year when he was nice to me—in the fall durin' deer huntin'. We'd walk up to the five-and-five field and he'd be a changed man. The only time I heard him laugh was one day we were target practicin'. We set a tin can on a fence post and stepped back about two hundred feet. He drew his thirty-ought-six up to his shoulder, aimed, fired, and blew that can right away, first shot. He laughed then and said, 'Hell, I guess I'm a good shot.'

"I brought my pistol along, the Colt .45 that's in the gun case. 'Course that golden bullet is just for show. I made a holder for it, but it's a dud. That .45, the live shells, and the fake one are the only things I can remember him givin' me. I used all the ammunition that came with it target practicin' and never bought any more. That day I was with my old man, I tried and tried hittin' the can, but missed every time. I couldn't hold that pistol steady if I went to hell. Every time I pulled the trigger, I shut my eyes and the noise would scare the hell outta me. He was calm. Finally, he said, 'Here, try my thirty-ought-six.' I did, and after two or three tries, I hit the can. He actually said somethin' nice to me. 'Good shot, boy, good shot!' Then he sorta talked to me in a nice way. 'Ya know, son, when a buck comes outta the edge of the woods in the late afternoon ta feed, 'n' you're hidden in the grass, say, behind that hardhack growin' on that ledge there. It's a calm day 'n' he won't get a whiff of ya. He walks closer 'n' closer; ya've got the one chance 'n' ya know it, so it better be good. Ya hold that Colt steady, draw a bead on that buck, don't blink an eye, then pull the trigger, 'n' drop that son of a bitch right in his tracks. When ya can do that, son, ya know you're a man.'"

Shirley is painting with rapid strokes but stops. "You mean your father believed you had to kill before you became a man? He was a nut."

"Why, you ain't a believer in that thinkin'?"

"I'm certainly not a believer in killing!" Shirley lays the brush down and rivets her eyes on Harold. She lowers her voice as if capturing a special moment. "Here's the way I'd tell it. You're hiding in the grass behind the ledge where the hardhack grows. It's late afternoon; the sun is low in the sky. You're holding the .45 waiting for that buck. From the edge of the woods comes this big ten-pointer with a perfect rack of horns. He's grazing, but he lifts his head and nervously looks around. He's dark brown as the sun reflects off his glossy coat. He moves as gracefully as a ballet dancer, placing his front foot smoothly, and follows with a rear foot in a precise sequence. He looks right at you, his black nostrils flaring with each breath. He's close to you now, so close his eyes pierce you with their brightness. He stops—then freezes for a moment in a picture book stance. Everything about him has been created to perfection. You hold the pistol steady with both hands, draw a bead, and are about to squeeze the trigger, when all of a sudden you realize that this buck is about the most beautiful animal you've ever seen. To kill this incredible creation would be a terrible mistake. At that moment, you've become a man."

"So you don't like killin'?" He runs his brush along the wall and stops a glob that's sliding down to meet the wainscoting.

"No, I don't. Why kill beauty?" She takes up her brush and resumes painting.

"I guess I never saw a buck just like the one you told about." He forgets about his paint-smeared hands and scratches his chin with his left index finger.

"That's because you've never looked for beauty. It's there. You just don't see it."

"Now, take a woman." He stops painting and emphasizes his point with his brush, pointing it at Shirley. Paint drips on the kitchen table. "I can see beauty in a woman."

"I know you can, but you missed my point." She smiles. "You're getting paint all over the place and on yourself."

Harold scratches his thin hair and leaves smears of white on top of his head. He glances at Shirley. *There's about the most beautiful woman I've ever seen, but all hell would break loose if I told her so.*

"That summer when Maria came to the farm, I thought she was beautiful even with her rotten teeth. Whenever she opened her mouth or smiled, just about all you could see was black. Between each front tooth was a big round black hole, about birdshot size. Her back teeth were all broken off and black. She spent most days just nursin' toothaches. Hell, you could smell oil of cloves all over the house. That was just before my ma died, and just before I started seventh grade.

"One mornin' I come to my ma's room and she wasn't there. She'd died in the night. Maria said my old man carried her to his truck and took her to the Sunset Funeral Home. The cheap bastard, all he gave her was a pine box.

"He looked more sour and ugly that mornin' durin' chores. We never usually talked in the barn, but when I asked him where Ma was, all he said was, 'She died last night.' We milked by hand then, and I think there were more tears in my pail than there was milk. He wasn't hearin' me cry. I hid it.

"The next day in the afternoon there we were, my old man, Maria, and I standin' by the grave. What a sorry lot we must have been. Two men were throwin' dirt on her wooden box. The man that owned the Sunset Funeral Home asked if someone was goin' to say a few words. My old man just said, 'Naw, cover her up.'"

Harold stands like a statue with the paintbrush in his hand dripping on the cloth. He's in a trance recalling that day. "Tears were rollin' down my face like a thundercloud had just opened up. My old man gave me a look that could have killed. I felt alone and cold even it bein' as warm as it was. Yup—I stood all alone and cold."

Shirley can see his tears as he stands recalling that day. "I can't imagine. Maybe I'm better for not knowing who my parents were." She has covered a large square of the wall with the off-white paint. She stands back to check for streaks left by her brush.

He continues slopping the paint on his section of the wall. "I changed a lot that summer. I grew tall, my voice changed, and I was sure sad. Come school time, I didn't want to go. My old man drove the fear in me right to my very bones. 'I want folks to know I've got myself a smart kid. Ya git ta school 'n' do good work, ya hear?' I tried, I really tried, but my whole life had changed. I wanted Ma so bad, and I was havin' these wild dreams. I wanted things the way they used to be. Even as bad as life was with Ma, sick and all, I felt better when she was alive.

"One mornin' I went to the barn to do chores; but this particular mornin', I told my old man I was sick and had to stay home. He didn't say nothin'. I finished chores and went to the house. It was fall, still warm enough for me to sleep in the upstairs north bedroom. I took off my shirt and bib-overalls and crawled into bed. Curled up in a ball and just cried. I was in a world all my own just cryin'. I heard the floorboards creak, and looked up. There was Maria standin' right by my bed—not wearin' a stitch of clothing. I wasn't believin' what I saw. I'd never seen a woman without clothes before, and I had no idea what she was up to. She pulled back the covers and got into bed with me. Her warm body next to mine felt so good and nice. She hugged me." Harold is sitting with his paintbrush tipped up, telling his story. He's in another world. Paint is flowing down the brush onto the handle, about to reach his hand.

Shirley is not comfortable with the direction his story is heading. "Gee, Harold, you've covered quite an area with your painting. You should brush out some of those globs you left, though. Isn't the room looking a lot better?"

"Yeah, if you ask me I'm makin' a hell of a mess." He continues in dreamland, with words flowing like milk from a pail. There is no stopping him. "She hugged me some more, rubbin' her softness into my chest. She was breathin' hard, real hard. All I could smell was oil of cloves. I was cold but her hands were warm and sweaty. She took me on a wild ride all right, to a place I'd never been before. Yeah—from that day on, my life took on new meanin'. At first it seemed kinda strange, but in a few months it seemed okay. She kept sayin', 'You ain't to tell your old man.' She made it sound bad, but I thought it was good, the best thing that had ever happened to me."

Shirley squirms thinking that Harold is telling the ugliest story she's ever heard. This woman was like no one she's ever known. What a pathetic life this house has seen.

"Maria picked me up every day after school. My grades were good now. We'd go into the house every afternoon right after we got home, and we'd go to my room. My old man was always workin' in the woods or in the barn. He never knew. Right from the first day, she always made me wear a rubber. She'd always say, 'No kids for me.' I'd go to the bathroom afterwards and clean up, get dressed and head out to start chores, and she'd start cookin' for supper. It was like a short break in the day that made our lives worth livin'."

He doesn't stop talking, but by this point he's speckled and spotted from head to toe with off-white paint. "I was enterin' Huntersville High for my freshman year. A lot of farm kids never went to high school in Huntersville 'cause farm kids were treated like shit. And I guess we stunk like it, too. The principal, Mr. Gifford, and most teachers made us feel like we came from the pits of hell.

"One good thing happened, though—Junior Campbell and I started bein' friends. Junior was the class clown, dared to do anythin' to get a laugh. He wasn't able to read or write. Every time he wrote, he tried to start ass-backward. In every class it happened that I usually sat behind him, in front of him or in a row beside him. I did his homework and fed him test answers; and to pay me back, he was my friend. He was tied to me like a baby lamb to its mother. He'd feed on my answers all day long."

Shirley breaks in, "I think it's time I got ready for chores, and I need to change and feed Steven."

"I'll tell you what, my hand feels darn good. I'll milk tonight after we get the cows in, and you can get supper and keep on paintin'."

Shirley glances at the job he's been doing. "Gee, that sounds like a good idea!"

Harold looks in the kitchen mirror. "Look at me. I'm plastered with paint. I ain't likin' this job much. Maybe you can get this kitchen back in shape faster without me."

Shirley laughs. "Don't bother to grain the cows. Joe can do that when he comes." She realizes he'd feed all the cows the same amount—and not enough.

She's excited thinking of seeing Joe and wants to paint as much as she can so he will be surprised to see what has been accomplished. He comes late, around six. He walks through the entry and is, as usual, the pleasant friendly Joe. They hug and kiss. "Harold says you want me to grain the cows?"

"Would you? You know Harold. He'd give them as little as possible."

"Wow! Look at the kitchen, and no dead smell. This will really look great when you're finished. Oh, by the way, I'm sorry, but I can't come again until Friday night. The extension service staff is driving to Burlington for a conference that will last all week."

Shirley is crestfallen.

"Hey, what's wrong with you?"

Shirley looks into his eyes. "I guess I'm beginning to think more of you and miss you more than I ever thought." She wants to ask if Dottie Candy is going to the conference, too, but decides against it. She doesn't want Joe to think of her as being jealous, which she has to admit she is.

Harold, Joe, and Shirley sit around the supper table in a disorderly kitchen. Harold looks at the ceiling and walls. None of the wainscoting has been painted. "We get the bottom half of the wall painted and we'll be done."

Shirley hates to break the news. "We've got to put on a second coat."

"What? Damn, I can't believe it. You're too fussy."

"It'll look a lot better with two coats."

"This is just why I ain't thinkin' it's a good idea for me to let you run the farm. I'd be hog-tied and whiplashed every wakin' minute. I know, we're supposed to be friends. Golly, if I haven't heard that lecture once too many times."

"I can see my offer of managing the farm won't work. Let's drop the subject. Forget I even suggested it." She jumps up from the table carrying dishes toward the sink. She whips around and returns to the table with a scarlet-red face. She elevates her voice. "I'll tell you this Harold Tully; we're making some improvements here so we can live in a decent home! I want to be proud of Pine Mountain and as it stands now, I can't say as I am! I love it here, but I'm sure not proud of it!" Her voice goes higher. "I'm not doing a half-baked job on this kitchen! It's going to look nice whether you help me or not!" She returns to the sink with plates and throws them into the dishpan to the sound of a loud clatter. Back to Joe and Harold, she presses both hands on the table for support, and leans forward into Harold's face. The veins are popping on her neck. "Sure, go ahead and run this place, do as you mind to." She yells, "But it's going to be done well!"

Harold sits up straight to get some distance from her. He growls, "Hell, if we're honest about the whole situation, you already run it."

Joe remains silent, and then he suggests, "I've got some time to help Shirley with this painting. Why don't I pour you a good stiff drink and you can go into the front room with a warm blanket and watch television?"

"You know, Joe, that's the best idea that's come my way all day. I need some peace and quiet away from the likes of Miss Power Woman." Joe helps Harold get settled and comes back to the kitchen.

Shirley says, "You're a lifesaver. I get so mad at him. I just don't know what to do sometimes." She shoves the kitchen table away from the wall for more room to paint. The legs stutter and squawk when they move across the worn linoleum. She picks up a magazine that's on the floor and throws it. It skids across the oilcloth.

Joe watches her. "Don't get so upset. He thinks you're great, but he just lacks your energy and drive."

Shirley walks around the table and goes toward the sink. "He's a little lazy, too."

"Well, yes, I was trying to be kind. Life will never run smoothly between you two, but you'll make out fine."

Shirley sighs, calming down from her high emotions. "Gosh, I wish I had your confidence." As they talk, they wash the dishes together and generously share their affection. The usual kisses are longer and warmer and the hugs closer and tighter. Joe picks up Steven and walks to the bedroom to get him ready for the night. Shirley starts painting, but feels the need to be near Joe. She goes to her room, shuts the door, and picks Steven up to nurse him while pulling on Joe's arm, wanting him to sit next to her. "I've never heard you talk about your folks." Shirley turns toward Joe. She can see a strained expression on his face and senses pain in his haltingly slow response.

"I guess—I guess—they embarrass me."

Shirley presses, "What do you mean?"

"Oh, you know my father's values. Both Mom and Dad are into the country club life and—and you can imagine what goes with it."

She senses the whole subject is off-limits. She stops questioning, and stands to put Steven to bed. Joe sits in a daze. She can see she's stirred in him the whole subject of family. She sits on his lap and kisses him. "I'm going to miss you this next week."

Joe responds warmly. "Last week was really special."

She continues kissing him, rubbing his back, then pulling his shirttail free, sliding a warm hand to feel his bareness. He kisses her ear and whispers, "What a wonderful armful I have—you thrill me." She pushes with her foot that rests on the floor and he easily lays flat-out on the bed. Their emotions begin to bounce breathlessly between each other. She presses herself against his chest. She feels a charge go through her, a strange new sensation. What seemed unthinkable only days before is now possible.

The whole wild process is moving too quickly for Shirley to stop and analyze future consequences. She feels no nagging pull or familiar twist in her stomach. She is relieved and pleased that she has discovered this new dimension of herself. He unbuttons her pants and he helps her slip them off. His hand runs up and down her smooth legs. He stands and drops his pants and throws them. His shirt is next.

She is delirious, discovering how lovers love. All of a sudden Harold's story and his relationship with Maria take on a different meaning.

Nature is parading its renewal before them every day—birds building nests and flowers being pollinated. She often hears the grouse thumping out its mating call. We, too, can answer that call and answer our hidden desire.

They lie on the bed under the one light suspended from the ceiling by a twisted cord. It is covered by a bonnet shade with a dangling brass pull chain. The dim light casts shadows across their near nakedness.

A light rain drums on the tin roof as she moves to her side and he pushes himself against her. He gently rolls her on her back. She loves his honest face, his hairy chest, and arms that she knows will never force her. She breathlessly anticipates the inevitable, while looking up at him,

Suddenly, he stops and sits on the edge of the bed. "What are we doing?"

"What's wrong?" She sits up on the bed with her legs curled beneath her. She's at eye level with his shoulders.

"I think we got swept away." He has his head in his hands acting troubled.

She is hanging her arm over his shoulder and resting her chin on him. He recalls, "It seems like only a few weeks ago we were talking about a barn fan and just a moment ago, I saw us standing at the alter."

Shirley can hear the rain pelting the window and through the dim light sees small rivulets, running down the glass. She pulls away in anger. "And whose fault is this? The dancing, coming to my room—who came up with those ideas? It sure wasn't me!"

She immediately calms her anger. She still wants him, and knows she loves him. But at this moment, there's a separation, and all the persuasion and pleading can't pull them back together. She's made a big mistake, being too willing, with no commitment.

Joe suggests calmly, too calmly, "Let's paint the kitchen."

Shirley and Joe work late into the night painting the second coat. He repaints the ceiling and she works on the walls. They talk very little. Harold comes to the kitchen. "You two have been paintin' up a storm. How's about me milkin' in the mornin' so you can paint the bottom part of the wall?"

Shirley remarks, "That sounds great, Harold. Maybe by tomorrow night we can have this place back in order. Joe, I think you should go along now. I feel guilty for keeping you. Thanks so much for the help!" Shirley feels bone-tired. They walk outside, and she gives Joe a memorable kiss, or at least one she hopes he won't forget.

She doesn't sleep well, dreaming nightmares of Joe. She wakes at her usual morning hour and is drained and emotionally exhausted, but she and Harold go about their work. The wainscoting covers very easily, but it needs two coats in some places. She paints the wall behind the refrigerator and on the side of the room by Harold's Morris chair and has the remaining painting nearly half done when Steven wakes.

She continues to feel tired and worn-out, but forces herself to forget about the previous night and continues to do her work. The dirty diapers have piled into what looks to her to be a mountain, but she pushes herself forward—doing the laundry, feeding the hens, and collecting the eggs.

Harold is milking, smoking his pipe, and seems to be enjoying himself.

She asks, "How's it going this morning?"

"Good. Cows are milkin' like hell. Nothin' like that good green grass." Shirley grains the cows and helps him finish.

"We've got a lot of eggs to grade before tomorrow. Do you want to do that while I finish the painting?"

"Oh, I guess so. Gradin' eggs has always been woman's work, but I'll do anythin' to get outta paintin'."

After breakfast Shirley and Harold put the television and the refrigerator back in their places. He sits at the kitchen table weighing each egg on the scale, its hand indicating: extra-large, large, medium, and small. When Shirley first brought eggs to the market, the manager weighed several cartons, and they were all heavier than the minimum weight required. Consequently, she was given a good price. The money paid was more than enough to buy the week's groceries. There was always extra money to buy what she thought of as fun things for the house. She had cartons printed that read HAROLD TULLY'S STRICTLY FRESH EGGS, HUNTERSVILLE, VT. Harold thought it was a good idea to buy the printed cartons because his name was on the box.

While she paints, she watches Harold. If the scale reads between medium and large, he seems to always put the egg in the box of large eggs. Sometimes he just looks at the egg and puts it in what he thinks is the appropriate carton.

Part of the job of grading eggs is cleaning any dirt or hen droppings smeared on the shells. She is bothered by his sloppiness in letting dirty eggs pass as being clean enough. She finds herself watching him more than painting, and realizes she's made a mistake letting him grade the eggs. She makes a real effort to not show her disappointment.

She comments, "There should be about forty dozen."

"Golly, what a mindless job."

"Harold, don't cheat on those weights! It's very important that you protect your good name. You know people buy Harold Tully's eggs because they get a good deal, and you know weights are checked." Harold sits in a sulk for a few minutes, and then starts doing a better job.

She's finished the second coat on the north and west walls. She steps back in the middle of the kitchen. "Don't you like the room, Harold?"

"Well, it does look a lot better. Hell, gradin' these eggs reminds me of Junior Campbell foolin' around—not doin' things just right. He was somethin' else in school."

Shirley sighs. *Now, more stories of Harold's morbid past.*

"Junior was sent almost every day to the principal's office where he sat in a small room they made up special for bad actors. Every time he was sent, Principal Gifford made him sit in front of a plaster head of George Washington. What do you call them? You know, you've seen them, Shirley."

"They're called busts."

He laughs. "I should've remembered that word. Well, Junior had to say this bunch of history about Washington every time he was sent to Gifford's office. The bust sat on a table right beside the principal's desk. Junior had to pull up a chair, look old George in the face within about six inches of the thing. He'd say somethin' like, 'I'm very sorry for my foolish ways. You were a great man, the father of our country, our first president. You fought bravely durin' the Revolution. If I'm goin' to amount to anythin' like you, I've got to change my ways. I'm ashamed I was sent to Mr. Gifford's office.'"

Shirley is painting with rapid strokes near her bedroom door. She feels exhausted, but pushes herself to complete the room as Harold drones on with his story.

"Then Junior would go and sit in the little room next to the principal's office for most of the day, and sometimes until after school. Near the end of his freshman year, Junior knew as much about how that school ran as anybody. He would stand on his desk and listen to all of Gifford's conversations through the heat register. Come June, the next to the last day of school, the final grades were figured. At the end of school, certificates were handed out to the students with the highest marks. Junior heard Gifford say, 'I can't accept this report. Here we have Harold Tully receivin' the highest-grade score for his class. This kid is a clod; he's not from one of our better families in town. Besides, he lives with that awful Maria Fullum we expelled. This makes a mockery outta the superior schoolin' we give our village students. We'll just move his name down a few places; no one will know.' Junior told me that and was I pissed—that son of a bitch.

"The next year I worked even harder. I was bound I was goin' to get back at that bastard somehow. Well, June rolled around. We took our finals, and I did good on them. That mornin' after exams we went to our homerooms. Junior went by the teacher's desk and slipped a tack in her seat. She was standin' and leadin' us in our openin' exercises for the day. She yelled at Junior to get back to his seat. He did just as she told while she went to her desk and kinda settled herself in her seat. It took a while for that tack to get through her corset, I guess, because there was a delayed reaction. In a minute or so she yelled and jumped about two feet up from her chair and was pickin' that tack outta her ass and at the same time screamin' at Junior to go to the principal's office."

Harold carries the apple boxes filled with egg cartons to the entry for storage until Wednesday. He stops midway on one of his trips, and rests the eggs on the edge of the wood box. He continues talking to Shirley, since she is now painting in back of the stove with her back turned.

"Junior, as he told it, sat in the detention room and waited for Principal Gifford to return. Miss Gibbons, the office secretary, was figurin' the final grades. When Gifford walked in, Miss Gibbons went to his office and locked the door. Junior could hear her clearly say, 'Harold Tully is by far the best student in his class. I don't think it's fair to him not to be recognized.'

"Gifford said something like, 'There has to be a reason—no extra activities. He's not a well-rounded student; that's the reason.'

"Miss Gibbons simply said, 'I don't know, but the numbers don't lie.'

"Gifford remarked, 'I'll explain his achievement when I present the award.'

"The assembly was held, and awards were given, and then the highest grade totals for each class were given with a certificate. When my certificate was handed out Gifford said that although I had gotten the highest grade total, I wasn't a very complete student. Just then Junior let out this loud, 'Boo.' Gifford looked up and you could have heard a pin drop. Golly, that made me happy he did that.

"When Maria picked me up after school, the weather was warm, and was she ever showin' off her spring finery. I was happy to see her, but more happy with my certificate. I could show it to my old man, and make him happy for a change."

Shirley inwardly groans. *Here comes some more of Harold's love life.*

Harold stands in a trance having just closed the entry door. "Maria was sayin', 'Ya know, the bathroom toilet plugged this mornin'—run all over the floor. Your old man's been a-workin' on it all day. I dunno why he's been fiddlin' around at the end of the pipe down in the pasture. He's got this old rusty pail in his hand. Looks like he's diggin' for fish worms, pokin' around with a stick.'

"We drove by the pasture and my old man was nowhere to be seen. We ran into the house, raced upstairs. I put my certificate on my bureau and stripped. I sat on an old oak wooden chair in the center of the room and Maria sat with her arms wrapped around my neck and the heels of her bare feet clingin' to the chair legs. The vapors from Maria's oil of cloves filled me and fed me like sweet drops of honey rollin' off her tongue. Just then the bedroom door crashed open. Son of a bitch, there stood my old man! He had rage in his eyes beyond belief. Here we were, caught red-handed. Slammin' the rusty pail in the middle of the floor, he left. We were both buck naked lookin' into the pail. Maria spoke first. 'Goddamn, that's one hell of a lotta rubbers.' I said, 'That there means one hell of a lotta trouble—big trouble.' I shut the door.

"The pail was two-thirds full of Maria's brand. I was tryin' to get dressed as fast as I could. Maria wasn't afraid at all. She was sorta laughin'. 'Your old man burns his in the wood stove. I see you flush yours down the toilet.' I could hear him boundin' up the stairs. Maria ran to me in the corner of the room. He was runnin' so fast that when the door crashed open, he tripped on the threshold and fell dead force with all his weight. His forehead smashed on the edge of the oak chair. His thirty-ought-six slammed to the floor, and he rolled to one side and let out one long groan. The bucket tipped over, draining its stink on the floor. Maria already had the gun in her hand, yellin', 'I'm shootin' the bastard.'

"I'm hollerin', 'No, no, he's my old man! He's gotta see my certificate.'

"She sat back in the chair and laughed hysterical-like. She was still bare, showin' her beautiful lean body. She had the prettiest face with long silky blond hair. There she sat with the gun lying on her lap. The fire that was in me just seconds before was now snuffed out. Maria was just a body now that needed clothes. I fumbled to my old man's side. 'See the certificate I got in school for bein' smart like you told me to be?'

"Blood was runnin' outta my old man's nose and the corner of his mouth. I was in a panic. His eyes had lost their fury. They were now just eyes. 'Maria, you've got to help me get him to a doctor.'

'That old bastard; let the son of a bitch die. I had ta sleep with the miserable grump for near three 'n' a half years. I'll be glad ta see the old puke dead.'

"I couldn't believe what she was sayin'. I yelled, 'But he's my old man! He ain't seen my certificate. Maybe he'd be happy if he saw my certificate.' I was draggin' him outta the bedroom, leavin' a trail of blood mixed with sewer water and rubbers. My heart was racin' and my gut felt like I was goin' to puke myself."

Harold continues standing at the entry door, his voice packed with emotion while talking to the backside of Shirley. She's touching up the paint job along the wainscoting.

"I grabbed his shoulders, swung him around, and pulled him downstairs. On each stair his shoes dropped with a loud thump. It sounded like a hammer bangin' in my head. I ran and got an old mattress, laid it in the back of the truck, and pulled him onto it, and then I put a quilt over him.

"His face was now lookin' blue. I hadn't drove much, but I put that pedal to the floor down Pine Mountain and damn near lost it on the hair-pin turn, but made it anyway to Huntersville to see the doctor. All I could think of was to show him my certificate. That would somehow make things right. I ran into the doc's office and he come out and checked my old man. 'Son, your father's dead.' I couldn't believe it. 'Take him up the street to the funeral home.'"

Harold slumps his shoulders as if living the very moment of his father's death.

"Drivin' home, I was thinkin'—the farm, the cows, it was all mine, and I didn't want it. It was all kinda a repeat. My old man took over young, and now I was goin' to have to run the farm. At the house, Maria was dancin' around. Hell, you'd think she'd been let outta prison. 'Hey, let's me 'n' ya go in on the old man's bed. It's yourn now, ya know.'"

His voice reaches a higher level and he turns and walks to where Shirley is following the top of the wainscoting around the room.

"I yelled, 'Damn it, my old man's dead! I've got to milk cows, shovel shit, feed hens, collect eggs and, bastard, hayin's comin' on quick.'

"Maria yelled, 'Ya goddamn fool! Sell the place. Ya 'n' me could have some real fun with the money.'

"I pleaded, 'No, he was my old man! He'd want me to keep the farm. That would make him proud of me.'

"The next afternoon Maria and I stood by the grave. The wooden box was lowered into the hole. The funeral director asked if I wanted to say a few words. I told him, 'No.' But, I wanted to put the certificate on the coffin. We watched the dirt bein' thrown into the grave and the certificate was covered along with my old man."

Harold walks toward the west window and sits in his chair at the table and looks at Shirley. She stands with paintbrush in hand in the middle of the room, critically examining the completed paint job. He says, "Well. I poured my guts out tellin' you all my life and you act as if you didn't give a damn."

Shirley is visibly pained by his comment and looks at him in sympathy. She sits and grabs his hand that's resting on the table. "I think you have a very sad story. Thanks for sharing it with me." She draws a deep breath. "I guess I was working too hard to finish, not giving enough attention to what you were saying."

Steven begins to cry. Shirley gets up from the table and goes to her boy. "Do you feel better? I think you do." She picks him up and goes to her room to change him.

Harold is still sitting at the table when she comes to the kitchen. He says, "I want you to hear the rest of my story."

Shirley sits at the table, taking in the view from the west window. "Okay." She feels sorry for Harold, and doesn't care to hear anymore; but as a friend, it's important to listen to a story that she's quite sure has never been told.

"Maria wasn't happy on the farm anymore. I knew that. She thought we'd be in the house foolin' around all day. I guess the work and the farm just made me change too much. I still loved her, but I was no match for her. I tried to think of ways to make her want to stay; maybe give her things she had never had before.

"One morning she was nursin' another toothache. I said, 'Go to the dentist and get those teeth pulled and get some false ones. I'll pay for it. Get rid of that black mouth of yours.' So she did. I gave her money to buy clothes, too. Hell, with a new mouth and fancy clothes, damn, was she a looker! Instead of her wantin' to stay, she was rarin' to go all the more. She asked to take the truck nights. Throwin' an old horsehair mattress in the back of the truck, she was gone. I'd hear her come home around midnight, one o'clock, all sweet smellin' and lay beside me as hot as a poker. She was always tellin' me I was her favorite and I knew she meant it. She had her freedom, and I had my Maria.

"In the mornin' after chores, I'd come to breakfast. She'd have on a light blue robe that just lit up her eyes. It didn't matter what the food tasted like. I just loved lookin' at her.

"But then it all changed. I come in from chores one mornin' and she had her coat on and was standin' next to her suitcase. 'I want ya ta take me ta Huntersville. I met a guy last night 'n' I'm goin' ta Albany, ta the big time. Make a lot of money, move ta a big house, throw big parties 'n' live a hell of a life.'

"I was pathetic. 'You ain't lovin' me no more?' I asked.

'Not up on this goddamn mountain. If ya want ta come I'll take ya.'

"I told her, 'I can't, my old man would want me to work the farm.' Well, that was the end of Maria. I cried for a week after she left; and to be honest, I guess I ain't never really got over it—a woman I loved, walkin' out on me." He ends the sentence in a whisper as if he really, to this day, can't believe the ending.

Shirley sees the tears running down his face. Wrinkles have deepened around his mouth and on his forehead—lines of sorrow that are all deeper than usual. She's looking at a man's face that appears much older than his years.

She realizes she was heartless not wanting to listen to his pain. "It's too bad you lost Maria, but it sounds as though she wasn't faithful to you. Eventually that would have caused you to be heartbroken." She inhales the paint smell again. "Maybe a newly painted kitchen will mean a fresh start for you after all these years."

"Yup, I know Maria wasn't tied to me, but she left. You can't bring back what you've lost."

Joe crosses Shirley's mind and she feels a wave of panic, but tries to repress it.

Harold looks around the room and really can't believe what a change has taken place in his kitchen. The late afternoon sun strikes the west window and floods the room with bright light. It glistens off the shine of the new paint. He smiles. "It looks damn nice!"

"Thanks for saying that." She glances at the clock. "Looks to be chore time. Would you help me tie up the cows?"

"Yup."

HUNTERSVILLE WEEKLY

May 17, 1948

Driblets of Honeydew
By Honeydew Mullen

Perry Bent has announced that he is a dealer for the Universal Four Wheel Drive Jeep. He claims that this vehicle is the answer to the small farmer's needs. It can be the family's transportation plus do most of what a small farm tractor can do such as: plow, harrow, saw wood, and plow snow.

The Huntersville Elementary School will hold its May Day celebration on the third Tuesday of this month. It has been postponed due to poor weather and the late blooming of spring flowers. Yours truly has been asked to lead the dance around the May Pole. I hope I can keep up with the kids.

Marty Stebbins, owner of Stebbins Hardware, has been warned by the Board of Selectmen that on Saturday nights there is too big a crowd gathered on the sidewalk watching television in his store window. They're requesting that he shut it off by ten PM. The Huntersville Temperance Society has reported drinking among some of the viewers. Public drinking is strictly illegal.

Louise Durkee, Huntersville's health officer, is making unwanted news. She claims she is being singled out by our town police officer for giving him dietary suggestions. Gabby Pilford ticketed her for running a stop sign at the corner of Elm and Main St. She claims she was hurrying home because she had two pies in the oven. Her appeal to the selectmen was denied.

CHAPTER FIFTEEN

The time is four-thirty. The morning light is just beginning to show through the pines as Shirley walks to the barn, reflecting on her and Harold's relationship. Today she hopes he accepts what she's planning, but she dreads the whole scene. She wishes Joe could be with them to help humor the situation, like only he can.

The previous evening the cows were let out for the first time for night grazing. As she walks through the milk room, she leaves Steven sleeping in his carriage, placing it near the milk cooler, so he'll be safe when the cows enter the barn. She opens the barn door, walks down the ramp, turns toward the pasture, and calls, "Come, Boss, come, Boss."

The cows are barely visible. The early-morning light hasn't revealed their places, as they lie on a green carpet of new grass, waiting for her call. A few get up and head toward the barn. They've calmed down since turnout time. She no longer needs help in tying them up. She locks them in their stanchions as they take their stalls. There is no rush; she enjoys seeing each as an individual while they lumber up the ramp and amble toward their stall. They know where to go, since they've stood in the same place for all their milking life.

She begins thinking through her day as it is Wednesday, errand and market day.

Thinking of The Market, she must remember to buy special ingredients to bake something tasty for Harold. The saying "Good food is the way to a man's heart" is certainly true in his case. He loves her cooking, especially if it's something sweet.

Shirley looks forward to seeing Attorney Iverson to discuss further the possibility of having the help of a young girl. She mentioned the matter the week before, and he promised to give her inquiry further thought.

Harold enters the barn to help finish up chores and to load the milk. Shirley walks from the barn, pushing Steven in his carriage, but stops to wait for him and to observe the new emerging life of spring. Robins are busy building a nest in the pine trees, picking up dead grass, flying with long bits of nest material fluttering as they dart toward the trees. Barn swallows swoop, collecting bits and pieces for their nests in the hay barn. The view to the west reveals all sorts of fresh new greens from the newly developed leaves. Harold walks up from the milk house to meet her. He is smoking his pipe, and takes his handkerchief from his back pocket. He wipes his brow. "These cows are makin' me work. Seven cans is the most I've ever loaded."

Shirley smiles and says nothing. He notices her expression. "Oh, I know I've got you to thank for bein' damn good with the cows—what are you standin' here for? I mean just standin'. You sick or somethin'?"

"I'm taking a minute to enjoy the beauty of spring and waiting for you."

He takes the handles of the carriage and pushes, while he talks to Steven. "Your old lady has somethin' a-brewin' in her head. She ain't never waited for me before."

She laughs. "Don't get nervous, I was just trying to be nice."

He smiles. "I know, that's what I'm worried about."

She cooks the usual breakfast, in between attending to Steven and grading the remaining eggs. The night before she made a list of needs and a grain order for Harold to buy at Butson's. He is listening to the morning news and reports to Shirley, "Looks like Governor Dewey will prob'ly be the Republican candidate for president. He'll beat the hell outta Truman. That no-good Truman, he's sendin' all our money over to rebuild Europe. The Fair Deal he calls it—some deal."

Shirley barely listens as she hands him the Butson's feed order and list. "Your breakfast is ready."

He steps to the table, reading the list. "Nine bags of fourteen percent? Last week it was twenty percent. I think the cows prob'ly have as hard a time with you always wantin' to change things as I do."

"Joe says the new grass is high in protein, and that they don't need twenty percent when they're grazing this time of year. He says it's just a waste. Fourteen percent is cheaper, too."

"Yup, it is; but I always fed sixteen year 'round. What's this? You want Bag Balm?"

"That doesn't cost much. I'd like to try it. Just being turned out, the cows have chapped teats."

"I've used lard for all these years, and now we have to use Bag Balm?" He continues reading the list. "And this? You want vegetable seeds?"

"I want to have a garden." Shirley sweeps her hair into place.

"And fifty pounds of seed potatas? Golly, you're gonna send me to the poor-house."

"Oh, you exaggerate. Your last milk check must have looked darn good."

"It was a good check. You sure know how to make me feel beholden to you."

"Remember, you loaded seven cans this morning."

"Oh, you're doin' one hell of a job. Really, do you want a garden?" he asks almost helplessly. "Golly, to have a good one, it takes a lotta work."

"I know it does, but you'll like the fresh vegetables. If you would only get it plowed and harrowed, I'll do all the rest."

"Plow? Plow—I ain't plowed ever in my whole life."

"Well, I saw a plow in the shed, and a set of horse-drawn harrows, too."

"They were my old man's. I ain't never used them."

"It can't be too hard. I'll drive the horses, and you hold the plow."

"Huh, us two plowin' would make quite the picture! That'll look good enough to be on the cover of some farm magazine."

She laughs.

He looks at his finger. "I guess it's healed enough to work at plowin'."

"I'll tell you what. You pick out a favorite vegetable, and we'll plant it."

He sits for a few moments in thought and then suggests, "You know turnips? My ma used to have a garden, and she always planted turnips. Damn, are they ever good to eat in the fall. Turnips and Green Mountain potatas; they're the best. They're, about the mealiest ones you can eat. Yup, I'll buy fifty pounds of Green Mountains."

I can't believe it. He's actually enjoying the idea of having a garden. On the way to Huntersville, I'll mention the idea of having a young girl to help.

They load the eggs that have been stored in the pantry and travel to the milk stand. He backs up to it. Zack and Alice are coming in their truck.

Shirley hasn't seen Alice since eating at the Coleses'. She gets out of the truck carrying Steven and lets Harold unload the truck. Alice rolls down the window. "Hi, Shirley." She appears gray and tired, but beams. "How are you? What a lovely jacket!"

"Isn't it nice? Harold gave it to me."

"He did? That's new for him. He's never given anyone anything."

"How have you been, Alice?"

"Good, just tired of all the work there is to do. Zack doesn't agree, but I think we ought to sell the herd and have him go to college. I just don't see a future in staying on a twenty-five-cow farm. We're in a narrow valley with no nearby land to expand. Frankly, there just isn't enough money in this business to hire the kind of help we need. I'm not sure it would be wise to expand even if we could."

Shirley remarks, "That's too bad."

"Zack keeps talking about having you come to work for us, but I understand if you just don't want to."

"I like Pine Mountain, and the chance Harold gives me to sort of manage the farm."

Alice looks at Shirley with searching eyes, so that she knows the woman is about to lead into a delicate subject. "Zack—he—he has deep feelings for you."

"Zack can only be my friend; I'm just not ready for anything more." Shirley tries to remain calm and casual, but she fails miserably in the telling of an out-and-out lie. Her face is getting red as Alice looks at her and through her. *She's too sharp a woman and knows I'm not telling the truth.* Shirley blurts, "I'm sorry, that's not true. Right now there's someone special in my life."

"Oh, really!" Alice's eyes rivet on Shirley. "Who's the lucky fellow?"

Shirley is intimidated by her and angry that now she is backed into a corner. She realizes Alice might have ties to Attorney Iverson, and she also realizes Joe might not appreciate her letting people know of their connection. Shirley regains her composure. "I'm sorry, Alice, but I'd rather not say."

"Okay, pardon me for asking." Alice looks straight ahead and loses her smile. The lines on her face deepen into a stern expression.

Shirley wants to rescue what good feelings the two might have toward each other. "I think your idea of Zack going away to school is a good one. It would be great for him to get out and meet people."

Alice remains cool. "It's very difficult, my dear, to plan someone's life."

Shirley remarks, "Of course that's right; I'll see you Alice. Harold is ready to go."

Alice doesn't give Shirley the satisfaction of eye contact and lapses into a tired stern demeanor, but does say, "Good-bye."

Riding in the truck on the way to town, Harold seems agitated and angry. He takes his pipe out of his pocket and sticks it in his mouth. Shirley says nothing. He yanks it out of his mouth and starts to load it from his can of Prince Albert. The truck is weaving considerably as they travel along. He has one hand on the wheel, and is holding the bowl of his pipe with the same hand. The can is in his other hand. He is shaking the tobacco into the pipe. The shreds spill on the steering wheel, in the pipe, and on the floorboard.

"Harold!" Shirley screams. "Watch the road!"

The truck is headed for the ditch. He yanks the wheel just in time. Striking a match on the open ashtray, he starts to smoke while rolling down his window.

Shirley's temper erupts. "What are you doing? You know I hate that pipe smoke, especially with Steven in the truck." Steven begins to cry. "He's telling you something, do you hear? And your driving—I hope we reach town alive! What's wrong with you?"

Harold throws his pipe on the dashboard of the truck. "That Zack's an asshole. He noticed we're shippin' as much milk as they are and I know that burned the kid. He looked at those cans as if he couldn't believe his eyes. He's makin' you out to be some kinda wonder-woman. Why hell, Zack thinks you walk on water and he's makin' me out a fool for never doin' as well. Of course you get all the credit."

"What Zack thinks doesn't matter to me, and it shouldn't to you."

"Yup, well, that's easy for you to say. You're in the driver's seat, I ain't."

Harold backs up to The Market's loading platform to leave the eggs. The stressful trip into town has ruined her chances of mentioning a girl. Maybe an extra tasty supper would help, and they can talk afterward. While shopping, Shirley notices waxed turnips and buys one. She settles up for the eggs, and has a few dollars' change.

She keeps the change for extra items and figures it is her money to spend the way she sees fit. The previous week she saw a nine-by-twelve linoleum at the furniture store.

It had a light and dark brown pattern that would blend perfectly with the beige and browns in the kitchen. Since the furniture store was right next to The Market, she bought the linoleum and asked the store clerk to leave it on the loading platform in back of the store. She parks the carriage and leaves the groceries in back of The Market and walks toward Attorney Iverson's office. Holding Steven, she enters the alley, opens the side door, and climbs the stairs. Seeing Attorney Iverson on Wednesday has become a regular routine, but she is a little anxious this day, hoping that he knows of a young girl to help, at the very least during haying season.

Shirley enters Iverson's office. He's sitting at his desk intent on reading a legal document. She clears her throat. "Have you given any more thought concerning a girl that could come and live on Pine Mountain?"

Iverson looks up and slides the document aside. "Are you sure you want to mother another child, and don't just want a babysitter?"

Shirley pauses. *Now he'll stand and begin that awful pacing.* "I'm sure—Mrs. Perkins was like a mother to me, she gave me a lot, and I would like to do the same for someone else. At the same time, I need someone to watch Steven when he starts to creep and move around." She looks down at the Persian carpet and watches Iverson's immaculately polished shoes travel the path.

The old clock, as usual, directs his pacing. "I have a granddaughter, Emily Ann, who is nine years old. I need to find a home for her, and you might be the solution. Her adoptive mother has had cancer for at least two years. Her adoptive father is a fisherman and is gone for long periods of time. He has asked me to help place her in a good home soon so that Emily Ann can make the adjustment before her mother dies. I see my granddaughter occasionally, and I'd like to have her live in the Huntersville area. They now live in Boston. I'd be willing to support her."

Shirley asks, "Where's her real mother?"

Iverson continues to walk back and forth. "I'd rather not talk about her mother. It's not necessary for you to know."

She watches the attorney. *That dreadful habit of his drives me nuts. How did I ever stand it when I worked here?* "And, her real father?"

Iverson stops. "He's not competent and probably doesn't even know who or where his daughter is. It's not necessary to know who her father is."

"So this child is supposed to be the daughter of Toby Perkins? Her grandmother is Mrs. Perkins?" Shirley reaches for her barrette, and nudges it into place.

Iverson stiffens. "There's no question. He is the father. How did you know that?"

"People know more than you realize."

The attorney sits down and adjusts his tie.

"Does this girl know who her real father is?"

"Yes, but in name only."

"Well, great, I would be assuming a liability, a future problem, call it what you will. You know full well my connection with the Perkinses and especially Toby. He could use Emily Ann as a reason to get back at me. He'll find out she's living with me. It's hard to keep secrets in this town."

Iverson becomes distracted by Shirley's last statement. He again adjusts his tie, and turns in his chair, gazing out the window. "Regardless of what child you have at this age, there's almost certain to be a problem. If the girl is a ward of the state, many times the true parents will want to take her back at some point and that can be a wrenching experience."

She ponders a bit and repeats herself. "Some secrets can be kept, but this one can't." Shirley is in a quandary. *Honeydew says that Emily Ann is a nice girl. At least the Iversons think a lot of her, but Toby Perkins is bad news.*

Iverson continues gazing out the window. His voice takes on a distant distracted tone. "Why don't I have Emily Ann visit the farm for a while? That would be advisable, anyway, to see how the two of you get along."

Her doubts concerning Toby Perkins linger. She sits, considering the offer. "I'll give it a try." She is puzzled by his mood change, and wonders what he's really thinking. He claims he's concerned for his granddaughter, but when she said, "It's hard to keep secrets in this town," the statement totally distracted him.

"My son Joe was away from town last week." He turns in his chair and directly asks Shirley, "Do you know where he went?"

I'm about to be caught in another lie—but no, I won't be! She tartly responds, "Ask him! Why do you think I would know?"

Iverson taps with a pencil. "Being away, maybe he'll have a change of heart."

"Change from what?" She checks Steven and straightens his jacket.

He sits stiffly, placing his arms and hands on his desk. He raises his voice. "You know what I'm talking about! It's one thing to have you raise my granddaughter, but quite another to have you involved with my son. I don't want him sucked into living on an old broken-down hill farm."

Shirley is enraged. "And take up with a lowly orphaned 'state kid' who got knocked up by your other messed-up son?"

Iverson snaps his head back and throws his chest forward and stands. "Jimmy claims he's been framed, that he's not the father of your baby. Tell me, what about Zack Coles?"

Shirley realizes she has said too much and that her anger has gotten the best of her. She calmly replies, "Discuss the matter with Dr. Plumbly."

"You didn't answer my question."

"Dr. Plumbly has my records. Talk to him."

"You still didn't answer my question."

"To use your legal language, because it's not germane to the point. The fact is I got pregnant, and believe me; I had no choice in the matter. Do you want to press me further and have me file charges for assault and rape? I've worked in here long enough to know that's a possibility!"

"No, no—don't do that!" He sits back in his chair. He takes a deep breath and sits quietly for a moment. "I can't possibly blame you for my son's behavior. I've heard good reports concerning your progress on Harold Tully's farm. You've amounted to more in a few weeks than he has in his whole life."

"Thank you, because I appreciate you and the help you've given me. I hope as the farm becomes more and more profitable that your financial help will not be necessary; and besides, if Emily Ann likes living on Pine Mountain, and we get along, you and I will need to be on good terms. I want that very much, so I apologize for my inappropriate anger."

"Your apology is accepted. I'm sorry, too, for perhaps overstepping my bounds. I do admire you. If Pine Mountain works for Emily Ann, she will have a good home. I'll be calling her parents tonight. If it meets with their approval, I could go to Boston, and bring her to the farm this weekend."

Shirley asks, "Could you bring her on Sunday, say about one o'clock, after dinner?"

"Fine, I'll do that."

Shirley, carrying Steven, walks out of the office, and to the loading platform.

She notices the truck coming. Harold is smoking his pipe with his jaw clenched on the stem. He gives her an angry glance, and backs the truck up, slamming into the platform. He gets out, and bangs the bowl of his pipe on the edge of a wooden plank. Avoiding her with a sour expression, he pulls his pipe apart, cleaning it while she loads the truck with groceries.

Shirley announces firmly, "I just bought a linoleum for the kitchen floor. It's in back of the furniture store. I'll walk over and wait for you to bring the truck."

Harold jumps in his truck and spins ahead and guns it backward, carelessly bumping the platform again before stopping. He gets out and angrily slams the truck door. "Living with you is hell. It's a bastard. Everyone thinks you're like a gift from heaven. You should have heard the shit I got when I walked into Butson's. Everyone is talkin'. 'Harold, what a good-lookin' woman you got this time. She's a worker, smart too, and makin' a lot of milk for you. I hear she's a hell of a cook.' It's Shirley this and Shirley that. Son of a bitch, do I ever get sick of the talk you've caused! Hell, everyone thinks I'm a nothing—can't do a damn thing without Shirley Mason. I never get credit for nothin'! Now you've gone and bought a new linoleum—never asked me! Hell no, why ask Harold? I don't matter! I ain't even worth a piece of shit! Take charge and do whatever you mind to!" Harold throws his arms in the air, yelling, "Just go ahead, like I wasn't around!"

Shirley, with Steven in one arm, angrily moves the boxes over the grain bags toward the front of the truck. Ramming the carriage into an open space, she slams the tailgate shut, leaps from the platform, brushing by the awestruck Harold, and jumps in the truck, slamming the door shut with enough force to break the glass, and drives away. She yells out her window, "You're acting like a spoiled kid!"

Harold stands in utter amazement. He hurries to climb the stairs of the platform, looking to see which way the truck is headed, as it leaves the parking lot.

As the truck returns to the parking lot it doesn't stop for him. It circles the lot again. It passes Harold standing on the platform; he just stares, not in anger, but more in disbelief. After circling again it stops where he's standing. Harold pulls the roll of linoleum onto the truck as Shirley gets out and hurries to the other side. He starts the truck and drives toward Pine Mountain with neither one saying a word.

As the truck climbs the hills to the farm, she yearns to see Joe. She waves at Mary Maple in passing: *After what happened today, I need to come down, sit on the bank, settle my nerves, and feel that calming spirit.*

He drives to the farm, and backs up to the entry door. "Harold, I'm sorry that I didn't mention the new linoleum to you. I should have, but I bought it with my own money, and it's for your house and for the both of us to enjoy."

"Where'd you get the money?" He stares straight ahead and methodically reaches for his pipe.

"It was egg money I didn't spend, after doing the week's shopping. I've been saving up for this." She reaches for her barrette and feels its warmth.

"Ain't you figurin' that money is mine?" He's loading his pipe.

"I've bought small things for the house with egg money before, and you've never questioned it."

"This ain't no small thing." He's methodically filling the pipe.

"Since when do I give you the leftover egg money? If you want all the egg money, you better start paying me at least thirty dollars a week."

"I can't. I ain't ever paid any money like that." The pipe is now in his mouth. He rolls a stick match between his thumb and forefinger.

"Yeah, well you've never had anyone who's worked like I do either." She sighs. "You know something? I came here, thinking I could make a good life for Steven and myself. I've tried as hard as I could so maybe you could come to appreciate me and enjoy life more yourself, but you can't stand it that way. You want a no-mind in the house half doing their job, rats running all over the place, losing money on your hens, having a bunch of slab-sided cows. I guess that's when you're the happiest. I'll tell you, Harold, I don't want to live here like that! If you want it your way, I'm leaving right now. I know the Coleses would take me in—no doubt about it."

Harold isn't taking Shirley's threats lightly, but he isn't going to bow and scrape to her either. There is a long silence. His move is the next to make. "Well, let's lay that new linoleum after some dinner. I want to listen to the noon news. Oh, by the way, you can keep the extra egg money for your own. You always get your way." He chuckles, and that breaks the tension. She smiles. "Well, being friends is difficult especially when you put the two of us together." She reaches and slaps him on the knee. They both sit for a moment and have a good laugh.

She takes care of Steven and prepares a light dinner. She reminds herself that the pasture situation needs attention. Maybe tomorrow she and Harold can get some fence fixed so the cows can have more feed. *I feel mentally exhausted and I miss Joe.*

The new linoleum flooring gives the room a bright and cheery look. It glistens from the light flowing through the west window. Despite this, Shirley begins to feel depressed. *I can't stop thinking about Joe.*

"Would you watch Steven for a while?"

"Yup. Where you goin'?"

"I'll be right back."

She runs out of the house and drives down the mountain to sit at the hairpin turn. Her whole world is silent. The hot afternoon sun causes Mary Maple to glow. Ferns are in full growth, covering the complete area surrounding the tree, making it look as if it is floating in the center of a natural soft garden of green. The ferns smell like newly mown hay. The two large sweeping limbs are fully leafed out. Imagined or real, she senses a presence and a relief from her stressful feelings. She sits soaking in the wonderful calm. In a short while, she returns to the farm.

Harold is sitting by the west window. "Where did you go in such a tear?"

"Just enjoying a calming moment with Mary Maple."

"Oh, really! Just long's you ain't decided to up and quit on me, but I knew you wouldn't leave Steven. Mary Maple has been there for a lot of people over the years. Maybe if Ma had gone to her more often, she would have lived longer; but hell, the evil of my old man rainin' down on her was too hard to have the good of anythin' help her in any way.

Thinkin' about it, maybe that's what life's all about; beatin' away the evil just enough to let the good win out. For me, I just ain't sure where I am in such a process."

Watching Harold study the view as he talks, she adds, "I'm not sure either."

By afternoon Harold and Shirley are outside getting ready to plow the garden. They drag the hillside plow out from underneath the shed. Harold has a thoughtful expression, as he says, "I think my old man bought this kind of plow so all the furrows could be turned one way on a hillside. I always heard it was damn hard to turn a furrow uphill."

They hook Jeanie and Lassie to a set of whiffletrees and place the eye of the evener onto the hook that is attached to the plow. Harold lays the plow on its side until they get to the planned garden site.

The horses pull the plow easily for the first pass. Shirley drives the team and Harold guides the plow. The newly turned soil gives off a fresh, bold scent similar to raw earth after a hard rain. Light brown earthworms move out of sight, trying to retreat from the light. They are easy to see against the rich blackness. The furrows resemble lines of spilled dominoes.

Shirley looks at the area and comments, "Your mother had a big garden. Let's make it smaller this year."

Harold mentally measures the ground. "Fifty pounds of seed potatas are goin' to take up a lotta space."

Shirley realizes he likes to plow as long as she drives the horses. Steven starts to cry in his carriage, which has been placed by the corner of the house. "I think this is going to be a big enough garden. I've got to take care of Steven."

Harold surprises her. "I'll plow a little by myself. My old man did. You don't have to plant the whole thing, but the ground will be ready just in case."

Jeanie and Lassie become familiar with the routine. Harold ties a knot in the rein-ends, slips them over his head, and slides them down to his midsection. He pulls on the left or right rein when he wants to turn the horses. Shirley watches while nursing Steven next to the house.

After a few passes with the plow Shirley says, "We have a big enough garden."

"Yup, we have, and we did a good job; hardly a single green sod shows."

"If you feel up to it," Shirley offers, "we have time to hook up the disk harrows."

The harrows are harder for Jeanie and Lassie to pull than the plow, but the plot isn't that big. Harold sits on a metal seat attached to the single gang harrows. The row of circular disks rolls over the plowed ground, pushing and spreading soil into all the dips, divots, and pockets of the newly exposed earth. The chinking of small stones can be heard as the disks roll. The horses pull the harrow easier with each pass over the garden, until it is smooth and ready for planting.

Shirley goes to the house, puts the turnip on to slowly cook, and makes a meatloaf for supper. She has also bought some ice cream for dessert, a special treat that was expensive. She keeps thinking about the closely grazed pasture, and hopes Harold will help her repair fence in the morning for some fresh pasture.

Being hungry, the cows come easily to the barn at chore-time. The lack of grass to graze has caused a drop in production. To help compensate, she increases their grain.

After chores she goes to look at the garden plot, and can't believe it, Harold is working in the garden. "Gee, you've done a good job. What are you planting?"

"I'm gettin' the ground ready to plant peas. They've got to go in the ground soon."

"I guess they have. Good for you!"

Later, Shirley serves supper, and Harold compliments, "By golly, this turnip tastes just like I remember my ma's did."

"I'm happy with the garden. Thanks a lot for your help."

"Well, you need the help. A garden is a great thing to have. As you said this mornin', it can produce a lotta good eatin'."

Harold is in his Windsor chair and Shirley sits facing toward the west window. She has her elbows on the table with her chin resting on her folded hands. She takes a deep breath and glances at Harold. "You know that Steven will be crawling around soon, and I'm going to need some help with him, especially during haying when we're busy. I saw Attorney Iverson today and he told me he has a granddaughter, Emily Ann. She's nine years old and needs a home. Her adoptive mother is dying of cancer, and he's willing to pay for her keep if we would take her in. I told him we could give it a try to see if we can get along together."

"Is that the kid they claim is Toby Perkins's?"

"Yeah, it is."

"What a worthless bastard he turned out to be. Where's the girl's mother?"

"I'm not sure; he wouldn't say."

"I'll tell you where she is—in a nuthouse somewhere. Hell, she's a real winner. Like her mother, she's a boozer. This kid you're talkin' about ain't got much of a chance with the parents she's got. What can I say? You've got the whole thing planned anyway."

"I think we should clean out the junk room. We could make it her bedroom.

"That room looks like the very hell! Plaster chunks fallin' off the wall, it ain't been used since I can remember. Let's put a small bed in your room."

"Good idea. Living on Pine Mountain will be a big change for the girl, plus having just left her mother."

"Well, I'll be damned. That's the first time you ever thought I had a good idea."

Shirley laughs and leaves to go to her room. Harold sits watching television. It has seemed to have given him more enjoyment than she ever thought possible and it may have softened him some. Whatever the case, she is thankful they have gotten through the day with him accepting change. *If we had a phone, I'd call Joe.*

CHAPTER SIXTEEN

A thick morning mist and dew cover the meadows. Shirley walks through the pasture in her pack boots to get the cows. The first few times after being let out, they came willingly to the barn, but now they seem to hang back, becoming more adjusted to their outdoor comfort. Babe is in the process of calving. She is on her side, very bloated, and Shirley wonders at first if she might be dead. She runs to the barn for a bottle of calcium, the intravenous tube, a needle, and a halter. She hurries back and easily finds a clean, protruding vein, just as Joe has shown her. Within seconds she has the fluid flowing into the cow's blood system. Babe starts to respond immediately by shaking and manuring, but it's necessary to get her to lie in a normal position to rid her of her stomach gases. Shirley tries with all her effort to get Babe to roll upright, but the cow can't do it herself, or even with Shirley's help. Joe has told her that cattle can die if left bloated on their sides for too long. Deep death groans are coming from Babe.

Shirley slips the halter on the cow. Digging her heels in the ground and pulling on the rope gives her enough leverage to help Babe finally roll into position. Now gases are easily passing from the animal's rumen. She is almost an hour later than usual, but she still wants to be sure and get the milk to the stand before the arrival of the creamery truck. When Harold farmed alone, he mentioned that frequently he didn't finish in time for the morning's pickup, and often had to drive to the creamery. *That's a complete waste of time.*

Harold walks in the barn at his usual hour expecting to load the milk. "You slept late. I can't believe such a power woman would do a thing like that."

"We had a cow with milk fever. Would you go out and see how she's doing?"

Harold comes back carrying a small bull calf with Babe following behind.

Shirley says, "I'll write a note to Stubby Demar and have him come for the calf."

"Naw, I'll take him to market myself."

"Well, not today. I'd like your help fixing some more fence for these cows."

Harold flips the wooden stanchion into place, and pins it to hold Babe in her stall. He yells, "Bastard, do you ever burn me! I try to get on with you, but every damn minute you're findin' more work for me to do."

Shirley blurts, "You were just out in that pasture! Didn't you notice that the cows have grubbed it so hard there's no grazing left?"

"Okay, okay, it's easy to see who's runnin' who on this farm." He stomps away.

Steven has slept later than usual in his carriage. She feels so badly for the cows' lack of grazing that she decides to turn them out into fresh pasture, fence fixed or not. She hopes they will be contented to graze, not bothering to find breaks in the fence.

She pushes the carriage to the back door, picks up her son, and goes in the house. She changes his diaper and then puts oatmeal, raisins, toast and coffee on the table. During breakfast she comments, "I hope Emily Ann is as much help as I expect she could be. Maybe she'll enjoy Steven."

Harold is still in a bad mood. "Don't be expectin' too much with the parents she's got. She'll probably be a whinin' snot-nosed kid that will drive me right outta my mind. Bastard, as if I ain't got enough to deal with already." He walks out of the house and heads down the hill with the milk.

After a short time, she's relieved to see the truck return. It would be just like him to take off for the village just to spite her.

Harold sits for a minute in the truck and lights up his pipe. *She'd throw a fit if I didn't get right back. I should go into town and see Honeydew. She'll be mad as hell I ain't been to see her, but 'course Shirley turned those cows out in new feed to make it so I had no choice but to help her fix fence.*

Half an hour later, Steven is in his basket in the fencing wagon. She harnesses the horses, takes them out of the barn, snaps their neck yokes in place, and slides the large yoke ring over the wagon pole. She goes to the back of each horse and hooks the tugs to the whiffletrees. She deals with Jeanie last, since she is good at backing to raise the pole, allowing for the last tug to be easily hooked. Harold is putting the fencing supplies in the wagon. Neither speak.

The dandelions are in full bloom. The new pasture looks like a sea of yellow. The June grass is beginning to show a light green bloom. She realizes, *it won't be long, and haying time will be here. I best not mention it today.*

Harold is driving fence posts with the mall, and she is stapling wire with a nail hammer. The fence doesn't need too much repair, but she's reminded that there isn't a wire along the back edge by the woods, which worries her. *If a cow wanders off, Harold wouldn't go looking for her. I'd have to do that, and where to look, who knows?*

They have the fence fixed sooner than she thought. "Harold, would you help me string a wire along the woods so we won't have any cows wandering out of the pasture?"

"Yup, I guess so; I ain't got any fight left in me. It's too nice a day to lock horns with you. 'Course, I think it's all hogwash havin' to do it."

They work saying nothing. Harold watches Shirley holding the end of the iron bar as the barb-wire reel spins a single line of fence between the two while they walk; Harold is holding the pointed end of the bar. The new sharp barbs shine from the late-morning light.

He chuckles to himself. *She really makes me laugh sometimes. Her drivin' away from me at The Market and around that parkin' lot. She was so mad I could see the smoke pourin' out her ears.*

He pulls the wire taut with his hammer while she staples it to trees along the edge of the woods. While watching her, he sees trickles of sweat running from beneath her blue cap. *She needs that Joe fellow to come back. He does for her what I sure as hell can't.*

Steven stirs just as they're about to finish. Shirley says, "I'm taking him back to the house. If you could finish this, I'll get dinner ready." She picks up her son. "Young man, you're growing up." He squirms, and rapidly moves his arms.

While eating dinner, she suggests, "Would you like to go to town this afternoon? I'd like to see Alice Coles, and you can pick me up before chores."

"Thought you'd be wantin' to plant your garden. You know, we've got to work every minute around this place." Harold smiles.

"Oh, go outside and smoke your pipe. I'll plan to work in the garden tomorrow."

He says, "Just take the truck and I'll stay home. Maybe I can relax for the first time in a month and a half. 'Course I should see Honeydew, but stayin' here is best for Harold Tully. I ain't up for any of her tongue-lashin'."

Shirley drives to the Coleses', bringing Alice a pie. She climbs the steps onto the front porch, but there is no answer when she knocks. She places the pie on the dining room table with a note and leaves. *I should visit Honeydew to thank her and show her my new jacket.*

Meanwhile, Harold searches in the shed for a ball of string his mother used in planting the rows in the garden. He finds it and the roll of chicken wire for the peas. *Peas are the first to be planted up here in the mountain. In fact, that's true wherever you live. Everyone should be given time to plant their peas. Maybe when Governor Dewey gets elected President, I'll write him with the idea that this country needs a National Pea Plantin' Day. 'Cause, when you think of it, puttin' that seed in the ground is the beginnin' of life. Yup, no one or no thing could live for long on this earth without the sun, the rain, the soil, and the seed.* Harold opens the bag of peas and grabs a handful. He examines them closely. *Golly, it's a miracle that this dried-up thing can grow a plant.*

He stands for a moment next to the string that stretches the length of the garden, holds the end of the hoe handle at arm's length, and bows his head as if speaking into a microphone. "I now declare this National Pea Plantin' Day and—and thank you, Harold Tully, for suggestin' it. Wait—wait, by golly, I hear the thunderous sound of applause for Harold Tully—no, it's actually Shirley from a distance, driving like hell over the just-graded road, stones pingin' the fenders of the truck, comin' home in a tear to do chores."

The next day, Sunday, Shirley is working in the kitchen in the late morning while Steven sleeps. She feels desperate thinking about Joe and wondering why he hasn't come to the farm. She reminds herself that, no doubt, their relationship had been moving too rapidly, and she realizes their last romantic encounter was a mistake.

Just then, Joe's Ford coupe drives in the yard. She can't control her excitement, and runs out to meet him. He gets out of his car and leans against the door. "Joe, I missed you; it's great to see you." She walks to meet him and puts her hand on his shoulder, since he has turned from having to look at her. "What's wrong? You seem so glum."

He begins rubbing his index finger on the car fender, leaving a shiny place where he's removed the road film, not giving her eye contact. He turns back toward her, his face is drawn with no smile. He puts on a front as if transacting business. "Shirley, I hate to tell you this, but I won't be coming anymore. I met a teacher this last week that I'm dating."

Shirley steps away from him feeling a crushing weight fall on her. She slightly bends from the instant ache in her stomach. She is surprised, yet not surprised. “Leave, Joe, you’ve said enough. Thanks for having the guts to drive here to tell me. I wasn’t good enough for you. I’m just an orphan that got knocked up.” Her voice rises to almost a scream; she reaches for the barrette, but it isn’t there. She wildly flicks her hair back in place. “I’m some poor catch for The Joseph Iverson, Agricultural Agent, who’s probably in line for some promotion. I’d be an utter embarrassment to you when you go off on your worldly junkets. All I can say is leave; get out of my life. I can see romance is chancy and cruel and your words feel like a knife that has just been driven through me.” Shirley screams, “You jerk!”

“I wanted to tell you that you’re strong, determined and you’re attractive. I’m still concerned about your fear and thought it better if I ended our relationship.”

She, again, sweeps her hair back with her hand. “Joe, you’re smooth, very smooth. The affable Joe with all the right information; but buddy, you just screwed up that last line! This move is your idea, and my so-called fear has nothing to do with you taking up with someone else. In fact, I know breaking up with me is just what your father wanted. He said something like, ‘I don’t want my son tied to some old broken-down farm.’ Or in other words, ‘I don’t want my son tied to some lowly orphan.’ Oh, but wouldn’t Shirley Mason sure smudge the Iverson name.”

Joe stands, seemingly speechless. His face is glowing in high color and he nervously jingles the change in his pocket. “But—but, I told you why I’m not seeing you anymore.” He sounds unconvincing.

“You’re weak, Joe, you’re weak—please leave!” Shirley rushes toward the house and slams the kitchen door. She wipes the table, and with all her force she throws the dishcloth toward the sink. It hits the faucet and hangs. She hears Joe’s car leave the yard and the loss feels like a club has just hit her knees. She scuffs to her room, with her shoes sounding like she’s walking on sandpaper.

She sits on her bed and stares out the south window. Jeanie and Lassie are standing side by side, head to tail, their muzzles resting on their rumps, each swishing the other's face with their tails, driving away flies—*paired for life.* She throws herself on the bed and cries until Steven wakes up.

Through sheer determination, Shirley forces herself to prepare for Emily Ann's arrival. She reminds herself that she's experienced broken relationships in her past. This was not new. However, romantic love was new, an emotion she has never known, but now those same feelings have turned to anger and despair. Shirley sets her jaw. *I've got to forget about Joe.*

A short time later at one o'clock, Attorney Iverson's sleek black car enters the Tully farmstead. Emily Ann gets out of the car. She looks sad, shaken, and frightened. Shirley greets her. "Have I ever been looking forward to meeting you! I'm Shirley and you're Emily Ann, and who do we have here?"

"This is Terry; my dad gave her to me. She's a border collie."

Shirley exclaims, "What a cute puppy!"

Iverson quickly says, "Good-bye," and leaves. He obviously doesn't want to have to meet Harold, and no doubt the feelings are mutual, since Harold hasn't left the garden.

Shirley and Emily Ann walk toward the house. She is tall for her age and slender. Her thin face is pasty white with big brown eyes showing signs of worry. Shirley leads her toward the house where they meet Harold at the entry. Shirley says, "Emily Ann, I'd like you to meet Harold Tully. Harold, this is Emily Ann Gray."

A very mature Emily Ann says, "How do you do, Mr. Tully?"

"Hell, you ain't havin' to call me Mr. Tully, I'm Harold to everyone I know."

Emily Ann just stares at him.

Shirley breaks in, "Let's go and see Steven."

They go into Shirley's room, where Steven is lying on his back in his crib, looking at his hands. Emily Ann brightens. "A real baby! Can I hold him?"

"Sure, let me nurse him and then you can take him for a walk with the carriage."

"That would be fun. I've never been near a real live baby before. I didn't realize babies were fed this way. I always thought they drank from a bottle."

"You're right, most babies are fed that way but this fits me better."

Emily Ann watches his diaper being changed. "Oh, he's a boy."

"Yes, he's built differently than we are."

"I can see that. I guess I never thought of it before."

"Let's put him in the carriage and you can go for a short walk. Cars almost never travel this road, so you don't have to worry about traffic. If he should cry or fuss, I'll be right here."

Emily Ann leaves the yard, pushing the carriage with Terry following behind. Shirley mentions to Harold as they watch from the west window, "Isn't that a cute picture?" She sits at the table and breaks down crying.

Harold stares at her in surprise. "Now what have I done? What's the problem, what's wrong? This ain't like you."

"Joe's dating another woman. She's a teacher. You know, class. What I'm not."

Harold pounds the arms of his Morris chair with his fists. "Bastard, you ain't talkin' like that, I won't hear it. That son of a bitch has a screw loose." He gets up and stomps around the kitchen. "You've got more class than any ten women. That's bullshit!"

Harold's support surprises Shirley, but it doesn't help her mood. She cries as she talks. "I don't feel up to chores, and anyway, I should spend some time with Emily Ann."

"That's okay, I'll milk. Golly, woman, I think you're tired too. That ain't helpin'."

"Joe has probably dated a lot, and no doubt he thought things were moving too fast. He certainly acted interested up until a week ago. Now he's dropped me like a handful of mud for someone with better credentials."

They walk out the door and stand together watching for Emily Ann. He glances at her, seeing her sad expression. "Don't try and figure the fool out. I like the guy, I'll admit, but he's no judge of a woman. You know, Shirley, you could get all the schoolin' possible, and you ain't goin' to be any different than you are right now. No—schoolin' don't change who you are. I ain't against learnin', but you're born with what you're goin' to be."

"Thanks, Harold, I appreciate your support." She wipes her face.

He reaches for her and puts his hand on her forearm. "You gonna be all right?"

"I'll be okay." She bursts into tears. In a shaky, tearful voice she continues, "Maybe Emily Ann will help with my sadness." She again wipes her tears away.

"I hope so. I can see this has hit you hard—the son of a bitch!" Harold leaves.

That night Emily Ann and Shirley sleep in the same bed. Their mere presence for one another gives sorely needed comfort.

CHAPTER SEVENTEEN

Shirley rises at the usual hour, a different woman, lifeless and tired. The memory of Joe just won't leave. *I have learned the hard way that love is fragile, a fleeting sort of thing. Love came and then left like a thief in the night. Joe—the louse!*

On the way to the barn, she feels no joy in the beautiful spring morning. The robins and barn swallows are just waking. A Baltimore oriole is calling out his song, perched on a wire leading from the barn to the house, but for Shirley, the sounds mean nothing.

She works in solitude and in the quietness of the barn filled with contented cows. She recalls that, except for the first nine years living with the Perkinses, her life seems to be riding on a winding road. What's around the corner is unpredictable. Staying with the Perkinses was great except for the ending. Life with the Ericksons was terrible. The loneliness was overwhelming, except for Willy Smithson. He was her friend and made life bearable. The Ericksons treated her like an outcast. Then came the Durkees. Louise hated her from the very first day. Their bull gave her nightmares. Over and over again in her dreams that mad Jersey bull was always chasing her. His head and horns were so close they rubbed her rear. She'd wake and let out desperate cries and find her back was rubbing the wall. Louise would never comfort her and she'd have a fit if Harry even came near her room. She'd sob until she went back to sleep.

Shirley looks up. Through the open barn door she can see Emily Ann pushing the baby carriage with Terry following behind. It's the cutest picture, and even in her glum mood, she smiles. Emily Ann comes in the barn like a natural, carrying Steven, and sits on a milk stool holding him while watching Shirley milk.

Harold walks in. "So that no-mind of a Joe split. I've thought about that a lot."

Shirley doesn't answer, and he can see that she isn't herself.

"That crazy bastard. I ain't believin' there's a better woman than you. He's too damn well educated. He needs his head examined. Another woman's caught his eye; but you wait, he'll come to see what he's passed up. That son of a bitch, he needs his ass kicked."

"It's just a fact of life. I know you may not see things the way he does, but it's over."

Harold walks away shaking his head. Shirley was concerned at first, having Emily Ann exposed to Harold's rough talk, but there are a lot of people out in the world that talk the way he does. She senses that the girl doesn't know what to make of the man. She probably has never met or seen anyone quite like him in the Boston area.

Haying is at least two weeks away, but Shirley is getting anxious over the upcoming season. She and Joe have already reviewed the condition of Harold's haying equipment stored in the shed. He summed it up: "Harold has an arsenal of tired, worn-out machines that don't look like they can stand another season."

At this point, Shirley can see two solutions to the haying problem: Offer to hay together with the Coleses, using some of Harold's equipment, and hiring no extra help, or spend some money to fix up the equipment, build a new wagon, rebuild the hay loader, and buy a new tractor and mower. If not the mower, the tractor is a must, and they would need to hire on at least one more person.

Emily Ann begins crying, pushing the carriage as they walk from the barn. "I miss my mom. We used to go for walks before she got too sick. We usually sat in the park and watched the pigeons and laughed when they fought over the bread crumbs we gave them. My mother always listened when I told her about school and things that made me sad. Of course, I told her about my good days, too. We never talked about how she was feeling. I know she's very sick and I'm afraid I won't see her again. I can't stop thinking about that."

"It sounds to me as though you have a very special mother."

"Oh she is, Shirley. I love her more than I think I could love anybody. I love Dad, too. He's great, but he's gone a lot and usually it's just me and Mom."

"After breakfast, we'll go and see Grampa Iverson and call your mom and see if you can talk to her."

Emily Ann with a worried expression says, "I hope she's okay."

"We'll find out."

Back inside the house, Emily Ann goes to change Steven's diaper.

Shirley remarks to Harold, "I know haying is two weeks away, but I want you to start thinking about it, now." She talks as she scrambles eggs over the woodstove.

"What do you mean, two weeks? I never start until after the Fourth of July. I've always done it that way, and that's the date we stick by."

"I don't have any energy to argue with you this morning. I feel totally depressed about haying. Your equipment is in sad shape. I wish we could just offer to work with the Coleses"—*If I can stand it*—"and forget trying to fix up your broken-down machinery."

She can see he's getting upset, but she doesn't care. "I'll tell you this, Harold Tully. If I stay here this winter, the cows and horses are not going to be fed the crap they had to eat last winter. That's got to change. Most of the farms I've worked on did their haying early enough so they were able to put up a second cutting. That kind of feed makes milk. We can do that ourselves by changing our ways and not dragging out first cutting into fall. I won't do it that way. You're the boss. Make some decisions and soon!"

"You know how to spoil my breakfast. I'll tell you right off, I ain't workin' with no Coleses." Harold raises his voice. "Who the hell do you think you are, anyway? Hayin's one big pain in the ass and you're goin' to make it worse by workin' with the Coleses. I'll tell you, that Zack is an idiot. Hell, he don't know which end is up most of the time."

"I agree. I don't want to work with them either, but we need to make plans—now!"

Harold sits down. "Well, I'm glad we've agreed on one thing. We ain't workin' with the Colseses."

Shirley washes a few diapers while Emily Ann does the dishes. "Emily Ann wants to see if she can talk to her folks this morning. I would like to take her to Attorney Iverson's office and call Boston, so I'll take the milk down. Is that all right?"

"Yup, I guess so. It will give me a break not havin' to think or do anythin'." He looks at the puppy. "I'll watch your dog, Emily Ann." He grabs the puppy and puts her in his lap. "You're one smart pup. You know how to use the newspaper already. Most dogs I ever had went all over the floor."

Shirley and Emily Ann, holding Steven, leave Pine Mountain. Emily Ann is excited on the way to town. She's an attractive, alert-looking child with dark hair and bright brown eyes. Although slender, she's not weak, since she can easily carry Steven.

Emily Ann breaks the silence. "Harold's a grump. You don't like each other, do you? You don't talk together like my mom and dad. They love each other a lot."

"You're lucky to have such great parents."

Emily Ann starts crying. "It doesn't seem fair that my mother is sick and I know she's going to die. That's why I came to Pine Mountain. I wish I could see her one more time. I miss her."

"You should. Regardless of what happens, your mother will be with you forever. You will think about her often, how she cared for you and all the fun times you had."

"Do you like Harold? He's not very nice."

"I hope you can get acquainted with him. He acts angry sometimes, but he likes me and I'm fond of him. We *are* friends, even though it doesn't seem like it to you."

"Well, if you say so, but he sure acted mad this morning."

"Haying is a hard time, and he and I deal with problems differently."

Emily Ann says, "I think he's lazy."

Shirley is surprised that she has already picked up on this trait. "Well, maybe he has a lack of interest. You see, he's lived on Pine Mountain all his life, and I think he's tired of having done the same thing for so many years."

They stop at Iverson's office and park on the street. For the first time Shirley walks up the front steps. She doesn't feel it's necessary to use the side entrance any longer. She reasons that many people know that Emily Ann is Iverson's granddaughter. They enter the law office, and are greeted by a secretary. "Attorney Iverson has a client with him. Why don't you take a seat? I'll let him know you're here."

Shirley sits, gazing off into space. Emily Ann asks, "What are you thinking about?"

"Oh, I guess my mind is wandering. Here comes your Grampa."

Emily Ann jumps to her feet. "Grampa, I want to call my dad and talk to him."

"Sure, just come into this side room, and Shirley will help you."

They sit in a conference room with a phone. Iverson shuts the door.

Emily Ann's excitement fades when she hears her father's voice. "She did?" Her face turns white and her bottom lip quivers. "When? Yesterday?...A funeral, when will it be?...Yes, she is." Emily Ann begins to cry in deep sobs.

Shirley takes the phone. "Hi, this is Shirley.... I'm so sorry your wife died.... Yes, I'll put her on the bus.... We'll see you on Friday when you return with Emily Ann."

John explains that he tried to call David Iverson earlier. He has checked and the bus will leave Huntersville for Boston at eleven. Iverson gives Shirley some money to buy a dress, other necessities and a traveling case for his granddaughter, since there isn't time to go back to Pine Mountain. Even though Emily Ann is shaken by the news of her mother's death, she is eager to return to Boston to be with her father.

They do their shopping and hurry to meet the bus. The bus stop is right next to the Huntersville Ford Tractor dealership. There is a brand-new Ford tractor with a mower attached parked in front of the building. Shirley looks at it. *That's just what we need.*

When the bus comes, Emily Ann isn't a bit frightened to take the trip alone. "Your dad said he would bring you back on Friday." Shirley waves with Steven in her arms, as the bus pulls from the curb. The engine roars like a dragon, and the muffled exhaust blows a round area in the street, clearing it free of dust and dirt. Shirley in her somber mood feels as though the enormous vehicle could consume Emily Ann and no one would ever know.

She drives back from Huntersville feeling depressed, thinking of Emily Ann and her loss. *I was the same age when I lost Mrs. Perkins—it was awful.* She wonders if Emily Ann will want to come back to Pine Mountain, and then, of course, there's Joe. She knows that if Joe were present, her conflicts with Harold would be made easier. The offer of her to run the farm is in the past. She realizes that a woman being Harold's boss is too much for him even though it's obvious he's sick of the whole farming business. The haying issue is critical, but she simply sees no hope for needed improvement. She stops at the hairpin turn and gets out of the truck and sits on the edge of the road. A cloud is passing over causing Mary Maple to look dark. Shirley can't feel her spirit. *Maybe it's gone.* She drops her head in her hands and sobs. *I feel desperate, drowning in a pool of panic.*

When she drives in the yard, she can see Harold working in the garden. Maybe he isn't lazy, but just needs a change.

Shirley walks weak-kneed to the corner of the house and sits to visit with Harold and to nurse Steven. A wave of exhaustion comes over her.

Harold asks, "Where's the girl?"

"When we called her dad, we found out her mother just died, and her father wanted her with him. I put her on the bus for Boston and her father's bringing her back on Friday. The poor kid really misses her mom. It's tough losing a mother at that age."

Harold looks at Shirley and wonders if she's all right. Her voice is wispy and shallow-sounding. "Damn it, why does life have to be such a bastard?"

"I think life is what you make it, but I must admit I'm feeling depressed right now."

"That dumb Joe!"

"It's over. He's out of my life." Her comment is forced. She feels for her barrette, but it gives her no comfort.

Harold is concerned watching Shirley. He looks down at the ground, and moves some soil with his hoe. He wants to say something. Shirley knows it and keeps quiet. Her colorless face reveals lines of grief and pain as she rests her head against the house.

Harold raises his voice. "Damn, I wish I could help! If I got my hands on that Joe, I'd shake some sense into him!"

He digs some more with his hoe, as clods as big as tennis balls roll off the blade and a rain of soil flies from the surface of the ground. "He's a fool, that's all he is—a fool." Harold pauses and then continues after a long silence. "About this hayin'—I hate it. I always did and always will. There's no easy way. You cut some down, rake it up, start to load the wagon, and the loader breaks, or it rains, or the stuff ain't dry enough. The whole subject makes me sick. I felt like pukin' when you were talkin' this morning. Hayin' just makes me sick."

She feels sick as well. A wave of exhaustion again sweeps over her. *I'm breaking—falling—falling into a pit from which I'll never recover. The cows, the hens, the eggs, the house, Steven, dirty diapers, Emily Ann, Harold, Joe, and now haying.*

She realizes her image to others—as a tough, energetic, take-charge person—is just not true. *Right now I'm weak and helpless.* In a listless tone, she says, "I saw a new Ford tractor with a mower. It sits near the bus station."

"Hell, I don't want to spend money that way."

Her combative mood has vanished. She has never been dishonest with Harold, but she feels like a defeated warrior with one shot left—trickery—acting as if she knows a lot about a subject that in fact she knows little. "Did you ever think of what's going to happen with your money when you die? The Internal Revenue is going to come into the bank and take it all. The government will get their hands on it—send it to rebuild Europe." She can barely utter the last few words.

"To hell they will. That ain't true." Harold looks at Shirley in questioning disbelief. She looks terrible, pale, black under her eyes, hair fallen in her face. Her barrette is sitting cockeyed on her head.

"You have no will. What do you think happens when people die who own property and have money and no family and no will? The court sends out an order. Everything is sold. The money is collected, and it's Uncle Sam's for the spending." Shirley begins to cry.

Harold stands leaning on the hoe, looking at her, wondering what to do for her and whether to believe her or not.

She begins to sweat and feel faint. She rests Steven on the ground. She stretches out flat then rolls to her side and sobs. "Harold, I've got to get away. You're going to have to drive me to Honeydew's with Steven. I feel sick. I have no strength. Take me to her house right now." She lies limp on the grass, tears streaming down her lifeless white face.

He springs into action and helps her to her feet.

"I feel faint. I can't focus on the heifers standing bunched by the pasture fence—will you bring Steven?" she asks in a whimpering voice. "I'll walk." She drags her feet, stumbling toward a black blob she knows is the truck.

"I've taken a lot of women down this mountain over the years, and I never saw most of them again, but you're different."

Her head is resting on the back of the seat. She slides down with her knees pressing on the dashboard. In her weak voice she says, "Go to the Ericksons and ask to have Willy Smithson help you for a few days—he's not what you think. He's good help. The best—I want you to have his help." Again, she sobs. "He'll come—just tell him Shirley needs his help—he'll come." She falls silent with tears streaming down her face.

Harold parks the truck. As Honeydew comes out of her little house, Harold blurts in a panic, "Shirley's sick!"

Honeydew takes her arm. "What's wrong, my poor dear? You look so pathetic." Shirley is sobbing as Honeydew brings her in the house and puts her in bed.

Harold walks in the house holding Steven with his head resting in one hand and his bottom in the other. The baby's blanket is draped over his outstretched arm. He offers his diagnosis: "She's tired and sad as hell. Joe left her, you know—damn him—Emily Ann has gone back to Boston because her mother died—and of course, there's hayin'. I have a box of stuff for Steven and his basket and carriage are in the back of the truck."

Honeydew, holding Steven, walks out to the truck and confronts Harold. "Since I picked out that jacket, I haven't seen a thing of you. I don't think you care about me anymore. I'm lonesome for my Archie."

"It ain't that I don't care. You know that!"

"No, I don't know that. How would I ever know?"

"Look, as soon as things get straightened out with Shirley, I'll be down."

"When you want something, you come running and like a fool I help you out."

Harold raises his voice. "Look, as I said, I'll be down to see you." He backs out of the yard and heads toward the Ericksons. He isn't surprised that she's mad at him. He really should have been seeing her more. *Now, jumpin' from one problem to the next.*

He drives into the Ericksons' yard, hating to take a hired man right out from under them. *Jules will shit his pants when I tell him I want Willy's help for a few days.*

Harold goes to the barn and luckily encounters Willy. He has a wide toothless smile that fills his face. His demeanor is that of a simple man in his late forties. As he walks toward Harold, he's slightly bent, swinging his arms rapidly, taking short quick steps.

"Willy, you remember me, Harold Tully? I want to talk to you. You know Shirley Mason works for me?"

"She does? I like Shirley a lot. The Ericksons treated her bad when she were here."

"Shirley's taken sick, and she wants you to come to Pine Mountain and help us for a few days."

"She does? I want to do that. Yes, I would. Jules will be awful mad. He treats me bad just the way he done to Shirley. 'Course I've worked here a long time." He nervously glances toward the house.

Harold doesn't want Willy to ponder the move too long. "Well, go get your clothes and I'll wait for you in the truck." He sees Jules coming out of the house, moving his big frame down the steps. "What's up, Harold?"

Harold stops, feeling like a thief, and sorry he has to confront the man, but he puts on a front full of confidence. "Shirley Mason, my helper, has just taken sick. I've come to get Willy's help for a few days."

"Who in hell do you think you are, sneaking around my farm and stealing my help?"

Harold flushes a bit. "I ain't stealin' him. He's comin' on his own. What do you think—you can hold him here with a ball and chain?"

"That slut, she's a smart-mouthed little shit. She set you up to this, didn't she?"

By this time Willy is in a crouch, humped, carrying his box of clothes and hurrying toward the truck. Harold is beside himself with anger, hearing Jules talk about Shirley in a disrespectful way. "You bastard! You ain't knowin' the Shirley Mason I know!"

Harold does an about-face, and stomps toward his truck. He sees a small stone in the yard and kicks it dead center. It flies and hits the side of the barn. Turning the truck around in the large yard, he floors it. Dust and stones fly from behind the truck, hitting and dinging the fenders. And Jules stands in a cloud of dust.

"I've got two errands to do, Willy. It'll take just a minute." He stops at the town clerk's office. In a short time, he comes out carrying an envelope, which he leaves at the county clerk's office. *There now, no government is goin' to walk in and take my farm and all my money.*

As they leave Huntersville Harold notices the new Ford tractor and mower parked near the street. They head toward Pine Mountain. Harold asks, "How much you wantin' to get paid, Willy?"

"Well—I guess nothin'. The Ericksons ain't never paid me. I mean, well, ya're goin' ta feed me, ain't ya? I'm goin' ta have a place ta sleep 'n' all?"

"Sure, Willy, but Shirley's stayin' at Honeydew's place for a few days. My cookin' ain't the best. She'll be back in a short while." *I hope real soon.* He continues, "I'll pay you ten dollars for the week. I expect Shirley will be back on her feet by then. That will give you some spendin' money."

"Gee, thanks, Harold. I ain't never had that much money."

The terms of Willy's employment are made as the truck enters the yard. Harold shows him his upstairs room. Willy changes into some fresh clothes, and is ready to do what he does best—work.

He collects the eggs, and feeds the hens, and starts grading the eggs, since the next day they have to go to market. Harold is surprised that Willy knows how to grade eggs. With his toothless grin he looks at Harold. "Mrs. Erickson learned me how ta do this. I graded eggs every week fer her."

Better him than me—what a mindless job.

Willy is impeccably neat. He is careful with each egg, taking great pains to make sure it's clean, wiping and scrubbing as needed. He places it in the white metal concave holder of the scale as if each one is the first he's ever weighed, squinting to see where the pointer stops, and then placing the egg in its appropriate box.

They do the night chores, and Harold again discovers that Shirley was right. Willy knows his farm work. Harold sees a cow in standing heat when they are driven to the barn. *I need to get a bull. I'll buy a fancy Jersey bull this year, that's what Shirley would want. I'll see if the Coleses have one they'd sell.*

Tuesday night Willy collects the eggs and heads toward the house for supper. Harold is no cook, but the television viewing makes up for the eating. Willy sits at the table grading eggs, letting the "tube" take him to a land he's never experienced.

Wednesday morning Harold loads the milk and eggs, and puts his bankbook in his pocket. He stops to see how Shirley is doing. Honeydew reports that Shirley has fed Steven and eaten a little, but is sleeping most of the time. Honeydew has regained her vibrancy. "I just love Steven. He's a lot of fun. I don't think I've ever had anyone smile at me as much as he does."

Harold puts on a coy grin. "Except me."

"That's a joke. You've only been smiling just lately, well—since…"

"Maybe it's 'cause of spring or somethin'. I'm intendin' to keep my promise to you." Harold is talking as he's getting in his truck. Honeydew stands in the yard and watches him leave, looking visibly crestfallen as her shoulders sag. She yells, "You don't care about me! You can't wait to get out of here!"

He yells back, "I'll keep my promise."

In The Market, Harold is trying his best to shop. He doesn't have any idea of what to buy except bakery products, loading his cart with cakes, pies, doughnuts, and white bread. Plus, they always need grape jelly. He is relieved that Willy is easily satisfied, but he feels awkward pushing a cart around The Market among nearly all women shoppers. Esther Erickson is coming toward him. He can see that a verbal head-on collision is about to take place. There is fire in her eyes; her cheeks are puffed out and her double chin is radish red. "If you don't have the biggest gall, Harold Tully, to drive right to our farm and snatch Willy Smithson from us."

Harold stops, tenses his neck, and sets his jaw. "Hell, he's been your slave most of his life, it's time he had a break. You're just mad that someone found out that he's one hell of a good worker."

"That smart-mouthed tramp of a Shirley Mason put you up to this, I know. That's the kind of person she is."

Harold flushes. *I'm itchin' to grab her flabby neck and squeeze it like I used to Ma's freshly churned butter. I could happily do that, and scare the bejabbers outta her.*

He looks Esther square in the face. "Willy Smithson is goin' to stay on my farm, because I'm payin' him, and he happens to like Shirley! You know why? Because she treated him decent when she worked, or I should say, *slaved* on your farm! It ain't hurtin' you fat-assed Ericksons one bit to do your own damn work!"

After that outpouring of anger, he moves toward the checkout counter. He wants out of the place, but Louise Durkee is in front of him with a pile of food that Harold estimates should last anyone a month. He sees her turn to look at him, but she does an about-face, and noticeably stiffens. He stands with his fingers nervously dancing on the cart handle. *What in hell's wrong with her? My clothes are clean. I ain't goin' to let her snub me.*

"Hi, Louise, you've bought enough food to feed an army."

She looks in his cart. "I only serve good wholesome meals, the basic seven. I see you're lacking most of them. All I hear from Harry is how beautiful Shirley Mason is, and how she's putting Harold Tully on the map. Almost no day passes but what I have to hear how great that woman is. Or I should say, girl. Well I'll tell you this, she doesn't know her foods." She sticks her chin out, raises her eyebrows, and turns around.

Harold laughs uproariously. "She's a corkin' good cook, and makes up a nice table, I'm sure with all the basic seven, whatever to hell they are. She's taken sick, and is stayin' with Honeydew for a few days. I'm doin' the shoppin'. I eat what I mind to." *And it's damn poor.* She turns halfway, not confronting him, and answers weakly, "Oh."

Harold leaves The Market and stops at the Coleses. He's comfortable going there, since his mission is to buy a bull. He heads straight to the barn. Zack is out back forking manure into his spreader. Harold comes right to the point. "Zack, do you have a yearlin' bull for sale?"

Zack looks surprised. "Well, I'll be, Harold Tully's finally going to buy some good stock. We do have one, a fancy young bull, about the best I think we've ever raised. Let's go to the barn, and I'll show him to you."

When they reach the barn, Harold looks over the bull, who licks his hand while he rests it over the edge of the pen. "By golly, he's fancy all right. How much you askin'?"

Zack's takes on an expression of panic. "I—I don't know, I'll have to ask Mother."

Harold remarks, "You bred and raised him, you ought to know what he's worth."

"I'll go in the house and talk to Mother. I'll be right back."

"Hey, look, if I'm dealin' with your mother tell her to come out here." Harold watches him leave. *The kid will never make it unless he's taught to stand on his own.*

Zack comes back. "We'd sell him for four hundred."

Harold reaches in his pocket for his billfold. He opens it and pulls out three hundreds and a fifty. "Here's three fifty, cash. Take it, or I'm buyin' somewhere else."

Zack grabs the money and just stands holding it, not saying a thing. He appears to be in disbelief that Harold Tully has just bought the nicest bull he's ever raised. Zack puts on a tortured expression. "The bull is out of our best cow, and by a top sire that's done well for us. I think the price is fair."

"I think it's high. Take the money, or forget it." *I like to see the kid sweat a little and make him realize that Harold Tully ain't just some dumb hermit.* Harold motions toward Zack. "Be satisfied with what I gave you or I'm still lookin'."

"Okay, I think it will be all right with Mother."

"It's about time you started thinkin' what's all right for Zack."

Zack stuffs the money in his pocket and hurries toward the house.

Harold drives up the mountain and stops at the hairpin turn, looking at Mary Maple. *Hope Shirley comes home real soon. I miss her.* He drives forward and notices a white flowering bush intermittently dispersed along the side of the road. *Golly, I ain't seen them white flowers in years. I think Ma called them shad. Yup, or shadbush, that's what it is, one of the first things to flower in springtime.*

CHAPTER EIGHTEEN

Shirley is waking at Honeydew's in a room of red: the floor, curtains, walls, sheets, pillowcases, and bedspread are all variations of rosiness.

Honeydew enters the room, holding Steven. She has a big smile that lifts the jowls of her puffy face. "Your son is hungry."

Shirley takes him and he snuggles in, searching for food. "Yes, you're hungry all right." As Steven is nursing, she looks up. "Wow, these past few days are a blank for me. I can't remember when I've slept so much. I'm grateful to you for taking care of Steven."

Honeydew is sitting in a chair by the bed. She remarks, "It's been fun except when he was hungry and I had to shake you so you'd come to your senses enough to let him nurse. I think you've been working too much, and losing Joe caused you to cave in."

"Maybe so. Living on Pine Mountain has been a challenge. I love the place, but it takes a lot of effort to get along with Harold. One thing is for sure: I don't want to move. Maybe that's why I've been trying hard—to prove to him that I can make a difference."

Honeydew frowns. "Don't worry about Harold. He thinks the world of you."

"Yeah, I know, but ever since Mrs. Perkins and I parted, it's been a fear—that again, I'd be told to leave. Frankly, Pine Mountain is the only place I've really liked, since the Perkinses. The Iversons were okay, but there was always Jimmy. He sure has a temper."

"I think Trudy Iverson messed up her kids. Well, maybe not Joe. She started to lose control right around the time that Toby Perkins supposedly raped their oldest, Curtsy. The girl was only twelve, but she was trouble. She developed at a young age and learned right away how to get the boys' attention." Honeydew shifts in her chair. "The Silvers live next door to the Iversons. Randy, their son, and Curtsy were often seen together. Trudy was, and still is, into the country club and didn't have any idea what was going on at home.

"Toby claimed that he followed Curtsy and Randy and saw them enter the Iverson home. Toby had no business being where he was. But according to him, he hid in the bushes for a while and then entered the house and went upstairs to find the two in bed. At that moment, Trudy came home and found Toby. Curtsy was screaming, 'Toby raped me! Toby raped me!'

"I guess Randy had left by the back stairs. Trudy probably had had plenty to drink and no doubt didn't have all of her faculties, but she did call Gabby and pressed charges."

Shirley's mouth drops open. "No kidding."

"Yeah, that's what I was told by Toby's oldest brother, Elbridge. He said that Toby was framed and wasn't guilty of rape. He said, 'My brother has a lot of faults, but he's not a liar.' However, his folks didn't support their son's claim of innocence because he did admit to being in the Iverson house.

"The Perkinses were embarrassed and shamed by the charge of rape. They let it stand, knowing that Toby was capable of doing such an act. He had just been released from reform school, having been sent there for sexual misconduct. So, of course, it was easy to believe Trudy and

Curtsy. Since Toby had previous misdemeanor charges, he was given a stiff sentence for breaking and entering and raping a minor."

Shirley remarks, "Harold has implied that Toby might not be Emily Ann's father but with no details. So you think he was framed?"

"Yes I do. Prentice Silver, president of the bank, is a big shot in town, and a good friend of Attorney Iverson. I think both men were anxious to clear their family names and pin all the blame on Toby."

"I never knew this Randy Silver."

"He got killed in a car accident right after the Curtsy incident. He was a bit on the wild side. It was right after that the Iverson boys moved to Janice and Jim's farm. Trudy told me it was so her sons could learn what real work was, but I think there were other reasons. Attorney Iverson knew that his brother Jim and sister-in-law Janice would make a good home for his sons. He also knew that Trudy had lost control of their kids."

Shirley, weak and wobbly, gets out of bed and carries Steven to change him. "Thanks for washing all his diapers." She looks out in the living room and notices two phones on her writing desk. "You must keep busy talking on the telephone."

"I need a lot of information in order to write my column. I only use about ten percent of it because most of what I hear isn't fit to print. You'd be surprised how people like to call and tell the misfortunes of folks they know. Some won't even give their name, but I recognize voices."

"I don't see your column every week."

"No, I only write it when I have enough material. The editor lets me be flexible."

Shirley sits on the edge of the bed, while Honeydew is holding Steven. Shirley stares out the window onto the street. "You probably know this teacher Joe is dating?"

Honeydew says, "No, I don't. Of course, he travels throughout the county so it's probably someone who doesn't live in town. Rejection is a difficult fact of life. I don't think I'm going to help you by discussing reasons why he's dating someone else. Just be thankful you have Steven and a good home on Pine Mountain. You'll have other chances. Heavens, you're young, attractive, and are making quite the name for yourself."

"Thanks, but you're right. I need to forget Joe."

Honeydew says, "Speaking of rejection, did you know that Harold and I have seen a lot of each other in the past? He doesn't come anymore, except when he needs me."

"I'm sorry about that. I've probably kept him too busy. He loves reading your column. He also loves watching television. I'll see if I can get you two together more."

"A television! No wonder he doesn't have time for me. Harold Tully has a television. This just doesn't sound like anything he'd buy. Heavens, they're expensive."

"Joe gave it to us. It was one that didn't work in town. It looks like the same one that came from his father's office, but he didn't say." Shirley pauses. "You know, I'm feeling great, good enough to go back to Pine Mountain."

"It's been fun to have Steven, and also to have your company. Although until now, you were, shall we say, out of it." They laugh.

Friday morning, Harold's at Honeydew's place. He promises, "Look, I'll be down to see you real soon."

Shirley remarks, "Bring her to Pine Mountain. I'd like her company."

Honeydew angrily says, "He's never taken me to his farm! He's too busy for me!"

"I just said, I'll visit you real soon!"

Shirley looks at Honeydew. "Thanks for the great rest, and caring for Steven, too."

"Oh my Steven is a sweetie, aren't you?" He returns a big smile.

Out in the yard, in the morning light, Honeydew closely examines his hair. "I think he's going to have dark curly hair."

Shirley looks too. "Maybe you're right. We'll see."

Harold starts the truck and backs out of the yard. Shirley waves as the truck pulls into the street. "How come you don't visit her more often?"

"Well, I really don't know. I—I guess Pine Mountain is different than when I was alone, or had some sad-sack woman rattlin' around the house. Then, it was a relief to get away. Now, you ain't sayin' another word about Honeydew, that's my business."

"I'm just asking. I enjoy her company. I like having a woman to visit with."

"You mean I ain't good enough company."

"Nothing against you, but it's not the same. Men and women see things differently."

"Really. I guess I ain't learned it all, yet'"

As the truck starts to climb the mountain Shirley says, "Look, the shad is in bloom." The white-flowered bush leans toward the road, lining the pathway to Harold's place.

"Yup, I noticed the other day."

"You did? I didn't think you'd—uh, well forget it."

"I know—you didn't think I'd know what the shadbush was."

"Something like that. You never seem to care about such things."

"Maybe I didn't used to, but I remember my ma always talked about how much she liked the flowering shad."

As the farm comes into view, the cows are grazing by the road and Harold stops the truck. Shirley screams, "Harold, you bought a bull! Wow, what a beauty! Where did you find him?"

"At the Coleses'. He's registered. Zack couldn't believe I'd be in the market for such a nice bull. Zack said he's the best bull he's ever raised. He's outta a hell of a cow that's made the most milk of any they've ever owned and he's sired by the High Life bull whose daughters are milkin' up a storm."

The young bull trots toward the fence and sticks his neck out to sniff while his tongue rolls beyond his muzzle to play with his nose ring. "He's a handsome fellow: good size, sleek coat, strong over the back and a good set of rear legs. Gee, I'm happy you bought him. He should make a big difference in your herd."

"Yup, that's what I was thinkin'."

They drive into the yard. Shirley screams again, only louder, loud enough to scare Steven. "I don't believe it! You bought that tractor, a new Ford and mower, and a new hay loader. Harold Tully, you old devil! You're so full of surprises!"

Harold smiles, seeing Shirley excited. "That loader is the new raker bar type. No more foolin' around with wood slats and ropes. I got to thinkin' about what you said about the government ending up with all my money, and I decided, by golly, we might's well enjoy life."

"That's right! Look at this, will you? Willy's mowing the lawn. Isn't he about the biggest dear? Joe or no Joe, I'd say I have about the two nicest men as my friends."

Willy pushes the lawn mower over to the truck and gives Shirley a toothless grin.

"Willy Smithson, aren't you the greatest coming to help out. I'm going to make both of you fellows a great supper."

Shirley carries Steven toward the house. She pauses and listens for the pines, a sound she hasn't enjoyed for some time.

Harold follows. "By golly, I want you to stay in this house for a few days. Stop worrying about the farm. That Willy's damn good with the cows. There's no need for you gettin' up early, the way you've been doin'."

Shirley ponders the request. "I can't completely forget the cows."

Harold puts on a scowl. "You stay in the house."

She glances at him without a comment. After Harold leaves, she looks out the west window and admires the view of the various hues of green, and the near and distant mountain ranges. *What a beautiful place*!

She watches Willy digging in his feet, pushing the lawn mower through an accumulation of snarl from forty or more years of neglect. *I hope he stays. Life will be great even after Joe.*

Late Friday afternoon John and Emily Ann arrive in an older-model Plymouth. Emily Ann runs to the house. "I want to see Terry and Steven."

Shirley goes out to greet John Gray. His face is drawn and he's solemn. Shirley says, "I'm so sorry about your wife."

He smiles slightly. "Thanks for putting Emily Ann—uh, on the bus. We've been able to give each other—uh, a lot of support." When Shirley shakes his hand, it is rough, but he has a firm grip, and a presence about him that makes her feel he's genuine.

John says, "This—uh, is a beautiful spot. I can't think of a better place—uh, for Emily Ann to grow up."

Shirley thanks him and says, "I want to prepare you for Harold. He owns and runs this farm, and he uses tough language; but underneath he's a good person. Also, right now, Willy works for us. He is mentally slow, but he's got a big heart."

"I'm not worried—uh, about these folks. I meet all kinds as a fisherman. You're going to be—uh, Emily Ann's new mother, and from what I see—uh, I think she's lucky."

"Thanks. Won't you stay the night? We have a room ready for you. Come in and have a snack."

They go inside and John greets the two men. Willy is on his way out the door to finish the lawn.

Shirley calls to him, "Willy, you sit down. I'm about to serve a snack."

Harold adds, "Sit down, Willy. That lawn ain't been mowed for over forty years. I guess it can wait another half hour." Willy can't be held down. He leaves quickly while drinking some lemonade and placing the glass on the kitchen sink. He heads out the door.

Harold comments, "Golly, I can see why Shirley wanted to hire Willy. They're both in continual motion, having to work at somethin' all the time."

John acts as if searching for conversation. His eyes scan the room.

Harold asks, "You been a fisherman most of your life?"

"Yes, I own my own boat—uh, so I feel I have to—uh, work it most every day. There are slack times—uh, when I pick up carpentry jobs—uh, to help make ends meet."

"A carpenter? You're just the man we need to rebuild a hay wagon for us."

"Really? You need—uh, some work done?"

"Sure do. We're goin' to get hayin' done in short order this year and need two wagons. They've got to be fixed up so we can hook the horses onto them as well as the tractor. I've bought a two-wheel rig with a pole and a hitch on back. When we get hayin' the field up back—we call that the five-and-five field—we can bring the wagons back and forth with the horses, and use the tractor to load. Pullin' a wagon and hay loader on these hills is hard work for the horses. With Willy unloadin', I'll drive the horse to run the hay fork. Shirley can drive the tractor, and we'll hire on someone to load the loads."

Shirley smiles. "Good for you. You've actually been thinking about haying."

"Well of course, what'd you think I bought all this equipment for?"

John suggests, "I'll take a look—uh, at your wagon, figure what we need for—uh, lumber, and get right at it tomorrow. I've got to go home—uh, to Boston Sunday afternoon. My wife and I have been taking—uh, Emily Ann to church. Sunday morning—uh, I'll plan to go with her."

The wagon has to be totally rebuilt. It is much more of a job than John anticipated. However, Harold, he and Emily Ann go with the truck to buy the needed lumber, bolts, nails, saw, hammer, square, and measuring tape. Harold has few usable tools on the farm and John has left his in Boston.

Later that day Shirley is working in the kitchen, getting a meal ready for five people. John is working on the wagon. Emily Ann is pushing Steven in the carriage. Shirley has a free moment to walk around the yard. The dandelions are starting to go to seed. She remembers a poem she learned in English class by Robert Frost, *Nothing Gold Can Stay*. "Nature's first green is gold/Her hardest hue to hold."

The June grass has grown its full height, and the orchard grass is fully headed out. Shirley looks toward the west. *More rain is due soon. It's a good thing John can work on the wagon under cover.*

She takes a look at what she now thinks of as Harold's garden. The peas are breaking through the ground and a lot of witch grass is poking pale green stems through as well. *This garden will take a lot of work, just as Harold said.* She walks down to visit with John. He needs help with the boards, since Harold has left for the barn and Emily Ann has gone with Steven.

John says, "I'm going to—uh, miss Elizabeth. She had a lot of courage—and uh, was in pain for a long time. She and Emily Ann were—uh, very close. They did a lot together. That's the bad part—uh, about fishing for a living. You have to—uh, be gone so much. I just had bought the boat when—uh, we found out that—uh, Elizabeth had cancer. It was like a trap. Our insurance wasn't that good, so—uh, if the fishing was good, I could keep up—uh, with the medical bills and make payments on the boat. After I sell the boat—uh, and pay off some remaining bills, maybe I can—uh, relocate near here so I can—uh, see Emily Ann more often. I didn't really want her—uh, growing up in Boston. I'm glad she's here."

Shirley asks, "Could you figure out what you need to get for your boat to pay what you owe and tack on enough more to pay your bills? Would that work? Ask that price and see if your boat sells. If it sells, you could move up here more quickly."

"I doubt that my boat—uh, would sell for that much, but maybe—uh, I'm seeing the glum side of things right now. It was hard to see—uh, someone you love waste away. Did you—uh, lose your husband, too?"

"No, I've never had one."

"Oh." His face slightly flushes.

Harold and Willy check on the progress. Harold remarks, "By golly, John, you're comin' right along. Maybe if we all work with you tomorrow, we can finish."

Willy adds, "I ain't no good at poundin' nails and makin' stuff. After chores tomorrow, I want ta work in Shirley's garden."

Harold looks at Shirley and frowns. Shirley looks at Harold. He laughs. "That's a good idea, Willy. I don't know whose garden it is, but if we all give it the attention it's been gettin', it's goin' to be a good one."

Shirley says, "I'll bet you men are hungry. Let's go to the house."

She serves roast chicken with potatoes, carrots, gravy, and chocolate pie with whipped cream. Willy is trying to chew with his gums. "Ya know, Shirley, this is the best eatin' I've ever et."

Harold agrees. "Little bit better than my cookin', huh, Willy?"

Willy lets out a big laugh.

John adds his praise. "This sure is—uh, a tasty meal, Shirley. If you don't mind—uh, Emily Ann and I will go to—uh, to the front room to read—uh, then I want to go to bed."

Willy helps Shirley with the dishes. She smiles. *His big joy in life is helping. He's just filled with generosity.*

Harold, John, and Emily Ann spend Saturday rebuilding the hay wagon. John gets up early and leaves the house about the same time as Willy—four-thirty.

Shirley likes her new role of just being in the house. Willy is a great help in the barn and with the hens and he does a good job grading the eggs. She is relieved that jobs she once considered hers can now be done by Willy.

Sunday morning, Shirley asks if she and Steven can go to church with John and Emily Ann. He agrees. They travel to town. John parks his car under the stately maples that line the street. They walk the marble steps leading to the front door, and enter the church, looking to be a typical family. Harry Durkee greets them. Shirley is wearing a rose-colored dress and high heels. She's put on lipstick. Emily Ann is carrying Steven. John introduces himself and his daughter to Harry. Harry beams at Shirley. "I'm pleased to meet you, Mrs. Gray."

She laughs. "Hi, Harry."

"Oh my gosh. It's you, Shirley!"

Several people are there that Shirley knows: Attorney Iverson, Alice Coles, Elmer Butson with his wife, plus Perry Bent and his wife, and the Ericksons, too. Mrs. Perkins sits alone. Louise Durkee is the only one she recognizes in the choir.

The hymns are fun for Shirley to sing: Faith of Our Fathers, In the Garden, and Jesus, Lover of My Soul. *As a kid, I thought I'd like to be a singer someday.*

The choir director announces that rehearsal will be on Thursday evening at seven, and new voices are needed.

I can do that. Why not? I love to sing.

After church, she makes it a point to greet Mrs. Perkins. She's looking old. Her hair is whiter than she remembers and the lines in her face are deeper. "Mrs. Perkins, I'm Shirley Mason." The older woman flings her arms around Shirley. Shirley knows that Mildred Perkins's life and burdens have been heavy, especially being the mother of Toby. As the two women cling to each other, she realizes that love overwhelms anything that might have happened in the past.

Mrs. Perkins's sober face breaks into a big smile. "How are you doing, my dear? You look absolutely great!"

"Fine! I'd like you to meet Emily Ann, Mrs. Perkins." Shirley takes Steven from Emily Ann. "This is Toby's daughter."

Mrs. Perkins hugs the girl and remarks, "My gracious, what a morning this has been. Hello, Emily Ann. I'm your grandmother. I remember when you were born and I wondered when and if I might see you again. I have a feeling that any grandmother would be proud to call you her own." Mrs. Perkins turns to John. "What a lovely daughter you have." John nods and thanks her.

They drive back from church and into the farmyard. There is a moderate breeze from the west; a clearing weather pattern is on its way. Shirley stops to listen to the pines' soft and tender sound.

They enter the house to find that Willy has the table all set. Shirley put a roast in the oven before church. She remarks, "Is this place ever hot!"

Harold agrees. "Golly, that old stove can really crank it out."

Shirley suggests, "Maybe at some point, we can get screens in the windows."

John mentions as he is eating, "I can fix those wagon hitches—uh, next weekend for you. It won't take long. I'll bring—uh, my tools along."

Harold asks, "You comin' back next weekend? Good, that'll give us a chance to fix all my equipment before hayin'"

CHAPTER NINETEEN

Willy comes running into the house at five in the morning in a panic. He yells, "Maria's down with the fever!"

Shirley jumps out of bed and meets Harold in the kitchen. "I'll take care of it. You go back to bed."

"You've still gotta meddle in the cow work. Son of a bitch, I thought you were gettin' easier to live with, but sometimes you're as irritatin' as a stone in my shoe, always havin' to take charge."

"Just go back to bed." Shirley smiles as she's leaving the house. "It's Maria, the cow, not your old flame." *He'd use that filthy dirty tire pump. And we'd probably lose the cow from a bad case of mastitis.*

Harold turns and slams the door.

Willy is at the point of tears. "Gosh, he's mad."

"Don't let it bother you. I'll feed him a good breakfast and he'll be himself again."

She goes to the pasture and kneels by the comatose Maria. She feels for the vein, bigger than the size of her thumb, allows time for the blood to pool and pressure to build, and then injects the needle. Blood flows from the needle. She connects the tube, holds up the 500cc bottle, and waits for it to bubble and flow into the cow's bloodstream. The liquid calcium does its miracle and Maria is up in a few minutes, walking toward the barn.

She looks at Willy and speaks firmly. "You let me know when a cow has the fever from now on. It will work a lot better that way. Harold uses the tire pump, and that's not the way to treat milk fever."

"I knowed, I knowed, it ain't a good way. I'll be sure ta let ya knowed. I'll let ya knowed; I sure will. I don't want him gettin' ugly, not me." Willy smiles. "I like it when you doctor the cows. Talkin' nice ta me 'n' all."

"Doesn't Harold talk nice to you?" Shirley tries to brush off the point she knows Willy is making and doesn't wait for his answer; she leaves the barn and takes a short walk through the back meadow. She wants to see if the manure has made a difference in the growth of the grasses. In a splotchy pattern she can see many shades of green in the undergrowth. In the places where manure landed, the growth is dark green, but in places where there was no manure, the growth is pale green. She remembers that Harry Durkee used commercial fertilizer on his fields especially after first cutting. It doesn't look to her as if the fields are very fertile. The grasses in general lack the lushness she remembers seeing. She knows from all Harold's other farming practices that probably commercial fertilizer isn't something he would buy. *Maybe Elmer Butson can sell Harold some fertilizer to get a better second cutting, and then I won't have to deal with him.*

She walks back to the barn. "Willy, how do you grain the cows?"

He smiles at her. "I give all the cows the same. That's what Harold told me ta do."

"In the next day or so, I'll work with you on a better way to grain them."

"Okay Shirley—so long's Harold ain't mad."

The production has dropped. I should weigh the cows' milk and make up a grain feeding plan by placing lines on each cow's card, since Willy can't read numbers. Each line can mean a can of grain, something that he'll understand.

Shirley meets Harold coming to the barn. "Bet you're glad I gave you a chance to get a little extra sleep."

He takes his pipe from his mouth and holds it in his hand. "Yup, you're just a queen. I mean a queen bee ready to sting me with your notions when I ain't expectin' it."

"By the way, Maria looks pretty good, since she's had a bottle."

He drags on his pipe and blows a buff of smoke. "Yup, I know for damn sure she looks better now than my Maria. If she's still livin,' she'd be in some gutter."

Shirley goes back to the house, which is quiet. She climbs the stairs and looks in Willy's room. Inspecting the walls, she realizes they have never been painted or papered. *Fixing up Willy's room would be a good project for Emily Ann and me.*

The men come in for breakfast. She serves oatmeal, popovers, and sausage.

Shirley asks, "Willy, how would you like Emily Ann and me to fix up your room with paint and wallpaper? Harold owes me some money from last week's eggs. I'll bet that will just about buy the supplies."

"Ya ain't got ta do that, Shirley. I ain't never had a nice room. I mean—this one is nicer than where I slept at the Ericksons—that one ain't even got a window. I slept on some paddin' on the floor. The chimney went right up through the middle. In the winter, I pulled my covers next ta the bricks, 'n' they kept me warm most nights. In the summer I was hot at night, bein' under the roof an' all, so those nights, I slept in the barn."

Harold comments, "Those Ericksons—what's wrong with them?"

As they are talking, a car drives in the yard. Shirley glances out the west window. "The devil himself is here."

Harold sees the car. "So it's Jules. Let the bastard walk to the house. Hell, he'll probably have a heart attack tryin' to make the grade to the back door."

Willy runs upstairs.

Jules is flushed as he knocks on the entry door. Sweat is pouring from his wide brow. With a blue-checkered handkerchief in his hand, he continually wipes his face. Shirley opens the entry door. "Come in and have a seat."

The heavy man continues to breathe gustily, emptying his lungs with a gush as he sits, sweeping his face again with the handkerchief, revealing that it is continually held in his hand during hot weather. "That's quite a climb from the car up to the house."

Harold shrugs. "Never noticed. We walk it all the time."

Jules continues, "You said you wanted Willy's help for a few days. I figure he's been helping you now for more than just a few days. I've come to take him back home."

Harold answers matter-of-factly, "His home is here now."

Jules raises his voice, "You think you can get away with coming onto my farm and taking a man right out from under me!"

Harold remains calm. "Jules, why don't you ask Willy what he wants to do?"

Shirley quietly leaves the kitchen and goes to get Willy. He is curled in a ball hiding under his blankets. She speaks in a tender voice, "Willy, you come downstairs and let Jules know what you want to do, go with him or stay here."

He comes out from under the covers and sits on the edge of his bed with his hands flat between his knees, slapping them as he swings his legs back and forth. "He'll be mad. I hate people ta be mad."

Willy's eyes dart around the room. He looks as wide-eyed as a wild cat. Deep lines spread from the corners of his mouth caused by his almost continual smile. Only, at the moment, the smile lines go straight down. He's nervously digging with his index finger at a small hole in his bib-overalls near his knee, twisting the blue denim.

"Do you want to stay here?"

"Oh, yes! With you, 'n' Harold, 'n' Emily Ann, 'n' Steven." He begins to cry.

Shirley sits, holding his hand. "Try not to be afraid. I want you to stay here, too, and I want to make your room a special place that you can call your own. We can paint and paper it just the way you want it."

Willy begins to relax, liking Shirley's plan. He momentarily forgets about Jules and looks at the walls. "I want my room ta be purty. I want it blue jest like the sky." Pointing with his work-worn finger, he continues, "Can ya paint a big red sun right there, so when I git up in the mornin' 'n' turn on the light I can see the sun? I ain't ever knowed anyone so nice as ya, Shirley."

"Thanks, Willy, and I feel the same about you."

"That ain't true because I knowed I'm dumb."

Shirley grips his hand tightly and directly looks at him. "People usually like you more for how you act with your heart than what you do with your head. You're all heart, Willy, and that's why I think you're special."

He smiles. "I like bein' with ya, Shirley."

"Willy, you'll always be like a son to me and this will always be your room. Emily Ann and I will paint and paper it just the way you want it. Now let's go downstairs and tell Jules you're staying. That's all you have to say: 'I'm staying.'"

"I'm scared of Jules, but I'll say that."

He hesitantly follows Shirley downstairs. When they reach the kitchen, Jules turns and looks at him while Willy stands in a tremble. "You get your things; it's time you came with me!"

Willy turns to Shirley. "What da I say now?"

"Just what you told me upstairs."

"I'm stayin', I'm stayin', I'm stayin'."

Jules replies angrily, exerting his power over Willy, as a demanding master would his dog. "Well hell, if this ain't a rehearsed state of affairs. You're coming with me!"

Willy's voice quivers, "I—I want—ta—stay." Big tears roll down his face and he sniffs. Shirley slips her hand in her apron pocket and hands him a hankie.

"Well, you half-wit dummy—you're coming with me!"

Shirley is bursting with anger. Harold looks at her and sees her sweep her hair into place. He has no such emotional tie to Willy, except he does appreciate his good help. *I can see why Jules wants Willy back, but it just ain't right the way they treat him.* Harold speaks firmly. "Jules, you might's well leave." He sticks his empty pipe in his mouth.

Jules barks back at Harold, "I didn't come here to leave empty-handed!"

"I don't know what more I can do. Willy ain't wantin' to work for you."

Jules fumes, "You came just like a thief and snatched him away! Now, tell him he's got to come home with me."

Harold takes his pipe out of his mouth and lays it on the table. "Damn it to hell, Jules, this is a free country. If the man wants to work for us, it's your tough luck. Let's end the subject. You're leavin' empty-handed. That's all there is to it!"

Emily Ann has been quietly giving Steven a bath at the sink. Shirley sits at the kitchen table acting as a bystander, yet nervous over the direction Jules and Harold's conversation seems to be headed. She spontaneously reaches for her barrette, and realizes she hasn't worn it for some time, yet resists running to her room to clip it in her hair.

Jules wipes his forehead again. His face is a brilliant red with blue blood vessels woven into his broad flat nose. He blows his words in a roar. "You people are trash—you've got quite the clan here. Shirley's prancing around as proud as a peacock with a kid. No one knows the father. She even has the brass to come to church. Here's a young girl, where did she come from? And Harold, you've had so many women in your life that no one could ever consider you nothing but an old whoremaster, and now you throw in a half-wit. What a mix! We decent folks don't like being around scum. I guess considering the situation, this is a good place for Willy. Let him stay with the likes of you people."

Emily Ann turns and puts her hands on her hips. Her brown eyes flare with anger. She blurts, "I'm Emily Ann Gray from Boston, my father's a fisherman and my grandfather is Attorney Iverson. I think you're nasty. I'm certainly not scum."

"Well, if you aren't a smart-mouthed little brat."

"I don't like you. You're an awful man to say what you did."

Shirley is startled that Emily Ann would talk to a strange adult as she does, and she nervously goes to be with her and Steven. She just wants Jules to leave, because she knows Harold is getting mad enough to be dangerous.

Harold warns, "You've got a choice—you can leave now, or I'll put you out of your misery, and goddamn, I'm mad enough to do it." He jams his pipe back in his mouth with authority, and bites hard.

Jules gets up with a great deal of effort and says, "You're threatening me?"

Harold yanks his pipe out of his mouth. "You're son-of-a-bitchin' right I am. Get out that door before you leave in pieces. If you don't, I'll blow your ass off with my double-barreled shotgun."

Jules snarls, "What a cheap bunch. I'm sorry I came." He wipes his brow.

Harold yells, "Believe me, you old bastard, I'm sorry, too!"

Jules threatens, "Here here, no one talks to Jules Erickson like that. You filthy old whoremaster."

"I'm sick of this. I'm gittin' my gun." He stomps toward the front room.

Shirley runs toward Jules. "Please leave right now before somebody gets hurt."

She stops Harold, who has just taken his gun out of the cabinet. "Put that away, this is getting out of hand."

Harold looks at her wide eyes, striking him, sending a message of fear instead of anger. He respects her emotions and turns to put the gun away. He closes the cabinet. With the *whoosh* of the door, he smells the remnants of wood stain and varnish, and rests his hand on it, taking a deep breath. His shoulders sag and his other arm drops limp. Shirley leaves the room. He walks into the kitchen and sits in the Morris chair.

He watches from the west window as Jules leaves the yard. "I'll show that son of a bitch that I am somebody. Jules and the likes of him are goin' to have to reckon with Harold Tully—they'll see—they'll sit up and take notice."

Shirley walks toward Harold to get his attention. "I hope you don't change from anything he had to say. He's got it all wrong, and you know it."

"Some of the things he said are true. I ain't amounted to a whole hell of a lot, not until—well you—you know." Harold's eyes water. "It hurt—just the same, it hurt what Jules said—to know what some people really think of me."

Shirley puts her hand on his shoulder and gently shakes it. "Listen to me. Harold Tully's twice the man that Jules Erickson is or ever will be—just remember, I know you both. Jules takes too much credit for who he thinks he is, and you don't give yourself enough credit for who you really are."

Harold looks at Shirley through blurry eyes. "I'm much obliged for you sayin' that. I ain't never thought I was deservin' of such talk." He turns and stares, taking in the view. "Since livin' through all the hurt and sorrow for all these years, I guess I figured I was someone maybe I ain't. Maybe changin' ain't such a bad idea after all."

Shirley quietly stands with her hand still resting on his shoulder.

He studies the distant mountain ranges and ridges. "Golly, the sky has a new take to it. It's blue and pure. It ain't only something to look at to forecast the weather, but it's more. Beyond the mountains and the blue I can see milky white clouds, big and soft-lookin' as a big pillow, floatin' my way. It looks like rain is comin', but beyond that, in the wide open sky, I see wonderment, thinkin' just what might be out there."

Shirley remarks, "The sky is a mystery—and beautiful, too."

That night a heavy rain does come from the west, giving the earth and Harold's little fields a good soaking. All the heads of the grasses are bent over toward the east. It looks like millions of tiny creatures, kneeling for morning prayer and bowing their heads to worship the majestic pines that tower on the hill before them. By midmorning the hot sun and a warm breeze dry the grasses. They stand now, and their flowered heads soak in the sun.

Shirley, Emily Ann, Steven, and Willy ride in the truck to the milk stand and then continue on to buy paint, plaster, and supplies for Willy's room.

"Do you think you want wallpaper?" Shirley asks.

"I dunno, ya tell me what I want."

"No, Willy, you tell me. This is going to be your room."

After shopping for paint and wallpaper, Shirley stops briefly at the Extension Office to pick up a leaflet on wallpapering. She once helped Janice Iverson paper a room, but that is the extent of her experience. She knows any sort of effort would satisfy Willy, but she and Emily Ann aren't about to do just any kind of job.

Shirley sets her jaw. *It will be well done, the best Emily Ann and I can do. Willy deserves it.*

Willy's room is small, just big enough for a single bed and bureau, a chair, and a small closet. The east wall is where Emily Ann will paint the mural of the rising sun. Later that day, the two start: Shirley on the woodwork and Emily Ann painting light blue on the east wall, planning to add crowns of green representing the trees. She saves a large space in the center for an orange-yellow sun. The green crowns will be drawn from a solid base of green at the bottom of the wall.

Willy charges up the stairs frequently to check on his room. Every time he looks in, his face lights up, and with a big, toothless grin he says, "It looks so purty."

At night chores, Shirley, as she promised Willy, starts weighing each cow's milk to set up the system of lines for graining. Harold uses a quart coffee can to measure out the grain. The full can weighs a pound.

Shirley remembers that on the farms where the cows produced the best, they were usually fed one pound of grain for every three pounds of milk. She has a black crayon she uses to draw the lines on the white cards hanging over each cow. She weighs Betty's milk—fifteen pounds. Shirley draws five lines on her card.

Willy looks at the cards. "That's a lot more grain than I've been feedin'."

"It probably is; but do you understand how they should be grained? For each line you give the cow one can of grain."

"I knowed, I knowed, but what if Harold ain't likin' it, 'n' gets mad?"

"He'll be in the barn in a while, and we'll talk about this. Now see, Willy, Susie only gave three pounds so she should get only one can."

"I've been givin' all the cows four cans night 'n' mornin'."

"Susie has been getting too much. Probably when we finish, we can see that the whole herd won't be fed more grain, but the cows that need to have the most will be fed right. I should do this again in three or four days, then we can change the lines, because the fresh cows will increase in production and they'll need to have more."

Willy smiles. "I like ta have ya ta talk ta when I milk."

"Harold is usually here, isn't he?"

"Not fer very long. Anyway, Harold ain't you."

"I like being with you, too, Willy, but remember you're like my son. I'm your mother, and you're my big boy."

"That don't matter ta me, I just like being near ya. Someday maybe ya could teach me my numbers so ya ain't havin' to draw lines."

"Sure, that would be great. I think Emily Ann would love to do that with you."

Harold walks in the barn. He sees Shirley, and immediately scowls. "What in hell are you doin' now?"

"I'm trying to set up a system so Willy can better grain the cows."

"You ain't leavin' your nose out of the barn—are you? We were gettin' on just fine without you!"

"Sure you were. The cows have dropped three cans a day. Doesn't that tell you something?"

Harold takes his pipe out of his vest pocket and starts banging it on the barn wall. "The cows always drop after the first flush of milk from new grass."

"They don't need to drop as much as they have if they're grained right."

"Bastard, woman, you burn me!" Harold's can of tobacco is tipped up as he fills his pipe, watching Shirley and carelessly spilling it on the barn floor. His jaw is set as he stares at her.

Willy milks the last cow, and she draws the appropriate marks. She walks up to Harold and gives him a big smile. "Do it my way and you'll make a lot more money."

"No one ain't never goin' to say that I ain't easy at lettin' things go your way." He draws on his pipe and blows a copious quantity of smoke at her. Shirley backs away and laughs.

Later that night she leaves the farm to go to choir practice. It's dusk in the village and nearly dark inside the church vestibule, but there's enough light from a window to see to open the door into the sanctuary. Walking on carpet, she's able to enter without being heard. Mustiness mixed with furniture polish wafts in her face.

There's a ceiling light shining down on the organ. Frumpy, gray-haired women are standing under the light, holding sheet music. Mrs. Forman, the organist and choir director, is playing and intermittently stopping to rehearse a difficult stanza.

Shirley stands at the end of a pew, watching thirty feet from the group. *It was easy to say I'd like to sing, but now I feel out of place. Even though I'm standing in darkness, I hope my guardian angel is with me in this. I'm not hidden from you, you know my every thought and right now I'm scared.* She reluctantly takes a few more steps forward.

Mrs. Forman sees her. "Oh, welcome. You've come to rehearsal?"

"Yes, I—I've come to—to sing."

"Well, well, isn't this wonderful, ladies? We have a new member to join us."

Shirley can hear Louise Durkee sneeringly remark, "It's Shirley Mason!"

At the same time, she hears a chorus of cheerful voices saying, "Welcome."

I feel like a young chick entering a circle of old hens.

Mrs. Forman says, "So you're Shirley Mason. I'm so glad to meet you. It's great to have a young voice! Let's see, do you sing alto or soprano?"

"I have no idea."

"Why don't you try a line or two of this familiar hymn?"

Mrs. Forman plays while Shirley sings:

Our God our help in ages past,
Our hope for years to come.
Our shelter from the stormy blast
And our eternal home.

She can hear a swarm of spontaneity, "A beautiful voice!" And one cutting response, "Oh, she does everything just perfectly!"

Mrs. Forman, a short, white-haired, woman, says, "Wonderful tone and volume. Do you read music?"

"No, I don't."

Mrs. Forman offers, "If you'd come a little early each week, I'd give you lessons."

"Thanks, that would be great! I'll plan on it."

"Here's a folder of sheet music. The piece we're practicing is on page sixteen. Why don't you stand next to Louise Durkee? Have you two women met?"

Shirley says, "Yes." There's no response from Louise.

Mrs. Forman directs, "You'll both sing soprano."

Louise raises her chin and turns away from Shirley. She mumbles, "I've been a member of this choir for almost twenty years and can't read music. Do you think Her Highness would offer me lessons—not a chance! But Shirley Mason waltzes in here and instantly grabs the spotlight."

Mrs. Forman taps the top of the piano. "Quiet please."

Shirley smiles and holds her music high enough to hide her expression. *There was a time when I had to take her crap. Now, it's different.*

They practice a bit more and during a pause, Shirley lowers her voice and remarks to Louise, "Your husband invited me to church. I just thought I'd make the most of it."

Louise jerks her shoulders back, standing erect. Shirley can see the veins pop on her neck, and red bloom from the hem of her collar to her hairline. She hisses, "I swear Harry worships you!"

"Louise—really! We're just friends."

"Baloney!"

"Well, you can think what you want. Let's drop the subject, I've come to practice." Shirley glances at Louise's music. "It's page sixteen, not eighteen. No wonder you haven't been singing."

"No I haven't been! I was doing just fine until you came!"

Mrs. Forman taps the piano again. "Let's start from the beginning."

The next morning, Shirley gets up at the same hour as Willy to begin the papering project. She starts over the north door, working from right to left. She figures that by the time she reaches the sloping south wall, her papering skills hopefully will have improved. She places the first piece over the door, and is ready for a strip next to the door.

She discovers that the door casing isn't square. If she moves the paper to abut the casing, the paper isn't square with the ceiling, or with the mop board. She tries moving the paper in all sorts of directions to solve an unsolvable problem. While trying to straighten the paper by pressing with the palm of her hand, a piece the size of her hand tears away and slides across the slippery surface of the wall. Quickly lifting her hand, she sees an accumulation of wet wallpaper resembling the shape of an oriental fan. Now, trying to pull it back in place, she realizes the torn edges don't quite meet.

She stands back and studies the problem and wrinkles her nose at the lumpy, torn, crooked piece of wallpaper clinging to a crooked wall. She pulls the paper off and throws it. She glances at the clock. It's five-thirty. She decides to go to the Iversons to get some advice from Janice. *It looked easy when Janice Iverson and I papered.*

Steven and Emily Ann are still sleeping, so she leaves a note on the kitchen table.

She drives across town to the Iversons, and stops and walks to the milk house, having heard the jangling of pails rolling steel against steel in a washtub. Janice is doing the milk dishes. "Hi, Janice, how are you?"

She turns around. "Shirley Mason! It's been a long time since I've seen you. You look as bright and snappy as ever."

Janice has always been outgoing and friendly, but she has changed. Her hair has turned prematurely gray, and the lines of worry and fatigue are telling on her face. "Jimmy's downstairs in the stable. Let's say hello, and then we'll go to the house for some coffee and a chat."

Shirley, momentarily, had forgotten about Jimmy and doesn't care to meet him, but Janice is already halfway down the stairs.

When they reach the stable, Jimmy looks up from graining the cows and sees Shirley. "This is a surprise, seeing Shirley Mason at this hour. I hear those cows up on Pine Mountain are milking to beat hell."

"I guess so, considering they're small, bony, and a mixture of every breed going."

Jimmy's flannel shirt is unbuttoned, hanging over his blue jeans. His youthful face needs a shave and his straight blond hair is in wild disorder, but it all adds to his rugged good looks. He has that friendly Iverson manner, immediately reminding her of Joe. But Joe is more polished, and better trained at meeting people. She says, "I'm here to learn how to wallpaper from your Aunt Janice."

"You've come to the right place. She's the best."

As they leave the barn for the house, Shirley looks over the cows and is impressed with the size and quality of their Holsteins as well as the neatness of the place. *I wonder if Jimmy has changed?*

Janice walks around the house, showing Shirley how to deal with various wallpapering problems. Shirley mentions the slanting wall on the side of Willy's room.

"I always cut the paper where the slanting wall meets the knee wall. In these old farmhouses, the walls and door casings are almost never square, so you'll need to fit the paper to the wall before you paste it."

Shirley apologizes for having to leave and tells Janice she needs to go home to feed her son. The older woman looks disappointed. "I was hoping you could have breakfast with us, so you and Jimmy could get reacquainted."

Shirley tucks her hair in place. "I'm sorry, Janice, maybe some other time." She leaves, thinking the woman acts lonely, but a visit with Jimmy can wait.

She drives in the yard and runs to the house, hoping Steven hasn't been too much of a problem for Emily Ann. She enters the kitchen.

Emily Ann remarks, "Am I ever glad you're home! He's hungry!"

"I'm sorry to have left Steven with you. Has he given you much trouble?"

"No, except he's hungry." Shirley feeds him while Emily Ann is getting breakfast. Shirley raises her voice as she's sitting in her room with the door open. "I'm going to need your help with the wallpapering. I tried to do it alone this morning, but it didn't go well."

"I can help and finish painting the sun later."

By early afternoon the papering is completed. Emily Ann resumes painting the rising sun on the east wall. It is purposely drawn to be larger than life, emerging and hovering over the giant pines like a round kumquat nestled in a patch of deep green moss. She has squeezed generous amounts of orange and yellow from tubes onto a smooth board, using it as a palette. Swirling the colors with a large art brush, she continues filling the spaces between the trees with rays of orange-yellow, painting the morning sunlight filtering through the pines as soft light, yet realistic as a morning sunrise. Her imagination flows as freely as the paint, but thoughtfully. Willy comes pounding up the stairs and runs in and looks. "Wowee, look at my sun!" He jumps up and down clapping his hands. "My room looks so purty. Thank ya lots. Wowee, that sun! Jest what I asked fer!"

Emily Ann remarks, "It was fun painting the scene. Now Willy, I'm told you'd like to learn your numbers."

"Ya, could ya teach me?"

"Sure, that will be fun. Maybe you could learn to write some, too. We'll work on it nights when we have the time."

"Gee, thanks, Emily Ann."

John Gray drives to the farm that afternoon. He is pulling a trailer and his car is loaded. The rear bumper scrapes as the car enters the uneven gravel drive.

Emily Ann notices the car and runs out and hugs her father, and he throws her up in the air. "I've sold the boat! I can't believe it! It sold the first day. I even have—uh, a few dollars left after paying—uh, all my bills. Good-bye to Boston!"

Emily Ann is jumping with excitement. "You can live here. We can be a family."

John looks down at the ground and scuffs, moving larger stones with the sweep of his foot, pondering what to say. His slow words finally come. "Well, Shirley and I—uh, we—uh, aren't married. It wouldn't be right to—uh, stay here for very long."

"Why can't you live here anyway, Dad?" Emily Ann slumps in disappointment.

"Well—uh, we'll see."

She still looks concerned and pulls on her father's hand. "Dad, I miss school. Do you think it's all right that I'm not going?"

"Yes, it is. Your teacher said—uh, you did well in school. Your mother's death—uh, moving to Vermont—uh, was enough for you.

School begins again in September—uh, my guess is that—uh, it won't be difficult for you."

Harold comes out of the house to visit with John. He's happy to hear John's news.

"I can hire you for hayin'. If the weather holds we can get done in two weeks."

Shirley is standing by and hears the last remark, and realizes that Harold's plan sounds ambitious, but she's encouraged that he has forgotten about his firm beginning date of July 4th. Willy is working in the garden. She remarks to Emily Ann, "Poor fellow, it seems like he's working even more now that we've redecorated his room."

Harold looks to the west at the sky and sees long, well-defined wisps of clouds or lines as fine as hairs. "Those mares' tails tell me we're goin' to get rain in two days. Maybe it will clear after and we can get to hayin'. We've got to have three sunny hot days to dry hay."

On Friday morning, all Harold can see is blue sky. The weather forecast calls for clear weather for the next few days. He realizes he should practice with the new tractor before striking off and trying to mow a whole field. He mumbles, "I ain't even sat on the tractor since it was delivered. The fellow delivering the thing showed me how the power take-off worked that moves the knives back and forth; but I ain't sure what he told me."

He walks toward the shed, kicking some stones along the way, and looks in at the shiny gray and red tractor with black shiny tires. He draws a deep breath and enjoys the smell of new paint, but the thought of sitting on something strange scares him. *This mechanical gadget is goin' to take some gettin' used to.*

When faced with a challenge, he instinctively knows he does better with his pipe in his mouth. The smell of tobacco and being able to bite on the pipe stem give him comfort.

Shirley is hanging out clothes and wonders why mowing hasn't started yet. Looking at the sky, she sees that the sun is getting high.

Harold is missing out on some good drying time. Maybe he has some sort of problem with the tractor.

"How do I start this damn thing, anyway? Before I worry about that maybe I ought to sorta stroke her for a while, like I do the team before a big pull."

Harold's hand slides over the smooth new paint. "So girl, so now. You and I are goin' to get to know each other just fine. Now, take it easy." His hand continues to rub the tractor hood, needing all the calming he can muster, and he doesn't notice Shirley fifteen feet away, watching from the corner of the shed.

She laughs. "You going to make love with your new toy all morning or are we going to get some hay mowed?"

Harold's hands fly off the hood while he jerks to an erect position in the tractor seat. "Oh bastard! You scared me! You're so smart; you know how to do everythin', 'course. What a girl wonder!"

"You make me laugh. I'm sorry. I don't know everything, but I did drive the Iversons' Ford tractor. This one's the same. Why don't you practice with it a little here in front of the shed?" Shirley shows Harold where the starter button is located, and points out the clutch and the brakes. "This is the left wheel brake and this is the right wheel brake. You have to push both at the same time for an even stop. If you push just one, it will pull the tractor to the left or right depending on which brake you push."

He starts the tractor and looks at Shirley and listens. "It purrs like a kitten."

She shows him how to raise and lower the mower. He pulls the throttle a little more, puts the tractor in first gear, and lets off on the clutch—but too quickly. Popping the clutch causes the front wheels to lift slightly due to the weight of the mower. He reacts with alarm and jams the left brake before pushing on the clutch. The tractor pulls to the left and the front wheel smashes out a post that is supporting the shed. There is a loud snap along with the squawking of rusty nails.

Shirley yells, "Push the clutch! Push the clutch!" When the tractor stops, the support post rests on the left rear tire, and the shed roof is wavering into a sag. Shirley can't help but uncontrollably laugh, looking at the results of Harold's first twenty-foot drive on his new tractor.

Harold turns to see the post resting on the tire. His face instantly turns red while he throws up his arms and hands. "You think this a big joke. You wanted me to buy this damn thing. If I'd hooked up Jeanie and Lassie half the field would've been mowed by now."

Shirley still has a grin on her face. "Oh, just relax. You're going to like mowing."

"Yup, after I flatten a few barns. Golly, the things I let you talk me into."

Shirley says, "John can easily put that post back in place. Help me swing this cutter bar into the mowing position, and you'll be going in just a minute."

They lower the cutter bar, and he practices raising and lowering the machine. He puts the power take-off in gear and mows some grass in front of the shed. He stops, lights up his pipe again, and heads for the field that slopes south in back of the henhouse. He throws his arm up in a wave as if heading for a new adventure. "I'll mow a few times around to get the feel of this rig."

The new cutter bar sounds like twenty or more sets of sharp shears opening and closing. He likes the way it mows compared to his old cutter bar which chattered, sounding like someone shaking a pail full of metal. It plugged and jammed all the time, and left wads of uncut grass. *Look at this contraption mow! I ain't believin' my eyes.*

He likes the feel of the tractor. The horses almost instinctively know where to go, but with the tractor, the direction it goes is entirely up to the driver. He mows for an hour, and begins to see a landscape of cut hay lying in neat swaths. They are as smooth and straight as a newly graded road. He knows where almost every stone, ledge, and hummock is in the field. Some obstructions can be easily seen, but some lie hidden, unmovable, and unforgiving, ready to break and foul the machine. He has mowed the field for over forty years, and the places of breakdowns are registered in his memory.

The beauty of the pattern he is creating inspires him. He mumbles, "This is goin' so good, I guess I'll mow the whole field—never have before, but by golly, Harold Tully's gone modern. I'll tell them at Butson's, "My hayin's all done." The farmers standin' 'round on maybe a rainy day ain't goin' to believe me, but ain't that goin' to be fun? This year I'm goin' to be at the top of the list of farmers who get their hayin' done first. I'll show the likes of that bastard Jules that Harold Tully ain't no slouch."

He has mown fifteen times or more around the field when he notices he's bothering a meadowlark. Due to the quiet purr of the tractor, he can hear it calling in a clear whistle, "see-you, see-you." *Prob'ly it's the old man, and his woman's sittin' on her nest.*

The call becomes louder, and more alarming: "see-you, see-you!" He continues to mumble. "I'm gettin' closer to her nest. I guess they could always plan on nestin' in Harold Tully's fields because they ain't never been cut very early. Not this year, I've changed my ways. Go down and nest in Zack's fields. He prob'ly ain't even started fixin' his hayin' equipment yet. Golly, I hate botherin' you birds, since you went to all the work of buildin' a nest. I'll leave a little standin' so as you can go about your business."

When Harold finishes mowing, the sun is high in the sky with no clouds in sight, and there is a slight breeze. It's noon and a perfect day to dry hay.

He drives by the shed. John is working on the kicker-tedder. "This machine is in rough condition. I see—uh, that shaft is badly worn—uh, those tines on the forks—are worn short."

"Yup, guess you're right. After dinner, I'll go and buy some new tedder teeth."

After the meal, and the drive to town, Harold buys the needed parts. He then drives to see Honeydew. He's heard she is in some sort of slump and hasn't seen her column for a while. When he pulls in her yard, she doesn't come out of her house like she always has.

He walks to the door and knocks. In a minute she appears and stands filling the doorway, looking totally changed. Her hair is in snarls with a face looking pale, and eyes that droop. "Oh, it's you."

"Who in hell did you think it was—Clark Gable?"

"You aren't funny, and you have some nerve driving in my yard. I'm nothing to you. Oh, but when Harold needs me, that's different."

"Golly, you've lost some weight, and you ain't fixed up like usual."

"Why should I be? You never come anymore."

"Get in my new truck. I want to take you for a ride."

"You don't have to do that."

"I know I ain't got to, but I want to anyway." He draws on his pipe and expels a large puff of smoke. "I'll wait in the truck."

"Okay, if you insist. I'll be right out."

He gets in his truck and slams the door, and mumbles, "Shirley's talkin' about friends has got me thinkin' on such things just lately".

After a long wait, Honeydew walks out of the house. She has changed her clothes, put on some makeup, her lilac perfume, and looks more like herself. But the different clothes and perfume can't do it all because she is definitely a changed woman. "Harold, I've felt lonely and sad lately. Maybe it's a woman thing, but most of it is YOU! I just feel awful. I haven't written for the paper since Shirley and Steven left. I just don't have the energy to do anything." She quietly sobs as she blows her nose and wipes her tears.

"Well, life can be a bastard, but at the same time it can be sorta fun. Maybe I can help you feel better."

"You—you make me feel better? All you've brought me is misery." Honeydew glares at Harold and wipes her tears again. "You've just up and stopped seeing me. Why, I can't imagine, and I can't help but feel jealous of Shirley. I know I shouldn't. She so nice and it was fun having her here with Steven."

Harold lifts the visor of his cap and scratches his head. "I should've come to see you, but there's too much goin' on at home, I just ain't had a chance. I'm bringin' you up to Pine Mountain. Hell, I'm runnin' a regular hotel up there."

Honeydew smiles. "You are? Good, I can see Steven and Shirley, and going to your farm will be a first."

He pulls his cap back in place and chances a slight smile. "That's because in the past we could handle what we had to at your house."

Honeydew glares at him. "Yeah, sex—period, period, period, and I always wanted more than that, but it never came from you."

"Maybe at the time I didn't have any more to give." He looks at her, and again observes her sagging jowls. She looks tired and older. Her familiar smelling lilac perfume doesn't cover the apparent hell she has been putting herself through.

Honeydew gives Harold a questioning glance. "You don't get it. Archie died last winter and then you stopped coming to the house. Isn't that enough to put me over the edge—being lonely?"

"You start writin' again. People miss readin' what you've got to say. Hell, it's okay to read about politics, crime, and bad things happenin', but really what's interestin' is what's goin' on in town."

"Harold, you've changed." She looks at him in disbelief.

"Yup, maybe I have. Up on Pine Mountain all these years, I had a nice mother, but a Hitler for a father. Holdin' on to my money like it was the only thing I had in the world. Nursin' my hurtin' over my old man—lookin' through a little peephole at life, thinkin' that way, I wasn't givin' myself a chance to be much. Hell, I've been lookin' at the worst of things all these years. I decided to change and look for the beauty, it's there to see. I guess I ain't never seen it before, until it come to me."

"'Beauty—beauty,' you've never used that word in your whole life. What's come over you? Who talks about beauty?"

Harold's voice rises and he clenches his jaw on his pipe stem. "Hell, Honeydew, do you have to know everythin'? I—I—I guess it come to me. I dunno—It just come to me."

"You've only seen beauty in one thing since I've known you."

"Maybe I've changed. Hell, I'm not sayin' I don't turn my head when I see a good-lookin' woman, but there's a lot more goin' on. Bein' sad like you are, you're killin' all the beauty. Life is great most days. Look for the beauty, it's there. You've just got to find it."

"What's happened to you, Harold?" She stares at him. "You've never talked this way. You're like a different man."

"Oh hell, Honeydew, you're makin' too much of what I'm tellin' you. I'm just thinkin' a little different." The truck begins to climb the steep hills to the farm.

"My goodness, this is quite the mountain." The large maple limbs, laden with leaves, hang out over the road. The undercover of shad, box elder, dogwood, and cherry also lean toward the narrow pathway. To Honeydew it appears as though the truck is climbing a hill through a dark tunnel of green and it makes her nervous. "All I can see are trees and bushes." She makes a snide crack, as the tip ends of the brush touch the sides of the truck. "What a place! You sure you live way up here, or have you got some other perverted idea in mind?" She nervously adjusts her big frame in the seat and braces her feet against the floorboard.

Harold laughs. "What'd you think, I'm takin' you parkin'? What's on Pine Mountain is real. Hell, you've lived in town too long, lookin' out your window at cement."

In relief, she remarks, "Oh, I guess there is life up here! Those your cows?"

"Yup, they make most of my livin', them and my hens."

"Oh, that must be Emily Ann with the dog?"

"Yup—she's a cute kid. Her father's here helpin' with hayin'. Willy Smithson is helpin' too."

"You mean half-wit Willy? What do you want him around for?"

"See, Honeydew? Damn it, you've been lookin' at the small-minded side of life too long. Willy's a good guy with a heart as big as Pine Mountain."

"I can't believe this! You've changed."

"I ain't really, you just never knew this side of me before. I've been savin' it up for my last leg in life."

Honeydew exclaims, "There's Shirley and Steven. I want to hold Steven."

Harold watches her go in a mix between a run and a waddle toward the clothesline.

Shirley is taking the laundry off the line. She drops the basket she's holding, and greets Honeydew. "Welcome to Pine Mountain, it's great to see you! Let me get a chair for you, then you can hold Steven and we can talk while I take down the laundry and fold it."

Shirley reaches to pick up Steven and gives him to Honeydew, whose face brightens. "You're such a dear. Yes, you are; and look at the big smile you have for me." Honeydew looks toward Shirley. "With Steven and housework, you must keep busy."

"Yes, but with Willy and Emily Ann, it's much easier."

"You told me she was living with you when you stayed at the house. I just don't believe Toby Perkins could father such a bright child. Has he been up here yet?"

"Heavens no! Don't suggest it! As if I don't worry enough about it. The Perkinses must keep him close to the farm, because Harold hasn't mentioned seeing him, and I know he would have because he knows what's gone on between the two of us."

John comes walking up across the lawn. Shirley introduces him.

"I could—uh, use Emily Ann's help—uh, for a while. Is that all right?"

"Sure."

Honeydew studies John, looking at him and through him, trying to discern his character as he turns and leaves. "So he's the one that adopted Emily Ann. Seems like a decent sort." Her affirmation of John sounds tentative, because he didn't give Honeydew a second look. "Slow-talking people make me feel uncomfortable." She reaches in her bag and pulls out her small mirror. She fluffs her hair and slips the mirror back.

"I don't know John well, but he treats Emily Ann wonderfully." Shirley picks up the basket of folded clothes. "Let's go and see our garden."

Terry is lying in the shade, watching while Willy hoes with quick motions, clipping every weed seedling in sight. "Willy, do you know Honeydew Mullen?"

"No, guess not—hi." He gives her his big toothless smile.

Honeydew says, "Your garden looks beautiful."

"It ain't my garden. It's Shirley's, 'cause she's always nice ta me."

Shirley says, "Thanks, but you work in it all the time. I think we should call it yours." From where she is standing, she can look up and down the rows of potatoes, beets, carrots, beans, and tomatoes and there isn't a weed in sight. Harold made sure to dust his Green Mountains for bugs. The Paris green powder still clings to the leaves.

"Willy, you make sure to stay away from that powder and keep Terry away from it, as well. It's arsenic powder. The stuff can kill you."

"Oh, I knowed about it. The Ericksons' cows got out in the potata patch once 'n' it killed some of them."

"Better the cows than you. I wish we didn't have to use the stuff. Willy, it's chore time. We're going to have a big supper tonight." Shirley turns toward Honeydew. "You'll stay, won't you?"

"Ask Harold, he's driving the truck."

"We'll talk him into having you stay for a meal." They go to the haymow where he's standing on a long hardwood beam, threading new rope through the hay fork carriage.

Shirley yells up at Harold, "Can Honeydew stay for supper?"

"Sure can, I'll bring her home afterward."

A few minutes later, Willy comes running to Shirley. "We've git a cow missin'. She's gettin' ready ta calve. I'm guessin' she crossed the fence 'n' she's in the woods."

Shirley asks Honeydew if she would hold Steven in the shade of the pines. Honeydew quickly says, "Sure, I'd love to."

John, Emily Ann, and Shirley set out to look for the cow. Emily Ann tells Terry, "Go find the cow. What's her name, Shirley?"

"I think it's Betsy."

"Go find Betsy, Terry. Go find Betsy."

John and Shirley start looking for tracks, where the fence is low, and soon find fresh ones. Terry charges ahead, and the dog finds Betsy with her new calf.

Emily Ann jumps with excitement. "Terry you found her!" The cow is standing, but swaying with droopy ears and eyes glazed. Shirley checks the calf. "It's a heifer." She tells John, "We need a bottle of calcium, the IV tube, the needle, and a halter."

While John is gone, Shirley and Emily Ann sit on a moss-covered ledge. The green softness makes for a comfortable seat. The ledge is in a small opening among a sparsely growing stand of young red cedar. There are a few white strawberry blossoms that look striking against the deep green foliage and the dark green mosses. Scattered throughout are patches of chalky white reindeer moss. Giant ferns surround the opening, and the delicate maidenhair fern is growing in clumps near the ledge.

The calf stands, staggering on weak legs. She's searching for her mother, poking and hunting for a teat with her black muzzle. In a few minutes she finds what her instinct says is there, and starts sucking vigorously. Betsy gives generously to the calf while leaking steady streams of milk from the other three teats.

Shirley and Emily Ann are sitting closely together, quietly observing the calf and their natural botanical surroundings.

Emily Ann breaks the silence. "Do you like my dad?"

The question startles Shirley like a clap of thunder. She thinks through what she hopes will be the right answer for Emily Ann. She is still angry and brooding over the loss of Joe. John is so quiet and unassuming that he could easily go unnoticed. She frankly hasn't thought much about him, but for Emily Ann's sake she decides what she feels is her honest answer. "I think he's a good man. You're lucky to have him for a father."

"Well, I was thinking of maybe more—maybe someday we could be a family." Emily Ann begins to cry. "I miss home so much. It's fun to be here with Dad, but I just can't believe that I'll never see my mom." She breaks into a sob. "If I can't be with her again, I want us to at least be a family."

Shirley puts her arm around her. "I feel badly for you, but your father and I wouldn't think of marrying, at least for some time. You know you're talking about—about love and deep feelings. Your father and I are suffering inside, remembering our losses. It's difficult to put two hurting people together—if you see what I mean."

"What happened—did your friend die?"

"No, but it's similar to death. He met someone he liked better. Being told that hurt me more than you can imagine—a different hurt than when someone dies. We don't need to be talking like this. It's grown-up talk."

"That's okay, I think I understand. What's his name? Did he work and live here?"

Shirley takes a deep breath and looks away. "Joe—he's our county agent. He travels the county giving advice on better ways of farming. Let's change the subject."

At that moment John comes back with the supplies. It is easy to halter Betsy. They have no problem giving the calcium, since the cow is subdued by the milk fever. John puts the calf over his shoulders, resting her midsection around his neck, holding her legs with his hands. The cow almost instantly recovers from her stupor and willingly follows her calf. Shirley and Emily Ann walk behind and Terry lingers, sniffing all sorts of smells.

As they enter the barn, Shirley notices the swept floor. The freshly bedded cows are standing in contented fashion, some searching the smooth manger floor for any morsels of grain they might have missed.

The lost cow finds her stall, and John lays the calf in front of its mother. Shirley instructs, "Willy, don't milk this fresh cow until tomorrow morning, and then take only two or three quarts. If her ears are cold, I should give her another bottle of calcium."

"Okay, I'll do just as ya tell me. I sure will."

She walks to the house across the nicely kept lawn, again being reminded, as she so often is, of all the work Willy is doing.

She and Emily Ann prepare supper. Honeydew is sitting with Harold in front of the house, holding Steven, who is asleep in her lap. They are watching the setting sun in the western sky. Honeydew remarks, "It's nice sitting here with you, Harold. This is a beautiful spot. I've never seen such a view."

"Yup, it's a decent view and sittin' beside you makes it all the better."

Honeydew stares at Harold. She fluffs her hair. "Thanks. That was sweet of you."

"Yup, the new Harold Tully, sweeter than a bowl of honey."

"Well, let's not get carried away." They laugh.

Shirley calls everyone for supper. She has cooked a ham, potatoes, string beans, and chocolate cake for dessert. Everyone sits around the table enjoying the meal, especially Honeydew. "I haven't had a meal like this in years."

Harold glances at her. *She's tellin' the truth because she's never cooked a meal like this in her whole life.* He offers John a drink, and the two sit with glasses of scotch. Harold pours himself another full glass. "John, do you want another?" He shakes his head no. "Willy, how about you? Want a drink?"

Willy looks at Shirley. She shakes her head. "Shirley says, no."

Shirley is watching Harold. "Your drinking reminds me of old Jim Iverson. He drank all the time anyway, but during haying, he lost control."

Harold's blurry eyes look at Shirley. "I ain't no Jim Iverson. Hell, he drank enough in his lifetime to float a boat."

Shirley remarks, "Drinking and haying don't mix. I won't stand for it."

He isn't up to facing her iron stare and those riveting brown eyes. He leans with his elbows on the table, the near-empty whiskey glass in one hand, swirling the contents, watching the brown elixir as a diversion from Shirley's presence.

She waits for a promise, a comment, some assurance that the bottle won't mix with haying. He finally lifts his head and his words flow easily—creamy smooth. "You know, you're one hell of a good-lookin' woman. Why do you have to continually yak at me and spoil it all? Jus' loosen up for once, will ya?"

"When it comes to drinking, I'm not loosening up!"

Harold bangs his fist. "Let me have a good time tanight. Drop the subject."

"You've gone beyond the point of having a good time." She sits down at the table, with Harold, John, Honeydew, and Emily Ann. Willy has left for bed. "When I was almost sixteen, I moved to the Iversons; Jim and Janice and their nephew Jimmy. Joe had gone off to college and only came home periodically. They were the nicest family that I had lived with, since leaving the Perkinses—well, until near the end."

Honeydew interrupts, "Where else did you stay?"

"Let's see. The Perkinses, the Ericksons, the Durkees, and the Iversons."

"I understand why you liked the family. They would be my choice."

Shirley continues, "I can't forget Mrs. Jones's boardinghouse. What a dump! That was just before I went to Burlington. Oh, I was going to tell about my stay at the Iversons. Jim drank steadily, but he nearly always held it under control. Come haying time, the whole process made him a nervous wreck."

Harold is trying to fill his pipe, but tobacco spills over the table in front of him. He looks up. "Hayin's a bastard. It drives the best of us right ta the bottle." He's attempting to bring the loose tobacco into a pile with the sweep of his hand over the oilcloth. His pipe is now filled to overflowing. He is trying to put the spilled tobacco back in the can by taking a pinch and aiming it at the top of the slender can. He misses for the most part, causing the tobacco to fall around the can. Some of the shreds cling to his fingers, but most of the brown bits of moist Prince Albert fall back on the table.

"Yup, hayin's a bastard. The sun shines bright in the mornin'. You mow a jag, and hell, by night the mountains are socked in with a mess of clouds. If that ain't enough to send you right to the house for a good stiff drink."

Shirley adds, "More like two or three."

After a few drinks, Harold starts to stand, looking like he's going to dive onto the table, but he catches himself and stands to an upright position. "I thought I'd sit in front of the house draggin' on my pipe and watch the thunderheads roll in from the western horizon." He weaves his way across the kitchen floor, heading for the entry. He turns and wildly motions. "Come outside with me, Honeydew, and we'll do a little sparkin'."

"I'm not sparkin' with a drunk, but I'll come out and keep you company."

Emily Ann gets up from the table to go to bed.

Shirley notices that tears have filled John's eyes. "How are you tonight?"

"It's memories—uh, they cause me to—uh, think of just a few weeks ago. Grief is odd. I can be enjoying myself one minute, then—uh, feel sad the next. I like the farm. Working together is—uh, good for a family."

The setting sun casts orange light through the west window striking John's back. It dances off his light-colored hair on his arms as they lie on the table. His face is in the shadow of his sandy hair as it glistens in the late evening light. Shirley can see his full lips move hesitantly, cautiously grinding out words and thoughts, a characteristic she's come to know as normal. She thinks of holding his hand to comfort him. She feels compassion for the man, but not love; and holding is love, and it means losing sometimes. She'd only comfort him as a friend or an acquaintance, because that's all he is to her. The last man she held left—and the memory lingers. Instead of reaching out to him, she pushes away from the table and stands. "I agree—working together does bond people, if they're right for each other."

John doesn't answer, but looks at his folded hands, resting on the tablecloth.

She realizes he is caught in grief and can't talk. "I think I should take Honeydew home now. I'll see you in the morning." She carries the woman's knitting bag to the entry door and walks to the front of the house. "Are you ready to go home?"

Harold speaks, "She's sleepin' with me tanight." He drunkenly laughs.

Honeydew jumps up. "Why, Harold Tully! I'm certainly not sleeping here tonight. I have to feed my dog."

"I knew you'd put that damn dog ahead of me." He tries to strike a stick match to light his pipe, missing several times before the match grazes the bottom of his steel lawn chair. The light reflects off his red droopy face.

Honeydew says, "I'm leaving."

"Come again 'n' plan ta stay the night." He again laughs uproariously.

Walking away, she grunts in disgust. Shirley realizes it might be for her benefit.

Honeydew is in high spirits, while riding home. "I've had a wonderful time."

Shirley agrees. "I liked having you, and I know Harold did."

"I guess he did—I was surprised to see Willy today. I never realized how much work he can do. It's good to see he's among friends."

"I like Willy. We've always been friends. We used to help each other out when we worked for the Ericksons, living as servants next to their inner family circle."

"The Ericksons would be hard people to live with."

On Pine Mountain, the sun has now set, and all that is visible is an orange reddish glow on the horizon. Harold is looking out the west window. "Red sky at night is ah sailor's delight." Harold turns to John. "Is that really true? Did ya ever know it ta fail?"

"As a fisherman—uh, I know weather can—uh, fool you, but a red sky at night—uh, almost always means a good day is coming."

"Damn, I hope so. I cut a hell of a jag down—too much to put up in a day. I got on that new tractor and everythin' went so well I just kept mowin'." Harold pours himself another drink.

The next morning, John takes the milk to the stand with Shirley, since Harold hasn't gotten up yet. Emily Ann stays home, giving Steven a bath. John understands the routine, but Shirley wants to go along for the ride in case Zack happens to be at the stand. She realizes Zack will want to know who the stranger is. She also remembers Emily Ann's blunt question from the day before: "Do you like my dad?" She really doesn't know. Maybe their time alone will be a chance to get to know him. He sure isn't Joe, but why compare? He's such a self-contained fellow.

Shirley asks, "Do you miss Boston?"

"Not really—uh, I guess there hasn't been time to think about it. I miss my wife, though. She was—uh, a wonderful person. I can't believe—uh, she's gone."

She quickly glances at him as they sit in silence. He's wearing his white undershirt on this warm steamy June morning. The white straps lift as he swings his arms, steering the truck down the mountain. The bands of skin over his shoulders are as white as birch bark. His chest and broad shoulders are layered with muscle. He reminds her of Atlas, capable of resting the earth on his back, as he gracefully moves his arms over the wheel. She overlooks his rough complexion, while only noticing his endearing features. His quietness, though, comes to the point of being nerve-wracking, but she calms herself after a while, and decides being quiet is part of who he is.

Shirley and John unload seven cans. *Willy is doing well with the cows, now that they are being grained on the new system.* Zack doesn't come with his milk. The empty cans bang and rattle while they travel back up the mountain. She breaks the silence. "It's a great feeling to have a place you can call home. I love Pine Mountain. I'd be satisfied to call it my home forever."

John glances Shirley's way. "It's like being—uh, closer to heaven." The truck is now traveling next to the pasture fence.

"On the next rainy day, we ought to put up another wire on the woods side of this pasture. You probably haven't fenced before?"

"No—but it shouldn't be—uh, too hard to learn."

They drive in the yard and see Harold walking out in the field, having checked his hay. Shirley feels a little flat while getting out of the truck, because John hasn't offered much in the way of conversation or companionship. It was their first and only time spent alone, and he certainly didn't make any effort to be interesting. She reminisces for a moment about how much fun Joe was, and how much she misses him, and how much she once loved him. She's angry with herself for letting memories surface, and does an about-face, briskly walking toward the house.

Emily Ann has started breakfast. Shirley says, "Thanks for your help. I saw Terry at the barn with Willy this morning. I think he's trying to make a cow dog out of him."

Emily Ann comments, "That's great. I read that border collies are good cattle and sheep dogs. It would be neat if he came to be Willy's helper."

Harold comes in the house and plunks himself in his Morris chair. He speaks to Shirley. "Damn it, you were the one that got me to mow all that hay. It just come to me. Those words of yours were just a-pokin' in and outta my head. 'I'm not goin' to feed that crap to the cows and horses that was fed last winter.' Yup, those words just kept pushin' and pushin' me farther and farther till the whole blasted field was mowed."

Shirley sloughs off Harold's remarks and laughs. "Oh go soak your head. You drank too much last night—you're hung-over."

"This ain't no laughin' matter. You pushed me to do somethin' I shouldn't have done. You pushed me out of my schedule. Never start hayin' until after the 4th of July. I should've stuck by my rule. That's what my old man taught me."

"You mean I pushed you out of your rut. If you want to give me the credit, I'm glad to take the responsibility." She asks, "Have we got three good hay forks? When the dew lifts, you can start the kicker fluffing the hay, and John, Willy, and I can spread out any green wads the kicker misses."

Harold looks at Shirley. "I don't know's we do have three good hay forks. After breakfast I better go and buy a couple of new ones."

"If you go, don't stop at the liquor store. Haying time is hard enough without having to deal with ugly moods and a drunkard smashing equipment."

Harold jumps to his feet. "Bastard, woman! You like to rule over me."

She walks over to him and speaks in a calm voice. "Relax, forget about haying."

Emily Ann turns with a frightened expression when hearing the harsh words.

"That's okay, Emily Ann. We're going to have breakfast ready in a few minutes, and that will help our dispositions."

After returning from town, Harold starts tedding the hay at about eleven o'clock. He completes four or five trips around the field before the three head out with hay forks. Shirley realizes he is driving too fast for the tedder to do a good job, even though the hay is light, and there are only a few green wads.

It's a hot day. The smell of drying hay fills the air, like country perfume. Shirley is working the hay with her fork. John is behind her on the adjoining swath. She turns and speaks to him. "I hope that tedder holds together. He's driving too fast." Harold's carelessness makes her wonder. Walking to the truck, she opens the door, and pulls open the glove compartment to find a half-spent fifth of scotch. She is enraged. She takes the bottle and hides it in the henhouse and hurries back to the field. Harold is traveling toward her. The tedder wheels are bouncing off the ground, while traveling over uneven places in the field. The machine is completely missing the hay in many places. She motions for him to stop, and demands, "Get off that tractor!"

"What in the hell's up with ya, now? What's eatin' ya?" Harold swings his arms in drunken wildness.

Shirley doesn't answer him. She walks over to John and asks, "Would you finish tedding? I'm getting Harold away from this place."

John and Willy look in wonderment at her. Harold staggers toward her.

"Ya goddamn son-of-a-bitchin' woman! Ya've gone too far. Ya strut around this place like ya own it."

She fumes, "Harold Tully, I am furious with you. You're drunk. You can't take the pressure of haying, so you run for the bottle. This is exactly the way haying went at the Iversons; Jim was drunk most of the time. I'll tell you it was awful having broken equipment, tipped-over hay wagons, and worst of all, it was dangerous having a drunk around. You've got good equipment, good help, and children that could be hurt. I'm not standing for it. I'm taking you to Honeydew's to stay overnight—to get you away from here. John can get you in the morning when he takes the milk down. You've got to get away. This haying is driving you right to the bottle."

"Ya little shit. Ya think ya can boss me around. Well, ya can't. I ain't goin'." Harold stands in the field, swaying to the point of almost falling.

"It's best for you, Harold, and best for all of us. I'm telling you, you're going to Honeydew's. Come on!"

Harold follows Shirley, weaving toward the truck. He goes as willingly as he does because he knows where there is more scotch.

John is studying the new Ford. After a while he starts it, and at a more reasonable speed, continues to work the hay.

She calls for Emily Ann to bring Steven, and they travel down the mountain. "You little shit; ya might's well run this hayin'." He's trying to load his pipe with a tobacco can, but he's spilling it all over his pants and the floor of the truck.

"No, you're going to run it, but you are not going to be drinking. Relax a little—so what if the hay does get wet? It's not the end of the world. You've tried as hard as you can—let it go at that."

He thinks aloud, "Maybe I'll live with Honeydew, if she'd take me in. I feel like a prisoner goin' to jail. Ya know, Shirley, there ain't many women that could do this to me."

"Remember, we're friends."

"Yup, the friends speech again! I know I should be overjoyed that ya're yankin' me around like I was a little kid." He has yet to light his pipe and is searching for a match in his pocket.

"We'll all be the better for it, Harold."

Emily Ann sits ramrod straight holding Steven, while staring in disgust at Harold. She wrinkles her nose when the aroma of fresh tobacco fills the cab.

As the truck enters Honeydew's yard, she comes out of the house, waving her arms, her usual self again. "Oh, I'm so happy to see you."

Shirley is out of the truck first. "Hi, Honeydew. Could you keep Harold for the night? He's been drinking. Haying has gotten to him."

Honeydew quickly loses her good cheer. "I'll try. I don't like him much when he's in one of his ugly moods."

Shirley nods. "I know what you mean, but we need to get him away from the farm. John will come for him in the morning."

Harold opens the glove compartment. "Well, I'll be, she's too son-of-a-bitchin' smart fer her own good." He stumbles out of the truck. "Ya stole my scotch."

"You're right. We'll save that until we've finished haying, then we'll have a big celebration."

Harold glances toward Honeydew. "Where's that miserable dog of yours? I ain't goin' into the house until ya lock up that little nippy bastard." He turns to Shirley. "Ya're the livin' end. How could I ever have had such bad luck as to run into ya, and worst of all, let ya run things like ya do?"

"Cool down. Staying here is the best for all of us."

Honeydew has gone to the house and now returns. "It's okay."

As they leave the yard, Emily Ann says, "Harold's one big problem."

"He is when he's drinking, which is true with anyone. I remember one hot afternoon old Jim Iverson and I were loading hay on a side hill. The boys were at the farm unloading the wagons. Jim would build a load and I'd drive the horses, and the next load we'd switch." Shirley momentarily turns to Emily Ann. "I can clearly see the tin flask he carried in his bib-overalls. By late afternoon Jim was too drunk to stand and could only lean on the headboard of the wagon. I was really mad and tired because I had to handle all the hay. On our last load, he had totally lost control of the horses." Shirley tightly grips the wheel recalling the frightening scene. She raises her voice. "They were moving too fast and the hay was coming up the loader too rapidly to give me time to build a good load. I yelled to stop the horses, but Jim was too drunk to understand. It wasn't my job to watch where the horses were headed. All of a sudden the wagon seemed to tip a lot more than usual. Up ahead one horse was walking below a foot-high ledge and the other was walking on top of the ledge. I never had tipped over on a load of hay, but I screamed, knowing it was about to happen."

Emily Ann looks at Shirley. "That sounds scary!"

"It was, but farmers had told me in the past and Jim had taught me in a sober moment never to hang on to a wagon of hay that's about to tip over. Jim instructed me, 'If you're using a fork, hold the end of the handle, sit down with your feet and legs pointed in the direction the load is tipping, and let the hay carry you off to the ground, and you'll never get hurt.' I did as I was taught, and landed, standing beyond the hay. The horses stopped, but Jim didn't move. He was buried."

Emily Ann breaks in, "What did you do?"

"I pawed around in the pile of hay and found Jim, pulled the hay away from his face, and left him there. He was dead drunk, and I was ripping mad. Thank goodness the hay loader was still upright.

"I just sat, fuming, at the edge of the field, figuring the boys would eventually come. I remember how hot it was that day. The afternoon sun was beginning to drop lower in the sky. I looked toward higher ground and saw rays of heat, rising from the hay stubble, in the direction the boys were coming. They were walking, leading the hay fork horse. Joe and Jimmy had their forks resting on their shoulders, coming toward the over-turned wagon. They were laughing as if a tipped-over load of hay was an everyday event. I wasn't laughing. I was tired and there lay a worthless drunk, Jim Iverson, who was the cause of it all. They used the horse to pull the wagon upright.

"Each boy took hold of an arm and shoulder of their uncle and pulled him away from the pile of hay. They rested his straw hat on his head for shade. Seeing them do that made me realize they'd done the same thing before. Joe and Jimmy talked about school, and friends, and laughed about past events that had taken place just as if what had just happened was no event at all. I built the load as they pitched the hay up to me. The pile was cleaned up shortly and I drove the horses and load of hay home. They left their uncle in the field and walked home, leading the horse. The Iverson boys enjoyed life, totally ignoring their uncle's problem. Their attitude amazed me."

Emily Ann shakes her head. "Gee, I'm glad that wasn't me. Now I know why you don't like drinking. Why do people drink anyway?"

"For different reasons I guess; but in Harold's case, it's because he can't stand the pressure, the thought that the hay might get wet and spoiled. Mowing hay for drying is a gamble and Harold can't stand the thought of losing. The more he thinks about poor weather ruining his hay, the more upset he becomes, and he feels he just has to take a drink to get relaxed."

"This all sounds stupid to me. Harold's stupid anyway."

Shirley glances toward Emily Ann and catches her look of self-righteousness. "Just remember, none of us are perfect. There is goodness in Harold."

"Maybe, if you say so."

Shirley begins thinking about the next day. She decides that when John goes to the village to get Harold, he can bring Honeydew back as well. She can baby-sit Steven. The next day is going to be busy. Harold will be in the mow leveling the hay. Willy will be unloading and Emily Ann will be leading Jeanie, pulling the grapple fork rope. John and she will be loading hay in the field.

They pass Dr. Plumbly's office on the way home. Shirley glances toward the building and reminds herself to make an appointment with him to discuss her medical record. When she took Steven for his shots he was away on an emergency call.

When they drive in the yard, Shirley looks to the west. It is now one-thirty, and the sky shows light clouds. She can see the weather sign that Harold calls mares' tails. At four, she will ask John to rake the hay. It is drying well, but she knows the rake will pick up some that's still green. The sun is intensely hot.

HUNTERSVILLE WEEKLY

June 7, 1948

Driblets of Honeydew
By Honeydew Mullen

Ron Burnham, of Ron's Texaco, is nursing an injured black bear that was hit by a car. He said it's questionable if the animal can ever be released due to a crippled hind leg. All are welcome to stop by to see the bear. Although he didn't stipulate, when there, it would be real nice of you to fill up with Texaco. Veterinarian Dr. Wheatherhead has declined an invitation to examine the beast. He said, "Horses, cows, cats and dogs are my specialty." He likes closely observing wild animals only after they've visited the taxidermist.

Harry Durkee, chairman of the upcoming Huntersville parade, sponsored by the Grange, has announced that this year there will be an elaborate gold-plated trophy awarded to the first place float. He said, "The trophy will be given in an effort to attract better competitive entries." The parade will be held on Saturday, July 3.

Gabby Pilford, our town policeman, has been released from his probationary period imposed by the Board of Selectmen for sleeping too much in the town's cruiser. In fact he has been given an extra week's paid vacation, since recent imposed motor vehicle fines amount to more than his salary. While in the village, watch your driving.

Elmer Dobson reports that his Guernsey bull got loose and caused quite the ruckus at their place. He charged a wagon full of loose hay, putting his head and neck under the rack and tipping over the whole load, tumbling it into his yard. The bull then charged the clothesline and tore up clean sheets that had just been hung on the line. Thelma, his wife, says, "Elmer will be sleeping on a bare mattress if that bull ruins any more sheets."

CHAPTER TWENTY

Harold wakes with a start from a nap at Honeydew's. It's late afternoon and the low sun fills the rosy red room. Rays of light bounce off the woodwork and wallpaper, appearing to give the room a fiery glow. The different shades of pink and lavender cause Harold to momentarily imagine he's sitting in the midst of a giant heap of raw hamburger. He's hungry and disoriented, having stumbled onto the bed drunk. He sits on the edge, nearly blinded by the sun flowing through the west windows. He moves to a chair facing away and looks around the room. "Well son of a bitch, I'm at Honeydew's." He groans in a loud voice. "Oh bastard, am I ever hung over."

Honeydew hears him and enters, seeing Harold holding his head. "Let me put some water on for coffee."

"Yeah, bring me a sandwich, too. I'm hungry as hell."

A while later Honeydew returns with a tray, carrying coffee and a peanut butter sandwich. The white bread is pressed into the spread making it look more like a wafer. With hunger overcoming appearance, Harold picks up the sandwich and cautiously takes a bite. He sits more erect and looks at Honeydew who sits in a chair next to him. "Thanks. How did I ever end up here?"

"You were drunk—remember?"

"Oh yeah, it's comin' back to me. The queen of Pine Mountain lugged me off down here. Damn, when she gets on a tear—watch out. Wild horses can't stop her."

Honeydew remarks, "The plan is that John will pick you up in the morning. She smiles. "You can spend the night."

He chuckles. "Just like old times. The only trouble is I'm feelin' a lot older than those old times."

"That's okay, we can still enjoy each other's company."

He slides the tray onto the table next to him and holds the coffee cup in his hand. "Yeah, we might's well."

Honeydew remarks, "When I was shopping this morning, I met Elbridge and had a long talk with him."

"Elbridge—Elbridge—who's that?"

"The Perkinses' oldest son. He told me in detail why Shirley had to leave when she was just a young girl."

"Well, get me some more coffee before you start one of your long stories."

Honeydew bustles to the kitchen and returns with the coffee and sits down. "As I was about to say, Elbridge's father, Howard Perkins, never wanted Mildred to adopt Shirley, but Mildred insisted, because she had all boys. She took Shirley with the understanding that adoption papers would be signed at a later date, and for some reason the Leland Home agreed to the arrangement. Elbridge said his father expected Shirley to work just like a boy. Even though she was the youngest, she was stronger than his brothers.

"According to Elbridge it always bothered his father that Mildred spent so much time with Shirley, and seemed to favor her over the boys, especially Toby. Elbridge got along with Shirley just fine, but his brothers tended to gang up on her, teased and fought with her. He told me his brother Toby was weird even as a kid. He was continually grabbing and pinching her in the wrong places. Shirley fought back hard enough so he'd cry and run to his mother. Elbridge said, 'My mother hated Toby for the way he acted, but my father sided with Toby.' His father's defense of Toby was, 'Boys will be boys.'"

"Golly, for bein' such a good farmer, he was kinda stupid."

"Well, I guess. Can you imagine growing up in that situation? The girl Elbridge was telling me about, and Shirley, don't seem to be the same person.

"One day all the kids were sent to the haymow with pitchforks to level the hay. They had finished their work, and he said his three brothers ganged up on Shirley. He watched for a minute, and left, knowing she always took care of herself.

"His brother, Matt, later told Elbridge that they pinned her to the hay. They were egging Toby on, according to Matt. 'Screw her, Toby; screw her!'

Toby is the oldest of the three boys and was a big kid at the time. He first took off her bib-overalls, while each boy held her arms. She kicked like fury when he tried to remove her underpants. Matt told Elbridge that without thinking he relaxed his grip on Shirley. She yanked her arm from Matt and in a flash was on her feet with a pitchfork in her hand. Matt ran for the house, but she cornered his brother, Pete, long enough to drive the end of the pitchfork handle right into his mouth. He beat it for the house, bawling, with his two front teeth in his hand.

"Elbridge and his father knew Toby was in trouble, because he wouldn't stand a chance with Shirley. When mad, she fought like a wildcat. On the way to the mow they met her, crying, running toward the house wearing just her underpants. They found Toby naked and lifeless in the hay. They thought he was dead, but he was faintly breathing. He had red welts the full length of his body from being beaten with the fork handle, plus blood was running from his nose. They rushed him to the hospital, and he remained unconscious for days. Dr. Plumbly didn't think he would live."

Harold remarks, "I can see now why she has no problem bossin' me around. Golly, and I thought I had it tough as a kid."

Honeydew continues, "Elbridge said his father came home from the hospital and demanded that Shirley leave their farm. Since there were no papers signed, and she had no parents, a new home had to be found. I guess Mildred was beside herself with grief, and Elbridge admitted that he, too, hated to see her leave. Don't you remember hearing about that awful girl that almost killed Toby Perkins?"

"Well, maybe vaguely. 'Course I ain't never been in circulation like you."

Honeydew adds, "The Perkinses are well-respected folks in town, so most people, naturally, sided with Toby, wondering what kind of girl could be so violent."

"Prob'ly havin' Steven has been good for her. It made her go to the Leland Home, and that's where she met up with this Dr. Meyer. Golly, she talks about him a lot. He sorta helped in gettin' her thinkin' straight. Sometimes, I wonder if he helped her too much. She ain't always the easiest one to get on with; but hell, I ain't either. Quite the team, we are."

"I'll bet you'd miss her if she left."

Harold's eyes water and he turns his head toward the bay window. "I guess—I think of her as my daughter, and damn, that makes me proud. Huh, it's kinda funny how she takes on so about my drinkin'. Golly, can't she be wild, though?"

Honeydew pauses and their eyes meet.

Harold reaches for his pipe. "I can see you think she's right."

"Well—what do you think?"

"Now that I'm away from the hay field, I guess I'd have to agree."

On Saturday afternoon, some of the hay is dry enough to be put in the barn. Shirley knows because when she steps on it, the stems break easily, making a crackling sound. In case the weather changes the next day, she decides to load both wagons.

It would be a good idea to test the new loader to be sure it is all ready to go. Since the next day is Sunday, Shirley plans that the two loads can be unloaded before church. While she and John are at church, Harold could flip the remaining windrows with the rake, since the hay, lying overnight next to the ground, will be damp. She realizes that even though two loads are taken from the field, there will be plenty of hay left for Sunday afternoon. The crop is thin, but there is a lot of ground to cover.

Shirley drives the tractor, pulling the wagon and loader. She has briefly explained to John how to build a load of loose hay. It starts coming evenly and smoothly off the front of the loader, dropping onto the wagon. The tractor and new equipment work perfectly.

The next morning John takes the milk, and is given directions to Honeydew's house. He carries a note asking if she can come to the farm for the day. Harold is eagerly waiting. "Damn, I thought you'd never get here. What a borin' place."

John meets Honeydew coming from the house and hands her the note. She brightens and makes preparations.

Harold has started the truck waiting for John. "What in hell is this all about?"

"Shirley wants Honeydew to—uh, sit for Steven. She'll be coming back with us."

"Okay, but we'll be pressed tight to the doors. She's one hell of a big woman."

She comes with her bag of needlework, animated over spending another day at the farm. She climbs in the cab and John slams the door, both men squeezing against flesh, causing one mass of connected bodies. The heat of the day intensifies Honeydew's perfume, filling the cab with lilac.

Harold asks, "How's the hay lookin'?"

"I raked it last night—uh, we loaded two loads. It looked to be in good shape—uh, of course this is all new to me. The hay left in the field—uh, looked fairly wet this morning. There was a heavy dew last night."

Harold ponders. "By eleven I should be able to rake it again. I hope we get some sun this afternoon. The weather is changin'. This damn hayin's a bastard, tryin' to work around the weather."

Harold gets more agitated just thinking about the subject. He mumbles, "I guess I'll stop here for a minute." The truck is in front of the liquor store, parking parallel to the sidewalk.

Honeydew says loudly, "Forget it, you can't buy liquor on Sunday."

He stamps his foot in disgust. "Damn, women drive me crazy."

He carelessly pulls the truck back into the street. A car is coming in Harold's lane. They hear squawking tires. Three heads turn and see that the driver happens to be Gabby Pilford in his police car. Gabby turns on his siren but Harold doesn't stop. "Gabby, you ain't goin' to stop me, are you? That lazy bastard, all he has to do is bother people."

Honeydew yells, "You better stop!"

"Yup, yup, holy shit! The biggest hay day of my life, and this mealy-mouthed no-mind has to waste my time."

Harold pulls the truck over next to the sidewalk. Gabby gets out of the police car with a pad in his hand, and reaches into his car for a pencil.

"Why that son of a bitch! He's goin' to give me a ticket." Harold sits in disbelief, watching the policeman walk toward his truck.

Gabby pulls his pants up, and throws a half-smoked cigarette on the pavement. "Pretty careless this morning, ain't you, Harold? I nearly smashed into you."

"Damn it, Gabby, I've got a big hay day ahead. I'm tryin' to rush home."

"Harold, you ain't giving me that line. You never had a big hay day in your whole life. Of course, with Shirley Mason being up there, you might have some hay down."

Harold is blind with rage, but has the presence of mind to divert Gabby's attention away from having him write a ticket. "You know, Gabby, I have a gun collection I'd like to show you when you get a chance."

"Really? I collect guns, you know." Gabby bends over coughing with the ticket book in his hand.

"Yup, I know." Harold shifts into first gear and releases the clutch and presses the gas. He sticks his head out his window and the truck moves ahead. "I'll see you at the farm sometime."

Honeydew is looking back, watching him. She yells, "I'm shocked at you! You'll be in big trouble for this, landing in court for resisting arrest."

"Resistin' arrest! Hell, I ain't got time to sit around and listen to him cough, and anyway, he never wrote me a ticket." Harold sarcastically repeats Gabby's comment. "'Course, with Shirley Mason bein' up there you might have hay down.' Sayin' that sure burned me—as if he'd know. Everyone thinks that Shirley Mason can do anythin'."

A big cloud cover has moved in and is resting over Pine Mountain. It is now eight-thirty. Honeydew goes to the house. Harold turns to John who is at the shed, working on the tedder. "I'm so damn hungry I could eat a horse. Honeydew is the world's worst cook. I hardly ate a thing at her house."

John laughs. "I'll have Emily Ann get—uh, something for you."

Harold looks at John. "Now I want you and Emily Ann to use Jeanie on the hay fork. She's the best horse to work alone. I'll harness her up now, so we can get started on the loads parked in the haymow. This afternoon, if these clouds lift, Emily Ann will be leadin' her by herself. I want her to learn how it's done."

"Do you think—uh, she can do that?"

"Sure—I did when I was a kid. There's no reason she can't." Harold calls Willy.

"We're ready to unload."

Willy runs to the barn and climbs up the headboard of the wagon. He stands on top of the load and swings opens the four long tines of the grapple fork and points the tines into the load. Then he jumps on each tine, driving them deep into the hay.

"You see, the grapple fork is lifted off the wagon by that long rope that Lassie will pull." Harold points, continuing to show John how the system works. "The horse keeps pullin', and the carriage rolls on the track. When I yell, Willy will motion to you and Emily Ann to stop Lassie. Then Willy will pull the trip rope, and the hay will fall from the grapple fork onto the haymow floor. Then Lassie has to go back from where she started. We've got a big jag layin' in the field so I'll be in the mow, levelin' the hay."

John nods. In another ten minutes he and Emily Ann are leading Jeanie, as Harold has instructed. The haying disturbance scatters the barn swallows from their nesting places, near the hay fork track, but they will return by evening to reclaim their homes.

While standing waiting for Willy to load the fork, Harold has moments to admire the structure of the old post-and-beam barn. Hand-hewn beams stretch the width of the building at least twelve to fifteen feet above the floor. Beams were also hand-hewn with the ends cut to fit as support beams and are held in place by a wooden peg. *I can't imagine the time my grandfather put into buildin' this barn. I can remember walkin' the beams as a kid when there was hay below, and jumpin' off into space, and landin' on loose hay. It was one of the few fun things I ever did.*

Jeanie knows the routine and pulls easily and the unloading of hay goes smoothly. After unloading both wagons, Harold walks out of the haymow, brushing himself free of hayseed and chaff, and goes to the house. It's now almost ten o'clock. "Golly, Shirley, are we goin' to hay today or not? This weather! I wish these clouds would leave."

"I don't know. I'm going to church. I'll send up a little prayer for you."

"I'm serious. If I had that bottle I'd drink the whole thing. I need somethin' to calm my nerves."

"Sit down, I'll pour you a cup of coffee." Shirley looks out the west window. "I can see the clear sky coming. We'll hurry back from church and have a light dinner. Then we'll be ready to go by one o'clock."

At the Sunday service, the whole congregation is in a buzz over seeing Shirley, and hearing a new young voice. She spends some time afterward with Mrs. Perkins, since it isn't possible to visit her at the farm. *What would I ever do or say if I met Toby?*

Harold has just finished turning the hay with the side delivery rake when his helpers return. The sun is hazy, and the air hangs heavy. There is definitely a weather change on the way. Shirley hopes that Steven will be easy for Honeydew's sake because, barring rain, the afternoon is going to be a long one.

The haying process moves along smoothly. Emily Ann likes leading Jeanie, who pulls forty to fifty feet depending on where Harold wants to dump the hay. Terry follows the horse back and forth.

Milking is going to be late, because it is now four o'clock and the weather is still holding. Shirley gives John a break and offers to build the loads for a while. The raker bars of the loader lift and pull the windrow completely intact into the carrier bars, which in turn lift the hay up the loader and onto the wagon. The hay is light green, and rustles with a gentle sound while it's being placed on the wagon in a planned pattern for easy unloading. The stems of the orchard and June grass hay are fine and malleable, since it is early cut, and not yet mature enough to be stiff and scratchy.

The cows are beginning to gather at the barn door. Their udders are full, and their knowledge of the routine tells them it is time to be milked. There is no way milking can start, because everybody is needed to keep the haying process moving. By six-thirty the cows are bellowing.

Shirley announces, "Some of us have got to quit. There are about four loads still on the ground. Willy, you should start milking. Emily Ann, why don't you go to the house? I think there's some spinach that could be picked from the garden, and you can heat the pot roast. I've already made chocolate pudding for dessert."

Harold is disgusted with Shirley for taking control, but when he hears her plans for supper, he feels better. Harold and John build the next load, giving time for Shirley to be with Steven. Honeydew compliments Steven. “He’s been a perfect baby. He loves to be held. He and I sat in the shade most of the afternoon watching all the activity.”

By eight-thirty John and Harold are pulling the last two loads onto the haymow floor. They are as big as John dared build them. Harold is happy. “By golly, we did it. The field’s all cleaned up, and it’s damn good feed.”

A low-pressure system has settled on Pine Mountain. It is humid and warm. The air feels as if it might burst with rain at any moment. While they sit around the table and tiredly eat, Harold, in his way, thanks everyone for their efforts. “By golly, we all put up one big jag of hay.”

The weather gods aren’t as kind to the haying crew on Pine Mountain in the second effort to put up what Harold calls a big jag of hay. That small window of opportunity for three days of sun just hasn’t happened. The weather pattern has changed into a cycle of clearing one day or a part of a day, and then a small shower comes floating in over the mountain. The atmosphere draws the moisture from the earth’s surface, forming clouds, which open up and return rain within a few hours. It acts like a giant pump. This phenomenon does little to improve Harold’s disposition.

On the Wednesday following the big haying success, he mows another ten acres, the field below the barn, and a five-acre piece north of the cow barn. This hay is by far the heaviest and the hardest to dry since woods border both fields. The sun can only reach these fields either in the morning or in the late afternoon. Harold explains to John, “Because this hay is hard to dry, my old man used to lug it to the field we’ve just hayed. He used to spread it out so it could get the sun. We need to do the same to make decent hay.”

The cyclical pattern of sun and rain continues for about a week. The hay that was lush begins to turn yellow. The underside becomes slimy. Harold thinks, *This last hay I mowed might be a total loss, but this hot, wet, muggy weather is good for the pastures.*

Willy works in the garden. John works on small projects in the house, taking the windows apart and fixing them so they can open and close. Shirley buys several sliding window screens, and a screen door for the entry for John to install. Emily Ann and Willy work nights for short periods on his numbers from one to ten and he is beginning to learn to write his name.

Shirley, Steven, and Emily Ann visit Alice Coles. Zack sees the truck and comes in the house. Shirley thinks he acts more anxious than usual. She asks, "How are you Zack?"

He runs his fingers through his curly hair. He blurts, "We haven't even started haying yet. Of course why should I worry, Harold never starts until after the Fourth."

Shirley says, "We put in ten acres last week."

"Ten acres! When did you ever have the time to do that? I'll bet it wasn't dry."

Shirley adds, "I think up on the mountain we get more breeze than you do here in the valley."

"Oh, you probably do!" Zack's face turns red. He stamps his foot and turns to leave when Emily Ann changes the subject.

"I like your cows; they look pretty with their big brown eyes and dished-out faces."

Zack calms himself and asks, "How would you like to take a calf to the fair? You'd have to own it and train it to lead. You could be in a 4-H dairy club. There's one in town."

Shirley nods. "We can see if Grampa Iverson will buy one for you."

Zack adds, "Maybe you could win some ribbons. It would be good advertisement for the Coleses' well-known Jersey herd."

Alice says, "Let me take Steven while you're at the barn. My goodness, you're getting to be a big boy and look at those hands and arms fly."

Zack, Emily Ann, and Shirley walk to the barn. Shirley says, "It would be nice to have a quality purebred Jersey heifer in our barn.

Harold's are a hodgepodge of different breeds with swaybacks and sickle legs, and they are small."

Zack remarks, "I've never seen Harold's herd but I can pick a heifer that will be the best for Emily Ann."

Shirley asks, "How much will she cost?"

Zack pauses for a long time, acting as if he doesn't want to scare Shirley away with his asking price. "I ought to check with Mother, but we usually get a hundred dollars for one of this quality."

Shirley gulps. "Wow! I'll have to ask Grandpa Iverson if he's willing to pay that."

Emily Ann jumps with excitement. "Oh, I think he will want me to have the calf."

"It sounds like a lot of money to me. We'll find out on Wednesday."

Alice agrees that the animal is worth the asking price. "Steven and I had a lot of fun. He sure likes his rattle. Everything has to go in his mouth. Looks like he's going to have curly hair."

Shirley looks at his head. "Yeah, I've noticed. It will be dark, though. Isn't it amazing how we are made up of the genes of our ancestors? His hair could be coming from a grandfather or grandmother for all we know." *I don't think it's from his father.*

Alice looks at Shirley with her knowing stare. "Or his father."

Shirley tries but can't hide her emotions and knows her coloring is revealing. She says, "We should go now. We'll let you know about the calf."

Alice still holds her domineering stare on Shirley. "Thanks for coming."

Shirley walks toward the truck, holding Steven. *What is that woman thinking? I doubt she knows about the picnic.*

Shirley, Steven, and Emily Ann travel back to the farm. The warm, moist weather has started the grass growing in the field that was first hayed. The new growth sticks up above the cut hay that John and Willy placed in the field almost a week earlier. The sight of hay spoiling, especially in view of the house, has set Harold's nerves on edge. He is mumbling a phrase that he's been repeating constantly: "Damn this weather!" He sits, watching the test pattern on the television, waiting for the evening news with John Cameron Swayze.

John says, "Why don't you—uh, go fishing? Forget about haying. I'll bet they'd bite today. You could fish right off—uh, that bridge—the one you cross on—uh, the way to town."

Harold brightens up. "Now there's a good idea. I'm getting' sick of waitin' on this weather. By golly, I'm gettin' outta here."

"Take my car—uh, you don't have to be back—uh, any special time. You could stay at Honeydew's."

Harold scowls at John. "If I stay over at her house, I'll have to bring my own lunch. Naw, you ain't got to worry. I'll be back tonight, but I'll take your car. It'll be nice to ride in a car for a change."

Harold acts like a kid just let out of school, leaving in his waders and his fishing hat. "By golly, I ain't been fishin' in a long time." He's driving out of the yard and passes Gabby entering in the village police car. He's watching the narrow driveway, and doesn't look closely Harold's way as he passes. *That traffic maniac has come. I guess I've lucked out goin' fishin'.*

Shirley goes to the door, having seen Gabby walk to the entry. "Come on in, Gabby—take a chair."

He sits a minute, blowing air from his rattling lungs. After a long coughing spell, he announces his mission. "I want to see Harold. He told me he had a gun collection."

Shirley says, "Well, I don't know about a collection, but he has a gun cabinet."

"Mind if I take a look? I collect guns."

"Help yourself. They don't interest me much." Shirley follows Gabby, and is standing beside him.

Gabby turns the small cabinet key and pulls on the door, which sticks a bit. He reaches in and picks up Harold's Colt .45, which is the centerpiece of the gun display. The pistol is resting on a holder backed with red velvet. When Gabby picks it up, Shirley notices the red velvet outline of the pistol; the velvet surrounding the weapon has faded to a red-orange shade. A golden bullet for the pistol is also on display.

"Now here's a valuable piece, monogrammed handles and all." Gabby examines the other firearms. "The rest of these guns ain't worth much, but someone paid big money for this .45. It's unusual to see a golden bullet, a replica of the real thing made especially for a .45. This is valuable."

"Harold's father gave him both the pistol and shell. He told me he hasn't any ammunition for the handgun. I guess it hasn't been fired in years. The gifts prompted him to make this cabinet when he was in high school."

"Nice cabinet. I didn't know Harold could make such a thing." Gabby replaces the pistol and fake bullet. He carefully shuts the door. "I guess I'd better go now and get back to work."

She watches him out the west window, laboriously walking to his car, trying to keep his pants up, and intermittently coughing in the process. John is fixing a kitchen chair. Shirley says, "I don't think Gabby is capable of much more than to give people traffic tickets." While at the west window, she notices the sky. "I think I can see some blue sky coming our way."

John asks, "How much longer—uh, will I be working here?"

"We haven't cut winter's wood. That will take a while."

"Maybe I could start—uh, while we're waiting for good weather?"

"I'm guessing that tomorrow Harold will want you and Willy to work the hay. You should ask him what his plans are when he comes back from fishing."

The next day, Shirley, Steven, and Emily Ann are at the Coleses'. Emily Ann asks to again see the calf Zack chose for her. "What's her name."

Zack answers, "I don't know. Mother is away today, but I think I can find her registration paper." He searches on a shelf in the barn cupboard. "Here it is." Zack shows Emily Ann a very official-looking document. "Coles High Life Rose. That's her registered name."

Emily Ann runs over and hugs the calf. "I like the name Rose."

Shirley notices that the Coleses have several cats. "Would you want to get rid of two cats? I want to be sure to keep the rats and mice away from the henhouse."

Zack says, "Sure, we have too many." He finds a box and Emily Ann picks two cats she likes.

Zack comments, "Well, I mowed some today. It looks to be nice stuff. The alsike clover was in bloom, but the timothy hadn't headed out too much."

Shirley resents Zack mentioning hay varieties, since she knows Harold doesn't have any such quality. *I'm sure not telling him that, at this very moment, Harold is mowing the-five-and-five field, which is mostly paintbrush, daisies, and goldenrod, with some dead June grass mixed in.*

Zack asks with a smirk, "Tell me, did you have some hay down this past week?"

She becomes even more irritated with the question. *What's his problem? They have better cows, better buildings, and a better farm.* She comments, "Why? Are you in the market to buy some good hay?"

Zack's expression turns to anger. "Not really!"

Tuesday night, Shirley offers to go to town with the eggs the next day, and stop at Butson's, since Harold will want to work the hay. Emily Ann asks to stay home with Steven, the new cats, and Terry. Shirley suggests, "If Steven is hungry you can feed him some baby oatmeal and milk."

After the drive to town, the visit to Attorney Iverson's office doesn't go as well as Shirley expected.

"I think a hundred dollars is too much to pay for a calf!" is Iverson's reaction.

"It is a lot, but it will be good for Emily Ann to have the experience of showing her calf at the fair."

The attorney frowns. "Jimmy is into that sort of thing. I don't think it's done him a bit of good." He starts his pacing.

"Jimmy! For heaven's sakes, Emily Ann isn't Jimmy! You think showing cattle is what made him like he is?"

"No—I expect not. Why don't you use one of Harold's or have her father buy it."

"You know John has little money, and in regards to Harold's calves, do you want your granddaughter to place dead last? This is a purebred Jersey, a beautiful animal. There's no comparison between the Coleses' calf and any that we have."

Iverson, seated, still looks set against the idea.

When it comes to paying cover-up money, he seems more than generous. Now he's presented with a wholesome project, and he balks. She pushes on her barrette, and she feels her emotions building. "I'm disappointed with you. Toby Perkins is out of jail and someday he's going to meet Emily Ann. I'm worried about it. How would you like to be told that this creep, Toby Perkins, is supposedly your real father?"

Iverson frowns again. "Well, I—I don't know. What do you mean 'supposedly'?"

"I understand that he might have been framed on the rape charge."

Iverson jumps to his feet while his face flushes in anger. "The pervert was charged with the crime and all involved agreed he was guilty. Of course he claimed his innocence, but don't most criminals?"

I'd better drop this whole subject if I expect to get what I've come for. "About this calf, it's a lot of money, but it's a good activity for her. The girl should get all the support we can give her. I want you to buy the calf. You should want it for her sake, and show her that you care."

"Well, okay. I don't see it the way you do, but I'll admit I might be wrong."

He sits at his desk and starts writing the check.

Above the mantel, in place of the clock, hangs a large portrait of a distinguished looking man. Shirley is surprised to see the change, and observes the picture closely.

Shirley asks, "What happened to the clock, and who is the gentleman in the picture?"

"That's my grandfather. He was president, for years, of the Huntersville National Bank, and was given the Empire Clock upon his retirement. I'm having the clock fixed. Since it will be some time before it's repaired, I temporarily put his picture in its place. He's always been my inspiration."

"Wow, a handsome man and some head of hair!" *And does he ever look like Zack—same hair, broad chin, and deeply set eyes. Harold might be right, claiming Attorney Iverson is Zack's father.*

"Yes, I'm told in his youth he was known as Curly. But when I knew him, he was referred to only by his proper name, Joseph Jacob Iverson." He hands Shirley the check.

"Thank you. I know this will mean a lot to your granddaughter."

A few minutes later, Shirley enters Butson's yard. She changes her thoughts of Joseph Jacob Iverson's picture to matters at hand, such as fertilizer for second cutting. The salesroom is filled with more farmers than usual, probably because of the lousy haying weather. She has to stand in line. Alice Coles is there and greets Shirley. She is relieved to see a friendly female face, someone she can talk to. However, she seems to Shirley to continue to look tired and gray; but Alice brightens when given the check. "I'm happy that Emily Ann is going to have the calf Zack picked for her."

"Yes, so am I."

Shirley's turn comes; she passes Elmer her list.

"How are you today, Shirley?"

"Fine." Then she lowers her voice. "Do you suppose, the next time you see Harold, you can sell him some fertilizer so we can get a good second cutting? Please don't mention my name."

"I'll try my best. He only buys what he needs, and frankly over the years it hasn't been much. You know Harold. I can imagine it will be a hard sell."

Shirley nods her head. "I understand." Her low whisper stirs curiosity. Some of the farmers in the room have stopped talking, straining to hear the conversation.

Walking away from the counter, she comes face to face with the most menacing looking man she's ever seen. His eyes spell hate! He has deep scars on his forehead, an unkempt beard, and his arms display several poorly drawn tattoos. Shirley avoids eye contact and focuses on a tattoo on his forearm. It's a knife with drops of red dripping from its point. She nervously looks up. He towers over her and possesses a body of bulk and brawn. "I'm Toby Perkins. I have a score ta settle with ya, 'n' this time I'm aimin' ta git even. The next fight will go my way." He garbles his speech, and saliva like venom collects at the front of his mouth and coats his teeth.

She can feel a rain of specks, carrying his threats heavy with wrath. Her throat turns dry. She swallows hard and is speechless, while walking around him, out the door, and down the steps of the salesroom. She shivers, with her knees and legs feeling like jelly.

CHAPTER TWENTY-ONE

On the way home from Butson's, Shirley feels her depression returning. The events of her past surface, and make her feel like she's neck-deep in swamp water and sinking. She can't escape. Maybe it would be best just to move away, but that would be running. One thing is for sure: Steven is, without a doubt, an Iverson, since he is growing curly hair and his earlobes are attached as are both Jimmy's and Zack's. Seeing Joseph Jacob Iverson's picture, she realizes where her son gets his curly hair. And there's forever Toby. She knows the Perkinses are the sort that would keep him homebound. Harold would have said if he'd seen him at Butson's.

She stops at the turn and sits by the edge of the road, soaking in the presence of Mary Maple. *You're changing with the season. Your leaves have hardened. They have lost their tenderness of spring and have turned a dark green. I expect you've grown a little, but yet you're so quiet. Progress is made quietly day by day, one growth ring at a time. It will be okay. Toby won't really hurt me, and Dr. Plumbly will assure me as to who Steven's father is. I hope.*

Upon arriving home Shirley asks Harold if he'd seen Toby. He comments, "Toby's dad prob'ly thought it was innocent enough to bring his son to Butson's, not realizin' he'd meet up with you. My guess is they keep the guy under lock and key most of the time. Honeydew says they're proud. They feel badly about Toby, and really don't want folks to know how he acts. I think you just hit Butson's on a bad day. They no doubt keep the freak locked in a room, and slide food under his door most of the time."

The remainder of the week on Pine Mountain includes big hay days for Harold and his crew. The hay that has gotten wet a number of times doesn't look all that bad once it's dry. However, it does have a stale musty odor. Harold spreads it throughout each mow and he is satisfied that it is better than most hay he's put in the barn in past years.

They finish haying by early Saturday afternoon. Emily Ann is tired. "I'll bet I've led Jeanie a thousand times, back and forth, back and forth."

Shirley suggests, "Why don't you go in and rest, because we're all going to the big dance tonight. Right, Honeydew?"

"Sure, I'd love to go. Even without the dance, I've had a wonderful day."

Willy says, "Me too, I wanna go."

"Yes, you too, Willy. We'll dance some squares together."

"I ain't never done that befer, I guess I'll jest watch."

John marvels, "Where do you get—uh, all your energy? I think I'm just as tired—uh, as Emily Ann."

Shirley says, "You've done a lot of work. Why don't you go for a rest, too?"

Harold asks, "Now, Miss Smarty, where did you hide that whiskey bottle? I'm havin' myself a drink." Shirley leaves and returns holding the bottle.

Honeydew warns, "Now, Harold, just one drink. I want to go to the dance, too, and I won't go with a drunk."

Harold announces, "No, I'm only takin' one drink because I want to tell every farmer I see that I'm done hayin'. Especially Zack. I hope I see him at the stand tomorrow."

Shirley remarks, "Let's try to be good neighbors."

"I am a good neighbor. I just want to put that wiseass in his place."

Shirley adds, "Stubby Demar is bringing a calf up here for Emily Ann tomorrow. It's going to be her 4-H calf. She might even take it to the fair."

Harold takes a deep breath and sighs, while he's looking out the west window from his Morris chair. "Golly, the things I got to adjust to"; but he smiles. He likes the taste of the warm drink, and the good feeling to be done haying, when in past years he didn't even start before the Fourth.

Shirley asks, "Harold, would you help Willy with the chores?"

"Yup, soon's I finish my drink."

Shirley packs some diapers in her bag and feeds Steven just after serving a light supper. Harold and Honeydew ride to the dance in the truck. John, Emily Ann, Shirley, Steven, and Willy go in John's car.

They drive west of town, following the Sunderland River. The riverbed consists mostly of round boulders worn smooth by the water. A few people are fishing in the shallow slow-moving water. In passing, they can see casting lines, as they loop through the warm evening air.

Before crossing the river through a covered bridge, Shirley looks down at the water and sees the backside of a scruffy-looking man, carrying a burlap bag, cinched in the middle with his big hand. He's crossing the brook, jumping from stone to stone, heading in the same direction they are. They drive through the bridge, and in a few hundred feet, they park among the lines of cars on a lawn known as The Common. *I wonder who that man was with the bag. He's the size of Toby.*

While Shirley and her family are leaving the car, she hears Shorty Spavin, the dance caller's twang over the microphone, beckoning folks to form sets for squares. The hall is filling rapidly with eager participants. Shorty plays his violin as the White Family Trio—a piano, saxophone, and drums—join in to jazz up the atmosphere. Shorty continues to urge more folks to come to complete sets.

Harold, Honeydew, John, and Emily Ann are in the same set. Experienced participants join, to help them manage the newness of square dancing.

Shorty's voice blares out over the amplifier. "First couple, bow to your right, bow to your left, swing your partners one and all, promenade around the hall." Honeydew is already breathing heavily, with perspiration showing on her forehead. She tells Harold, "This dancing is hard work."

Shirley is sitting on John's car fender, while Steven is in the backseat sleeping. She enjoys watching the crowd, even at a distance. She can see Willy sitting on the sidelines, clapping his hands to the music.

Joe Iverson isn't part of the squares on the floor. Shirley watches him moving through the crowd, probably looking for a partner for an upcoming series of rounds. He notices Shirley and walks her way.

She turns her head to ignore him, and while doing so, she catches a glimpse of the man carrying the bag, sneaking between cars in a crouch. *I wonder who it is?*

She redirects her attention toward Joe.

He is smiling, in his amiable manner. "Hi, how's Shirley tonight?"

Shirley can't help but say what's on her mind. "You're such a charmer. You think you melt the heart of every woman you meet."

He frowns. "I was only being friendly."

"I know, that's just like you. It's sort of a come-on style like the trap you set for me. You like romancing a girl to see how far you can go, only to stop short when love begins."

"I only came over to say hi and to ask you to dance the next set of rounds."

"I know, but I'm not going to be lulled by your charm."

"Gosh, you know how to shut a guy off."

"Especially you! It hurt when you dropped me; don't you know that? You did a lot for me, came every night—acting like you cared. I thought you loved me. That's what was happening to me. I have my problems, but you have yours, too. It's called fear—fear of marriage—being tied to one woman."

Joe stands speechless. The distant sound of crickets, laughter, and music drift over the rows of parked cars. The air is heavy with cooling dew. Shirley looks toward the hall as if ignoring him. Darkness is rapidly creeping in, edging away the daylight. She sees the shadow of the crouched figure, running to hide behind the dance floor.

Joe, silent for a moment, says, "I admire you, Shirley. I made a mistake. I wish we could start over and rekindle an old flame."

"Why should I be interested in stirring the ashes? Have you somehow changed?"

Her jaw is set. She's dressed in a low-cut, white peasant blouse, and a gingham skirt.

Joe continues, "You're cool, very cool; you're strong, you're direct, you're beautiful and damn—you're blunt."

"Maybe I am, but you had your chance. Please, leave me alone. If I thought there was anything between us, I'd be interested; but at this point, nothing has changed."

"I just asked for a dance."

"And something about—rekindling—whatever that means to you."

Joe says, "You seem to know so much about the way I think, but maybe you're wrong. I admire you more than ever. I'd like it to be just like it was before."

"And you're not going to back away again?"

"Gosh, to get a dance with you, does it take a lifetime commitment? I'd just like a dance with a celebrity. You know, you're becoming sort of a legend among the farmers of Huntersville."

"I'm sorry that people are making me out to be more than I am. Maybe we all want a hero or heroine in our lives, but I'm just a plain simple person trying to put my life together one block at a time, in a slow quiet way."

"I see you as more than that."

"You don't see me as much more than that, or you wouldn't have left me for what you described at the time as someone with more CLASS!"

"I'm sorry! Would you dance with me just this one time? It doesn't have to mean a thing. I'll even let you keep on telling me what a crumb I am."

She reacts with an automatic smile that she hopes is hidden in the dim light. "Well, okay, I guess it can't do much harm. Remember, I'm not the greatest dancer."

Emily Ann comes running over to her. "Do you want to dance now?"

"Joe, this is Emily Ann, she lives with us."

Emily Ann proudly adds, "Yes—and so does my father."

Shirley is jolted by the comment, but smoothly recovers, and asks Emily Ann to watch Steven.

While walking with Joe toward the dance floor, she overhears Harold telling some farmers, "This is a celebration for me. I'm all done hayin'."

There is laughter. "It must have been a light crop." A voice is heard, with another comment. "Well, holy smokes, it don't take long to put up a few acres of ferns, paintbrush, and goldenrod."

Harold remarks, "What are you talkin' about? I've got better hay than that."

She notices one of the Erickson boys in the group. He seems to be talking the loudest. "Hell, you haven't put a bag of fertilizer on that place since you've been runnin' it. Besides, you rounded up one big crew to do a little job."

Harold's mood remains unchanged because he knows he's accomplished something no one else has. He's done haying. In a half-joking and half-serious manner, he looks into the crowd, no doubt for young

Erickson's benefit. "Hell, I pay my workers. They ain't workin' for nothin'."

Shirley has heard enough and is grateful to be out of earshot of Harold's boastful ways. As they walk onto the floor, she feels stiff dancing with Joe. She's determined to make it seem as though being on the dance floor with him is only an exercise. She locks her elbows, not allowing herself to dance closely.

He laughs. "Well, Miss Stiff, I see you're really enjoying yourself."

"I don't like your humor."

He laughs again and she stares at his expression. *That handsome smile.* She relaxes without thinking, and he pulls her so they touch. She remembers how good it felt. *I really miss him,* but she quickly pushes away. He laughs again. "This could get to be a game."

"One I don't want to play," she remarks in an unconvincing tone.

He pulls her closely again, and she relaxes in his arms. She likes it, but says, "This is your first and last dance."

He whispers softly in her ear, "Won't you let us try again?"

"I don't know. First, you've got to tell me exactly why you didn't want to see me anymore. I'm not going to be part of a love-and-leave thing again."

"That's a deal. I'll stop by and we'll have a talk."

"Don't hurry. I haven't committed to anything."

The music stops and Joe firmly grips her hand. "I'll look forward to our visit."

She walks back toward the car in turmoil. She vows that she'll be on her guard in any new relationship with Joe, but she has to admit that like it or not he *has* rekindled a flame—maybe more of an inner glow that will not leave.

Emily Ann acts distraught. "I thought you would be with Dad. That's the Joe guy who left you, isn't it?"

Shirley is startled, hearing the recounting of a failed love through another's voice. "Yes it is, but it—it was only a dance."

"While the music is still playing, why don't you ask Dad?"

Shirley sees him leaning on a post watching the crowd. "I'll do that."

She walks toward John. "You want to dance?"

"Sure."

She pulls his hand and walks onto the floor, going toward the back of the hall where there is more space. She also wonders about the man with the burlap bag. She looks out the open back of the hall and sees the outline of a figure seated on the ground with his back to the hall, guzzling from a bottle. "John, look at that guy out there."

"He's having his own—uh, private party."

"I wonder who it is? He looks similar to Toby, but he's too much on my mind. It's probably some tramp passing through town."

"You haven't—uh, seen him before?"

"I don't know. I don't think so, but I haven't gotten a close look at his face."

Shirley can immediately tell that John's a good dancer, one who can lead her through the rhythm of the music. She loves the feel of his strong arms and muscled back and shoulders. He is in control on the floor, holding her tightly, moving her through the steps with confidence. It's fun to be with him as he twirls and swings her around the smooth floor. He is solid, genuine, pure, no frills—just a good man. "I like dancing with you, it helps me to learn the steps since I'm not very good."

"You're doing—just fine."

Shirley glances toward the back of the hall and sees a head with its face down and a body the size of a boar hog climbing over the open side and landing in a heap on the floor. The man has ragged clothes. She has yet to see his face. Dancers nearby scatter as the individual drunkenly stands.

Shirley looks again and inwardly collapses. *It* is *Toby Perkins!* She squeezes John's hand and instinctively crouches to hide, pulling him to sit on the railing so as not to be seen. They both wait motionless.

She hears someone scream, "We have a drunk on the floor!"

The moon, the stars, the summer air, the music, the laughter, all the euphoria of the night is broken in that instant. There's complete silence and everyone stares at Toby. He is so drunk he can barely stand. He's wearing a worn, unbuttoned frock, bib-overalls, and black rubber boots. He resembles a Neanderthal man: long scraggly hair, beard, wild-looking eyes, scarred face, and drool streaming from his mouth.

"I've got a score to settle with Shirley Mason." Toby walks, weaving toward the center of the floor. The crowd pushes away, leaving a circle of open space around Toby.

John leaves Shirley's side, elbowing his way through the crowd to confront Toby.

"Leave!" Shirley sees John begin to push him toward the exit.

Toby towers over John. Toby grabs him by the head and throws him to the floor. He bounces to his feet and skillfully lands a vicious right at Toby's midsection.

Toby lets out a loud "Oomph!" John continues with a lightning-fast left in the same location. "Oomph!" Toby stumbles backward. John keeps coming with a powerful right and then a left. An "oomph" follows each blow.

Shirley can't see but hears a crash against the piano with a score of notes hit at the same time. *This must be how John settles his disputes while at sea.*

The crowd is quiet and awestruck with everyone frozen in place. In a second a gushing sound like a pail of water thrown on the floor comes from Toby's direction. Most onlookers let out an odd noise something between a gag and a scream. In seconds the dance hall is filled with Toby's stench.

She can hear a loud voice say, "Good heavens! He's puked!"

People scatter from the hall, walking in big circles away from the mess. She sits on the darker edge of the hall. She can now see him clearly, since he's sitting on the floor in the well-lighted bandstand. However, he has yet to see her. John, unfazed by the vomit and foul odor, starts to drag him by the feet toward the exit. Toby fumbles in the side pocket of his frock and pulls out a handgun and fires. John sees the weapon and ducks.

Shirley is horror-stricken, but relieved when she sees John scramble on his hands and knees, leaving the hall. Toby stands and laughs and wildly shoots a second time. "I wanna see Shirley and blow her brains out."

Joe runs onto the floor. Toby pulls the trigger for the third time, wildly aiming toward Joe, but missing. Joe pushes by the few remaining people. Shirley notices him frantically scanning faces. She stands from a crouch. Relief comes over him as he runs across the floor to be with her. Toby fires through the roof. "I want Shirley Mason or I'm blowin' someone's guts out!" He again wildly fires and shoots. The screaming continues.

Joe jumps over the backside of the hall, pulling Shirley with him. She's stunned.

Toby sees Shirley escaping and aims at the open side in her direction and fires. She stumbles to the ground in the area where she first saw Toby drinking beer. However, his shot missed.

He continues stumbling across the floor in drunken pursuit. He reaches the side railing and aims his handgun at what appears to him to be Shirley.

She looks up knowing the next shot may hit its mark, but she's helpless. Even though Toby can't see that much in the dark she can clearly see the outline of him and the gun pointed in her direction. Toby laughs. "My last shot won't miss!"

This can't happen!

At that moment John and other men tackle him from behind and he falls to the floor. Everyone can hear a click, but no shot. He's used up his ammunition.

Joe is holding Shirley. They are sitting in darkness. He asks, "Are you all right? It's over. He can't hurt you now."

She sobs, "I can't believe this…" She coughs and cries, "…that he's angry enough to kill me…" She gulps and blurts, "How can I ever be safe?"

Joe says, "He'll be sent to prison."

In a shaky voice, she cries, "That won't be the end! He'll get out someday."

Joe pulls her closer. "You need to be satisfied that, for now, he can't hurt you."

She raises her voice and pleadingly cries, "Can't you understand? That's not enough! I'll wake in the night with nightmares!" She forces her words while crying. "Even with him in jail it will always be with me. That endless fear." She drops her head in her hands and her whole body shakes with emotion.

Joe rubs her back. He's at a loss how to comfort her.

She calms somewhat and says, "I read on a Christmas card once, 'And the lion shall lie down with the lamb.'" She pauses. "Would that ever be possible?" She looks directly at Joe. "I mean peace between Toby and myself."

Joe says, "I doubt it."

"Maybe that's my deepest desire—that my awful fear of him and his hate of me can somehow end." She begins crying again and between sobs says, "Thank God no one was hurt, especially you and John!"

Joe adds, "Yes, and you, too."

Junior Campbell runs toward the police car and breathlessly yells, "Gabby, wake up! We need help on the dance floor." Gabby groggily comes to and stumbles out of his car, pulling up his pants while heading across The Common. A coughing spasm doubles him over midway to the dance floor.

A hysterical man can be heard yelling at Gabby, "You don't even own a pair of handcuffs." Someone has called the Vermont State Police. Several men are now holding Toby, waiting for help. Someone runs onto the floor with a hay fork trip rope. Men drag Toby toward a support post and sit him up while winding the rope around his arms and midsection.

Shirley, leaning on Joe, walks to John's car, gets in, and rests her head on the back of the passenger-side car seat. Harold comes over and talks to Shirley through the open car window. "That no-good ought to be shot. Hell, we can finish him off right here. Bastard, what trouble he's been."

Honeydew, in a high-pitched voice, exclaims, "I was just frozen. I felt totally helpless, and my gracious to think he was after you, Shirley! What a relief to know he'll be going back to prison."

When John opens the car door and sits behind the wheel, Emily Ann asks, "Who was that awful man?"

"His name—uh, is Toby Perkins."

"Is he the son of that nice Mrs. Perkins, my grandmother that I met in church?" The question is too direct for John to avoid.

"Yes—uh, he is."

"How is he related to me?"

John can't answer and looks grim.

Emily Ann matter-of-factly remarks, "He must be my uncle or my real father."

"Do—uh, you see now why some children are given to other people to—uh, raise and love?"

"I'm so lucky to have you, Dad, but Toby is my real father, isn't he?"

Shirley begins to regain her bearings and hears her question. *He is, until we know differently.*

"Yes—uh, he is; but I'm your father that—that's always going to love and—uh, care for you."

Willy is crying in the backseat, making very low sobbing sounds.

Shirley in a consoling tone says, "Everything's going to be all right."

"I was afraid he was goin' ta hurt ya, Shirley."

"I know; so was I."

Days and weeks later, Harold remembers the dance like most other folks, but he can also recall that it was the night he told everybody, "I'm done hayin'!"

In the small town of Huntersville people still talk about that dance. No one at The Common that warm summer night will ever forget what they witnessed—Toby Perkins trying to gun down Shirley Mason.

HUNTERSVILLE WEEKLY

June 28, 1948

Driblets of Honeydew
by Honeydew Mullen

Toby Perkins was arrested last Saturday night for drunkenness and assault with a deadly weapon. He will be serving ten years in Windsor Prison with no chance for parole.

The selectmen have been flooded with complaints regarding Huntersville's poor police protection in cases involving violent crimes. It took almost an hour for the Vermont State Police to travel from troop "C" in Rutland to apprehend Toby Perkins.

The whole issue of police protection has been brought to the local level. It is well known that our own Vermont State Representative, Hiram Smith, in 1946, had been an outspoken opponent against the formation of the Vermont State Police. Smith has been quoted as saying, "Establishing the Vermont State Police was a big waste of money."

Harry Durkee has thrown his hat in the ring and is running against Smith in the Republican Primary as a write-in. He said, "Huntersville needs better representation."

Louise Durkee says, "If elected, the legislature will be a good place for Harry. He'll actually be paid for talking instead of hanging out at Butson's and making my sons do all the work."

No Democratic candidate has stepped forward for the position. It's hard to find anyone in town to admit they're a member of the party.

Gabby Pilford, while fly casting on vacation, caught a fish hook in his earlobe. Ethel, his wife, said it was the biggest fish he caught all week.

CHAPTER TWENTY-TWO

Harold is taking the milk to the stand and thinking about the next big chore. *We've got to get goin' cuttin' our winter's wood.*

Last fall he was behind in his work and didn't start his wood pile until way into November. That green wood was tough to burn, causing the house to be cold. He even lost a couple of housekeepers because of it. Harold remembers how the first one stood around warming her hands over sizzling, spitting wood, wearing a cotton dress, standing with blotchy blue legs, shivering, and hugging the stove. She left and he hired another, but she only stayed until the end of January. The rest of the winter he went it alone, freezing, and he nearly died. He vows to start cutting firewood right away. He figures they will need twice as much as usual because they have to run the furnace. He also realizes that Shirley and her good cooking has burned up most of the pile of dry wood in the shed. They may run out, and that will mean bad food and a cold house. Just the thought of it causes him to press the gas toward the floor in order to get home to start making plans.

However, this year is going to be different because he wants to take a cutting from his woods and sell saw logs to raise money. The tops of the hardwood trees can be used for firewood. A landin' will have to be built so logs can be loaded. It will have to be in a good place, a large area where logs can be sorted according to their different kinds. There needs to be a place for pulp, too. Most of his woods haven't been cut in years, and only some when he was a kid. *Jeanie and Lassie will be darn good skid horses; havin' John and Willy, we can get out a pile of logs.*

Arriving home, Harold sits down to eat breakfast with everyone. Soon after, Stubby Demar drives his cattle truck in the yard. Emily Ann sees the truck. "My calf is here, my calf is here!" She jumps up from the table and is out the door.

Shirley mentions, "We have two cows that aren't milking much, and they apparently aren't carrying a calf. Maybe you'd want Stubby to buy them for beef?"

"Which ones are they?"

"I'll take Willy, and we'll divide them from the herd and drive them to the barn."

"We've got a bull calf to go, too," Harold adds.

The silky hide of Rose shines when she walks off the truck into the morning light. Born in early January, she is six months old. She is light brown, a similar color of deer after they've lost their winter coat. She has a small white spot on her head and is tall, long, and lean for her age. She kicks her heels and acts frisky, while Emily Ann gallantly holds the halter.

Stubby suggests to Emily Ann, "Jimmy Iverson has a 4-H dairy club you could join. I know he would come to the farm and help you get started trainin' the calf." Before Emily Ann can answer, Harold comes out of the barn and asks Stubby to look at a couple of cows he has to sell. The cattle dealer walks to the barn swinging his cane. "You know, beef is off this week."

Harold laughs. "Hell, you say that every time you come to buy beef from me."

The dealer quickly looks at the two cows that are thin and small, much smaller than most dairy cows he's accustomed to buying. "That's the truth, beef prices dropped this last week, but I'll tell you what. I'll give you a hundred dollars for the two plus the bull calf."

"Come on, Stubby, you're makin' too much! A hundred and a quarter or you leave with an empty truck."

"Well, I've already got one cow loaded that I picked up at the Coleses'. She's a big one, too, and in good flesh."

"What did you pay for her?" Harold pulls his pipe from his coveralls.

Stubby takes his hands out of his light blue bib-overalls and pulls a cigar from his vest pocket. His round red face is partly shaded by his fedora that he tips to the back of his head to more clearly look at the cows. He glances at the elm flooring of the empty stall he's standing in and pokes the cows' bedding with the tip of his cane. "I can't answer that."

"Why not? You gave them a big shot, and now you're tryin' to make it up on me."

Stubby pokes some more with his cane. He is obviously careful not to get in the position of comparing Harold's cows with the Coleses'. "I'll tell you what, Harold, we'll split the difference. I won't make any money, but I want to keep your business."

Harold laughs. "Stubby, you've told me that for the last twenty years; but hell, you're still in business, and you drive a pretty damn good truck."

"That may be true, but I never make much on Pine Mountain." Stubby rechecks the cows' height with his cane. Resting one end on their backs, he levels it and pulls the other end toward his chest. It comes just below the vest pocket of his bib-overalls. "No, one hundred twelve and a half; that's all I can do."

"All right. You did bring the girl's calf up, that's worth somethin'. I ain't never got much for my beef. I guess prob'ly they ain't worth much," he growls.

"You ought to buy some of the Coleses' cows. They're bookin' an auction."

"The Coleses? Alice is sellin' out?"

"Yup, I think so. Sometimes farmers talk and don't do anythin' about it, but she claims she's tired of havin' to work for barely nothin'. Zack didn't look too happy hearin' her talk, but it's clear she's the boss. Now *there's* a herd of cows! I guess you prob'ly know, but they are some fancy. Farmers will come from all parts to buy into that herd. She claims she wants to sell everythin': equipment, small tools, plus the whole place, if she gets a high enough bid."

"Golly, I ain't believin' this. Alice's family has farmed there for generations. Just as long as my folks have."

"She says the place ain't big enough. I'll tell you, Zack acted like a puke over the whole subject."

"That's Zack, but in this case, I guess I can see why."

Stubby leaves the yard. Harold decides he'll go to make contact with the county forester to make a date to look at his woods. He needs some advice, since logging is new to him. The forester will know of an honest trucker as well as an honest mill to sell to. *I ain't wantin' to be swindled, especially someone like me who don't know nothin' about log prices and is ripe for the pickin'.*

Harold owns three good axes, two crosscut saws, one for pulp and one for hard-wood, as well as a one-man crosscut saw. He finds John working in the barn, and he tells him, "I want to show you how to sharpen these tools. By golly, they need to be kept sharp. The sharper the tools the easier it is to work in the woods."

John listens to Harold's instructions and, shortly, Harold leaves in his truck for Butson's. Shirley has suggested that Harold should do the errand to buy grain. He understands because of the farmers she has to face, but in fact she wants Elmer to have a chance to give his pitch for fertilizer. Harold has chosen Tuesday because on Wednesday he plans to be organizing his logging project.

Harold's milk checks are now the biggest he's ever seen and the biggest Elmer Butson has ever seen. Elmer is looking at the face of the check while Harold is talking. "By golly, Elmer, my hayin' is all done. Damn, does that ever feel good."

"Why don't you spread some triple ten on your best hay fields? A good second cut will make you a lot of milk this winter. Since you're about the first in town to be done this early, commercial fertilizer will give that grass a big boost."

"I ain't never spread commercial fertilizer." Harold considers the thought as he takes his pipe out of his bib-overalls pocket and starts loading it.

"How many acres have you got that's good hay land?"

Harold presses the tobacco into the bowl of the pipe and ponders the question. "About twenty."

"Well, if you bought three tons of 10-10-10 you'd see a big difference. I've got a spreader you can use, too. Just hook it onto your tractor, and you'd have it spread easily in a couple of hours."

Harold knows Elmer to be an honest and reasonable man, but in all these years, he has never tried to sell him anything. It's odd that Elmer seems to be giving him a push to buy and spread fertilizer. Harold lights his pipe.

From the group of farmers standing around in the feed mill, one comments, "Harold ain't wantin' to feed good hay to his cows this winter. That would make too much milk for him to lug." All the farmers laugh.

He draws on his pipe, turns, and blows his lung capacity of smoke toward the few that are in back of him. It would be the first time he's ever fed any second cut and the big milk checks could keep coming, like they never have before. "Well, Elmer, could you deliver that fertilizer and spreader tomorrow by early afternoon?"

"Sure can. It'd be good to spread it by tomorrow. It's supposed to rain by midweek. That will get that fertilizer working right away."

Harold pays for the triple ten and leaves. He meets Harry Durkee on his way to the truck. Harry says, "I'd think you'd want to have your new truck in the parade this year. Have that cute kid that's staying with you ride in the back with a calf. You could put a sign on the side of your truck: The Pride of Pine Mountain. You know, doing that you might win that big trophy we're giving this year."

"Harry, that's quite an idea. You know she just got a real fancy calf from the Coleses. Maybe she would like to do that. I'll see."

"Well, if you do, show up Saturday at about ten in the school yard, and we'll sign you up right there, just before the parade begins."

Harold gets in his truck, lights up his pipe again, and feels very satisfied with himself. *Golly, I would like to be in the parade. It would show Huntersville I'm somebody.*

A memory comes to him of Shirley saying, "If I'm the one that gets you out of your rut, then I'll gladly take the credit." *Elmer has never pressed me quite so hard to buy somethin', as he did today. I wonder if Shirley is behind it.* He chuckles to himself. *The fertilizer is a good idea, but I'd never have bought it if Elmer hadn't talked me into it.*

As he drives up the mountain it's nearly noon. *John is good help. Willy and John would be a good team on the crosscut saw. I'll skid with Jeanie and Lassie while they do the cuttin'. I've spent a good many years on the end of a crosscut, cuttin' my winter's wood. It will seem good to turn it over to younger fellas. That is damn hard work, usin' a crosscut all day.*

Harold pulls into the yard and walks to the shed to see if John is still sharpening the tools. He's pushing a file over the bevel of a steel tooth. Gray filing dust is floating onto the workbench. "Looks like you're doin' a good job."

"Oh, it's—uh, easy to do."

Harold empties his pipe on the door and blows on it to clean the stem. "You know, I'd like you to stay on and help us with loggin' and the wood supply for winter. I just heard logs are bringin' big money right now, so I could give you a good week's pay. Say fifty dollars and your board and room. There's a good winter's worth of work in my woods."

"Probably Emily Ann would—uh, like that, and the pay is—uh, good, but I don't feel it's proper. You know." John shifts some floor dirt around with his foot in search for words. "I'm not—uh, not married. I'm not sure—uh, how it would look."

"Hell, no one hardly knows you're here. We live our own lives on Pine Mountain. You know what the truth is, that's all that matters."

John continues moving dirt with his shoe. His head is down. "Well, I'll stay."

That night everyone is sitting around the table eating. Harold announces, "The county forester is comin' tomorrow. I want John to be with us. Maybe we can both learn somethin' about cuttin' logs. I've cut a lot of firewood, but loggin' is a different matter." He looks at Shirley. "Butson's is due here tomorrow afternoon with some fertilizer and a spreader. Could you get that spread with Willy's help?"

Shirley asks, "How much did you buy?"

"Three tons, sixty bags of triple ten. I figure we'll only spread the fields down here around the barn. Elmer said he'd have the rig all set when his men deliver the fertilizer."

Shirley leaves the table and goes to the sink, smiling. "Sure, I think Willy and I can do that."

Harold continues, "I saw Harry Durkee at Butson's. He wants me to be in the Fourth of July parade with my new truck, with Emily Ann and her calf. We can make two nice signs, The Pride of Pine Mountain, and put them on either side of the truck. Polish the rig up so you can see your face in it, and decorate it with red, white, and blue crepe paper—maybe we can win that big trophy."

Bouncing with excitement, Emily Ann asks, "Can I bring Terry?"

"Sure." Harold nods. "We've got just a few days to work on this."

As much as Shirley hates the thought, she remarks, "Jimmy Iverson ought to be asked if he could come and help train the calf. At this point, the calf sure isn't ready to ride in the back of a truck with just Emily Ann holding her."

The county forester is helpful to Harold and John as they walk into the woods at the upper end of the five-and-five field. "This poplar should be cut right away for pulp. They have to be cut in four-foot lengths, and peeled to get the best price. May and June is the time to peel them. By mid-July the bark will be too tight to the tree. You have a lot of it here at the edge of the woods in the general area you want for the landing and workspace. We call these weed trees, because of their low value; therefore, their growth in a woodlot should be discouraged. Pulp will be a low-value byproduct of your logging." He marks hardwood trees that are in poor condition for firewood. "Firewood should be cut now, too, at least what you need for burning this winter."

Harold adds, "Yup, I want to start cuttin' a wagonload of four-foot firewood every day. We'll build a pile by the back entry to be sawed later with the saw rig."

They continue to walk. "You have valuable timber here." The forester instructs John on how to get the best value out of a tree by cutting various lengths. He explains how board feet are measured. John seems to understand, and seems eager to learn.

Harold remarks, "I ain't wantin' my woods stripped. We've got to leave trees for the young folks."

In the upper end of the five-and-five field near the woods, the forester points out a good landing site, and instructs John how to build it out of hemlock logs.

It is now late afternoon, and Shirley is just finishing spreading the fertilizer.

Harold has returned from the woods. He checks on Shirley and picks up a handful of remaining fertilizer. He looks at the gray, white, and red particles. "I hope Elmer didn't sell me a pig in a poke. I can't believe this stuff does all that they claim it will."

Shirley remarks, "You wait a week or so. If we get a good amount of rain, I think you'll see a big change in the grass."

Harold draws on his pipe and exhales, studying her expression. "How do you know so much about fertilizer?"

"Oh, I've seen it used before. Just wait for the rain and watch the grasses change."

The next evening, Jimmy Iverson is at the farm, helping train Emily Ann's calf. Shirley watches. *He reminds me of Joe. I wonder if he still has that terrible temper?* His T-shirt reveals his bronze tan. His honey blond hair flutters free in the light mountain breeze. *He looks like a model for a Montgomery Ward catalogue.*

He acts relaxed and natural leading the calf, like a woodsman swinging an ax. The calf and Jimmy move and flow gracefully together while he's instructing Emily Ann. John and Shirley listen intently at what he has to say. "Always hold her head high, move with her slowly, place her feet squarely under her when you stop, and keep the rear right leg back a few inches when in a standing position. You should always move as one unit with the calf." He looks at Emily Ann. "If you want to train her to stand in the truck, you've got to lead her for a short time at least twice a day and more if you have time."

He also shows Emily Ann how to wash and clean her calf and how the calf should be clipped for the show ring. "Gosh, there's a lot to this," Shirley blurts. She is holding Steven, watching Jimmy fully engrossed in what he knows and does best. She looks to Emily Ann to take Steven, while she and Jimmy walk with Rose back to the barn. They visit with small talk for a while, and for the moment she feels safe in his presence. He unexpectedly offers, "I've thought a lot about us. It was terrible what I did to you, causing you to leave. I wish you'd give me another chance. I would never do that again."

His admission of guilt relaxes her even more. *Must be he's learned to control his temper.* His tender smile and soft, low voice captivate her, a reminder of how she felt with Joe. As they walk out of the barn, she notices that he is as tall as Joe, moves and talks like Joe, and for the moment, she imagines he is Joe.

He comments, "You sure have grown up in the short time since living on our farm."

"Yes, and you've changed yourself."

They lean on his truck. He says, "Remember how we used to visit every night? I think about that—often. Could we meet at the bottom of the mountain tomorrow night and just talk? We could get to know each other again, and if you would like we could go to The Common Saturday night after the parade."

"Sure." *I'll see how our visit goes. He seems to have changed.*

Emily Ann calls from the entry door, "Steven is hungry."

Shirley presses her hand on Jimmy's forearm. "Thanks for your help; I'll see you tomorrow night." She runs to the house surprisingly energized and feeds Steven.

Emily Ann is in a grump. She cries in a low tone, "I want us to be a family." Tears fill her eyes.

"We're almost like a family."

"Jimmy Iverson and you looked awfully friendly down by his truck."

"Well, we are friends. He wants to take me to The Common Saturday night."

"Just the two of you?"

"Yes, we'll see. Isn't that all right?"

"No, it isn't. I want you to go with Dad." Emily Ann starts crying.

How can we be a family? Especially since I can't ever imagine feeling any attraction toward John.

Later that night, Shirley lies in bed wide-awake. She can hear the night sounds out her window. The horses in the pasture are drumming their hooves on the hard ground, racing to the far end of the small pasture to free themselves of flies. A slight wind is whispering through the window, promising a shower. Insects splat against the screen, flying wildly out of control. She listens to Steven's breathing, and the deep breathing of a little girl, who now depends on her for comfort and love. *I have asked for this, and wanted Emily Ann, but now I'm trapped.*

If she allows herself, she could fantasize about a love affair with Jimmy. Maybe he has grown up; after all, he apologized, and seems genuinely sorry for what he did to her. *It's easy to forgive a charmer, and he said he could never do anything like that again.*

Joe's presence looms before her. She can feel being in his arms, pressing herself close to him. Her breathing quickens, and her hands dampen. *Maybe it's the hot night.* She needs to control her emotions. If only she could erase her promise to meet Jimmy and had said no to the dance at The Common.

A hard rain comes during the night, washing in Harold's fertilizer.

The next morning the news of Shirley's date breaks into the sounds of breakfast. Emily Ann matter-of-factly announces, "Shirley's got a date with Jimmy Iverson. They're going dancing at The Common. You know, where the shooting was. She's going right back there."

All eyes around the table look at Shirley. Everyone freezes in place. Momentarily, the breakfast scene looks like a group of wax figures. Harold has a half piece of bacon stuck out of his mouth, Willy's forkful of scrambled eggs stops in midair, John reddens with embarrassment with his fork resting on his plate. Emily Ann wears a smug look, her eyes squinting, with her mouth clamped shut. Her glare is fixed on Shirley, who holds Steven in her lap. "Look, I only accepted an *offer* to go dancing Saturday night. I've known Jimmy Iverson for a long time. Is it okay with all of you if I go? Do I have to ask permission?"

Harold resumes chewing and swallows his bacon. "You've built one damn big pile of responsibility for yourself right here on Pine Mountain. Now don't go and blow it on some flash-in-the-pan across town."

Willy says, "Ya'd never leave here, would ya, Shirley? I mean, I mean…" and tears begin to run down his face.

John assures, "Let's just be—uh, be reasonable. Shirley's only going—uh, to a dance."

Harold bears down. "A hell of a lot can happen at a dance. Let's not fool ourselves."

Shirley remarks, "Hey, it's only a date. It'll be okay."

Harold won't let up. "It ain't you we're worried about. It's what you might leave behind, one hell of a lot of shattered lives."

Shirley has nothing to say, but sits in turmoil.

After breakfast, John, Willy, and Harold head for the woods to cut pulp. Shirley and Emily Ann are still at odds. Doing the best she can to deal with the situation, Shirley suggests that they think about the upcoming Fourth of July float. Since it is Wednesday, they're going to town, and they could buy supplies. Plus, Steven is beginning to eat some solid food; therefore, baby food is on the grocery list, as well as evaporated milk.

Shirley is driving and Emily Ann is holding Steven, looking sour and unhappy. After leaving the milk stand, Emily Ann says, "You know, I miss my mother so much, and I feel sorry for Dad, too. We were a happy family." She begins to cry. "I hate life the way things are. I don't care about any stupid float. The Pride of Pine Mountain—what does that mean, anyway? It sounds dumb. I wish we didn't even live here, so how can I be proud of anything on Pine Mountain? If I have to sit in that truck, I'm going to look just the way I feel—sad. In Boston there was a lot to do. Things were exciting, even when my mother was sick. We had *fun*."

Emily Ann's talking this way makes Shirley feel badly. Any fantasies she had the night before concerning Jimmy Iverson now seem a distant memory.

It's a hot day. The freshness of spring is only a memory. Dirty roadside dust coats the scraggly brown grasses. They show their worn and tired look. Here and there clumps of daisies are growing, seeking what nourishment they can get from the dust and dirt. The dampness in the road from the night's rain has quickly evaporated from the oppressive heat of the day.

Shirley doesn't know what to say to Emily Ann. Nothing short of not going Saturday night will help. Her thoughts turn to the men working in the woods. She could buy some cold drinks and drive up there. She'd pack a picnic. Maybe Emily Ann would enjoy being with her father for the rest of the day. Shirley doesn't want to suggest it now, because Emily Ann would balk at any idea. "I'm not going to force this float on you. If you don't want to do it, fine. It's Harold's idea. We could just have Harold in his new truck decorated with red, white, and blue crepe paper. Maybe *he's* The Pride of Pine Mountain."

"Yuck! Harold, The Pride of Pine Mountain? I doubt it. There are only two people on Pine Mountain I'm proud of. It's Dad and Steven. I love Steven—he's always happy and I think he likes me. He only cries when he's hungry. And Dad, well, he's the greatest."

On returning home, Shirley suggests, "Let's make a picnic and drive up and see what the men are doing. We can bring Terry. Wouldn't you like to spend the afternoon up in the five-and-five field?"

For the first time all day Emily Ann brightens. "Oh, could I? It would be fun being with Dad." Shirley is as interested as Emily Ann is excited to go to see the logging project. It is now eleven and already the thermometer at the outside entry reads ninety degrees. There isn't a breath of cool air in the kitchen, even with the new screens in the windows.

She prepares a picnic and brings ice water in a gallon jug, root beer soda she has just bought, and some Devil Dogs for snacks. She's never purchased snacks before, but she knows Harold will like them.

When they enter the five-and-five field, Harold is driving Jeanie as she pulls a limbed-out tree-length poplar. Jeanie pulls the cut tree on top of two small hemlocks that have been set in place. Willy, with a bark spud, cuts the bark the whole length of the tree. John and Harold turn the tree with their peeves, and Willy again cuts the bark on the opposite side. With their axes, they lift the edge of the bark, and it is pulled off easily on each side, leaving skinned creamy white wood. Their hands are black from the sticky sap. All three stand and watch Shirley and Emily Ann coming in the truck.

Harold remarks, "Golly, is it ever hot today, but we have a slick system. Willy cuts the trees and limbs them out, while John and I cut up the four-foot lengths."

Shirley takes John aside. "Emily Ann is upset with me, and I thought maybe she could help in some way this afternoon."

"Sure she can. She can pile the bark—uh, after we've peeled it from the trees."

After leaving the field, Shirley enters the house, carrying some electric fans she has purchased while in town. One each is for Willy's and John's rooms, and one for the kitchen. She plugs them in to try to get some air moving, while she starts what looks to her to be a huge laundry.

Since she knows everyone will be tired from their first day of working in the woods, she leaves the house, pushing Steven in his carriage, because it's time to drive the cows to the barn. The pastures are beginning to dry up, and she's noticed that the milk production is slipping; but at this point, she doesn't know what to do about it, except to increase their grain. The last hay they put in was too musty to help the cows much and all the good hay is buried in the mows.

About an hour later, the crew sits in the house taking a break before chores. They look bushed. Emily Ann is especially quiet. Shirley announces that she has put the cows in the barn. Even Willy can hardly muster a smile, but says, "Thanks."

Harold remarks, "That fan is a good idea. It sure as hell cools down the kitchen." Ice clinks in his glass while he's gulping his tea. Shirley tells John and Willy she hopes their rooms will be cooler with their new fans. Steven smacks his lips while Emily Ann feeds him applesauce. Hand-feeding him is a new responsibility, but for Emily Ann it's another joy in the act of childcare. In between mouthfuls, Steven bangs his highchair tray with a spoon he's holding. Emily Ann devotes her full attention to him.

Supper around the table is very quiet. Everyone eats well, but no one talks. They all are tired except for Shirley, who is wound up, thinking of her planned meeting with Jimmy. She is nervous, leaving the house without telling anyone, yet at the same time she's excited. *Maybe he has changed to be more like Joe.*

She plans to be gone for only an hour, and doubts Steven will wake up. Just in case he does, she fills a baby's bottle of milk for him, and writes a note to Emily Ann.

Everyone is in bed by early evening. Wanting some distance between herself and Shirley, Emily Ann is sleeping on a cot next to the window. Shirley dresses in the outfit she wore at the dance, and touches her neck and face from a bottle of cheap perfume that's been collecting dust on her bureau. She feels for the note in her skirt pocket, and leaves it on the kitchen table. Walking out the door, she gets into the parked truck and coasts out of the drive. There is still enough light to drive a short distance with no headlights. Jimmy is waiting at the stand with a beer in his hand. He offers her one and she accepts. When his truck door opens, the dome light gives her a glimpse of empties on the seat and floor.

The valley is warm but the night is beginning to cool. A light fog gathers. Crickets and frogs sing from their changed world of darkness. The smell of brew and perfume mix and make for a warm relaxed feeling. They sit on a blanket outside the truck, with their backs leaning against the front bumper. He chatters cow talk. "Few, if anyone, can ever win over an Iverson entry."

She listens, recalling the past when he sat on her bed night after night, extolling his remarkable achievements dealing with Holstein cattle. She feels herself relaxing from just drinking the one beer. They have slipped down and are lying on the blanket. Her head is in a slight spin, but she feels in control and refuses the offer for a second. The romantic emotions that passed through her mind earlier have vanished. Maybe it's the sight of the empty bottles and the thought of a heavy drinker that gives her chills, or maybe it's his conversation that is totally about himself; he's reminding her that Jimmy is no Joe.

His strong arm pulls her close and he kisses her. She pulls away and quickly stands. He stands, too, and starts to hold her again; but she pushes, and he almost loses his balance. Jimmy sneers. "What's wrong with you? You don't act like the Shirley I saw last night."

"You don't act like the Jimmy I saw last night. You're half drunk. I don't know what I'm doing here, anyway. Somehow, I thought you might be different, more like..."

"More like who—Zack? You and he are seeing each other—ain't you? He's the one that knocked you up, ain't he? Tell me the truth!"

"Dr. Plumbly examined me after you came close to killing me, and he claims you are. You know what went on after I blacked out. I sure don't."

"You asked for it."

"For what, Jimmy? Tell me—for what?"

"What all girls want. What do you expect?"

"Not this one! While I was out cold—you're sick!" All her fears of Jimmy come rushing back. "I'm leaving while I'm still able."

"NO! Don't! You ain't leaving now! I told you I was sorry!"

"Saying you're sorry isn't enough. I'm leaving."

"No, you ain't!"

"I am!"

He holds his arm around her waist. She lets her hand fly, slapping him hard in the face, sending his jaw cockeyed. He's momentarily stunned, stumbling backward, while she runs toward the truck. He recovers, and quickly reaches the truck, clinging to the door.

"Don't leave, I'm sorry, don't leave!"

While the truck is moving and her head is half out the open window, Shirley blurts, "Forget about the dance, forget about me, forget you even saw me. We aren't for each other—that's all there is to it!"

Stumbling and falling, he yells while flat out on the ground, "You dirty bitch!"

When she passes Mary Maple she sighs in relief. She continues on her way home. She pulls the truck to the side of the road before reaching the farm, and again reminds herself, *Jimmy isn't Joe. There's no use in fooling myself. He hasn't changed.*

She sits in the truck for a few minutes, while tears of relief freely flow down her face—relief of being free of Jimmy. *No, he's just the same. What was I thinking?* She shivers, realizing the consequences of being locked in his grip. After calming herself, she leaves the truck by the side of the road and walks to the farm.

She loves the alive-world of darkness. The cool air and quietness calm her. Night creatures are only visible by the light of the moon. She watches bats, swooping, collecting their food from an ample supply of bugs. Fireflies zigzag, zooming out of control, looking as if they've lost their flight plan. The crickets chirp their summer song.

The moonlit night makes for easy walking. She spots a skunk up ahead, ambling in the shadows over the short grass, taking evening ownership of what she thinks of as Willy's lawn. Jeanie and Lassie stand next to the fence, their heads and necks hanging low. They welcome her with their soft chortles, the same as they do when she grains them. She stops for a moment and strokes their heads. *What a friendly greeting.* Their sleek summer coats warm her hands, while sliding over their faces. Walking across the well-mown grass, she jumps, and then chuckles when a toad crosses her path.

The fans pleasantly hum upon entering the kitchen. She rips up the note left on the table, lifts the stove lid, throws in the paper, and watches it crinkle and turn black from the glowing light of a tiny ember.

She undresses for bed. Emily Ann and Steven are sound asleep. She stands for a moment, still feeling thankful to be free of Jimmy; but she thinks of Joe while pressing and rubbing her hands against herself, remembering how it felt being in his arms. Beginning to breathe faster, her hands moisten from emotion, enhanced by the heat of the night. Emily Ann rolls in her bed, and Shirley abruptly slips on a light cotton nightie. She is sleepless. It's Joe—she wants Joe; but is it only a dream? *Can it ever be like it was?*

Shirley rises early the next morning to drive the truck into the yard, and backs it up to the milk house, and checks on Willy. He looks tired and isn't his pleasant self. A pall has fallen over the spirit of Pine Mountain. She wonders if it is her, the hot weather, or the hard work.

Breakfast, again, is quiet. Emily Ann is somber, but she continues to be attentive to Steven's needs, a natural little mother.

Harold remarks, "If this hot weather keeps up, peelin' pulp is goin' to be too hard. I guess prob'ly by the end of the week we'll have to quit. The forester claimed we would, 'cause the sap will be all in the leaves and the bark will cling tight—too tight to peel. Yup, it will cling tight all right, just as tight as two lovers in the night." He looks Shirley's way for a reaction. She passes her hand over her hair, collecting strands to tuck in place. He continues, "How come the truck was parked at the milk house this mornin'? It wasn't there last night. What'd you do, step out on us—run off across town to meet young Iverson? I've seen it before, a woman gets an itch she can't scratch, and off she goes."

Shirley feels like a crumb, and is angry that Harold has figured out that she left the farm. "Hey, I know everyone here is upset with me. I'm trying to be helpful. You are all working hard, so I bought some fans, got the cows in last night, and backed the truck up to the milk house. I'll bring you all lunch and cold drinks again today if you want me to. Maybe you all would rather I didn't."

Willy says, "Gee, I like what ya do fer me. My room is nice with the fan. I slept good."

John speaks up, "The fan was—uh, nice and the cold drinks are sure good by mid-morning."

Emily Ann looks at Shirley. "I'm going to help all day in the woods. I like being with Dad—someone who cares about me."

Shirley looks at her. *That girl really knows how to cut me down.*

Harold is cleaning his plate with a piece of toast, soaking up streaks of egg yolk. He doesn't look at her. "Did you see Iverson last night?"

Shirley runs her hand over her hair again. She feels guilty, but isn't about to lie. "I don't have to answer to you for all that I do."

"By golly, when it comes to a matter like this, you do. Just admit it: you've gone over fool's hill."

Shirley gets up to wash the dishes. Although she's made a decision regarding Jimmy, she wants more time to think about the whole matter of dating, especially regarding Joe. Maybe Honeydew could help her. "Harold, I've worked to help you make Pine Mountain a better place. I'm not going to leave it on a whim, just because I've seen an old friend. You draw all these wild conclusions. I'm not answering your questions, because I don't think it's any of your business."

Harold jams his pipe in his mouth and leaves the kitchen in a huff.

Emily Ann accuses, "So you did leave last night, and didn't even bother to tell me. I think you're awful."

"I left a note telling you what to do in case Steven woke. I was only gone for less than an hour. Everyone is being so dramatic over me seeing someone."

"It isn't just someone, it's Jimmy Iverson. If you keep seeing him and get married, you're going to take Steven and leave me. You aren't like a mother to me. You aren't even a friend. All I've got is Dad and I miss my mother." Her eyes well and tears stream down her face.

Shirley sighs. "I'm not going to *marry* Jimmy Iverson. Don't worry about it!"

"You still left the house last night without telling me!"

"I'm sorry. I don't think it's as big a deal as you're making it."

Everyone but Shirley and Steven leave to go to the woods. Shirley looks out the window. Emily Ann is sitting in the back of the wagon with her legs dangling as the horses and wagon passes the house. She has a pout on her face, appearing as though she is about to cry again.

After leaving the milk, Shirley drives to the village to visit Honeydew.

Honeydew welcomes her. "Come in, Shirley, it's so good to see you. How are you?"

"Fine, but I'm here to ask some questions, to see how well you know the Iversons."

"Why the Iversons?"

"Because I'm wondering about Joe. Why would he stop seeing me? Now he's changed his mind and wants to begin our relationship again. I visited with him at the dance Saturday and he acted interested, but I wonder if he really is. And Jimmy is a mess. I just wonder if you know any more than you've already told me."

Honeydew frowns. "Jimmy Iverson? Shirley, he's all window dressing. He's dated a string of girls lately, and has had some of them work at the farm; but they all leave him. It's his drinking. Mildred Perkins's daughter-in-law told Louise Durkee, and Louise Durkee told me that some nights after chores, Jimmy is so drunk Janice has to help him to the house. I think that's why he can't keep a girlfriend. As for Joe, he's totally different than his brother. I know his folks have big plans for him, but he's disappointed them in the job he's taken. No offense, Shirley, but Trudy and David would have a fit if they knew you two were seeing each other."

"Yeah, you're right, yet Attorney Iverson thought Pine Mountain would be a good home for his granddaughter."

"David Iverson is a hard one to figure. Farms are all right as a home for children, but once they're grown, he doesn't think farming, as a career, carries enough prestige, at least not for his own sons."

"Do you think Joe would ever go against what his parents want for him?"

"I think he might. He's a county agent, and they sure didn't want him to do that."

Shirley says, "Maybe he'll be at The Common Saturday night. How would you like to go again this week?"

"Oh, I'd love to."

"Can you come with me now? We'll shop for cold soda and Devil Dogs, and then we'll go to the woods. We'll ask everybody if they would like to go to the dance Saturday night. I'll bet they'd like to."

Back at the farm, Harold is skidding a large poplar log out of the woods with Jeanie. He stops her for a rest at the edge of the woods. He looks down across the five-and-five field. *By golly, I think that's Joe comin'. It is him.* He yells, "Well, I'll be! Never thought I'd see you again. Glad you've smartened up and have come a-callin'."

Harold and Joe shake hands and Joe says, "Good to see you, and hi, Emily Ann."

Emily Ann reluctantly smiles. "Hi, Joe."

"Shirley around? Thought she'd be working up here."

Harold says, "She's not to the house?"

"No, no one is. The truck is gone. I noticed the wagon tracks leading up here and I thought this is where she'd be."

"Why that little sneak. I'll bet she's off seein' your brother again. You know, Joe, you come to your senses a little late."

Emily Ann adds, "She left the house in the middle of the night just to be with him."

Harold adds, "Romancin' makes you do some damn fool things sometimes."

Harold notices Joe's reaction: His face takes on a sober look and he fidgets with the change in his pocket, while standing speechless. He methodically makes small talk for a few minutes, then leaves Pine Mountain.

Shirley and Honeydew finish shopping by late morning and head to see the loggers. They bounce over the rough field road. It's another hot day. Honeydew is wiping her brow just sitting. "Goodness, this sweat is washing my makeup away."

The men and Emily Ann stop working when they see the truck coming up across the field. The crew looks tired, especially Harold, and it isn't even noon yet. Their hands and arms are black with sap and dirt from peeling the pulp. Shirley has brought along some warm soapy water and washcloths.

They're eager to clean up. John says, "Thanks, this pulp is—uh, sure sticky."

She's aware that the others have no comment, but are at the same time washing their arms and hands. There are already several cords in a pile. They sit enjoying the break, guzzling huge quantities of drink.

Harold mentions, "Joe Iverson was here; 'course you weren't to home. I told him, you—you know what I told him? You were off seein' his brother."

Shirley blurts, "That isn't true! You've got a one-track mind." *Darn it, I missed him!*

Honeydew comes to Shirley's defense. "Harold Tully, you're wrong; she was at my house. Shirley and I are going to the dance Saturday night. Would anyone like to come?"

Harold remarks in a tired tone, "What are we supposed to do, stand around and watch Shirley and Iverson fall all over each other and see a great love affair blossom right before our eyes?"

"I'm not going to the dance with Jimmy. It's all off. Honeydew and I are looking for others who might like to go."

Emily Ann jumps up from her sitting position and runs over and hugs Shirley. "That's great news! I know Dad will go." Shirley glances at John. Sweat is streaming down his face, while he is trying to clean his arms and hands. He smiles. "Dancing isn't—uh, on my mind right now, but I'll go."

Harold says, "Well, I'll be, you are about as good a woman as I thought you were. For a day or so, you weren't actin' like the Shirley Mason I know."

Willy has his big smile. "I'll go ta the dance jest ta watch."

Harold sighs as he slowly lifts himself up. "I suppose we've got to get goin' again."

Shirley watches him. "Why don't you let me take your place?"

"Golly, I like the sound of that. I'll go and tell the trucker we've got a load of pulp."

Honeydew leaves, carrying Steven, and rides to the house with Harold. Shirley sets her feet and takes hold of the pulp saw handle and John does the same. The saw's sharp teeth cut the soft fibers easily. John's pull on the pulp saw cuts, while Shirley's pull clears the sawdust. The crosscut rides back and forth cutting quickly and easily, sawing four-foot lengths of pulpwood. They get to know each other through silence, while the saw glides through the white poplar wood, leaving piles of sawdust the size and shape of ant hills to dry in the sun.

Harold drives slowly down the field road to the house, relaxing after the work he's been doing all morning. "Golly, am I ever happy Shirley shut off Iverson. I could see that was headed for no good."

Honeydew adds, "You mean no good for Pine Mountain. She's a very desirable woman, and beautiful to look at as well. Isn't it natural that the Jimmy Iversons would want to take her out? You probably haven't seen the last of her dating. She's young. She should be thinking about finding a man."

"I know that. I just wish I could light a fire under John, but he's still thinkin' about his last wife. I can't imagine a man bein' tied as tight as he was to a woman, but I guess that's the way he is."

Honeydew laughs. "John Gray doesn't think like Harold Tully. You don't have an ounce of commitment in you. You'd turn your head at anybody who wore a skirt."

"You're making me out to be some loose-minded sort, rovin' over the countryside lookin' for any female I can find."

Honeydew laughs again. "Well, aren't you?" They have stopped at the house, and Honeydew gets out, holding Steven.

Harold turns her way. "I want you to know, you're the only woman in my life, and that's been the case for some time." She walks from the truck, smiling, raising her hand to check her fluffy hairdo.

Harold loads his pipe, strikes a match, and looks toward the barn. *Whose car is that parked by the barn? Oh damn, I'll bet it's the milk inspector. Bastard, we jump from one crisis to the next at this place.* He drives to the barn, mumbling to himself, "This is like walkin' to a hangin'." *I just know he's goin' to find a bunch of things wrong. This guy ain't goin' to pass me. They never do at first and then only after a lot of hassle. You never see the same face; they rotate inspectors so they don't get thinkin' kindly toward the farmer. They must keep them locked in cages and feed them raw meat, 'cause they sure as hell are ugly by the time they make it to my place.*

Harold enters the milk house. The inspector is writing his report. He's wearing a fedora and spotless coveralls that look like they've never seen a day's work. A small, slight man, he has the nervous habit of stretching his neck and adjusting his shirt collar. His skinny neck is accentuated by a black leather bow tie snapped to his shirt collar. He's sporting a carefully manicured toothbrush mustache.

Harold doesn't say anything, but goes to the sink to wash his hands and arms to remove the remaining black dirt and stickiness left from the pulp sap.

In an authoritative manner, the inspector starts reading from a list, explaining why Harold isn't going to pass his inspection. "You've been running some high bacteria counts probably because you aren't cooling your morning's milk properly. Milk should not be taken from this farm unless it is cooled down to forty degrees."

He continues, "I want the cobwebs swept down and the barn whitewashed. The door to the milk room was left open; it should remain closed at all times. The water in your cooler is dirty; it must be drained and the cooler washed. The cement on the milk house floor is badly cracked; I want that repaired. You need all new rubber parts on your milking machines. These teat cups are stretched out and cracked, and the air tubes are porous. I don't see how you can possibly milk a cow considering their condition. I'll give you several weeks to get things in order, and if you have not done so in that period, I'll write a cease and desist order." His long skinny neck stretches high off his collar and he tips his head forward. "Oh, by the way, you need to paint your milk room, too."

Harold is livid. "Well, if you ain't the biggest namby-pamby I've ever met. You know what I'm goin' to do with this report?" Harold yanks it from the inspector's hands. "I'm goin' to shove it down your throat along with that fake bow tie."

The inspector is hurrying to his car, his voice breaking in a high-pitched tone. "Remember, I'll be back. You'll have no market unless you follow my orders."

Harold watches the milk inspector's car leave the yard and grumbles, "He's the most power-hungry son of a bitch that has ever come to the farm. The more they come, the worse they get."

Around the supper table that night the Pine Mountain crew looks way more tired than the night before. Harold is recalling his confrontation with the milk inspector; this afternoon he purchased the new rubber parts for the machines and has made arrangements to whitewash the barn. "From now on, we ain't loadin' the milk until after breakfast. That little whiny bastard of an inspector says our bacteria counts are too high, our milk ain't been cold enough when it reaches the plant. He's prob'ly right. Why ain't milk inspectors ever nice to you? They always have to act like they're dictators. Bastard, do they ever get me ripped! Oh, by the way, Willy, next rainy day we need to paint the milk room. I've gotten by with it the way it is for all these years. My old man was the last to paint it."

No one has the energy to remark. They just look at their food. He continues, "This is the last of the pulp cuttin'. Tomorrow is Friday. We've got to work on our float. The parade is on Saturday. Emily Ann, you've got to keep workin' with your calf, and John, maybe we can put a headboard and side rails on the truck so the calf ain't tempted to jump over the side."

Emily Ann asks, "What am I supposed to do when I'm in the back of the truck?"

Harold suggests, "Wave to everybody; you're The Pride of Pine Mountain."

Willy adds, "That's good, we ain't got ta cut pulp. I can work in Shirley's garden 'n' mow the lawn."

Shirley looks out the west window. "A storm is coming our way. We could use the rain. Maybe it will cool us down and give a boost to our second cutting."

They all go to bed early. Even Harold isn't tempted to watch television. Shirley thinks about the day while lying in bed. *I'm sorry I missed Joe.*

Emily Ann is on the cot. "I'll sleep here again tonight, not because I'm mad at you, but because it's too hot to be together. I like it when you and Dad have a good time working. It's like we're a family. It's fun."

"It was. I liked it, even though we all got black and sticky from our eyes to our elbows." They both laugh and fall asleep. A heavy shower comes in the night, dumping a copious quantity of rain on Pine Mountain, but not a soul wakes in the Harold Tully house.

Friday morning, Shirley starts planning for the float. The Fourth of July parade is like homecoming for all the folks of Huntersville. Many area towns don't have a parade; therefore, she knows there will be out-of-town folks watching as well. She decides Emily Ann should do more than just wave at the crowd while standing in the back of the truck. She should throw little gifts, such as candy kisses, flag buttons, or whole peanuts.

While looking out the west window, Shirley continues planning as she feeds Steven and watches Emily Ann, leading Rose. After Steven finishes, she carries him out in the yard and speaks to Harold. "Honeydew needs to be here to help, and I'll bet she'd be willing to ride with you in the parade."

"By golly, that's a good idea. We're goin' all out for this float."

She's never seen Harold act so charged, while he washes his truck with unusual care. Shirley suggests, "Willy could string some beads so Emily Ann will have them to throw to the crowd, as the parade moves along. I bet he'd like doing that."

Harold has a long list to fill when he goes to Huntersville. He buys several boxes of candy kisses, flag buttons, a big box of colorfully wrapped small vanity soaps, several boxes of unshelled peanuts, colored beads, and red, white, and blue crepe paper.

Willy doesn't like giving up his garden time, and he really wants to mow the lawn, but stringing beads is fun for him. Honeydew works making the signs.

Shirley plans for Rose to be tied toward the back end of the truck, since Emily Ann is going to be busy, giving away all the items Harold has purchased. Pine bows and red, white and blue crepe paper neatly decorate the truck. Harold stands back, inspecting the float. His face breaks into a big smile.

Saturday morning, John drives the horses to take the milk to the stand. Harold, Honeydew, and Emily Ann drive with the float to the school yard. Emily Ann has left the truck cab and is sitting in back with her calf. Honeydew is checking herself with her hand-held mirror, getting every last hair in place while closely inspecting her makeup.

Parked at a high point, Harold looks over the jam-packed school yard. "Golly, look at the crowd, must be twenty or so floats here."

Honeydew continues to check herself in the mirror. "Aren't you a little nervous?"

"No, I ain't, 'cause we did a good job."

"No, I mean you and I—being seen in public. On display for the first time."

"Hell, no, you look like a queen and I've shaved and am wearing my new clothes. Remember, we're The Pride of Pine Mountain."

"Well for me it's like an announcement that you and I are sort of a pair—maybe you could call it late-life dating."

Harold laughs. "You're only catching up with what folks in town have known for the last thirty years. We've been seen dancin' at The Common."

"This is different. We're going to be in a parade."

"Well, just relax, let's enjoy it." Harold looks over the crowd again, and views all the floats. *I should forget about winnin' any trophy.*

Emily Ann is wearing a crown of daisies with a light yellow, short-sleeved summer dress with dark yellow buttons. She patiently sits on her wooden seat that her father made. She's feeding Rose handfuls of grain in an effort to keep her calm, with the plan to feed her some fine hay that Willy dug from the bottom of the mow once the parade starts.

Harold watches Harry Durkee frantically trying to line up the participants. He's trying to make order out of chaos in the crowd that spills over into the street. Harry remarks to Harold, "This is the biggest parade Huntersville has ever had."

Shirley is waiting by the side of the street while Steven sleeps in his carriage. Dottie Candy greets her in a friendly manner. Shirley introduces her to John and she greets him with a "Nice to meet you." And at the same time she coolly nods Willy's way. It seems to take forever for the parade to begin. Willy is uneasy. Shirley suggests, "Run up the street, Willy, and you can come back and tell us when the parade begins."

Dottie giggles. "I'm waiting to see Jimmy Iverson's float."

Shirley looks up the street, watching Willy's bobbing head dart through the crowd. "Why his float?"

"He's taking me to The Common Saturday night."

"Oh, you're dating him again?"

"Well maybe." She continues to nervously giggle. "I'll see how it goes. I think we've grown up a lot, since the last time."

"Good, I hope you have fun." She continues to look up the street, waiting for Willy to return, not wanting to give Dottie eye contact. *Better her than me—the sicko.*

Willy comes racing down the sidewalk, dodging people and jumping over obstacles, wearing his big smile, happy to be a reporter. "It's started! It's started!" He continues to jump up and down.

Shirley can hear the band from a distance. Heads and necks crane forward as the crowd patiently waits and waits. The sound of drums grows louder as the parade comes closer for review. Flag bearers lead the parade. They are older veterans. She looks at their faces. *These guys could tell stories of war and tragedy that wouldn't remotely resemble the peace of Huntersville.* A platoon of World War II vets passes, marching in step. Most have flushed round faces and tightly fitting uniform pants and shirts, so tight it looks like buttons are about to fly. They show that home cooking has put on some pounds, in the three or more years since the war. The VFW Band goes by, playing favorite marches.

The Huntersville fire truck is next. Junior Campbell is dressed up like a clown and acts like one, hanging on to the back of the truck, running to children who are lined along the street and throwing them dime-store balloons. The Masonic Lodge float passes; local men are dressed in black with black stovepipe hats. HUNTERSVILLE LODGE is printed on the side and another banner on the back: IN GOD WE TRUST, 1948. The float looks as though it has been around for a while because the 194 is faded and the 8 is a newly made number. Dottie remarks, "They have the same float every year." The Huntersville Grange float passes with the lettering, TILLERS OF THE SOIL. Women in Pilgrim dresses and bonnets sit in a circle with a quilt on their laps. Dottie remarks again, "That's about the same, too, but I think they've made some progress on the quilt."

Several beautifully groomed riding horses prance by with highly polished saddles and bridles. Jimmy Iverson is driving his new Ford tractor, pulling a hay wagon decorated with green and white crepe paper. There is a big 4-H clover on the headboard. On the side of the wagon is written in green, HEAD, HEART, HANDS, AND HEALTH. Six or eight kids are seated on the wagon wearing green and white 4-H shirts. Shirley chortles, "Is that float the same, too?"

Dottie swoons. "No, of course not. Isn't he the greatest?"

"Depends."

Dottie urges, "What does that mean?" Shirley smiles but doesn't answer. One of the Erickson boys passes driving a pair of oxen. They are beauties, a well-matched pair of speckled roans. The Jolly Town Homemakers are behind the oxen. Their motto is A GOOD LIVING THROUGH BETTER FOOD. Four boys on bicycles with wheels all trimmed in red, white, and blue ride by. Next, Uncle Sam walks by, elevated on stilts, bowing and nodding. After Uncle Sam come two floats drawn by horses, with signs reading DRINK MILK FOR HEALTH. Governor Belcher is seated in an open convertible waving to the cheering crowd. The selectmen and school board ride in several brand-new Chevrolets. *It looks as though Perry Bent has used every new car he had on his lot.* Huntersville's Vermont State Representative, Hiram Smith, is next. He's riding in the backseat of a brand-new red Jeep with the top off. Then, THE PRIDE OF PINE MOUNTAIN comes into view. Shirley is bursting with joy. Emily Ann is in her glory. Harold is smoking his pipe with the window down waving at people he barely knows. Honeydew's window is rolled up. She's seated, acting as if a million eyes are glued to her.

Emily Ann is wildly waving at John and Shirley, and throwing her favors with the other hand. Rose acts contented, munching on her hay.

Shirley claps and turns to John. "Emily Ann is about the cutest kid I've seen."

John nods. "I think so."

The next floats that pass go unnoticed as Shirley is fixated on theirs, as it moves out of view. The Huntersville High School Band ends the parade. Gabby Pilford, riding in the Huntersville police car, follows in back of the band, smoking his Pall Malls while coughing up a storm. Shirley shouts, "Hey, Gabby, are you going to win first prize?" He waves and laughs.

The Grange is putting on a big meal at The Common, and most follow in their cars to the next event. Shirley folds Steven's carriage and puts it in the trunk of John's car, while asking Dottie if she wants a ride. "Sure." Dottie comments, "What a crowd." They all pile into the car.

Shirley says, "I wonder who'll get the prize for the best float this year. Harry did a good job."

Dottie says, "I was in the office when he called asking Joe to pick the three judges." Shirley asks, "Who did he pick?"

Dottie pauses. "I think he chose Alice Coles, his father, and Perry Bent."

Jokingly, Shirley says, "They should be impartial. Of course Joe didn't know we were going to be in the parade, but Attorney Iverson bought Emily Ann's calf. Alice Coles sold her the calf and Perry sold Harold the new truck."

John adds his opinion. "It was—uh, the best float!"

Willy nods. "I liked it. I really did."

Dottie, sitting in the backseat with Shirley, quickly says, "I liked the 4-H one."

Shirley twits, "How would you know? You only looked at the driver."

"Well, maybe. Isn't he cute? Especially the way he keeps his wild blond hair." Dottie giggles.

Harold is waiting by the turn to Pine Mountain. "I'm goin' to the farm to unload, then I'll join you at The Common. Governor Belcher is goin' to give out the trophy to the winner."

Willy jumps out of John's car, wanting to help Harold, while John continues to follow the line of traffic to The Common. Shirley's mind wanders toward Joe. She can't resist asking Dottie a question that really sounds out of context once it was out of her mouth. "Have you ever been on a date with Joe?"

Dottie looks at Shirley and pauses, watching Shirley's face turn pink. "Wow, does someone have a crush or what! Look, you and everyone else would like to get that guy. No, I haven't! I overheard the boys, in Joe's office, saying that their father wants them out of town so they can meet some more *qualified* women!"

"Oh, really. Do you think that will happen?"

"Hey, I've got a date with Jimmy, haven't I? He likes the down-home kind." She shivers and shakes to emphasize her point, revealing her voluptuousness.

Shirley is watching the line of cars ahead. "What about Joe?"

"Who knows? We never talk about our personal lives; he's so professional, it's sickening."

People are flooding onto The Common, rapidly filling the seats. It's a scorching hot day with the noon heat bearing down. Shirley is trying to shade Steven from the direct sun.

The Master of the Grange greets everyone. Hiram Smith talks about matters of legislative importance. He takes too long. Governor Belcher is introduced and has way too much to say, as well. Everyone in the crowd is wilting from the heat. Everyone is fanning themselves with their programs. Babies are beginning to cry and even good-natured Steven won't stop fussing. Emily Ann picks him up and heads for a shade tree.

Harold becomes agitated and in a loud voice grumbles, "If this ain't the biggest bunch of bullshit. This heat is killin' us." Several around Harold nod.

Finally, Harry Durkee is introduced. He says proudly, "This is the biggest parade Huntersville has ever had. There were many fine floats, but only one can be the winner and take this beautiful trophy home."

He holds it high for all to see as the gold plating glistens in the sunlight. Harold is sitting ramrod straight in his chair, sweat running down both sides of his face, his mouth hanging wide open while his tongue dances over his teeth. Harry is searching for the decision of the judges. "I know I have it here somewhere." His hands nervously duck and dive from one pocket to the next. Shirley smiles, watching Harold alertly sit as if he's about to spring from his seat like a jumping jack out of a can.

Harold gulps. "Well, golly, Harry, how long are you goin' to torture us?"

Relief comes across Harry's face as he pulls a paper from his shirt pocket. He's adjusting its distance with his arm for better focus. "The winner is—is—the winner is, The Pride of Pine Mountain."

Harold acts in disbelief. He jumps about two feet off the ground with a loud "Yay!" He hurries to the platform and is presented the gold-plated trophy. Gold columns support a medallion inscribed, HUNTERSVILLE PARADE. FIRST PLACE, JULY 3, 1948. He shakes hands with Governor Belcher, holding the trophy high with an expression of delight. At that moment, the Huntersville Weekly photographer snaps a picture.

Without the least bit of hesitation or intimidation, Harold grabs the microphone and gives due credit. "I want to thank Emily Ann Gray who was the star of our float and all those who helped: John Gray, Willy Smithson, Honeydew Mullen, and Shirley Mason, who was the brains behind the whole creation."

Harold runs off the stage and everyone claps. He smiles as he hurries toward his seat. "Damn good for old Hermit Harold, I'd say."

Emily Ann, carrying Steven, runs from the shade to inspect the trophy. "Wow, I've never seen anything this nice before."

Shirley adds, "You were just great, Emily Ann! Of course Harold won the thing because of his natural good looks." Everyone seated near them laughs.

As they leave for home Shirley catches a glimpse of Joe, but he makes no effort to speak to her. She's angry that Harold didn't tell Joe the truth about her relationship with Jimmy. *Now he'll probably never come to see me.*

That night the Pine Mountain crowd returns to The Common. Harold brings along his trophy, offering everyone a chance to examine his elaborate prize. After the dance, a huge fireworks display ends the day.

CHAPTER TWENTY-THREE

Monday morning the logging crew goes to the woods and timber harvesting resumes in earnest. John and Willy are a good team, handling the saws. John looks up at a standing tree, figures where it will fall, and then he and Willy saw an eight-inch-deep cut. Willy swings the ax, slicing the wood, completing the notch. They then plant their feet, holding the saw by the handles, and, in perfect back-and-forth rhythm, they cut on the opposite side above the notch. The blade slowly buries itself, forming a slender hinge across the circumference of the tree. Within seconds the tree slowly tips, picking up speed while crashing to the ground. Harold keeps busy, skidding, since his cutters are fast, efficient, and tireless.

For the next few weeks, a carload of dancers leaves Pine Mountain every Saturday night for The Common. The dancing starts at about eight, and except for Harold and Honeydew, they dance almost every number until midnight. Emily Ann sits for Steven in the early going, until Honeydew is eager to sit out for the remainder of the night. By mid-summer Janice Iverson comes with Jimmy and often joins the Pine Mountain crew. Janice especially likes being paired with John. Joe

Iverson is usually there, but he doesn't dance much, only visits, since he knows most of the people. Shirley's impulse is to confront him concerning her ties to Jimmy, since it's obvious that she is not there with his brother. But she decides she would be acting too forward.

She's emotionally sick over the whole lack of communication between Joe and herself. After a strenuous square dance with John she feels the need to lie down because after all the spinning of the dance, she feels physically sick as well. She walks to John's car. Emily Ann has gone for some refreshments and has temporarily left her sitting position on the fender of the car. Shirley uses Steven's diaper bag as a pillow and lies on the front seat.

It's dark; light comes only from the dance hall and the refreshment stand, which are a considerable distance from John's car. Shirley feels the car dip as Emily Ann returns and sits on the front fender. Through the open window she hears voices. *It's Joe talking to Emily Ann. How embarrassing to eavesdrop.*

He asks, "How are things on Pine Mountain? I was there a lot this spring. It's a great place."

"You left Shirley and that made her really sad. At least that's what she told me. Now I think she loves my dad a lot. I think they're going to be married soon. Then we can be a family. Steven and I will be brother and sister, won't that be neat?"

That little liar!

"Gee, that's interesting. The last time I was at the farm, she was dating my brother, but that must not have lasted, because he's here dancing with Dottie Candy most Saturday nights."

"We were all pretty mad at her for even thinking that she could leave Pine Mountain to date your brother. I guess she got the message and likes my father more and more every day. At least that's what she told me. You know, we're in the same room, and we talk often in the dark, just before we go to sleep."

"I see." Joe's jingling the change in his pocket.

He's nervous.

"No, her seeing Jimmy didn't work out. Harold was mad. You know him, how he talks funny. He said something like, 'By glory.' He really didn't say glory, but you get the idea. 'By glory, you ain't leavin' a heap of a mess behind to go to young Iverson.'" Emily Ann laughs, tickled with herself that she can talk like Harold. Joe laughs with her.

He adds, "You're quite the actress. I actually liked Harold, once I got to know him, underneath all that gruffness. Tell Shirley congratulations for me on her engagement to your father."

She's getting a piece of my mind!

Emily Ann nervously laughs. "Did I say something wrong? You look so glum."

"I was thinking how much I miss Pine Mountain."

"Come on up for a visit and see us all: Steven, my dad, Willy, and old Harold." She laughs again as she lowers her voice to say his name. "But I wouldn't come to see Shirley, because she's ripping mad at you, and you know how that is when she gets mad."

I cannot believe the gall of that girl!

"Yeah, I know. It was nice talking to you. Maybe I'll come to visit you and old Harold, someday."

Shirley snaps up and watches Joe walk away. When he's at a distance, she demands, "Emily Ann, I want to see you in this car right now!"

Emily Ann blurts, "I didn't know!" She jumps from the fender and walks with her head down and shoulders slumped, and opens the door, and sits.

Shirley hisses, "Yeah, you didn't know I was here and heard every word you said. I can't believe what you told Joe. Most of what you said was out-and-out lies. You should be ashamed of yourself!"

"I'm sorry." She begins to cry. "I want us to be a family so much!"

Steven, waking, begins to cry. Shirley lowers her voice. "You can't make relationships happen when they aren't meant to be."

"How do you know they aren't meant to be?"

"At least at this point, a romance between your father and me isn't possible. Look at him now. He loves dancing with Janice. The two of them glow from head to toe when they're together. I think it's great. Lying to Joe can't change the feelings they have for each other."

"Can't you at least try and like Dad?"

"I do like him. He's a very special person, but it doesn't mean I love him. Someday you'll understand all this. But for now, don't try and force us into a family."

"I'm really sorry, Shirley. I won't do it again."

"Thanks, honey. With my luck, you probably won't have another chance." They hug. "Why don't you go and dance with your father and pull him away from Janice?" They both laugh.

HUNTERSVILLE WEEKLY

July 11, 1948
Driblets of Honeydew
By Honeydew Mullen

The big news of the week is that Harold Tully won the coveted trophy for placing first in the Fourth of July Parade. I'm mentioning it in my column because yours truly rode in the front seat of the winning float.

The Ernest and Susie Frost family who farm on the Branch Road had quite the surprise early Sunday afternoon. The family and friends were visiting in the kitchen. Teddy Frost, their son, was bragging that they had the best cow dog in Huntersville. "When we say Buster, go get the cows—" Just then Buster, thinking the command was for real, woke from his sleep and sprang through the glass window of the kitchen door. Buster wasn't hurt, but before they could stop him, he was in the pasture rounding up the cows for night milking. It was only one in the afternoon.

Mr. Floyd Howell, the newly appointed Huntersville High principal, is introducing new curriculum for the health class. He wants parents of students to review the materials at a public meeting at 8:00 on Wed., July 28. He claims the recent rash of teenage pregnancies are an indication that young people don't have any idea how human reproduction occurs. The proposed curriculum is sure to stir considerable controversy.

Joe Iverson, Huntersville County Agricultural Agent, says there is an economic crisis on most of our dairy farms. He reports that in 1945 there were 26,490 farms in Vermont. Joe said, "Agricultural economists predict that at the current rate of exiting, by 1950 there will only be about 19,000 Vermont farms left in operation." He blames lagging milk prices as the prime cause.

CHAPTER TWENTY-FOUR

At breakfast in early August, Harold announces some surprising plans. “We ain’t goin’ to the woods today. I’m goin’ to show you, John, how to sharpen the circular saw. You and Willy can start cuttin’ up that pile by the entry and puttin’ it in the woodshed.

“I’m goin’ to spend some of our money we been workin’ to earn. We’re goin’ to have a phone. It’ll cost a lot, but hell, it’s time we went modern. I’m also goin’ to the Coleses’ auction. I’m buyin’ their best and sellin’ our cows. We’ll get rid of the runts and drag bags we have in our herd. I like Emily Ann’s calf and I figure if the prices ain’t too much I can replace most of our herd with log money we’ve earned. I ain’t wantin’ to own no more scrub cattle. They’re all goin’ to look as good as Rose and the young bull we bought. I’m spendin’ every last cent I have. We’re paintin’ the house and fixin’ the barn, too. I figure part of bein’ a success is lookin’ like you *are* a success. By wintertime, we’ll have a nice lookin’ barn, full of good hay and full of good cows to feed it to. We’ll have a nice white house with a woodshed full of wood, and the cellar shelves loaded with Shirley’s and Emily Ann’s cannin’. If there’s money left over, and I think there should be, we’re buyin’ a new four-wheel-drive Jeep so we can tote Emily Ann back and forth to school. No need to worry about makin' the mountain when you own one of them four-wheel drives."

Shirley remarks, "I can't believe what I'm hearing. We've gone from rags in April to riches by August. Now, that's quite an accomplishment to say the least. How about buying a barn fan and having John install it? We'll need it as soon as the cows are tied up for the winter."

"Golly, that's right. John can do that on a lowery day we don't go to the woods. I'll order one from Butson's."

John says, "Sure, I'll—um, be glad to."

On his way home from ordering the barn fan, and making arrangements to have a phone installed, Harold stops at the Coleses' to closely look over their herd. He walks into the barn. It is midmorning and Zack is getting ready to turn the cows out after having fed them hay. "'Mornin', Zack, thought I'd like to take a look at your cows."

"What for?"

"I want to buy a bunch at your auction."

Zack acts shocked at Harold's newfound interest in quality cows. "You—our cows are worth big money, maybe you can buy one or two. Stubby says he's gotten inquiries for our sales catalogue from all parts of the country. You'll be left in the dust, trying to be the final bidder on most of these."

"Maybe so, but hell, you'll take the time to show me your herd, won't you?"

"I guess so. Here's a catalogue."

Zack points out a cow. "This is one of our foundation animals you could probably buy. She's fourteen and still milking well."

"I ain't interested. She might have been a good one some years back, but she looks a might over the hill—low bag and all. I own plenty of them already."

"Not as good as she is; look at her production!"

"Could be, but she ain't got much mileage left."

"Well, here's a nice young cow sired by the High Life bull—the same as the sire of the bull you bought from us. She milked really well her first year."

Harold studies the cow, dragging on his pipe. "You have a fancy-lookin' herd. She's a looker, but I don't care for her feet. She walks on her heels too much. What about this young cow? She's a beauty."

Zack agrees. "She's one of our best. It's going to take a lot to own her."

Harold leafs through the catalogue, noting with a pencil mark the animals he wants to own. Since Shirley and Willy handle cows so well, he decides to buy their best.

Zack laughs. "You're selecting only the top of the herd. They'll sell sky high."

Harold draws on his pipe. "Well then, I'm only buyin' sky high."

Zack goes to the next cow. "Here's a fancy one."

"By golly, she is." He notes Zack's slight smirk. "What's wrong with her?"

"Nothing—she's bred back and due late fall."

Harold glances in the catalogue. "Milkin' to beat hell, too." He squats by her and looks at the teat ends and squeezes for some milk as his fingers turn white. "Damn, you have to crank on her to get any milk to come. Who wants a hard milker?" *The wiseass, he'd let me buy a cow like that.*

Zack laughs. "I wondered if you'd notice."

"Thanks a lot, NEIGHBOR!"

Zack stamps his foot, and runs his fingers through his curly hair. "You aren't going to buy any of these cows. I'm wasting my time showing them to you. You just don't have that kind of money."

Harold growls, "Show me your herd; you ain't knowin' what I can or can't do!"

An hour later he leaves the Coleses' with the sales catalogue. He knows one thing. He's buying quality, and it will no doubt take a lot of money; but they have almost a month of cutting before the sale. After winter's wood is sawed, he plans to strike right into the red oak, the Cadillac of log values.

The summer season is moving into mid-August. The winter's wood supply on Harold Tully's farm is nearly all split, piled, and stacked in the woodshed and cellar. Each day, John and Willy can be found sawing wood on the circular saw. The belt-driven saw is powered by the new Ford tractor's pulley. It zips through the pieces of firewood with ease. John sharpens it frequently, which makes the teeth, cutting the dense fibers of the wood, sound like the cry of a bobcat, echoing throughout the hills. Anyone within a mile of the farm can tell winter's wood is being sawed.

The second cutting of hay is all in the barn. Two stretches of good weather have allowed time for the dark green grasses to dry sufficiently. The twenty acres of fertilized ground yielded far more the second time than they did the first. The bays in Harold's barn are filled to the peak.

Harold's remark to Elmer Butson is in his fashion. "I looked at a handful of that stuff you sold me, and it looked like some damn phoo-phoo dust, but those withered-up pale grasses took hold and grew tall, greenin' up like fury."

"I believe it—I sold it to you." Elmer smiles, realizing he has a repeat customer.

Shirley and Emily Ann are busy canning almost on a daily basis. Since the garden is being harvested, Willy has begun painting the house. Shirley is no longer nursing; therefore, Emily Ann takes almost the complete care of Steven.

In spare moments, Emily Ann and Willy work on his numbers and some short words. She says to Shirley, "He knows how to write his name and can write words like 'cat', 'dog', and 'cow'. It's fun working with him because he wants to learn."

Shirley, Emily Ann, and Steven are at the barn. Shirley is looking at the registration papers of Emily Ann's calf and Harold's bull. The bull's name is Coles Farm High Life Shasam. Shirley is printing his name on a card to be placed over his pen.

Emily Ann is pushing Steven in his carriage in the empty barn. She races up and down the walk. The speed and bouncing of the carriage causes Steven to breathlessly laugh. She stops for a moment to check out Shirley's printing. "Shasam. That's a funny name. I don't like him. He scares me."

"You're right to be frightened of him. Bulls can never be trusted. Jersey bulls are the ugliest of nearly all breeds. Harold should go to the expense of having the cows bred artificially before this bull gets too much older. I was happy when he bought Shasam, but the first sign of him turning ugly is the time to get rid of him."

"I agree. The other day I was pushing the carriage by the pasture, and Shasam came running up to the fence. He made a loud bellowing sound and pawed at the dirt. It went flying, landing all over his back. He also put his head down and snorted. I laughed at first, but at the same time it scared me. Terry started barking at him, and I don't think he liked it one bit."

"Is that right? You should have told me earlier. Just a while ago he wasn't acting like that. I've got to talk to Harold about this. I don't want Willy getting hurt, or any of us for that matter."

Emily Ann asks, "Can a bull really hurt you?"

"They certainly can. When I worked at the Durkees' they had an old Jersey bull that bellowed and roared terribly every time I went to the barn. He never acted up when Harry or his kids were around, but for some reason he didn't like me. When a cow came in heat, they'd put her in the pen with the bull. One morning after a cow had been served, Harry opened the pen gate, but he couldn't hold the bull; I guess because I was just coming in the barn. He was a mad bull on the loose. He ran after me, right out of the barn."

Emily Ann listens intently. "What did you do?"

"The nearest protection I could see was the pickup truck. I opened the door and had just enough time to jump in and shut it. The bull rammed the door. When his head hit, I sat frozen in horror. The window was rolled down, and I could hear the glass crunch. He backed up and charged the second time."

Emily Ann's mouth is slack jawed, and her big brown eyes stare at Shirley.

"Harry was yelling at his kids to get them out of the way, and I was screaming. The truck rocked to the point of almost tipping over when the bull struck the second time. Harry had a pitchfork in his hand, and he jabbed it into the bull's rear end. He roared and turned, and then ran after Harry who was headed for the barn. I don't know what happened immediately after that. All I know is that I had never been so scared. I went to the house, crawled under the covers of my bed, and just sobbed."

Emily Ann says shakily, "I'm so scared. I almost feel like crying."

"There was no one to talk to; no Mrs. Perkins to make me feel better. Louise Durkee sure couldn't. She tried to blame me for the whole scene. She and I never got along.

"After a while I looked out my window toward the barn. The bull was in the barnyard, and Harry had a gun, but I couldn't see everything because the barnyard was partly hidden by the fence and the buildings. I heard a loud blast—then I relaxed. Harry announced at the next meal, 'We don't have to worry about that bull any longer—he's dead. All of our cows are going to be bred artificially from now on. Bulls are just too dangerous.'"

Emily Ann nods. "No wonder you don't like bulls."

That night at the supper table, Harold shares his plan. "Starting tomorrow, we're cuttin' all the red oak we can for the next three weeks. I'm hirin' a second trucker to move the logs off the landin'. I think we can cut two loads a day if we get a good start. Shirley, I'd like you to take the milk to the stand. Then we can leave early for the woods."

Shirley is in wonderment. "What's the big rush?"

"The Coleses' auction. We are goin' to be ownin' all their good cows, heifers, and calves. You and Willy deserve the best, and I want a chance to show the likes of most folks in town that Harold Tully ain't no damn backwoods hermit, but can keep up with the best of farmers. Besides that, I want money to buy a Jeep. We ain't ever goin' to have to worry about makin' it up the hill again or bein' stranded like we were this spring."

Shirley breaks in, "If you've got money enough for a new Jeep, why can't you buy an electric stove? Emily Ann and I have been suffering all summer, cooking and canning with wood heat."

"Well, maybe we can buy a stove. I'll see after the auction. You know what I did? I ordered a load of alfalfa hay from the Champlain Islands. That's goin' to shock the hell outta everybody. Yup, it sure will. We're goin' to start testin' our new cows. We'll put them on official Dairy Herd Improvement Association testin'. You know, Elmer says cows milk like hell bein' fed second-cut alfalfa hay. He wants me to order some seed for next year, too. Everyone will go bullshit when they see how our cows are milkin'."

Shirley frowns. "I think you have some good ideas, but for all the wrong reasons. I hope you aren't testing and buying good feed just so you can show up other farmers."

"I took shit for years from Zack, Jules, and a lot of other farmers because I wasn't doin' much up here; but now folks are goin' to sit up and take notice."

"Harold, I don't want to talk you out of buying cows, and a new Jeep, or testing cows and buying good hay; but let's not do this just to show everybody up. How about spreading lime on your fields this fall, and plowing some so we can grow timothy and alfalfa of our own?"

"We can do that and buy phosphate, too. I think we'll have the money, so long's we keep those oak logs a-rollin' outta here."

"It's a good thing you didn't let me run this place. You act more ambitious and want to accomplish more than I would have ever thought possible."

Shirley wants to visit Alice and yet at the same time dreads it, because she feels a slight responsibility for the Coleses selling out. She knows she made the right decision, staying with Harold, but just thinking of Alice and not working for them brings the whole subject back into focus. She hopes the visit will settle any strain they might have in their relationship.

She leaves Emily Ann home cutting green beans, because they have plans for another big day of canning. Even though she is getting to be very dependent on Emily Ann caring for Steven, she brings him along, thinking that Alice will enjoy seeing him.

As she drives through the narrow valley, she notices how the goldenrod and Queen Anne's lace are beginning to bloom beside the narrow road. Withered grass has struggled to grow in the middle of the road. A few dried maple leaves are scattered along the traveled way, promising that fall will soon arrive.

Shirley, holding Steven, climbs the stairs onto the porch and knocks. Alice answers the door looking worn and haggard, which is a look that Shirley is getting used to seeing in the woman. "Come in, I've been *wanting* to talk to you."

Shirley is brought up short, since there is no smile in Alice's greeting or in her comment. Instead, she sounds very businesslike, not offering to have Shirley sit. Shirley feebly tries to recover from being surprised at the greeting and weakly comments, "You've been on my mind. Having an auction must be very difficult."

"It's for Zack's sake, not for mine. He continues to mention you. I know you're constantly in his thoughts. I would best describe him as mourning the fact that you didn't come to work for us. He knows that would have made the difference, and I wouldn't have made the decision to sell."

Shirley feels chills of intimidation.

Alice stands staring at Steven.

Shirley asks, "Is something wrong?" She takes a quick look at her son, feeling that Alice must be seeing something she's missed. They continue to stand at the doorway.

"No, I think his hair is turning more auburn in color since I last saw him, and it still appears to be coming in curly."

Shirley looks at his head. "Yes, I've noticed the same thing."

"It might tell you something. Tight curly hair is hereditary, you know."

"I really don't care what his hair looks like."

Alice stares off into space. "His hair looks just as Zack's looked at that age and his ears; they aren't like yours, they're attached at the lobes, the same as Zack's."

Shirley's stomach tightens, but outwardly she keeps her composure. "Oh really." Her response is fine, but her voice cracks on *really*—like a singer missing a high note. *Alice is a keen woman, and I'm no match for her. I should leave right now.*

Even though Alice's hair and clothing need attention—gray strands hang by the side of her face, her shirt has holes at the elbows, and her pants need patching—her unkempt appearance doesn't detract from her strong, overbearing manner. "It's been brought to my attention that Zack may be the father of Steven. I must admit the thought is somewhat of a shock to me, but this might explain his depressed, almost reclusive behavior. I want to know if this is possible. The innocent boy Zack is, I can imagine that you might have pushed yourself onto him."

Shirley tucks her hair into place. She raises her voice. "Explain what you mean."

"Well, being who you are, and the homes you've lived in, I expect you've learned quickly that certain favors can be won through sex."

Shirley rivets her brown eyes on Alice. "Oh, yeah! And how could you ever have come to that conclusion? It must be through your own experience, because that behavior has not been familiar to me. By my medical records, Dr. Plumbly has confirmed the father of Steven." *It's Jimmy.*

Alice's face slightly flushes. "Oh—oh. You think Dr. Plumbly can tell what went on between you and other men?"

"He can tell a lot, concerning the chain of events. I have made a promise that I will never tell who Steven's father is, and I don't intend to tell you, except that his father is an Iverson. His curly hair and attached earlobes come from his great-grandfather. Just look at his picture hanging in Attorney Iverson's office."

Alice takes a deep breath as if Shirley's words were like arrows mortally wounding her self-assurance. She backs away with her shoulders visibly caving and arms hanging by her side. "I need to sit." She plops in an overstuffed chair in the living room. Her back is turned. She's some distance from Shirley, who's still standing in the doorway holding Steven. Alice says, "Sorry, but I'm exhausted. Forget about the whole subject." She has lost interest in her guest and sits as if in semi shock.

Shirley backs out the door and weakly says, "Good-bye, then."

After leaving, she vows to never again visit the Coleses. There seems to be too many issues for her to ever be close to Alice. She's satisfied that Dr. Plumbly was able to tell her for sure that Jimmy is Steven's father. At the time of the senior picnic, she was already pregnant.

She stops at the stand, hearing a log truck rounding the hairpin turn. Trucks are a common sight coming from Pine Mountain. Relief comes over the driver's face as he smiles and runs a hand across his forehead, signaling that he has once again made it safely down the treacherous hills of Pine Mountain.

That night everyone is sitting around the table talking about the big day of canning twenty-four quarts of string beans. They all look at the quart-size Ball canning jars tipped upside down on the counter.

Emily Ann jumps up from the table, starting to examine the pale red rubbers on the covers of the jars to see if she can discover any telltale bubbling, indicating a poor canning seal. "They all look good to me; twenty-four more to put in the cellar." She writes the number on a chart that hangs by the kitchen sink in the column labeled *String Beans.* It's her idea to keep an inventory, a record of their work.

Harold encourages, "Now that's a good idea. 'Course the record of our work in the woods is restin' in my back pocket. It's gettin' big, feelin' like I'm sittin' on a stone."

Shirley adds, "In case you didn't know, the bank has checking accounts. I would think that would be a safer place to keep your money."

"Yup, I know, but it ain't goin' to be there long. I'll spend most of it next week at the auction, plus buying my new Jeep. I'll also have to pay for that truckload of second-cut alfalfa hay from the islands. Since the bays are full, we'll stack it on the barn floor, and feed a little bit of it every day along with our own hay."

Shirley remarks, "My word, you're spending the money all right."

For most of the summer, John and Janice Iverson have been dance partners every Saturday night at The Common. Shirley has only occasionally danced with him, and figures that was only due to Emily Ann's insistence. Therefore, it surprises her when John leans over at the table and asks, "Let's take a walk up to—uh, the five-and-five field tonight."

"Sure, I'd love to."

On their return, Shirley is pleased having had time alone with John, but she has no romantic attraction toward him, and she senses he feels the same toward her.

The next morning everyone is still seated around the breakfast table except for Willy; he's standing at the sink doing the dishes. Emily Ann asks, "Am I going to take Rose to the fair?"

Shirley draws a deep breath. "I think we should pass that up, since you'll be going to school in a few days. If you take Rose to the fair as a 4-H member, we would be dealing with Jimmy Iverson, and that's reason enough not to go."

"That's right, I don't want to see him again," Emily Ann remarks.

"Hell no, we've got to keep Shirley under control." Harold laughs. "Let's go to the woods so we can keep these logs rollin' outta here."

Mid-morning, Shirley goes to the woods to tell Harold that his load of alfalfa hay has arrived. After returning, she notices a package on the kitchen table marked SPECIAL DELIVERY. She unwraps it, thinking it must be some sort of bad news. Instead, she is surprised. It is a framed picture of Harold holding the float trophy, shaking hands with Governor Belcher. "You did a great job for Huntersville" is written on the picture and it's signed by Governor Belcher.

"Look at this picture, Emily Ann. Harold is as happy as I've ever seen him."

Emily Ann remarks, "He'll be so puffed up we won't be able to stand it. I'm taking Steven out in front of the house to feed him."

Shirley hangs the picture in the kitchen, just above the trophy placed on a shelf John has made. She stands by the west window, and watches the hay being unloaded. She shakes her head. *He's having the time of his life, spending log money.*

Shirley makes up a drink for the men, realizing they will need it after unloading the hay. There are plenty of tomatoes to can, but she'll wait until tomorrow morning before poking up the fire. Shirley calls the crew. "It's time for a break. I've got something for you to drink."

Since their walk, John is becoming more at ease around her. He frequently hugs her around the waist so quickly that no one realizes, except for Emily Ann. When she notices her father's affection toward Shirley, happiness fills her face.

The men sit around the table, with Emily Ann holding Steven. Shirley stands behind John, wanting to place her hands on his shoulders, flexing her fingers and imagining the feel of his strength. But she clenches her fist, thinking it would send the wrong message. She's reminded of Joe, and tucks her hair into place.

Harold breaks the silence. "That was a damn good load of hay. You should see the green leaves fall from those bales when they're handled."

Shirley smiles. "So you're in the milk production race, hoping to pass everybody in a cloud of dust."

"You're damn right. I'm goin' to have some fun, just seein' how much the new cows can milk."

"Why don't you start breeding your new herd by artificial insemination? Use some good proven bulls. Get rid of Shasam before he hurts someone."

"He ain't goin' to hurt no one. He ain't botherin' you, is he, Willy?"

"No, not yet; 'course I'm his friend. Some mornin's he makes a lot a snortin' but Terry always comes with me. Terry ain't goin' ta let him hurt me. I jest laugh at him."

Shirley reminds Harold, "Older Jersey bulls can be ugly. I think it's foolish keeping him much longer."

"He's a good-lookin' bull. I'm keepin' him for the winter."

"Good looks doesn't mean a thing when you've got a sixteen-hundred-pound bull bearing down on you. That's a pretty small barn to find a place to hide, with a mad bull on a rampage." Shirley drops the subject, but she is hoping someone will get a good scare from Shasam without getting hurt, an incident that would change Harold's mind.

After a brief silence, she comments, "I'm surprised none of you have noticed what we got in the mail today. I hung it on the wall above the trophy." The three men get up for a closer look.

Harold remarks, "Golly, wasn't that the day, and Belcher signed it. That's prob'ly one of his best days since he's been in office. At least he was tryin' to make friends. You know I can't remember a damn word he said, but I'll never forget bein' on that dance floor, and him puttin' on that fake smile, shakin' my hand sayin', 'Congratulations!'"

Shirley laughs. "Yeah, just an average day in the life of Harold Tully."

"In a way that was the first good day of my life. Before that, I was just a piece a shit everybody laughed at and kicked around."

That night John and Shirley take an evening walk up the hill in back of the house. Harold and Willy are glued to the television watching wrestling. Harold gets up from his chair during a commercial and goes to the front room, having watched Emily Ann go there earlier. He wonders what she's doing in a room with no light?

Harold stands at the door of the front room and can barely see the outline of Emily Ann's head and shoulders. She's kneeling on an over-stuffed chair, resting her arms on the back. Her chin is resting on her hands with her attention fixed toward the side window that faces the field road. She leaps out of the chair, throwing her arms up in the air, acting like a cheerleader at a ball game. In the process she notices Harold standing in the doorway. He says, "What in thunder are you doin' in here in the dark, jumping around like you just landed in a bed of hot coals?"

"Oh—you scared me! What are *you* doing staring at me?"

"Just wonderin' why you're in a dark room. Unless it's to watch your dad and Shirley."

"Well—that's why I'm here. Is that okay?"

"Sure is. If she likes your dad, it'll keep her from fallin' for another Jimmy Iverson."

"I sure hope she doesn't." Emily Ann resumes the position in the chair.

"I agree."

John is thinking out loud as if Shirley weren't with him. "I'm going to—uh, visit Janice on the day of the auction."

"Fine, why don't you? Aren't you and she about the same age?"

John scuffs his feet. "Yes, but don't jump to—uh, any conclusions."

"Hey, she's attractive, lonely, and needs a man. That's a great combination."

He continues moving his feet, with his head down. "You're attractive…"

"But I'm too young. After all, I'm still a teenager." She laughs and rests her hand on his shoulder.

"Don't say that. I think of you as being—uh, older." He hugs her and quickly releases his arm. "I don't think—uh, this is right. That I—uh, hug you alone in the dark."

"I don't mind. I'll tell you when it doesn't feel right."

"Okay, but I'm—um, just not sure."

"Don't be attracted to me because of Emily Ann or because it's convenient."

"I understand."

The next morning is busy for Shirley. She rises early to can two batches of tomatoes. She has started early because the ripe tomatoes are getting ahead of her, and the Wednesday trip to town will take up a big part of the day. She also wants to remind Harold that an electric stove is needed, to keep them from suffering in the heat of the wood fire. After removing the quarts from the hot canner, she turns the Mason jars upside down.

At breakfast Harold remarks, "Golly, woman, you tryin' to drive us outta this place? Damn, is it ever hot in here."

Shirley serves breakfast. "Look under your plate."

He pulls out a piece of paper: "ELECTRIC STOVE."

"Okay, okay, I get the point. Why don't you buy one when you go to town?" He reaches in his back pocket, pulls out his wallet, and lays two hundred-dollar bills on the table. "Golly, you're one crafty woman. It's just goin' to take that much longer before we can have that Jeep."

She laughs and jumps like a kid. "Thanks, Harold! I figure if you can have your hay, it's time we had a stove."

"Oh, I know. I got carried away buyin' that load of hay, but we're into a good stand of oak right now, and these logs are bringin' good money. Oh, did anyone notice? The milk inspector came back and passed me. The son of a bitch, if he didn't there'd be hell to pay. Apparently coolin' the milk during breakfast has kept our bacteria counts down. I don't know's it's always forty degrees when it leaves the farm but it must be good enough or he sure as hell would have let us know."

Emily Ann and Shirley make The Market their first stop. Shirley meets Mrs. Perkins. She asks warmly, "Hi, how are you? It's good to see you."

Mrs. Perkins says, "I was thinking not long ago that you must go by a big maple at the foot of Pine Mountain. You know the one I'm talking about?"

"Sure do. We call her Mary Maple."

Mrs. Perkins laughs. "That's what most folks call it. When I was a young girl, our Sunday school traveled out to see the tree. Our teacher told us it was a sacred tree, because its limbs represented the loving arms of the mother of Christ. Someday I'd like to visit you and see it again."

"Gee, why don't you? I'd love to show you around Pine Mountain."

Mrs. Perkins says, "I'd like to invite you to our place but two of my boys see things differently than I do."

"I realize that might be the case."

They hug and Mrs. Perkins talks through her emotions. "I've always missed you, since the day you left. But you've made out all right and I'm proud of you. Seeing your silver barrette reminds me of the day I gave it to you, years ago. I remember at the time you were excited to have it."

"There's almost no day that passes but what I think of you." The two hug again.

"Thank you, Shirley, for saying that. My goodness, we'd better say good-bye. We're making quite the scene here in The Market."

"I'm glad we had a chance to visit."

Next, Shirley and Emily Ann buy school clothes, and then they're off to look at electric stoves at Marty Stebbin's hardware store. Marty shows them one and says, "This will be a great stove for you."

"I'm sure it will be." She slides her hand over the enamel surface and remarks, "We're now modern on Pine Mountain."

The next day, Shirley picks all of the remaining beans, loads them in a wheelbarrow, and pushes it toward the shed. She plans to dry the beans on the wooden rack of a hay wagon.

While walking to the house, she stops to listen to the pines, since a cool breeze is beginning to blow from the west. She realizes she hasn't listened often enough to the singing pines. The fall colors are nearly at their peak. The near and distant mountains glow with vibrant colors of yellow, orange, green, purple, and red. The scene resembles a painter's pallet struck by water, since the colors mix and run together. She doesn't know why, but she feels filled with gratitude. Maybe it's her visit with Mrs. Perkins?

CHAPTER TWENTY-FIVE

Harold leaves the milk at the stand, and for the first time in recent memory, the Coleses' cans are already there. He's headed toward town. Honeydew had called and asked to be taken to the auction. He mumbles, "Golly, look at all of these folks from outta state, even a few Cadillac and Lincoln cars with New Jersey plates." *Bunch of down-country people prob'ly, comin' to buy the place. They'll turn it into a hideout for gangsters and gamblers, who'll howl all night with their wild women.*

He feels for his wallet that is stretched to the limit. He stops the truck at the side of the road, pulls out his wallet and puts the big roll in the front pocket of his bib-overalls. *Old Harold's goin' to keep his hand on the till, bein' in amongst the likes of these people.*

Honeydew is all dressed up waiting in her yard for Harold. He chuckles. "Golly, we ain't goin' to the country club."

"I might be interviewing some very important people. I guess I know more about this than you do."

"That ain't hard. This is the first auction I've ever been to."

Honeydew remarks, "Word has it that a group of out-of-staters from New Jersey are buying the farm. Moneyed folks—who knows what will happen to the place?"

"Golly, that will be a change. Instead of puttin' up with Zack's bullshit, I'll prob'ly be starin' down the barrel of a sawed-off shotgun."

"Well, I don't know about that. Aren't you being a bit dramatic?"

"Prob'ly, but people dressed in fancy clothes, ridin' in fancy cars make me nervous."

"I did call Attorney Iverson, and asked what he knew. He wouldn't say much, but he said Alice advertised the auction in the *New York Times.* I bought the paper. Here's the ad." Honeydew hands him the clipping.

> **Sleepy little farm at the end of the road,**
> **Sells by auction.**
> **Tues. September 2. Huntersville, Vermont.**

Harold sighs. "Wouldn't you know Alice would do something like that—draw in a bunch of foreigners to make a few extra bucks."

Honeydew replies, "She's a smart woman. Anyone who's worn the same dress for as long as I can remember has to have stashed away a lot of money. She never spends any."

"I don't suppose anyone knows the real Alice Coles, not even David Iverson. Even though she's churched and all, there's a hard side to that woman. I think Shirley and she had a fallin' out. Don't ask me over what, but she wouldn't come with us. She didn't want any part of it. Golly, look at all this traffic and all the people millin' around. They even put up a big tent."

A young fellow is motioning for Harold to keep driving toward the back of the barn. He stops and lets Honeydew out. "Save me a front-row seat under the tent." Harold drives through the back meadow all the way to the pasture to park.

He slips the marked catalogue in his back pocket, and leaves his wallet in the glove compartment of his truck. The environment of strange cars and strange people gives him a sick hollow feeling that his little corner of the world will never be the same. He feels as if he should be on guard, but just how to do that he isn't sure. The act of locking a truck, a door, or anything is completely unfamiliar to him. He is slightly mad at Alice Coles, because in an attempt to earn a few extra dollars, she is willing to sell the serenity and security of living next to Pine Mountain. He feels like he's walking to a funeral over a pasture that will never again see a cow, and through a meadow that will never again be farmed for a need of hay or a crop. *It will probably be hayed by some idiot that won't give a damn about the results, but only usin' his equipment to play a little.*

He mills through the crowd, most of whom he doesn't know and others who are only vaguely familiar to him. He sees Stubby chewing on his cigar as if he's about to swallow the whole thing, nervously running around, getting ready for the auction. Harold sits in his seat and turns to Honeydew. "Stubby looks like he's in way over his head. He's as nervous as a long-tail cat tiptoein' through a room full of rockin' chairs. Hope he doesn't pass out before this thing begins."

Honeydew offers, "Alice tells me that Zack has left for school already. He didn't want to be here."

"The more I see today, the more I've got to admit I'll miss the jerky kid."

From his front-row seat, Harold is looking up at a small roped ring that is bedded with sawdust. In back of that is a high podium painted white, wide enough for two people to sit behind. STUBS AUCTION SALES is printed across the front in bright green letters. Stubby is about to take a seat behind the podium, and so is a man in a white cowboy hat, wearing a white suit jacket over a green shirt with a blazing red tie. Stubby speaks into the microphone. "Ladies and gentlemen, please take your seats. Let's settle in for what is goin' to be a great day for Mrs. Coles and a great day for all of you who have come to bid and buy into a nearly complete farm that has been in the Coles family for most of two hundred years. Mrs. Coles has taken a few items from the house to furnish her small home in the village, but other than that, it all sells. We have a long day ahead, so let's get started. Gordy Strobavitch is our auctioneer today. Do you have a few words before we begin?"

"I sure do. Seldom, and I mean seldom, do we get a chance to be the last bidder on quality. Right from the house to the barn. What a day this will be. I know Mrs. Coles wants to say a few words."

Honeydew turns to Harold. "I wonder if she'll buy a new dress after this is over. She's wearing the same outfit even for this big day."

"I don't know, but the wad of money I've got my hand on could buy out the whole of F.D.'s Women's Boutique." Harold looks over the crowd and can see Harry Durkee, Howard Perkins and his boys, Janice Iverson, and Jules and Esther Erickson and their boys.

Alice, holding the microphone, stands in front of the podium. "I'd like to welcome you all to the Coleses' farm today. Stubby and his crew have done a great job with the cattle these past few days, getting them ready for the sale. I know you'll enjoy working with these fine animals that have been raised and bred for generations right here at the Coleses' farm. All items sold here today will be honestly represented. If you don't think an item is accurately presented, please see Stubby before the close of the sale. I want everybody to leave here a happy buyer. Thank you for coming."

Harold comments, "Golly, she handles herself like this was nothin'. She's a cool one that Alice is. Now, if that was me and I was sellin' Pine Mountain, I'd be standin' there meltin' right into the sawdust."

Honeydew says, "You aren't Alice. She's traveled more roads in her lifetime than all the folks in Huntersville."

Stubby announces, "We're sellin' the small tools and farm equipment first, the household furniture, and then the cattle. At one o'clock we'll take a break, and then sell the farm, which includes the house, farm buildings, and two hundred and fifty acres of land. Mrs. Coles reserves the right to have the last bid on the farm; everything else goes to the highest bidder."

Gordy begins the sale. "Here we go, folks, a dandy wheelbarrow loaded with all sorts of nuts and bolts. Ten dollars anyone? Nine—eight, yes and half, yes, and nine—nine—nine, sold to the young fellow in the blue cap." The gavel bangs. "Forks, hoes, and shovels; get a buy here today, eight dollars anyone?"

Harold stretches his legs. "We've got a long wait, Honeydew." He takes a walk to again look over the cows, heifers, and calves to be sure he hasn't missed anything in his selections. The barn is full of farmers doing the same thing, examining each animal very judiciously.

Jules Erickson is checking out the nice looking young cow that's a slow milker. *I hope to hell he buys her; it will serve him right.* Harold leaves the barn and is approached by a young couple with two small children. The husband asks him, "We're looking at this place. If we buy it, would you be interested in working the land? I understand you're the Coleses' neighbor." After a pause, he adds, "I'm joining a law practice in town and have no use for it."

Harold feels relieved to actually meet the people that could be his new neighbors. "Sure, we can work something out, but you ain't bought it yet. You might be biddin' against some high rollers from down country."

"We know, we're from New Jersey ourselves."

"No kiddin'. I guess you outta-town folks ain't all bad." They laugh and Harold walks away, saying over his shoulder, "Good luck, I'll be rootin' for you."

After waiting for almost two hours for the small tools, farm equipment, and household items to sell, Harold starts thinking through his strategy. If he's going to end up owning most of the cattle, he's got to bid on all of them until he's bought the ones he wants. If he doesn't some would throw in a fake bid just to see him pay high prices, figuring he's willing to pay any amount.

Stubby announces, "Okay, folks, this is what we've all been waitin' for, to get a chance to buy into the finest herd of Jersey cattle that can be found anywhere."

As he talks, Stubby nods to Gordy, who is holding the tool of his trade, a brown wooden gavel. "I travel the Northeast and have sold a lot of cattle, but these are the best, production and type, all in one package and some fancy! Let's start with lot number ten. Isn't she sweet? Calving right at twenty-eight months, and is she ever big with a perfect udder."

Stubby jokes, "I'll bet our leadsman will even bid on this one. I'd like you all to meet Jimmy Iverson, the best showman in Huntersville. He's known for his Iverson Holsteins, but isn't she about the finest Jersey? Ain't she a show winner, Jimmy?"

"Sure is!"

Gordy drones his auctioneer call. "Eight anyone? Seven-six-five-four; yes, we have four and now four fifty-fifty-fifty, four fifty. The bid is right here in the front row."

Stubby stops Gordy and warns, "Folks, you've got to get in early on these fine cows, because there ain't an unlimited supply. The first one always sells cheap. Harold Tully has the bid. This man knows his cows."

"Yes, five and now fifty, yes, and now six, come on let's keep this goin'. Six fifty-fifty-fifty, six fifty anywhere? Going"—*bang*—"going"—*bang*—"sold to Harold Tully.

"Now, her heifer calf, just a month old by the High Life bull. He's worked well in this herd. Right here in the front row; Harold offers fifty, now seventy-five, yes, and a hundred, one hundred-hundred-hundred, yes, yes, yes, now a quarter, one hundred and twenty-five anywhere?" Gordy holds his gavel, looking over the crowd—*bang.* "Sold to Harold Tully."

Stubby resumes, "Lot one. Take your eyes out of the catalogue, folks, and just look at this beautiful cow. Wow, Gordy, this cow can also show. She's dry and just springin' right in her weddin' clothes, ready to go to work for you, by the great, great High Life bull."

Gordy drones, "Eight hundred to start—anywhere? Now we have five in the front row, five-fifty, now six, and six-fifty, seven-seven-seven anyone? "Seven hundred for this great, great cow?"

Harold yells, "Six seventy-five."

"Okay, six seventy-five, now seven-seven-seven, anyone? The bid's on Harold Tully."

Stubby interrupts, "Harold Tully has lived all his life as neighbor to the Coleses, and he's been waiting all his life for a chance to buy into this herd. He knows his cows. Successful bidders always watch the good cow men, they'll spot the best ones every time."

"Seven anyone, going—going—gone"—*bang*—"sold to Harold Tully for six seventy-five."

Honeydew whispers, "Gracious, I never knew cows cost this much. You sure are spending the money today."

"Yup, my bankbook's flat and all the log money I could muster is goin' into these cows. It's the future of Pine Mountain." The next cow enters the ring, and Harold yells, "Four hundred."

"Harold has the bid at four hundred for lot number two. Do I have fifty, yes, now five?"

I'll scare off the bidders. "Seven!"

Gordy stops. "Folks, we have a man here that's going to take away this whole herd. He knows quality. The bid is at seven and fifty anyone, anyone at seven fifty?"—*bang*. "Sold for seven hundred."

A hush moves over the crowd. All eyes are on Harold in disbelief at the prices and the money he's spending. Lot number three enters: an old cow, one he doesn't want, but he starts her at one hundred. The bid moves on to one fifty and then two. He's hoping for a raise to two fifty by another bidder and gets it. He refuses to raise the bid.

"Sold to the man in the plaid shirt."

He's successful on the next five lots in the three-to-five range as the quality has dropped slightly. The slow milker comes in the ring and he starts her at two hundred. Jules Erickson bids to two-fifty. Harold chances a bid at three hundred. Jules counters to three-fifty and Harold stops.

Gordy continues, "Now, boys this is too good a cow to sell at three-fifty. Fancy, fancy. Right, Jimmy?"

"You betcha." Jimmy leads her around the ring and places her to show her off.

"Four anyone?"

Harold pauses and then nods. Gordy screams, "Yes, yes, yes, we have four on Harold Tully." Esther Erickson pokes Jules, looking angrily at Harold. Jules looks pained as he nods. "Four fifty; wise choice, don't let Harold Tully buy all the good ones. Now five-five-five, anyone five hundred for this fancy, fancy cow? Going"—*bang*—"going" *bang*—"Gone—a good buy to the folks over here at my left."

Harold chortles to himself. *Damn, am I havin' fun.* He continues to set the pace on all the good cows, heifers, and calves until Gordy stops as promised for a break at one o'clock. Harold adds up what he's spent.

Honeydew looks at the column of figures. "My word, I wish I owned a few cows. This doesn't seem real."

"There's only a couple more I'd like, then I'm done. I'll have spent every last cent I have until my next milk check or until more log money comes in. I'll even have to ask Elmer Butson for credit on grain, something I've never done; but golly, it's been worth it."

Honeydew sighs. "I hope so for your sake. Look at the bunch that's stepped forward interested in the farm." Most of them are men in silk suits, wearing sunglasses, all except for the young couple with the two small children.

While Stubby is holding up a survey map, explaining the acreage and the boundaries of the farm, and what the final bid will entail, Harold pulls the young couple aside. "What you folks aimin' to pay for this place?"

The young attorney says, "Well, it's appraised by the town at five thousand."

"You ain't gettin' it for that."

"Well, maybe we could go to six."

"Look at that bunch over there, they ain't stoppin' at any six thousand. Think more like ten or twelve."

The young attorney shakes his head. "Oh, we can't do that."

Harold asks, "Would you pay six for the house, barn, and five acres around the buildin's?"

"Oh, gladly."

Harold offers, "Okay, I'll buy the place, and sell the buildings and five acres back to you for six."

"Do we need a sales contract?"

"Nope, up here a handshake is good enough." They shake hands at about the time the auctioneer starts the bidding.

The atmosphere is electric; everyone holds their breath to see who will buy the farm. Gordy calls for the first bid and Harold jumps up and yells six thousand. Stubby runs from the podium to Harold's side and takes his soggy cigar out of his mouth. His round red face looks like it could burst. "Are you makin' a joke outta this sale? Since when do you have that kinda money? We'll need a five percent deposit by the end of the sale."

"You ain't needin' to get rattled. I know what I'm doin'."

Gordy's voice goes to a fevered pitch. "Six thousand on Harold Tully. Six-five, six-five, six thousand five hundred—anyone?" Gordy scans the crowd for a bid.

The group of silk-suited men starts milling around, talking loudly to one another, arguing in a language no one understands. Stubby runs to them asking for a bid, but the arguing continues among them with no one offering. All they say is, "Too much—too much!"

Gordy waits, but no further bid is offered. Alice nods her approval to sell the farm. Harold turns to the young couple. "I guess you folks own the whole place. Just what you wanted to pay for it. What are your names? 'Cause you folks are my neighbors."

"Donald and June Tuwiliker and this is Stephie and Peter."

"Pleased to have you ownin' the place. Come up to my farm when you can, and meet my big family."

CHAPTER TWENTY-SIX

The morning after the auction, Shirley can't believe that all the beautiful animals walking off the truck are now Harold's. It takes Stubby four trips and he buys and trucks away almost as many as he delivers. Harold is keeping a few of his original herd; such as Babe, Shirley's favorite—Daisy, and, of course, Maria. But they look very common compared to his new herd. Shirley hugs Harold. "I'm so proud of you."

Harold is surprised to find himself choked with emotion and at a loss for words.

That same day in the late afternoon, Shirley drives into the school yard. Emily Ann runs to the truck, asking, "Could we buy a softball and bat? We're playing softball tomorrow and I don't know how. Dad could help me tonight. So I won't look too stupid tomorrow."

Shirley agrees and drives to Huntersville to buy the ball and bat. On returning, they find the men in the house taking a break before evening chores.

Emily Ann enters carrying Steven. John looks at his daughter. "How was school?"

"It was great, Dad, but I'm worried that I don't know how to play softball. Can you teach me tonight?"

Harold adds, "I know what she means, I could never play either. Why don't you help her, John, durin' chores? Part of bein' good in school is feelin' as though you ain't stupid. I know all about it. I did okay with the books, but when it come to recess, I wanted to run and hide because everybody played softball. I couldn't hit that damn ball if I went to hell; and so when teams were chosen, I was always picked last. Golly, did that ever make me feel bad."

Steven is put in his new playpen, and Shirley, John, and Emily Ann start practicing softball. Emily Ann quickly learns how to hit. She is easily connecting with John's softly thrown pitches. Shirley catches the ball, until Steven begins to fuss. When John starts throwing the ball faster, she continually misses. "Watch—uh, the ball when it leaves my hand," John encourages. "Concentrate—uh, on the ball. Emily Ann, why—uh, don't you—uh, practice throwing the ball to me." John hits them lightly back to his daughter for a while and then they break for supper.

After the meal Emily Ann bathes and feeds Steven and puts him to bed. She also gives Willy some words to write on a practice sheet, and asks her dad and Shirley if they can play ball for a while longer. The sun is setting. There is a beautiful orange-yellow sky on the western horizon. Harold is watching the nightly news, and viewing the sunset from his Morris chair by the west window.

Emily Ann is doing well, since she has better-than-average eye and hand coordination; therefore, hitting comes easily for her. However, when John throws the ball at a fast speed, she misses it more times than not.

Emily Ann asks Shirley if she would like to hit for a while. Shirley agrees saying, "It's been some time since I played softball, but I used to like it because I could hit the ball a long distance."

John continues pitching and is throwing Shirley fast stuff. The sun has almost set and she can barely see the ball. Emily Ann is standing in back of Shirley and is getting a lot of practice throwing the ball back to her dad. He is instructing Emily Ann how to throw, telling her to use her whole body rather than just her arm and elbow. *This is not like John to throw me difficult pitches to hit.*

Shirley is beginning to feel silly, fanning at the air as the ball passes. John is chuckling to see her so inept at the plate. She begins to laugh out loud at how badly she's missing the ball. John encourages, "Watch the ball as it leaves my hand."

"How can I, when all I can see are shadows?" The ball leaves John's hand. In a fraction of a second the bat connects for a solid hit, but late in the swing. The ball travels high in the air and has some distance to it. It's heading toward the house right in line with the window on the northwest corner, which still reflects a slight orange from the sun that is about to be hidden behind the mountains. The ball hits the windowpane, right where Harold is sitting. He is captivated, watching Ted Mack's "Original Amateur Hour." The glass explodes.

The three ball players run to the house. Shirley turns on the light as Harold stands leaning on his chair. His face is white and he's shaking. Broken glass is scattered all over the kitchen floor. Harold isn't cut, but he still has shards of glass on his clothing.

"Son of a bitch, you tryin' to test my heart? Golly, did that ever scare me! I thought someone had fired a gun." He looks at Emily Ann. "You're goin' to be one hell of a ball player to hit a ball that far."

Shirley grabs his arm. "I was at bat. It was my first hit. Are you okay?"

"Yup, I guess so. I should've known it was you. You prob'ly aimed it right at this window just to scare the hell outta me." Everyone laughs.

Shirley picks the glass from him. "I'm glad you weren't hurt."

John looks at the window. "I'll fix it—uh, tomorrow night—uh, after we come home from the woods."

The next night at supper all Emily Ann can talk about is the ball game they played and won. She was the only one on her team that wasn't a Stark. "Roy Stark always picks his brothers and sisters for his team. He needed one more player so he picked me. He's a real good pitcher and the best hitter in his family." She continues explaining how they won over the rest of the kids, who usually beat the Starks.

Harold is listening intently to the description of the game. "Golly, that's a great story. Those Stark kids deserve a break once in a while. Ethan Stark works like a bastard to support that family. He's a cutter for the Soule Lumber Company. Hell, what he brings to that family for money in a teaspoon they lug away in a scoop shovel, bein' as big a family as they are."

Emily Ann is in deep concentration. "I want the whole school to come here on Saturday for a ball game. We can play it like it should be played. Dad, you can call balls and strikes. What do you call that person?"

"An umpire, but—uh, I wouldn't want to do that. Sometimes players get—uh, mad. I just don't want that. Umpires have to be tough—uh, tell players sometimes what they—uh, don't want to hear. I wouldn't like that."

Emily Ann sits, thinking, and turns toward Harold. "You would make the perfect umpire."

"Who, me? I ain't never watched a game, say nothin' about bein' a—what?"

"An umpire. You can tell us kids what's a ball and what's a strike. If they don't like what you called, that wouldn't bother you. You'd sort of run the game. Be the boss."

"Hell, I don't know about this. Maybe Honeydew can help. She's always listenin' to the Red Sox. John would have to show me what's a ball and what's a strike."

"Sure—uh, we'll practice. We've got time until—uh, Saturday. You need protection—uh, the umpire gets right down—uh, where the ball comes over the plate. He needs padding—uh, something to—uh, protect his face, but yet be able to—uh, see the ball."

Emily Ann looks in the cupboards, opening the doors and searching through the pots and pans. After some clank and clatter, she pulls out a colander. It has two handles and a large round dish-shaped strainer. She holds it to her face. "I can see you, Harold. If we make two of the holes larger with a nail, it would be perfect for your face and you'll be able to see."

John adds, "You need a pad for—uh, your neck, chest, and stomach."

Emily Ann won't back off. "We can make one, stuff it with feathers and use cloth we've sewed together."

This girl is determined. Shirley suggests, "Janice Iverson is a good seamstress. Maybe she'd come tomorrow night with her portable sewing machine and make up a pad. I could bring Honeydew at the same time." Shirley looks at John. He acts nervous, moving his feet and rubbing the back of his neck. He looks at Shirley, and sees she is watching him, studying his reaction. He quickly looks at the floor.

John explains to Harold in some detail what umpires do.

Harold scratches his head. "Golly, I ain't goin' to remember all this."

Emily Ann says, "We'll help."

The next night Janice is busy on her sewing machine, making the chest protector. She has some heavy muslin that is well suited for the purpose. She could have done the same at home, but she wants to come to Pine Mountain, since it is a first for her.

John comes to the kitchen after his practice with Harold and Honeydew. He is confident that the game will go all right on Saturday. They are country kids, not sophisticated, not bound by perfectly executed rules; they'll just want fairness.

John sits at the kitchen table drinking some iced tea. Shirley is aware that he's watching Janice with her long slender hands, being nimble with the cloth. Her fingers are worn and tough on the underside, but smooth and delicate on the other. Her hands pull, flatten, and feed the muslin to the machine that chatters as everyone quietly watches. John just holds his gaze on Janice. She glances his way, aware of his focus.

Honeydew and Harold leave to sit in front of the house to see the last of the red mottled sky disappear behind the mountains. Emily Ann starts mixing a batch of cookies, getting ready for Saturday. Shirley goes to the junk room and finds two old pillows and then starts bathing Steven. John just sits sipping his iced tea, concentrating on Janice. Her hands move like fluid over the cloth, like the balm of warm oil. Her fingertips are quick and experienced, flattening the muslin as the needle and presser-foot unite the cloth. It is her hands that make it happen, creating the match, bonding the cloth.

Janice says, "I'm ready, John. Let's fill this thing outside."

Shirley continues to wonder about them. After drying Steven she carries him to her room for bed. Afterward, she walks to the front room, and sits in the dark. The light in the entry is enough for her to clearly see them filling the muslin pad with feathers.

John has been glancing at the door while dealing with feathers. He shakes the opened pillows into the sewn muslin. Feathers float up and stick on his moist face and lips. Janice laughs, and leans her face close to his, picking them off. He gathers the feathers that cling in her hair. She quickly kisses him. *They look like a couple of love-bugs.*

The entry door slams. He jumps and stumbles backward. Emily Ann is adjusting her eyes to the dimness. "Is that you on the ground, Dad?" John comes to his feet, brushing off his back end.

Emily Ann laughs. "There's a white feather sticking on your nose."

Janice pulls a needle and thread from her pocket. She laughs. "Your dad just stumbled. He backed up from the feather dust and lost his balance."

Shirley smiles. *Yeah, Janice, John just fell.*

After the padding is complete, Harold holds the colander to his face and the chest protector to his chin and squats. His voice is muffled, sounding like he's talking into a tin can. "Let's play ball." Everyone laughs.

John takes Honeydew and Janice home. Much later that night, Shirley wakes, hearing the floorboards creak. The clock by her bed shows one o'clock. *Wow, it's late! John is just getting home. He's been with Janice all this time?*

Saturday morning, Shirley calls Janice and asks her to bring Honeydew when she comes. John and Harold leave in their vehicles to pick up the school kids. Emily Ann has asked Willy to mow an area in back of the henhouse. It's the best place she can find that is somewhat level for a ball field. She figures the building will stop passed balls and wild pitches. She spots an open window, covered with chicken wire, by the granary and decides it would be a perfect place for Honeydew to sit to help Harold. She can be inside the building, behind the chicken wire, and look right over home plate, and record balls and strikes while Harold calls them.

Harold and John drive in the yard with the kids, and they all gather in the field. John places flat stones for the bases. "Let's do some-uh, practicing. I'll pitch so you—uh, boys won't be all tired out for the game. This will give Harold some—uh, more practice, too."

Steven is in his high-chair while Shirley prepares dinner for the kids. She's cooked a big pot of beef stew to be served with milk. She plans to have Emily Ann's cookies for dessert with some ice cream.

Emily Ann is supervising Willy and helping her dad. There are a few minutes before the noon break, so Shirley brings Steven with her to watch the practice. Emily Ann has placed some chairs for people to watch, and for players to sit. Janice is the only one seated. Shirley walks toward her. "Hi. How's everything going?"

"Good—Harold looks like a steam engine with that colander in his face. I think he likes being the umpire."

Shirley comments to Janice, "Aren't you looking snappy this morning, with your cute terry cloth jersey, lipstick, and hair all in place? I like your gold necklace and matching earrings."

"Thanks. It's not very often that I'm invited out to a ball game." They both laugh.

Shirley realizes there's a change in Janice and it's obvious. Her expression has changed. She's lost those facial lines of tension and eyes of grief. *John's in her life and maybe in a big way.*

Shirley looks at her own loafers that need a polish, and socks that were once white and have lost the elastic. They continually slip down, like dirty snow sliding off a barn roof. She reaches and pulls them up, and looks sideways at shiny brown loafers and white, white socks pulled in place on a slender leg; even the ribbing is straight.

Shirley glances at her own baggy blue jeans with rolled-up cuffs. Janice has on a pair of finely knit tan chino slacks that fit snugly over her flat front and trim waist. She looks at her own light blue work shirt with rolled-up sleeves and tails that hang, and then at Janice's terry cloth sleeveless jersey that fits smoothly over her attractive figure. Shirley tucks her hair into place and wonders how the woman next to her always keeps her hair under control. *We're here, John, on review. Which one do you want? I really don't want to be in the contest; to do so would only be for Emily Ann's sake.*

Janice asks, "Do you want me to hold Steven? Shirley—Shirley do you want me to hold Steven?"

"What? Oh—of course."

"Gosh, you're really into this practice. You've hardly said a word."

"Sorry I haven't been good company. I was just watching. Look at Harold, he's having more fun than the kids. And Honeydew, perched up there looking through that chicken wire. What a picture."

"She reminds me of a prisoner of war sitting behind the fencing, only a little too well fed." They both laugh to the point of being silly.

The laughter puts Shirley in a light mood. "And John, he's happier than a kid with a new toy." Shirley continues to laugh.

Janice turns toward Shirley. "Just what do you mean by that remark?" Janice has a slight smirk.

Shirley stands. "I guess you know." Shirley lightheartedly laughs. "I think it's time we served some dinner."

"Great, I'll help you."

Shirley finds right away that she hasn't prepared any too much food for the kids. Janice is serving the stew. She turns to Shirley. "It looks like you and I will be breaking out the peanut butter and jelly." They laugh and Janice continues, "Gosh, can these kids ever eat."

Emily Ann's cookies and the ice cream are a big hit. Roy Stark yells, "Forget the ball game, it's worth coming here just to eat. Thanks, Emily Ann. Pine Mountain is a lot of fun." Roy's remarks are followed by everyone saying, "Thanks."

Harold has a big smile. "It's damn nice you all came."

Shirley notices Roy Stark, a kid with a bit of a swagger, handsome, and a natural leader. If he had a bath, and put on some decent clothes, he'd make any mother proud. She can see why Emily Ann talks about him so much.

Out in back of the chicken house, on the area now called the ball field, the kids gather around Roy. Emily Ann suggests, "Let's have the same teams we have at school.

Harold throws a half dollar fifteen feet up in the air.

Before it lands Roy calls, "Heads." And Teddy calls, "Tails."

Teddy's team is first at bat.

Harold slips his arms into the cloth straps, looks to see if everyone is ready and yells, "Let's play ball." He bends over the catcher, a little second-grader. Teddy Frost is up first. Roy throws a flamer; the speed of the ball scares Harold, so he steps aside. The little kid who is the catcher doesn't even try for the ball and ducks out of the way. It hits the henhouse with a bang, and the hens start cackling, acting like they've just laid a hundred eggs. Honeydew yells, "Strike!" and records it with her pencil. Teddy digs his feet in, concentrating, ready to connect with Roy's next fastball. Roy winds up, acting as if to throw it fast, but the ball barely floats over the plate. Teddy swings way too early. The next ball is medium speed. Teddy doesn't get a good swing, and pops it up, and Roy catches it.

A kid named Mickie is next up, and again Roy starts with a fastball that is high, but Mickie swings. The little second-grade catcher timidly sticks up his glove. Harold plants his feet, not wanting Honeydew to take his job. The ball hits the colander and jams it into his face. He pulls it off, rubbing his forehead and chin. "Strike two. Bastard, that hurts!" Mickie pops up on the third pitch and Roy catches it. The third batter strikes out. Harold learns quickly to step aside if a fastball is coming, because the little second-grader is no match for a high-speed ball. *That Roy is a good pitcher.*

The next side is up. Harold speaks to Teddy, the pitcher. "You got someone who can catch the ball? Golly, I'll be ready for the grave if I get hit all day." He's still rubbing his forehead and chin.

"My sister can catch. She does all the time at home."

Roy is up first. He is his team's best hitter. Teddy throws only balls, because a walk is better than a home run. Harold feels more relaxed doing his job because Teddy's sister is a good catcher. The next batter is up. She hits Teddy's first pitch. It's caught and Roy is tagged running to second. The third batter is up. Teddy throws it right over the plate, but low. Harold yells, "Ball!"

Honeydew yells, "Strike!"

Harold throws up his hands. "Before this game goes any farther, I'm gittin' somethin' straight." He steps to the granary window. "I know this is goin' to be damn hard for you today, but you keep quiet. You hear?"

"But it was a strike."

"I don't care what you think. The pitch was a ball."

Honeydew sarcastically yells, "You need glasses."

Harold motions for the game to continue.

The batter hits the next pitch, but Teddy catches it for the third out.

Roy looks at his team and speaks to Harold. "My only good player is Charlie, but I'll have him catch so you won't get hit."

"That's good." Harold is still rubbing the two welts on his chin and forehead.

The game is a standoff going into the ninth inning. No one has scored. Roy's good pitching makes up for his weak team, and the good defense behind Teddy makes up for his mediocre pitching.

In the top of the ninth Roy continues to mix up his pitches, not allowing a hit. At the bottom of the ninth, Teddy is tiring, and has lost his control. Roy can see what is happening. He tells his players not to swing at the ball unless it's a strike. Harold is getting tired, too, and keeps standing, putting his hand in the small of his back. Teddy looks at his team. "I wish someone else could pitch. My arms feel as limp as rubber."

No one offers. Teddy throws easy stuff to the next two batters; however, neither reaches first. Harold's back is paining him constantly. Roy is up next. Teddy throws an easy-to-hit ball right over the plate. Roy blasts a hard grounder that goes past the second baseman into the outfield. Roy is running as fast as he can for home. The play will be close. Harold bends further forward to watch. A back spasm hits him and he falls to the ground, writhing in pain. Honeydew yells, "Safe!"

Shirley and John run to the aid of Harold. Emily Ann is all smiles. Her team has won and the Stark kids are jumping up and down in celebration of their victory. Teddy is a good sport. "I got tired out. Good pitching can always win the game, especially if there's an umpire."

The kids all form a circle around Harold. Roy asks, "You going to be all right?"

"Yup, I'm okay; just my back." He lies flat out relaxing.

Roy leads everyone in a cheer. "Yay, Harold, yay, yay, Harold!"

He rests with a big smile. *I'm lookin' at the bluest sky I've ever seen.*

HUNTERSVILLE WEEKLY

September 20, 1948

Driblets of Honeydew
By Honeydew Mullen

Harry Durkee easily won the Republican nomination for the Vermont House of Representatives from Huntersville. He will be automatically elected in the November election, since there is no Democratic opposition. He won on the promise that he will fight for better law enforcement for southern Vermont. The Toby Perkins incident brought to the forefront the need in the minds of most voters.

Dottie Candy, as newly appointed Huntersville High cheerleader coach, has caused quite the controversy. Attendance at the games has increased among the fellows even though Huntersville has never had a winning team. Esther Erickson said, "Jules has never been interested in football until this year. The cheerleaders' skirts are way too short and those cartwheels and all those bare legs, my goodness!"

Alice Coles reports that her sale was a success. Her cattle averaged to sell for $440. The national average for registered Jerseys is about $330.

She plans to move to the village and has been hired by Attorney David Iverson's law firm.

Principal of Huntersville High, Floyd Howell, has been surrounded by controversy over the introduction of sex education in health classes. A number of parents are calling for his resignation. Louise Durkee says, "Health to me is teaching good nutrition and cleanliness. Sex education has no place in the curriculum."

CHAPTER TWENTY-SEVEN

Shirley opens out a large tarp on the edge of the front lawn. Wheeling loads of dried beans to the canvas, she is dumping them in the center. She begins beating the dried bean pods with flailing sticks. When all the pods are broken, she brushes the shreds away. She lifts each corner of the canvas, the beans gathered in the center. The day is warm and breezy for early November, a perfect time to be thrashing the beans. Steven is sitting in his stroller, cooing and banging a clothespin.

Shirley remembers that the last time she swung and beat anything this swift and hard was on Toby Perkins's limp body. The red kidney beans remind her of the welts on his back and the blood that flowed from his nose. She's never told anyone how in her moment of rage, she enjoyed what she was doing. Maybe that's the human part of it all: the secrets kept, one's closely hidden side, the drives, the demons inside that we can't or don't want to control.

Most of the people she knows have a hidden side. Attorney Iverson is upright and distinguished; yet he's a man with secrets. Then there's Harold, and his shabby treatment of women in his past. Something he never talks about; that is certainly his dark side. Alice Coles, without a doubt, has secrets. Zack is surely Attorney Iverson's son. And then there's Joe and his mysterious side; so guarded he can't say why he really left her. And why did Honeydew keep her secret romance with Harold going for so long?

She dumps a fresh bunch of red kidney beans on the canvas and continues to flail at the pile, splitting the pods at the veins while red beans pour onto the canvas, reminding her again of Toby. He is still living, drooling saliva, waiting in his jail cell for the day of revenge.

She kneels and scoops the beans with a cup, letting the gentle breeze blow the chaff as the beans fall from the cup onto her open hand, filtering through her fingers and spilling onto the pile. She then scoops the beans into small bags and clears the canvas.

She next flails at a different variety—soldier beans. They are almost all white with just a hint of darkness. Every bean has that same brown spot found in the same place, where it was connected, sucking and drawing nourishment from the soil.

John is almost pure white like the beans she's looking at. He hasn't told her much; maybe he, too, has an unknown side of times when he was docked at night in distant ports, drinking and carousing, but she doubts it. He wouldn't have mourned the loss of his wife and be as attentive to Emily Ann, if he were that sort. However, he is trying his best to hide the fact that Janice is somewhere in his life. And yet he seems to like living on Pine Mountain, being with Shirley and doing for her: the broken cooker handle fixed, the spring on the entry door replaced, and the leaky faucet repaired. She never has to ask. He just sees what needs to be fixed. The puppy play and flirting confuse her. Why does he act that way? Maybe as with that brown dot on the bean, he has a bit of darkness.

She whips the sticks, sending them singing through the air, and crashing them onto the pods. The white beans pop from their shells, showing their brown spots. Perhaps the brown spot is like a desire of John's, an ego thing, to hold claim to more than one woman.

When nearly finished, she can hear a car coming. Holding Steven, she waits to see who it is, as she stands next to her collection of beans. An older gray car comes into view. The driver stops. Shirley greets the man behind the wheel. Glancing in the back seat, she recognizes his paraphernalia, and knows, right away, why he's come to the farm.

He sticks his hand out the window. "Hi, I'm Ivan Pendergast. I'm planning on testing your herd tonight. I don't usually give notice like this, but seeing as this is your first test, I thought I'd better stop by. I suppose you know I'll be a-puttin' up at your house tonight. I'll do my work on the kitchen table in the morning, after breakfast."

Shirley remarks, "I remember you from when I lived at the Perkinses'. That was ten years ago."

He now wears glasses. Deep wrinkles have developed, but he still has that continual smile that she recalls. He ends every sentence with a slight chuckle. "By jingoes, that's right. You were the cute little girl that was always a-checkin' my work. That's where I knew you from before. I hear your name talked about a lot around to different farms. All good, you know, but I never made the connection."

"You didn't test at the Iversons?"

"They're in a different testing association. I'd like to test that herd, but for some reason they belong to a northern association. Well, what time do you start milking?"

"Around five."

"All your cows' names and registration numbers need to be in order. That'll save a lot of time. I know you wouldn't be like this, but some folk's information is in one heck of a mess. By jingoes, you wouldn't believe it."

"I tacked up new cards the other day. All the registration papers, breeding, and freshening dates are in order."

Ivan takes a small packet from his shirt pocket and reaches inside for a pinch, which he places inside his cheek. "Good, I'll see you tonight." The car chugs forward to turn around and passes by Shirley. Ivan throws up his hand in a wave, wearing his smile.

Shirley puts Steven in his stroller, packs the bags of beans in a large paper bag, rakes up the shreds, and throws them over the fence. While pushing the stroller toward the house, she is wondering where Ivan can sleep. She brings the beans in the house and takes lunches out of the refrigerator, puts them in the carrying pouch of the stroller, and heads for the logging site. *Someone will have to sleep in the front room. Maybe John?*

Pushing the stroller up the hill with Terry following, she forgets about the coming evening, and loses herself in the beauty of her surroundings. The brilliant leaf colors of red and orange have faded to a dull brown. A gray squirrel is leaping across the stone wall, rustling the dry leaves. Its mouth is full on its way to store beechnuts. *We're not the only ones thinking of winter.*

The logging operation is making the five-and-five field look like a grand staging area. Rows and rows of piled four-foot pulpwood are beginning to accumulate. It's mostly spruce, fir, and hemlock. Hardwood is being stacked on the side of the field for a firewood supply to be used in future years. Harold reported that they are still cutting oak, and continue to get good prices, which is lucky for him, because he is worried about his lack of money since the auction.

Shirley pushes the stroller along the skid road and walks deep into the woods. The ground underfoot gives as she follows the freshly disturbed path, the soil being loosened by the continual skidding of logs. Steven begins to fuss. She hands him some toast that he loves to suck on.

She reaches the crew. Harold stands on high ground waiting for a tree to fall. He remarks, "That's one hell of a big oak."

It is at least three feet across and growing taller than most of the trees in the woods. John's and Willy's legs are spread and their feet are planted, with each man bent over pulling the crosscut in perfect rhythm. The saw moves back and forth in a moderate steady pace while sawdust spills out on both sides of the cut. John stops, grabs a sledgehammer and wedge, places the wedge in the cut, and drives it three or four inches. Each strike of the hammer, steel against steel, sends a high-pitched note singing through the woods. They resume cutting and the tree ever so slightly starts to tip in the desired direction. The saw passes three or four more times, sounding similar to a porcupine's gnawing. Shirley can hear the strong fibers of the wood snap, reminding her of a boot breaking through ice-covered snow. The tree is on its descent, falling faster and faster and now it crashes, booming as it lands. Dead leaves fly and scatter. The ground shakes from the weight of the huge oak. Shirley observes that even though the cutting is being done, Harold is leaving smaller trees for a future harvest.

Willy and John walk up the slope, having seen Shirley standing beside Harold. Both smile, eager for a break. The four sit on logs, forming a circle with Steven in the center on a blanket sucking and gumming his toast. Shirley announces, "The milk tester's coming tonight, and staying over. I don't know about the sleeping arrangements."

"Hell, you mean we're finally goin' to be tested. He's at least three weeks late." Harold takes his pipe and fills it, strikes a match on a small stone, and draws a big puff of smoke. "I can fix the sleeping arrangements for one night." His mouth turns up at the corners as his weathered facial skin wrinkles slightly in a smirk.

"I don't want to hear it from you, Harold. Don't say it."

"I won't. Hell, I was laid up for a month after I only stood at your doorway."

John's shoe is gently poking the side of Shirley's leg out of view of the other men.

Shirley doesn't think he's funny and moves out of John's reach, and suggests, "I thought we could put the cot that's in my room in the front living room. Emily Ann can sleep with me tonight."

John offers, "I'll give up my room—uh, I'll sleep on the cot. It won't bother me for—uh, one night." He's slid toward her and continues poking Shirley's leg with the toe of his shoe. She doesn't change her expression. *The flirt. Is he getting some sort of pleasure from this?*

Willy is devouring Shirley's egg sandwiches and drinking large quantities of iced tea. "Gee, that's nice of ya, John. I'd miss my room. I'd miss my sun when I git up in the mornin'."

Shirley adds, "Soon we'll have to keep the cows in nights and probably most days. Don't you think, Harold?"

"Yup, I guess, especially when we begin to get nasty weather. We'd better break work early, to be ready for the tester. I'm also goin' to town to get my new Jeep. John, you can come with me to drive the truck back. Today is also Election Day. Everything looks like Dewey will be a sure winner; but, just the same, I've got to go to town and vote. There's also a bunch of others to vote for. I just check the box at the top, Republican." He pauses. "I'm happy Harry Durkee will be our next representative. He's a darn good man. At least it was 'cause of him I have that trophy."

Shirley adds, "Yeah, Harry's a good man. The trophy is real important. I would vote for him, too." She laughs.

Harold looks at her grin. "You have a real wise mouth, sometimes."

"Oh, by the way, I've got the names and registration numbers all posted over the cows and all their papers are in order. Tonight, the tester will only take butterfat samples, and weigh each cow's milk. Tomorrow morning he'll want to read some ear tattoos, but he probably won't look at every cow if he sees they're in their own stalls. The new cows are taking their stalls all right now, aren't they, Willy?"

"Ya, I jest let a few in at a time. That's the way I do it. I give 'em a little bit of that nice hay 'n' they come a-runnin'. Terry helps, too. He comes with me every time I git the cows; he goes right after Shasam. I like Terry. He helps me a lot."

Harold smiles. "'Course the nineteen-year-old girl-wonder here knows all there is to know about testin'. Hell, here I'm three times her age and don't know nothin' about it. Will you allow us to at least come down from the woods five minutes early so we can shake the guy's hand?" Words flow from Harold like the whine of the circular saw to sassily zing Shirley's self-assured manner.

Shirley laughs. "How do you know it's a guy? It might be a Rockette dressed in bib-overalls."

"Okay, a half-hour earlier, if that's the case." John and Shirley laugh.

"The man's name is Ivan Pendergast. I knew him when I lived at the Perkinses'. He's an easy fellow to get along with. I'll do the paperwork with him in the morning. And Willy, we'll have to change the grain the cows get after Ivan leaves."

"Ya, this time ya use numbers. Emily Ann learned me numbers. I can write, too. Every night she learns me new words. I leave my writin' on the table 'n' Emily Ann checks it in the mornin'."

Shirley looks at Willy. "I'm real proud of you for wanting to learn to write and for learning your numbers too." She pauses. "Harold, you go to town and take as long as you like. I'll be here for any questions Ivan might have."

Harold shakes his head. "No, I'm goin' to be here for milkin'. Hell, if you were any more efficient you could be our next president. I know you'd do one hell of a lot better than Truman, but I guess that's not sayin' much." Harold lays down his pipe and is enjoying a piece of Shirley's apple pie. "On second thought, you'd better stay here. One thing I've never doubted about you, and that is you're one hell of a good cook."

John has moved closer to Shirley and is again poking the side of her pant leg. Shirley doesn't know what to make of him. His actions embarrass her.

Harold remarks, "Well, golly, woman, you don't have to get red in the face just because I tell you you're a good cook."

She stands and picks up Steven. "I'm leaving. I love the attention I'm getting—too much of it."

Harold belts out, "Well damn, I suppose I ain't been a-complimentin' you enough."

"You don't have to, I know you think I'm about the best and the worst thing that ever happened to you." She's now pushing the stroller away, traveling the bare earthen skidding path. Harold picks up his pipe, turns, and raises his voice so Shirley can hear. "I hate to admit it, but most of the time I think it's the best."

She turns and waves.

Harold lights another match, draws in a quantity of smoke, and exhales, blowing smoke. "Now there goes about the most beautiful woman God ever created. John, I'd think you'd give her more attention before another Jimmy Iverson comes along."

"You think—uh, I should?"

"Yes, damn it, yes."

John and Willy walk down the slope to continue their afternoon's work.

Shirley sits down on a flat stone at the top of the five-and-five field to feed Steven. She remembers sitting on the same stone that spring and enjoying the birth of a new season. Now all she sees are logs piled in orderly fashion covering the whole upper end of the field. She knows the site will be cleaned up, but logging has temporarily ruined a beautiful landscape. In her moment of relaxation she wonders about John and the way he teases her. Would he like their relationship to be more? If he does, she doesn't think she's ready, mostly because of Joe, and then there's Janice. John would never say, but it's obvious something is going on between the two.

She pushes the stroller downhill with ease as the sticky earth-caked wheels pick up leaves and become larger until the wheel-scrapers clear the accumulation. Steven falls asleep. An empty feeling fills her. *Joe has never come to see me.*

Ivan Pendergast arrives at five. He gets out of his car, puts on a pair of bib-overalls, reaches in his pocket for a pinch of snuff, and places it in his cheek. Then he picks up his pail, milk scales, and dipper in one hand and carries a box of sample bottles in the other. He heads toward the barn.

Harold acts like a ten-year-old kid, all questions, in regards to the testing process. He starts pumping Ivan for information about other herds, and how well they are milking.

Ivan is evasive. "Well, these first few cows here are milking up a storm."

"Better than any other cows you test?"

Ivan chuckles. "It's hard to know, yet. Each month a letter is sent telling how the different herds are milking. You'll find out next month."

Harold discovers quickly that Ivan doesn't talk very much about other farmers, just weighs each cow's milk on his calibrated scales, and records the weight beside each name on a barn sheet. He uses his scoop to stir and sample the milk and pours it into a small glass sample bottle. He fills it halfway to leave room for a like sample to be taken in the morning.

Harold doesn't lose interest and mentally records the milk weight of each cow. Ivan is weighing the last cow's milk. "By jingoes, these cows have been producing like Holsteins. Ain't sure as I've ever seen Jerseys milk like this before."

Harold bursts with pride. He tells himself he doesn't care how much the service costs, it's worth every cent, just to know how well his cows are milking.

Meanwhile, Emily Ann is racing up and down the drive, giving Steven a bouncy ride, causing him to laugh.

John and Shirley are moving the cot into the front room. John is carrying the front and Shirley the back end. Every few steps he stops and presses backward. Shirley pushes forward, and then he lets the pressure off and she rushes forward, causing her to yell, "John, stop that, I'm going to drop my end!"

She gets to giggling over his playful behavior. They place the cot in the front sitting room. Shirley goes to get sheets and bedding and feels the bow of her apron pull. She turns around quickly. John laughs as her apron falls loosely, hanging only from her neck. She swings to slap his hand and he catches it and pulls her close to him and hugs her. She is helpless in his grip. She gasps in surprise. She laughs, "You're too much. I've got to get this bed made before supper."

"I'll make my own bed—with you in it." He lightens his grip on her.

Shirley gently pushes away, and feels her color building.

He looks her in the eyes and whispers, "I love you, Shirley—I want to marry you."

She's filled with emotion. "What are you asking? You can't be serious."

He reaches for her arm, and repeats, "Yes I am. Will you marry me?"

She starts to cry, staggering to sit in a chair. "Why are you asking without some romance? This all seems too contrived, too automatic, too convenient. What is your intent? To plant one foot in a house of bliss, climbing the stairs to the marriage bed, while having your second foot in another life, living in adulterous bliss?" *On the other hand, since there's no Joe, this might be my only chance.*

John kneels by the chair and holds her hand. "No, I—uh, love only you."

She wipes her tears and looks at him saying, "Let's give this some time. Let me think about it." She openly cries, wishing the circumstance could be different—such as loving the guy. Suddenly she hears voices. She tries to settle herself, wiping her tears again, waiting to calm her emotions. John leaves to bring back the bedding. He tells Emily Ann to start putting supper on the table. Shirley doesn't know why, but she continues to cry. She knows she is capable of being John's wife. He would understand her weaknesses, her incompleteness. He would be gentle and wouldn't abuse her. Whatever the case, this is embarrassing, to be emotionally out of control. John comes back in the room but he's at a loss what to do for her. All he can say is, "I guess I'm guilty of—uh, poor timing." He kneels with his arm around her, trying to comfort her, but that brings on even more tears. He finally leaves and goes to help Emily Ann serve the meal. Emily Ann looks concerned. "Is Shirley sick?"

"No—no, she'll be all right—uh, in a while."

Harold inquisitively looks at John, realizing that he doesn't act himself. He wonders what has happened between the two. They sit down to eat without Shirley. A wave of insecurity passes from person to person, except for Ivan Pendergast, who's enjoying his meal. No one else says a word. They all stare at John. He's obviously lost his appetite, since he's not eating. Harold, Willy, and Emily Ann are looking to him for answers. He turns whiter and whiter. He leaves the table and goes to the front room to rest on the cot.

Tears start to stream down Willy's face. Steven is banging a clothespin on the tray of his high chair. Emily Ann runs into the front room to see what's wrong.

Being left alone, Steven begins to cry at the loss of Emily Ann as well as having to look at the stranger, Ivan Pendergast. The milk tester finally breaks the silence. "This is a mighty good-tastin' meal."

Harold is at a loss what to think or say. Emily Ann comes running out to calm Steven. She's all smiles. Harold studies her and normally would have asked what was going on, but checks himself because of their guest. Emily Ann looks at Willy, who is still silently whimpering. "It's all right, Willy, my dad just asked Shirley to marry him."

Harold remarks, "Well, damn, I told your father today that he ought to pay more attention to her, but I didn't think he'd propose to her on his first try."

John lies face up and flat out on the cot and Shirley checks in the mirror to see how badly her face looks. He gets up off the cot. They walk in the kitchen together. Emily Ann wildly claps. Willy regains his smile and joins her. Harold would join them, but he takes one look at Ivan and decides against it. John sits down and Shirley stands in back of John. She rests her hands on his shoulders. "John has asked me to marry him, but I want to wait for a bit."

Harold turns to Ivan. "I want you to know this ain't a normal supper on Pine Mountain." Then he remarks to Shirley and John, "Well, I hope you can work things out. You'd make one damn good pair. Shirley, you'd have a good man that will never fail you; and John, you'd have a good woman. She'll say everything for you and at times will say more than you want to hear."

Shirley says to Ivan, "I'm sorry for the disruption. John, momentarily, swept me off my feet."

"That's okay, Shirley. You still cooked a good-tastin' meal, though. I must say I've run across a lot of different happenings in farm homes, but I never came across one quite like this."

Harold looks at John and then Shirley. "Well, when's the weddin'?"

"I think this whole idea needs to wait." Shirley tries her best not to sound too negative. It's hard for her to take John's proposal seriously.

Wanting to lighten her heavy heart, she flips out a plan to bother and challenge Harold, taking pleasure in seeing his reaction. "It definitely will be a church wedding. I'd have you give me away."

He immediately acts worried. "Well—well, I dunno how to do that. Damn, another new thing to learn: Where to sit, where to stand, what to say. Ah—give you away? Hell, I never had you."

"It's a custom at weddings for the father of the bride to give his daughter to the bridegroom. You know, you march down the aisle with me, and announce to the whole church and the minister that you're setting me free."

Harold clears his throat. "All the times I've taken the Lord's name in vain, I'll be struck dead as soon as I enter the church door. I ain't never been to church before." He looks at Shirley and sees the smirk on her face. "You little whip, you like to bother me and get me a-churnin' inside."

"I mean it, though, you deserve to give me away, if anyone does. That's just the problem, there's no record of who my father is or was. You're as good to me as any father could be."

Harold reaches for his pipe, being nervous, hearing Shirley's plans and her openness in front of company. He rubs his pipe in his hands and turns to Ivan.

"Yup, Ivan, Shirley kinda woke me out of a deep sleep to get me to shape up this place."

Now she feels embarrassed, knowing he isn't supposed to talk like this. On the other hand it isn't like her to lose total control, nor like John to speak so freely of his desire for her. Harold is right. This isn't a normal supper on Pine Mountain.

Harold changes the subject. "Golly, I like the way that new Jeep drove, zipping up the mountain like nothin'." He pauses. "I voted. Everybody I met was for Dewey. He's goin' to make a great president. Ivan, if you'd like, we'll watch television tonight and see how badly Truman gets beat."

"By jingoes, you folks are the only people I know of who have a television."

Emily Ann is getting Steven ready for bed and John and Shirley have left for a walk. Shirley feels more at ease being alone with John. He holds her hand and she responds with a squeeze. She stops and looks at him standing outside the entry. He is facing the entry door. The dim light allows her to see his face. Shirley takes the opportunity to further question his proposal. "What brought about this change of heart? The last I knew you thought I was too young, young enough to be your daughter. And then there's Janice. What's between you two? She's changed and I think you've been part of the reason."

Shirley watches his expression. It is painful to see him try to get the words to flow. He scuffs his feet and continually rubs the back of his head. "But—but I—um, love you." He moves dirt in a circular motion with the toe of his shoe. No more words come.

"That's not enough, John. I want answers to my questions. When you first came to the farm you were grieving. I can understand that. In recent weeks you haven't even mentioned Elizabeth's name. That's okay. But I just wonder if we'd be acting too soon, simply because I'm here, and Emily Ann wants us to be a family."

He draws her closely and holds her for a long time. She feels warm, secure, and comfortable in his arms. She kisses him on the lips, but she feels troubled that she can't say those three expected words.

A cool breeze is blowing from the west. She can hear the scattering of leaves moving up the drive toward them. She realizes John is not about to calm her concerns in regards to what she thinks of as a quick marriage. They stand in silence while she is waiting for him to explain himself. John and she hug and she says, "Good night."

Later, Shirley lies in bed thinking. What it would be like sleeping with John instead of Emily Ann? The idea doesn't thrill her, but she would be a part of a typical family. *Shirley Gray is all right but Shirley Iverson sounds better.*

It's early morning. Harold, Ivan, and Willy are leaving the house. Terry has come from the barn and is waiting at the entry door. Willy pats him and they walk together toward the barn; the ground is completely white with frost. Lights from the barn cast shadows across the waiting herd. A light over the entrance ramp is turned on. The cows are ready to be milked and wanting to be fed. Beyond the ring of grouped cattle, Shasam is mounting a cow that's in standing heat. Willy, with Terry's help, starts letting the cows in the barn. The dog controls the number that enters by sitting at the top of the entrance ramp. When Willy calls "More cows", Terry lets a few more in the barn. When Willy calls "Stop", the dog returns to the top of the ramp. Harold and Ivan wait in the milk house for the cows to be tied up.

Harold has just gotten word from a radio in the milk house that Harry Truman has won the 1948 presidential election. "Ivan, can you believe there are that many stupid people who voted for Truman? I don't know as we can stand to have him be our president for another four years. I just don't understand it!"

All the cows stand in their places eating hay. The cow in heat goes to her stall. Willy swings the wooden stanchion into place and pins it.

Shasam follows and mounts the cow. After a moment, he dismounts. Willy is standing in front of the line of cows, protected from the bull. He speaks to Terry. "Sic 'em."

The dog barks at Shasam, lightly nipping a front foot. The bull turns and charges at Terry, heading away from the entrance, chasing the dog to the end of the barn. To avoid the bull, Terry darts between two cows. Shasam turns around and charges toward Harold, who is looking at the floor of the walkway, unaware of any danger while mumbling about the election. Terry is chasing behind the bull. Bellowing a guttural roar, Shasam puts his head down. He is ten feet from Harold, coming at full speed. Willy yells, "Watch out!"

It's too late. Shasam hits Harold in the midsection and lifts him off his feet. He grabs the bull's hips, as his chin is now bouncing on the bony spine of Shasam. Harold's legs stick straight out and his thighs are cradled by the bull's horns. His outstretched arms and hands continue holding the bull's hips. Terry is still aggressively chasing the bull as he turns and rumbles down the entrance ramp. Willy charges for the house, screaming and crying for help. Terry sees Willy running, so chases after him. Ivan hurries out through the milk house to try and help.

Shasam stops and lowers his head to the ground, and Harold slides forward, while the bull's horns continue to cradle Harold's midsection. Now standing, but bent over the bull's head, Harold is dazed and makes no effort to escape.

Shasam snorts at the ground, blowing holes in the frosty loose soil. In an instant, he flings his head and muscled neck skyward; a neck with the strength of an oak log. Harold blows a thunderous groan and flies over the barnyard fence, rotating with extended arms and legs. He lands facedown and motionless with a thud.

Willy is back from the house, crying, "Are ya hurt, are ya hurt?"

Ivan rolls Harold over. He groans, holding his chest. His chin and face are bruised. "By jingoes, Harold, I thought you were a goner."

Shirley has followed Willy outside. She says to him, "Don't get upset."

Willy is crying. "Ya sure he's goin' ta be all right? I was scared."

Shirley assures, "We'll just have to see."

With a pale face and irregular breathing, Harold sweats and grips at his chest.

Shirley looks for the truck. "We'd better take him to the hospital."

He has the presence of mind to whisper, "You ain't takin' me to no hospital."

They try to help him stand, but he's in too much pain. John comes from the house, carrying a mattress. Ivan, Willy, Shirley, and John carry him to his bedroom. Shirley searches in the bathroom to see if Harold has any pain pills left from his earlier accident. She finds them and has him take two.

Shirley calls Dr. Plumbly. "He doesn't want to go.…I know it's a long way up here.…Oh thanks, Dr. Plumbly."

Harold starts to rest easier, but he's still pale and his breathing is irregular.

In a half hour the doctor arrives and goes straight to Harold's room. Shirley is standing by for a report. "He should be brought to the hospital. His heart rate is not normal and his blood pressure is low. I can't feel that his ribs are broken, but I'm just guessing at this point."

Shirley speaks gravely, "He asked us not to take him to the hospital. I'm sure it would be best for him if he went, but I'm not about to go against his wishes."

"I'd take him to the hospital regardless, but it's your call."

"I need to respect his wishes."

"I'll leave some pain pills so he can rest easier, but that's about all I can do. Try and convince him to come to the hospital."

"Okay. Thanks for coming."

After Dr. Plumbly leaves, Shirley calls Stubby Demar. "We have a bull to sell. Please come right away!"

The table is cleared after breakfast and Ivan brings in a Babcock Centrifuge and places it on the kitchen table with a box of testing supplies and glassware. He uses a glass pipette to draw milk from each sample bottle and transfers it to a test bottle. Using sulfuric acid, a hot water bath, and centrifuge, Ivan is able to separate the butterfat from the milk.

"By jingoes, Harold has a mighty good herd here. These totals are high for Jerseys, and they test good, too." Ivan holds each test bottle in the light and uses his dividers to measure the width of the yellow butterfat column. "How's Harold doing? He'll be laid up some from that business I saw this morning—wonder it didn't kill him."

Shirley says, "He's resting quietly. We'll just have to see. I know one thing: that bull is leaving this farm!"

Emily Ann is doing the dishes while she waits for her father to take her to school. "I'm glad my dad wasn't hurt. You told Harold to get rid of the bull, but of course he wouldn't. I feel badly, but I think he got what he deserves."

"Just remember, people make mistakes. We don't want anyone getting hurt—do we, Emily Ann?"

"No, I guess not." She changes the subject. "Willy is doing super on his writing. He's so neat. I put his work on the table in the front room, if you'd like to see it."

"I'll look at it later. I think it's great that you're working with him."

Ivan packs up his testing equipment. "I'll see you next month. Hope Harold gets feeling better."

Shirley thanks Ivan and then goes to check on Harold. He is waking up. "I don't feel as bad as I did, but golly, am I ever weak. That bull knocked the stuffin' right outta me. I gotta get feelin' better. Deer huntin' is comin' on soon."

Shirley looks at him and speaks firmly, "I think you'll miss it this year. You're in no shape to go deer hunting. By the way, that bull is leaving this morning. That's one decision we agree on, isn't it?"

"Oh, I know you're right. He should've left a while ago. 'Course I used to keep a bull until Christmas, but they never acted like this one."

"As a matter of fact, Stubby just drove in the yard."

"Send him in the house after you load the bull. That sly fox will buy him for a song if you don't."

Shirley walks toward the barn. The sun has melted the early morning freeze, but the dead weeds and grass are limp from the hard frost.

Willy is afraid of Shasam at this point and doesn't want to go in the pasture. He calls the cows. Since they haven't been out very long, they don't budge from their resting positions, and are chewing their cud, having just been fed hay and grain. Shasam comes running and bellowing in low tones. He stops. Pawing the ground, he throws grass and sod in the air. Stubby takes a cigar out of his pocket and lights it. The men and Shirley are standing outside the fence. Stubby comments, "That's one hell of a nice lookin' bull. You really want him to go for slaughter?"

Shirley says, "He'll be a lot better looking to me once he's loaded on your truck. He came close to doing Harold in this morning. I want him away from here."

Willy points toward the barn. "Terry, sic 'em, go ta the barn." Terry barks at the back end of the bull. The bull whips around, snorting and pawing more grass and soil. Terry aggressively comes at the bull and lightly nips Shasam's nose. He throws his head and neck in the air. Terry nips at his front legs and continues to bark. The bull turns and runs toward the barn. The dog charges at his hind legs. Shasam is now running at full speed and heads up the ramp with Terry barking right behind. When Shasam runs to the end of the barn, Willy shuts the door and calls the dog.

Stubby backs his cattle truck up to the entrance ramp and lets down the tailgate. John finds four two-by-sixes and nails two on each side of the ramp. He drives a fence post on either side of the tailgate and nails the two-by-sixes to the posts, making a temporary chute that hopefully will direct Shasam onto Stubby's truck. Stubby studies the makeshift chute and listens to the bull. He concludes, "There's no way these planks are going to hold that bull."

Shirley puts her hair into place, trying to think of a safe plan.

Stubby bites the end of his cigar and spits it on the ground. "By the sounds of that bull, he's ready to charge anybody or anything."

John has figured out the solution to the problem. "We've got—uh, room here; let's back those two—uh, hay wagons up to—uh, the outside of these planks. I think they should hold the—uh, chute in place." After John backs the hay wagons where he wants them, he checks the tailgate to be sure they can close and latch it after the bull runs onto the truck. "Shasam is going to—uh, come down that ramp and—uh, want to turn to get back out to pasture. I've never handled cattle but—uh, that would seem to be a normal thing he would try and do."

Shirley agrees. "Terry better be driving him so he won't have a chance to turn, then with some luck, he'll run straight onto the truck." Willy opens the door of the barn at the top of the ramp and runs in front of the stanchion line for protection. Terry is panting, acting nervous in the presence of Shasam. The bull is accustomed to Willy and Terry and, therefore, is relatively calm. John yells, "Start him coming!"

Willy yells, "Sic 'em, Terry," and runs out through the milk house to stand on the hay wagon. Terry has Shasam on a full run toward the door. The bull rumbles down the ramp. Dust and dirt fly and the barn shakes. He wants to turn right, but his momentum is so forceful that he continues straight ahead with Terry barking and nipping his hind legs. He has no choice but to run into the truck.

John, Willy, and Stubby race to lift and shut the tailgate and drop the bar that holds it in place. The bull is at the height of anger now as he turns around, rocking the truck and charging the tailgate. The entire vehicle's mud, manure, and road dust fall to the ground from the force of Shasam's impact, but thankfully the truck body is strong enough to hold the beast.

Stubby lights another cigar. "I think you should pay *me* to take this one away. I ain't seen a bull that worked up in years."

Shirley mentions, “Harold wants to see you.”

The cattle dealer laughs. “He might be laid up, but he ain’t lettin’ me leave without payin’ for his bull.”

Shirley turns to Willy and John. “Thanks for your help. Terry saved the day. If Emily Ann had been here, she sure would have been proud of her dog.”

A log truck is slowly moving down the hill by the house. The driver stops and speaks to John and Shirley. “Soon as we get freezin’ weather, I ain’t haulin’ any more logs out of here. Even with chains on, I can’t hold a truck on this mountain; if I ever lost a load, I’d be a goner. I’ll get some pulp trucks in here and we’ll clean up what you have in the field. I’ll only haul on warm days, if we get a few before deer huntin’.”

John understands the driver’s concern and agrees to have all the remaining logs ready to load at the landing.

CHAPTER TWENTY-EIGHT

It's Wednesday, and Shirley has done her shopping and has dealt with the eggs. She is walking up the steps of Attorney Iverson's office, carrying Steven, and happy that this will be her last visit. His secretary offers her a chair. "It will be just a minute and the attorney can see you."

She sits and notices carpenters remodeling, making ready for the law office expansion. She talks to Steven. "My goodness you're getting to be a heavy boy." Steven gurgles his laugh and smiles.

Attorney Iverson walks from his office. "Come in, Shirley." He goes to his desk and hands her the usual envelope.

She sits with Steven on her lap. "I've come to tell you that I no longer need support for Steven. I've been grateful for your generosity over these past few months." Since Iverson is standing, she reaches to pass him back the envelope.

He takes it and starts his pacing. He holds the envelope by a corner with his thumb and forefinger and taps the edge on his open hand. The Empire Clock hasn't returned. She looks at the picture of Joseph Jacob

Iverson. The attorney seems to be in deep concentration. "Why the change?"

"For several reasons, but mainly, I just don't need it."

"I deserve to know the reasons."

"You act as if you're cross-examining me on the witness stand. Why does it matter? I don't need the money. John is supporting Emily Ann and the farm is doing well."

"You said there were other reasons."

"Our arrangement was and is a very private matter. I understand Alice Coles is going to be your secretary. Since that's the case, confidentiality would be difficult."

"Yes, that's true, but could it be that you're not sure that Jimmy is the father of Steven?"

She feels her anger, but tries to control herself. "Dr. Plumbly has reviewed my records and assures me that Jimmy is the father of Steven."

"Where does Zack Coles fit in to the picture?"

She raises her voice. "Why does it really matter? You're the father of both the boys! Regardless of whether it's Jimmy or Zack, Steven is an Iverson!"

Iverson turns white and stops in his tracks. "What right do you have to make such a statement?"

"Look at the picture of your own grandfather. Zack is the spitting image of him. I'm surprised you still have it there, since Alice must have visited your office."

"This conversation has gotten out of control."

"I agree! Both Jimmy and Zack raped me, but by the time of our class picnic, I was already pregnant. Dr. Plumbly confirmed that fact from the dates on my records. Now are you satisfied? I've said way too much!" She stands and carries Steven out of his office, choking back tears while slamming his door.

After sitting in the truck to calm herself, she drives to Honeydew's house. Honeydew comes rushing out. Her arms are raised and are swaying back and forth as she waddles toward the truck. "I want to see Steven. How is my little boy?" She takes him from Shirley, who is standing next to the truck. "Have you got a smile for Honeydew?"

The baby stretches his legs then bends his knees and kicks in delight, having heard her voice.

"Hi, Shirley. You look terrible. What's wrong?"

Shirley tries to lighten her mood and smiles. "Oh, I'm fine. How would you like to come with me and visit Harold after I go to Butson's?"

"I'd love to. Is Harold any better?"

"Not really. He needs to be put in the hospital, but he won't go. He spends most of his day in bed, but I know he'd like to see you."

"I'll be right with you." Honeydew goes back to her house to prepare for her visit.

Meanwhile, Harold is sitting in his Morris chair, looking out the west window. *Golly, I wish I felt better. I've got to go huntin'. If I can't do that I might's well be six foot under.*

The phone rings. Harold staggers to pick up the receiver. "Hello—this Gabby?…Son of a bitch, what a low-down snake. How'd he escape prison?…Well, they'll find him. I ain't tellin' Shirley. That'd send her off the deep end. Hell, he'll never find his way to Pine Mountain anyway.…Thanks for callin', Gabby. Let us know when you catch him." He hangs up. *What a problem!*

Honeydew is holding Steven as the two women travel toward Pine Mountain. The day is typical for late fall: windy, gray, with a misty rain. The trees and bushes have come full circle since April. They've lost all their leaves from the wind and rain and the leaves' brilliant colors have turned to dull gray. The pastures and meadows are withered to brown. As they travel, heifers and cows are seen huddled and humped from the damp windy day. "Honeydew, let's stop and look at Mary Maple."

"This tree must mean a lot to you."

"It does. It somehow comforts me—like nature's milk. I usually feel a spirit when I sit in its presence." Honeydew doesn't get out of the truck with Steven, but rolls down her window. Shirley sits at the edge of the road just a few feet from the truck. She says in a reverent tone, "Mary Maple looks especially beautiful today, even having lost all her leaves. The ferns that surround her seem dead—brown and bent. They spent all summer filling their crowns and roots with water and food, enough to survive the long winter ahead. The world around her may be crazy, but she remains peaceful and quiet and at rest with the season. Winter storms will whip at her and howl, but she will stand solid and strong."

Honeydew comments, "It's a pretty setting, but nature and me never connected."

Shirley looks skyward at the tree's graceful limbs. "See the sun breaking through the clouds? It's causing the wetness on the branches to shine. They seem to come alive. See, Honeydew, the heat from the sun is changing the mist to a light fog, filling the open space between the branches. I can slightly see a friendly smile forming between the branches. I call it the spirit of Mary Maple. It's wonderful sitting here, relaxing, knowing there's someone greater than me that I can come to for comfort."

"That's wonderful." Honeydew's voice has an unconvincing tone. She strains to see what Shirley has just described. After a minute she gives up and pulls out a small mirror from her bag to check her makeup and hair. Steven is still sleeping in her lap. Shirley hops back in the truck, and they travel up the mountain.

"Harold will be surprised to see you and happy you made the effort."

"Well, maybe. He has changed, but I haven't seen him pleased over much in the last thirty years I've known him. When he won that trophy this summer was the happiest I've ever seen him. Oh, and spending all his money on those cows. He was in high form that day. But I do love the man and after all these years, I can't figure out why."

They arrive at the farm. Shirley holds her son while he rests his head on her shoulder. She slightly arches her back from his weight while walking to the house with Honeydew. The entry door slams behind them as they go to check on Harold.

When he sees them he mumbles, "Well look who's come to see me! My lover!"

"Oh, Harold." She stands by his bed and bends to kiss him. "You look terrible—*lover* is only in your dreams. You're barely able to hug a pillow, to say nothing about me."

"That's right. I'm weak as a bastard. I can hardly make it to the bathroom and back. That ache begins in my chest and runs down my arms every time I stand. Odd as hell, don't you think, after all this time? But I'm goin' huntin' just the same."

Both women reply in unison, "No! Don't do that!" Shirley leaves to change Steven.

"If I die, I'd hell of a lot sooner be lookin' down the sights of a rifle than doing anythin' else. You know that was the only time my old man made me feel I was okay."

Honeydew sniffs, "Don't talk that way. I'd miss you terribly."

"Oh, I ain't goin' to die. I'm too tough, but I was no match for that bastardly bull."

"I wish you'd forget about deer hunting."

"Well, I ain't. I'll have John get my new Jeep ready. I'll shoot my deer right from the seat."

Shirley reenters the room and passes Steven to Honeydew. "There's some applesauce in the refrigerator. He would like some of that."

"Oh, I'd love to feed my little dear!"

Having heard Harold's comment, Shirley remarks, "You don't give the deer much credit. If they see your bright red Jeep drive into the five-and-five field they'll beat it into the woods, and all you'll see is the flash of their white tails."

"You know, Shirley, you amaze me, bein' an authority on any and all subjects. You may be right, though, I probably will have to park at the entrance and walk to that clump where the ledge is and the hardhack grows, on the lower end of the field where we didn't mess it up from our loggin'. I'll lay by the ledge in the tall dead grass and wait—wait for the pain to leave and the deer to come feedin', outta the edge of the woods."

"Well, I'll worry about you. I want you around for a good long time. I don't want my life to be too simple." Shirley pokes Harold and they both laugh.

"Hell no, I've got to hear that friends speech a few more times."

Shirley leaves Harold's side, goes to her room, and looks out her south bedroom window. Jeanie and Lassie are waiting by the gate for Willy to take them in for the night. The barren trees, the dead grasses, and the weeds whip and wave, being blown by an occasional breeze. She turns toward the mirror, removes her silver barrette, combs her hair, resets it, and starts preparing for supper. Two log trucks pass the house, and she knows John and Willy will follow, since it is nearly chore time and time for John to get Emily Ann from school. She starts a roast cooking and goes to Harold's room again. He's sleeping. She says to Honeydew, "I think his color looks better."

"I hope so. Wouldn't you know that all he can think about is hunting."

"I know."

That evening Harold comes to the table and eats a small meal. "Yup, I can't wait for deer huntin'. I can finally get outta the house and have some fun."

Shirley snickers. "Maybe you'd better send John up ahead to put a salt block out to make sure the deer will be waiting for you."

"John, you know, you asked one smart woman to marry you. She gets smarter every day, and even knows all there is to know about deer huntin'."

Honeydew adds, "I don't think the deer will have to worry much with the shape you're in."

Emily Ann says to Harold in disgust, "Why do people have to shoot deer?"

"'Cause, here in Vermont, deer huntin' is like Christmas. It's a holiday for most fellas. It comes around every year."

Shirley laughs. "I'll speak to Reverend Comstock this Sunday and see if deer hunting is included in the holy year. I'm sure he'll know."

"I'll tell you, John, if you two decide to get married, you'll be gettin' a real winner. Oh, by the way, next time you're out in the yard, would you park my new Jeep on this side of the shed, headin' it toward the road? That way I can see it better, admire it a little, and have it ready to go up the hill to the five-and-five field."

"Sure—uh, I'll do that."

A half hour later, Harold and Honeydew are sitting at the table, Willy is doing the dishes, Emily Ann is putting Steven to bed, and John and Shirley have gone to visit Don and June Tuwiliker, their new neighbors.

Honeydew reaches across the table and holds Harold's hand. "My goodness, your hand is cold."

"Yup, to tell you the truth somethin's busted in me. Prob'ly it's my heart. Maybe in time I'll get feelin' better."

"You be careful deer hunting. You won't be out long, will you?"

"No. I just want to get out and see the five-and-five field. I'll enjoy the day and lay and think about my last days. They've been better than I would ever have thought."

She starts crying and sniffs while talking. "You act as if this is the end for you."

"It ain't no end, but let's face it; I can't do a damn thing. I hardly have the strength to grip your hand." He looks at her. "I'll tell you something I'm a little worked up about." He lowers his voice. "Now don't say a thing to anyone here, especially Shirley. Toby Perkins has escaped prison. Gabby said he'd let me know when they catch him, but I ain't heard from him yet. I thought he'd have called by now."

"Oh, goodness! That is a worry. He'd never find this place, would he?"

"That's just what I'm thinkin.'"

"Well, let's hope he doesn't."

While driving down the mountain to visit their new neighbors, John pulls Shirley toward him. He stops the car where the road levels. The car lights shine on the dead sausage-like brown heads of the cattail, standing erect at the side of the road as if in vigil, waiting until the heavy snow breaks them over. He holds her and kisses her. "I love you."

"John, you're a good man. I'm lucky to be wanted by you." She then fills in the blank spaces, as she imagines they are, trying to get him to talk, to deny what she is saying. "Janice seems right for you. I think she loves you. And for you, she's as pleasing as a mouthful of apple pie. I know Janice has changed. I'll bet you'd rather be holding her, while you're trying to convince yourself to love me."

"No—uh, I love you."

"Will you answer my questions, and calm my concerns?"

"I like Pine Mountain—uh, I can be a faithful husband—uh, and live as a family with Emily Ann, you, and Steven."

"I know that, without a doubt. You would do it out of duty. But there will always be Janice, standing in the recesses of your mind, waiting, and waiting. I don't know what you think, but in matters of love, I think you follow your heart, not your head."

He releases his hold on her, and continues driving. "Maybe you're—uh, right."

On their way home, John is quiet and Shirley chooses not to talk, since she is in turmoil over their relationship.

When they return from their short visit, Honeydew is seated by Harold's bed. She's holding his hand and he's sleeping. She says in a low voice, "He has absolutely no strength. He could hardly make it from the table to his bed. I'm terribly worried about him." She starts to sniffle. "He wants me to come again tomorrow afternoon when he comes back from hunting. Are you going to be able to get me?"

"Sure. It's good for him to have your company. I'll take you home now."

"Well, you know, I just love coming here."

Shirley wakes in the night, hearing the spruce flooring creak. Her luminous alarm clock shows it's ten o'clock. Harold cries out. While going to his room, she hears the new spring on the entry door stretching, sending its distinctive sound throughout the house, like an off-key violin string being tuned. She realizes it's John, leaving to see Janice. She asks, "Harold, are you okay?"

"Yup, I must've been dreamin'. Somethin' woke me." *I hope it wasn't Toby snoopin' around.*

"John just left to see Janice."

"Why in hell is he seein' her at this hour?"

"Get your rest. We'll talk about it in the morning."

Shirley decides to rise early to work with Willy. There is no hurry, so she fills the furnace and kitchen stove with wood, and starts heating some water for a cup of coffee on the new electric stove. She likes the quietness of the morning, a good time to think. She feels irked, knowing John left in the night. She wonders if their talk has caused him to rethink his marriage proposal. She doesn't have a clue and might never, knowing him. He can talk freely of Elizabeth and fishing, but in matters close to home, he acts as closed as the steel lid on the kitchen stove. She glances at the paper on the table that Willy worked on the night before, but doesn't look at it closely.

She walks to the barn, noticing and feeling the chill of a frosty mid-November morning. While shining her flashlight on the dead grass bent over from the burden of the freeze, she notices footsteps leading to and from the henhouse.

The stable lights cast their oblong window shapes onto the gravel drive. The fan hums. The warm barn air beats back the chill of fall and allows the grass to thrive beneath the shroud of the fan. Her thumb presses the latch, and she pulls open the door and enters the fresh warm barn.

"Good morning, Willy. How do you like the new cows?"

"I like 'em a lot, but I ain't sure how ta grain 'em."

"Let's weigh their milk and see if the numbers on the cards need changing. It's been a while since Ivan tested." They work together, adjusting the numbers. "I'll have to weigh this milk a few more times to be sure these are correct."

Afterward, she goes to the house to get breakfast. Harold comes out of his bedroom, looking white and in pain. He flops into his Morris chair. Shirley says, "I'm worried about you." She bites her lip and her eyes water.

"Hell, don't worry about me. We all die someday."

She cries, "Don't be so flip about life! Pine Mountain can't be the same without you. I wish you'd go to the hospital."

"I ain't goin' to no hospital." He draws a deep breath and grunts to lift himself from his chair, heading back to his room.

Later, they all sit around the table eating breakfast. Harold notices Shirley's face is drawn and tense, looking to be close to tears. Shirley asks, "John, did you leave the house in the night?"

He sits up straight. "No—uh, no!"

Shirley stands. "Then what was it I heard? A ghost?" She points toward the door. "Somebody left this house at ten o'clock. I heard the floorboards creak and the new spring on the door stretch." She rivets her eyes on John. "That spring sounds like nothing else in this house. Harold cried out and I got up to see how he was. When I went to his room, I heard the floorboards and heard the spring stretch. Now don't tell me you didn't leave this house!"

She sits back down, but still holds him in her line of sight. Emily Ann is worried, looking at her father. Shirley feels for her barrette that isn't there.

He shuffles his feet. "No—uh, no—I—I—uh, didn't leave in the night."

She jumps up from the table and runs in her work shoes toward the hallway. She yells back. “Now this is what I heard. Don’t anyone make a sound.” She walks out into the kitchen. “Did you hear the flooring?” Without waiting for an answer, she turns toward the entry, opens the door, and pushes. The spring stretches, making its distinctive sound. “Hear that?” She walks back to the breakfast table, sits down, and stares again at John. “That wasn’t YOU?”

John’s face starts turning red. “No—uh, no it wasn’t me.”

Emily Ann blurts, “I’ve got to go to school. I’m already late. Oh, Willy, I couldn’t read all of your work. Some of it didn’t make sense. Maybe you were tired. I put it in the front room with your other work.”

“I’ll try better tanight, Emily Ann.”

John clears his throat. “Since we—uh, aren’t—uh, going to the woods, I’m going to—uh, the Iversons to—uh, do some carpentry.”

Shirley says, “Willy, will you please help John with the cans? John, I’ve got to speak with you for a moment.” Emily Ann continues to look worried while leaving the kitchen. Steven begins to cry. Shirley picks him up and walks toward the entry. She and John go outside. She says, “You’re going to be at the Iversons today. Think of what we talked about last night. If you’re drawn more to Janice than to me, then let it happen. Emily Ann can adjust.” She raises her voice. “If you try and have it both ways, it won’t work. I won’t stand for it.”

She turns and goes back to the house, not believing how he lied at the kitchen table; but the man is becoming more and more of a mystery. He seems totally unable to give her some answers. She’s beginning to feel those familiar symptoms of a breakdown—weakness and blurred vision. Steven grabs her hair and it distracts her. “You like to grab Mama’s hair, you little monkey.”

Harold looks bewildered as he gazes out the west window. He hears her entering. His eyes follow her as she sits down. He says, “I feel hog-tied to help you in any way.”

She looks pale and nervous. "John's proposal to me is a joke. He's doing it only for Emily Ann. He doesn't love me; maybe he respects me, but he doesn't love me. Make no mistake about it, Janice Iverson is his woman."

"Well, I'll be. How do you know?"

"They danced a lot this summer at The Common, which was innocent enough, but they've gotten to know each other better than we think. I encouraged him to have a relationship with her; but he was hesitant, I think, because of Emily Ann. Then the night she was here sewing, John took Honeydew and Janice home, and he didn't come back until late in the night. Didn't you see her at the ball game? Snappily dressed, with a happy look, like she'd just walked through a candy store and been showered with sweetness. And then last night—how could he lie?"

"I ain't sure. Emily Ann bein' right here and all, he might. Damn, those hot-blooded Iversons, they've got a way of throwin' a wrench our way and havin' it land in our monkey works." *I hope it ain't Toby that was in this house.*

"Janice Iverson is a good woman and attractive, too. If he wants her and she wants him, why not? I say let it go." She looks at Harold. "You know I don't feel about him the way I did Joe. You talk, often, of your Maria. Well—I had my Joe. He was right for me."

"So, you still think about him?" Harold looks at her, wanting to help, but helpless.

"I can be honest with you. Yes, I do."

"Bastard, what ever got into that guy anyway?" A chest pain grabs him and he walks toward the bedroom. He staggers and flops on his bed. He stares at the ceiling, thinking about Joe and why he might have left.

Willy comes back to the house and goes to the kitchen sink to start the dishes.

Shirley starts sweeping the floor. "You and I are going to take care of the rest of the garden today. We'll dig the potatoes and turnips, and we'll put away the onions that have been drying in the shed."

"Good, I like workin' with ya, Shirley."

Harold wakes and feels better, encouraged that he will be hunting after all. He gets up and sees Shirley and Willy working in the garden, and goes to the phone. He hates new things. But for him, it's easy to call Honeydew because she does all the talking, however this call is different.

He forces himself to pick up the receiver. He presses it to his ear. "Operator, I want Joe Iverson. Yup, I guess that's what you call him. I want to talk to Joe.…Hi, Joe.…

Dottie—you mean this ain't Joe? Oh…okay—Joe, this is Harold. I've been a-missin' you. I need you to come to the farm. Everythin's shot to hell. It ain't in the barn, it's in the house. Shirley's a mess and I feel bad for her. She tells me this mornin' that you're the one that can fix it. She loves you! You damn fool. She's the best woman that ever set foot anywhere. You musta known that already.…Well, that ain't happenin'. Janice Iverson's caught his eye. I got busted up by our bull, and all I can do now is eat and talk. Can you come early tomorrow mornin'?…Really, you can? Thanks, that makes me feel better. You know, tomorrow is the first day of deer huntin'—I'm goin', even if it kills me." Harold laughs. "Thanks, Joe. I'll see you in the mornin'. Come for breakfast if you can and eat some good cookin'."

Harold hangs up, feeling relieved, and sits in his Morris chair, watching Willy and Shirley as they pass by the house with Willy pushing a wheelbarrow and Shirley pushing Steven in his stroller.

His chest tightens while looking across the lawn toward the farm drive. Gabby's vehicle, two Vermont State police cars, and two Sheriff's cars pull into the yard. They look to be in some kind of hurry. The road dust hasn't settled yet, and the fronts of the cars dip down when the vehicles skid to an abrupt stop. He watches them talking to Shirley. She's working her hair, acting a wreck. Harold realizes they're gettin' her upset, and for what? What have I done? He mutters, "Here I am barely able to walk, and it takes a bunch of them to take me away?" *But no—maybe it's Toby.*

They walk toward the house, and as they come closer, he can see Shirley more clearly. Her face is white and she looks to be nearly staggering. She's left Steven behind. Willy is pushing the stroller following the troopers. She rushes into the kitchen. "Toby has escaped prison. The police know he's in Huntersville. They found an abandoned car that he stole in Windsor down on the branch road, near the school."

Harold falls back in his chair. "Why, that no-good. I know he scares the hell outta you, but can you settle yourself a little?"

Willy has brought Steven in and Shirley puts him in his high chair and sits at the table, looking to be in shock.

Harold groans, "Of all the times."

A policeman follows them in and announces, "We've borrowed a bloodhound. It's on the way. We're searching your property."

"Go right ahead. I hope you find him and shoot the bastard. As I think about it though, he ain't got brains enough to find Pine Mountain."

Harold can hear Gabby, who's been thrown into a coughing spasm in the entry. Harold says, "Hope we ain't dependin' on him for our protection."

Gabby enters the kitchen. "Can I have a seat so I can catch my breath?"

"Damn, Gabby, this is one hell of a situation. They think he's up here somewhere?"

"Just checking, just checking." The policeman, wheezing, stands and pulls up his pants. He walks to the front room. "What'd you do, sell your .45 and that golden bullet?"

Shirley runs to the front room and sees the faded red velvet outline the shape of the pistol. The Colt .45 is gone and so is the fake golden shell. Harold struggles into the room and stands beside her. "Son of a bitch, that was taken last night! Yesterday afternoon I cleaned my rifle and it was there."

Gabby says, "That golden bullet ain't no good. And Harold, you didn't have any shells for that pistol. That's one thing that's workin' in our favor."

"That's right, he ain't shootin' nobody with that .45."

Shirley turns to Harold. "You yelled in the night at ten o'clock and that scared him. He must've been the one I heard leaving the house. Oh my God, oh my God! I wonder if Willy's sloppy work was actually a note from Toby? It was on the kitchen table included with Willy's writing." Shirley quickly finds where Emily Ann left Willy's paper and scans it. "This isn't Willy's. I can barely read it."

> *Shirl I noya are hear I anit slep in 2 daz I slep*
> *in the mow. I burn the barn if ya call gaby. I hav a gun*
> *n 1 shell. I anit wastin it on harold. I seeya when I wak*

Shirley hands Gabby the note and says, "Tell the police where Toby is and have one guard this door." Steven starts crying in the kitchen and Shirley runs to be with him. "What can I do? What can I do?" She phones Janice. "John has to come right now. Pick up Emily Ann at school and come to get Steven. Can you put them up tonight? Toby Perkins is in our haymow and has threatened to burn the barn. I want the children away from here, but I've got to stay to be with Harold and Willy."

Harold is standing beside Gabby in the front room. "You know you can do me one hell of a big favor."

Gabby wheezes, "What do you want?

"Will you go right now and find Joe Iverson? We need him here and fast. Damn it, don't stand there lookin' at me with big questions in your head. Do as I say. Now go, quick as you can. He's out and about the county somewhere. Ask his secretary where he's at." Harold shuffles to his Morris chair and sits. "That no-mind is sayin' he's burnin' the barn. Hell, we're outta business if that happens. If he strikes a match to that hay, the barn will be flat in an hour." He feels another chest pain, and gets up, staggering to his room.

Shirley puts Steven down in his crib and flops on her bed. She looks at the ceiling and at the dangling light. The whole room is moving, she can't focus on anything that is stationary. She sees double then doesn't. She's trembling, cold, and sick. She gets off her bed and stumbles to the bathroom and dry heaves into the toilet. She can't stop. Her responsibilities seem like mountains. She knows Harold is extremely sick and she needs to stay sane for Steven; but now Toby—when will he wake, and see all the lawmen? Will he burn the barn? There's no way they can stay on Pine Mountain if there's no barn. And what if he ends up killing her? She remembers the verse she recited that awful night at the common: "And the lion shall lie down with the lamb."

She continues sitting on the edge of the bathtub with her head hung over the toilet. "Oh please, Mary Maple, I know you will make everything right." Just visualizing the day before and her time sitting on the bank, in the presence of the tree, helps her to relax by forcing herself to remember those peaceful moments.

She goes to the entry door and calls Willy. He comes from the henhouse, running with the eggs he's collected. "What ya want, Shirley?"

"I want you to stay in this house where it's safe. Did you feed the hens before you did chores this morning?"

"No, I ain't tended ta the cats 'n' chickens until now."

"Well, someone was in there."

"Ya look worried, Shirley."

"I am. But we'll be all right if we stay in the house. You see that line of police cars? They'll protect us." She feels for her barrette.

"What's wrong, Shirley?"

She nervously glances toward the barn. "Toby Perkins is in the haymow."

Willy begins to cry. "He wants ta kill ya, Shirley."

She rests her hand on his shoulder. "Why don't you go to your room?"

A policeman is guarding the door as Shirley has requested. John comes with Emily Ann and they take Steven. She paces the kitchen floor, then goes to her room, combs her hair, and clips the silver barrette in place. Harold comes back to the kitchen and sits in his Morris chair, watching out the west window. "We've gotta sell all those nice cows if that son of a bitch burns our barn. We've got to think of a way to stop that bastard."

Joe arrives, and before he can come inside, Harold walks to the entry and yells, "Let all the animals out. We're about to have a fire." Joe runs toward the barn.

Just then a burning wad of hay is thrown out the mow door and a ball of fire slides down the side of the barn, landing in dead grass next to the building. The fire ignites the grass and the flames lap the siding. Joe stomps on the burning grass. Harold, watching from his chair, passes out.

Shirley cries, "Harold, Harold wake up!"

He moans.

Shirley calls for help from the entry. The police come running and pull Harold onto the floor and elevate his feet and legs. He starts to come around.

After a few minutes, Joe comes breathless into the house. "How can we stop that maniac?"

She looks at Joe and quickly hugs him. "You've come just in time. Would you be here for Harold? I'm leaving. We aren't going to let him burn that barn and have our whole livelihood go up in flames along with that wonderful hay." She leaves the house and hurries toward the barn, saying to the police on the way, "Stay clear and let me see what I can do. He says he'll burn the barn if threatened by you guys."

She climbs over the barnyard gate and Jeanie and Lassie whinny. *I know you don't know what's happening—poor things.* She stands among restless cattle and under the open door. Another ball of burning hay flies out the window. She jumps to avoid it and the cows clear away from the smell of smoke. She stomps on it when it hits the ground. "Toby, this is Shirley. Stop your fooling around with fire!"

"Only if ya come up here, 'n' see me 'n' bring me some food 'n' sompin ta drink."

"Okay, but it'll take a minute."

"Ha, ha, that's a deal, but no cops—jest you, or I'll burn the place. I ain't et in two days 'cept for raw eggs 'n' I'm goddamn thirsty."

Shirley runs back to the house, carrying a nail hammer. *I hope this works.*

She speaks to the guard at the entry. "Don't any of you law folks go near that barn. You fellows can wait in the shed. If I scream that will be your signal to run up the high-drive to take charge."

Joe in a panic asks, "What are you up to?"

Shirley's eyes slightly squint, showing she's on a mission. Her quick hands fly. "I'm making a plate of food for Toby. Go in the bathroom and get Harold's pain pills. Take this hammer and crush them into powder and then add the powder, plus a half cup of sugar, to that pitcher of iced tea that's in the refrigerator."

Joe counts the pills. "Wow, there are eight here; this will knock him for a loop."

Her hand nudges her barrette. "That's the idea."

She cuts pieces of ham and places them on a plate with a huge helping of leftover potato salad. The banging of the hammer brings a staggering Harold to the kitchen. "What in hell do you think you're doin'? You can't face that no-mind and come out alive."

"'And the lion shall lie down with the lamb'. What does that mean to you, Harold?"

He pauses and looks at Shirley as if she's lost her mind. "It sounds something like, 'And the fox will sleep with the hen'." He asks, "Have you gone crazy?"

Shirley snaps, while she continues to prepare Toby's food, "Go back to bed and pray, asking Mary Maple to watch over me. I'm hoping my plan works."

Joe says, "You better do what Shirley tells you, because this situation is close to being out of control."

"I guess, but there ain't no tree that's goin' to listen to me." He shuffles toward his chair and mutters, "And the lion will *kill* the lamb."

Shirley glances his way. "Don't sit there. Do as I say and go back to bed. You'll get too upset and faint on us again."

"By golly, I got to see what happens." Harold watches out the west window. "Well, I'll be. Those lawmen are down at the shed sittin' and standin' by my tractor as if they were havin' a party when my barn is liable to go up in smoke. All the hard work that's gone into that buildin' and some idiot comes along and it's leveled in the blink of an eye."

Shirley places silverware, the plate of food, half an apple pie, and the pitcher of tea with a glass on a tray. "I feel like I'm walking to my last supper and it isn't even noon."

Joe smiles. "How can you make a remark like that at a time like this?"

"Because I'm scared to death and to carry this off I've got to act lighthearted and not a bit afraid. I figure an outward sign of fear is what he enjoys most. I'm not about to give him the sadistic pleasure, thanks to a dud of a bullet, a generous quantity of spiked tea, and a group of police."

She and Joe hug. He says, "Be careful. This could be dangerous."

"I'm confident this will work." She leaves the house, carrying the tray, and walks toward the shed. The police all stand and look at her with solemnity as she passes by. Walking up the high-drive, she feels her bravado of moments ago fading. *I've got to control my fear.*

The barn swallows have left for warmer places, but she can hear sparrows chirping as if this quiet haven is the safest spot on earth. The long loose hay at each side of the center drive smells country fresh. Each stem encapsulates sweetness as it lies like lace. The hay hangs over the bays, similar to a warm winter quilt hanging off the edge of a bed. The alfalfa bales are in front of her, neatly stacked on the barn floor.

She sets the tray on a bale and sits next to it, draws a deep breath, and swallows. "Toby, your meal is ready!"

No answer comes from up on top of the mow.

She packs force into her voice. "Toby come! I have your food!"

She feels he is watching her, but she remains seated with her legs crossed gazing straight ahead from the dull shadows of the mow into daylight.

"I'm warnin' ya. You're a dead duck as soon as I git my hands on ya."

She automatically checks her barrette. "Eat first!"

She glances up and sees Toby high in the mow with his head nearly touching the rafters. He sits on the hay and slides down, landing on his feet with a thud. He's standing near her with the .45 aimed, poised to shoot.

She turns toward him. "Sit and enjoy your food." Expressionless, she turns back, continuing to stare off into space. "Have a drink of tea." *God, he looks like a cave-man.*

Shirley notes that while in jail his beard has been shaved, revealing scars on his face. His eyes are set wide and are wild looking, with hair scruffy and snarled. He's tall, but stooped with the bulk of a bear.

She watches him hesitantly sit on the bale next to the food. The tray is resting on a bale between them. He grabs the pitcher handle with one hand and drinks from it, while still pointing the .45 at her. His swallows croak like a bullfrog, but he continues to drink, looking like he will drain the whole thing.

"Put the gun down and enjoy your meal. I'm not going anywhere."

"You ain't afraid?" Drool mixed with tea runs down his chin.

"No, I guess not. I figure you need someone to talk to. Someone that will understand your problems."

His chin is nearly on the plate. He's shoveling the salad into his mouth—a mouth that's almost as big and round as a baseball. He mumbles, blowing words past food. "My whole goddamn life is a problem."

Shirley focuses on him in a relaxed manner. "It doesn't need to be."

He's chewing a huge forkful of salad. He garbles, "Oh, ya. Sit your ass in prison fer ten years 'n' see how ya like it."

"I can't imagine."

"Well, I was framed. That pecker-head—Randy Silver—was doing Curtsy Iverson. It wont me!"

Shirley continues in a relaxed manner, "But you got caught in the house."

"Ya, old lady Iverson comes home 'n' pins the rap on me. Curtsy runs around the house screamin', 'Toby raped me! Toby raped me!' The little whore!"

She asks, "Did you tell the judge that?"

"Ya, but no one believed me." He leans toward Shirley and raises his voice. "Randy, the candy-ass, had a clean record."

"But you didn't."

Toby's shoulders start caving forward as he gulps a piece of pie. "No, I ain't."

"If what you told me is the truth, I'd be willing to help you clear the rape conviction. It's important that you don't serve time on a false charge, and Emily Ann should know who her real father is."

"That would be good not servin' time fer somethin' I ain't done. 'Cause that kid ain't none of my doin'. I ain't even been told her name 'till you said." He swipes his mouth with the sleeve of his jacket. "You'd do this here checkin' fer me?" He gulps another forkful of pie.

Shirley says firmly, "I will. I think it can be proven by a blood test. I'll ask Dr. Plumbly."

He suddenly stops eating. He closes his eyes and puts his head in his hands. "I'm dizzy as hell. I guess I et too fast."

Harold and Joe are watching from the west window. "Golly, you 'spose she's okay?"

Joe leans forward for a closer view of the high-drive. "I don't know. She's had a lot of time with him."

Harold's face is almost pressed against the glass. "Well, I'll be. Here she comes carrying that tray. She's talkin' with the police."

Joe smiles and hurries toward the entry. "This is amazing!"

Harold laughs and slaps his knees. "There they go runnin' up the high-drive. I'll bet he's out cold."

Joe says over his shoulder, "He should be, with the pills she gave him. I must say she has a lot of courage."

Harold has gotten up from his chair and is standing in the entry in back of Joe. "Yup, and you go and dump her. You're a smarter man than that. I know she ain't perfect, but hell, none of us are."

Joe says in leaving to meet Shirley, "I'll admit, I made a mistake."

Harold raises his voice so Joe can hear. "Well, good. I'm happy for her."

Joe walks beside Shirley carrying the tray. She comments, "Whew, I'm glad that's over! I acted so calm, but inside I was a mess. I even have the .45 and the golden bullet."

He remarks, "I can't believe what you just did."

"I really can't either. I guess the fear of losing the barn drove me to it. You might say the lion fell asleep by the lamb." They both laugh.

Joe looks at the barnyard. "We need to put the cattle back in their places."

They enter the house. Shirley says, "Willy can help. Poor fellow, I can hear him pacing in his room." She walks to the stairs. "Willy, come down. You can help Joe put the cattle back in the barn."

Willy comes running out of his room. "Everythin' gonna be all right?"

"Yeah, we're safe. Toby has left."

Joe says, "Willy, we'd better get these animals back in the barn before they break through the fence. They're acting hungry."

Harold says to Shirley, "Ain't we lucky to get this mess straightened out?"

She draws a deep breath. "Yeah, we sure are. All it took was befriending a desperate soul. It sounds simple, but it took all I had to make it happen and a few pain pills besides."

"Golly, you and your friends. What a ragtag bunch we are."

Later that evening Joe and Shirley are sitting in the front room. They're on the couch and Joe has his arm around her. "It seems ages ago that we were here in this same place under a blanket, making farm plans."

Shirley remarks, "Yeah, the only difference is we now have the wood furnace. Joe, I've missed you so much. I didn't think you'd ever come back."

"In my defense, I must say I wasn't given any encouragement. First I hear you're dating Jimmy, and then Emily Ann tells me you're marrying her father."

"Yeah, the little devil. Why did you leave me in the first place?"

"Like you said at The Common the night we talked—it was my fear of commitment. I just didn't think at the time that I was ready to settle down. I've had the summer to think and I can't imagine being away from you. I know my folks will be horrified to know I'm marrying you. But I've come to the conclusion that marriage is a decision I'm making, not them. You're the one for me, if you'll have me, I know for sure I love you and want you for my wife."

Shirley starts crying and smiles through her tears. "I love you, too." She sniffs and wipes her nose. "Will this be a problem for us, knowing your folks don't approve? I have to tell you that I got mad at your dad when he pressed me about Steven's father. You probably surmised already that Jimmy is the father of Steven and that your dad has been supporting him. It was a secret that I promised would never be told."

"I didn't know." He's surprised. "Jimmy told me Zack is Steven's father."

"That's what your dad wanted to believe. However, it was nearly six weeks between the night Jimmy raped me and the day of our class picnic. Dr. Plumbly explained it all to me. Before Steven came, I knew very little about sex, pregnancy, and all that goes with it. So I wasn't absolutely sure until Dr. Plumbly reviewed my record."

Joe smiles. "If we have another Steven, I'd be thrilled. It was horrible what Jimmy did, but I must say it will be a joy to help raise my nephew."

"I agree. But let's give the idea of marriage a little time to be sure we both feel right with it." She presses her finger into his chest. "And no coming to my room at night. The next man who lies on my bed will be my husband."

Joe squeezes Shirley with a hug. "This all sounds reasonable to me."

She kisses him. "Will you stay the night?"

"Sure."

Joe leaves for the barn, and she sits for a moment on the old couch and glows. She can't believe how her life has changed. All she had this last spring was a beautiful son, a bag for him, and a cardboard suitcase. Now, a wonderful man has come into her life and she has lovable old Harold for a friend. Most of all, Pine Mountain is her home. She wraps her arms around herself and squeezes.

While Joe and Willy do the chores, and after Shirley makes plans for supper, she puts on her jacket and goes for a walk with an empty basket on her arm. Leaving the house, she looks off at the mountains in the dusk of the early evening. She can barely see the outline of the peaks and valleys. The sky is gray and the air is cool, but she still sees beauty in the awesome view. She turns and looks at the house all painted white and the lawn, green and lush even for late fall. She walks to the back of the house and sees that Willy has cleared all the garden trash away. *I must remember to spread some lime before winter.* Next year she plans to have a bigger garden with sweet corn. *That will be fun, I can taste it now.*

She glances up at the giant pines and pauses in silence to see if there's enough wind for them to make her favorite sound. The air is too calm, so she walks ahead and starts collecting a few pinecones for a wreath she plans to make for the front door. She walks up the five-and-five road and stops at a balsam fir. She breaks off ends of branches and places them in the basket. Darkness is rapidly creeping in. Walking down the hill toward home, she looks toward the dark gray sky. Light snowflakes are scampering through the air. She feels them collecting on her face, and hears the lonesome call of a crow, and smiles, remembering first coming to Pine Mountain. She leaves the basket in the entry and enters the house to prepare supper.

Willy and Joe come in from the barn. Harold is back in his Morris chair. "Are the cows okay after that ruckus this mornin'? Golly, that was a close call."

"They seemed to be. By gosh, you've put together quite a herd of cows, what a change since spring! And that hay, too. You don't see any as good as that around the county." He sits down at the table.

Shirley stands in back of Joe with her hands resting on his shoulders. Her index finger races over the edge of his shirt collar. Warmth from the friction consumes her and thoughts of love for Joe fill her. *And it all started with the talk of a barn fan.*

Harold offers, "Yup, these past few months have been the best time of my life. To think I would have done it all anyway and Shirley just happened to be along for the ride." They all laugh.

Shirley glances Harold's way. "You don't feel well, do you? Is that pain coming on again?"

"Yup, but I'm goin' to bed to think about that buck I'll shoot when I go huntin'."

Joe and Shirley sit at the table after the meal. Joe asks, "Will John stay on here?"

"I don't know. My guess is that he would welcome the chance to move in with Janice. I'll have to talk it over with him and Emily Ann. For now, I think you better plan to visit nights and wait and see what the arrangement will be."

"That sounds fine to me." Joe squeezes her hand. "Well, I'm ready for bed."

"Joe, you're my lifesaver." They hug and kiss good night. She feels the rush of joy from her toes to the top of her head as her face glows bright red.

Before bed, she checks on Harold. She turns the light on and finds him staring at the ceiling. "You see that big water mark up there? I lie here imaginin' that it's the sky and those little brown specks in the middle are people floatin' on that big puffy cloud. I've been a-watchin' them lately. Thinkin' about my ma, when I look to the west, wonderin' if she's somewhere out there floatin' on the clouds. Maybe when it rains, she drops down to see us, and gives us all a drink. Then *poof*—she goes back, climbin up the hair of a mare's tail to rest on a cloud."

"Those are wonderful thoughts. Let's hope you have a good night's sleep." She reaches for Harold's hand and squeezes it, her eyes fill with tears. He notices and clears his throat. She turns off the light.

In spite of Harold's condition, she lies in bed thinking she's never been so happy. *Joe Iverson wants to marry me!* She kicks off her blankets and springs out of bed, literally jumping for joy. She beams and gets back in bed. Sleep is slow to come.

The next morning, she wakes, prepares breakfast, and sits waiting for her family. She ponders the previous day and remembers that she must apologize to John—accusing him of leaving the house in the night. She calls Janice and Emily Ann answers. Shirley asks, "How are you?…It's all okay now. Toby has left and is back in prison. I'm going to see if I can help him with the term of his sentence.…I don't have to fear him anymore. He understands that I will befriend him.…I feel differently toward Toby than I did.

I feel sorry for him.…I'm glad you had a good time with Janice. I miss you, though, and Steven, too."

Shirley calls Honeydew to update her on recent events. "Harold, Honeydew wants to talk to you."

He comes from his room and plops in his Morris chair. "Hi, beautiful.…Yes, I'll be careful. Shirley will get you this afternoon." He continues telling her all about the Toby incident.

After Harold hangs up, Shirley says to him, "I wish you looked better."

"Well, maybe I ain't feelin' the best, but because I'm ailin', it gives me a chance to be smarter. You wait and see. I'm gettin' my deer."

"What are you going to do, have Joe mount your rifle on the hood of your Jeep?"

He smiles. "The remarks I have to take from you. If you weren't so good-lookin' and my FRIEND I'd get mad as hell at you." He wears a smirk as he scuffs and totters across the kitchen floor. She watches and really doubts his ability to leave the house, especially to go hunting.

"I guess I'll drive my new Jeep up to the five-and-five field and park it just outside the entrance and walk to the ledge where the hardhack grows, then lay and wait. Joe, would you load my thirty-ought-six, and take it to the Jeep for me? I'll sit here awhile."

Shirley suggests, "Why doesn't Joe go with you? I'm sure he would like to see what a great shot you are." She glances toward Joe and casts her eyes toward Harold.

Joe adds, "Sure—I'd like to go with you."

"No, huntin's a private thing for me. It's my chance to be with nature. Anyway, if Joe comes, I'd be a-talkin'. Huntin' and talkin' don't mix."

Shirley watches him with heightened concern. "You're being foolish, going hunting alone, considering the shape you're in."

He remarks, "Don't talk about me anymore. You keep tellin' me how bad I look and I'm goin' to start to believe it."

He slips on his boots and his red-checkered hunting jacket and hat, and unsteadily makes his way to the Jeep. Joe helps him. Shirley stands at the entry door, nervously watching a feeble Harold.

The accident has aged him, especially since he hasn't shaved. He sits slumped over the steering wheel, shakily filling his pipe with tobacco, spilling as much in the Jeep as in the pipe. He fumbles, unbuttoning his coat, and puts the Prince Albert in his bib-overalls pocket. He strikes a match, draws on his pipe, and starts the Jeep, slowly creeping up the hill. Joe walks back toward the entry, seeing Shirley shake her head. She says, "That man's stubborn, but who are we to deny him some pleasure?"

Shirley and Joe walk toward the back of the house. They stand, looking at bare soil. Shirley says, "This garden really sparked Harold's interest. In the process of preparing and planting the garden, he started seeing things in a more positive way. It was like a beginning for him. Now the garden and he have entered their winter season."

A couple of hours pass, and no word yet from Harold. Shirley asks Joe, "Should we take the truck and see how he's doing?"

"I think so."

They drive up the field road and walk to the spot where the ledge is and the hardhack grows. Harold is flat out, facedown next to the bushy cover. They roll him over. He's sweating and his face is as white as his stubby beard. She unbuttons his coat. He seems semiconscious. Shirley kneels, holding his cold hand, worriedly looking at him. His lips are blue. His eyes are sunken. He speaks in a low whisper. "Stop—don't leave. You know, Shirley, I want to hear the pines play their song one more time."

Joe and Shirley wait, quietly, to hear the light wind whistle through the pines, causing the giant trees to play their haunting melody. His breathing is shallow. His words are barely audible. Shirley bends closely to hear.

"I saw that buck—he was a beauty—just like you said. I had time for one shot, but then it come to me: 'Why kill beauty?'

"Will you give Honeydew a hug for me? Pine Mountain is yours. The papers are in town." He labors for his last breath and falls silent as the light from the metal gray sky reflects off the red Prince Albert can that's half tucked in the pocket of his bib-overalls.

978-0-595-38502-7
0-595-38502-8

Printed in the United States
63554LVS00003B/70-999